THE LAST QUEEN OF THE GYPSIES

ALSO BY WILLIAM COBB

Coming of Age at the Y

The Hermit King

A Walk Through Fire

Harry Reunited

Somewhere in All This Green

A Spring of Souls

Wings of Morning

THE LAST QUEEN OF THE GYPSIES

A novel by

WILLIAM COBB

NewSouth Books
Montgomery | Louisville

NewSouth Books
105 S. Court Street
Montgomery, AL 36104

Library of Congress Cataloging-in-Publication Data

Cobb, William, 1937-
The last queen of the gypsies / by William Cobb.
p. cm.
ISBN-13: 978-1-58838-242-9
ISBN-10: 1-58838-242-7
1. Teenagers—Fiction. 2. Abandoned children—Fiction.
3. Romanies—Fiction. 4. Florida—History—20th century—Fiction. I. Title.
PS3553.O198L37 2010
813'.54—dc22

2010015024

First Edition

Design by Randall Williams
Printed in the United States of America by Sheridan Books

This book is set in Adobe Caslon Pro

Join the discussion about *The Last Queen of the Gypsies*
at www.facebook.com/newsouthbooks

For
Jonathan
and
Sara Beth

CONTENTS

1

CENTRAL FLORIDA

NOVEMBER 1932

They put her out along a deserted road, put her out the way you would an unwanted puppy or a croker sack full of kittens that you couldn't quite get up your nerve to throw in a creek and drown. Just drove off and left her. For one thing, she had one green eye and one blue one, which her mother knew from the ancient times was bad luck. And the old gajo preacher at the migrants' camp where they had been living for the last six months said it was a mark of the devil to have mismatched eyes. And she was another mouth to feed, which, in that passel of children, stair-stepped from three years old up to sixteen, didn't make that much difference, as far as she could see. But her mother obviously didn't feel that way. "She's the one too many mouths to feed, I've done told you," her mother had said. "Then put me out, too," her big sister, Evalene, had screamed. "It ain't right, Mama!"

Minnie could still hear her sister's protesting as they went on down the road, the old Ford roadster shaking and trembling over the ruts in the dirt road, half-heartedly paved with crushed oyster shells. The other children were crying, too, trying to jump out of the car, and Minnie could hear her mother wrestling with them, yelling at them, biting off her words like she was chomping at an apple, and Minnie could see in her mind's eye her father, his stained old black felt hat jammed down low on his head, nearly covering his intense black eyes, just staring straight ahead down the road between the tall saw grass and twisted live oaks to where the road went on toward Tallahassee, where they were headed, her father looking for work, any kind of work, not just fruit picking because there was too much competition now he said. Or at least find some bread lines. But you could get killed in a bread line if you were a Gypsy. Hungry gaje folks were dangerous. Minnie stood there thinking about her father getting killed in a bread line. "Good riddance," she said out loud, to the live oaks alongside the road. It was not clear even to her whether she meant the eventuality of her father getting killed in a bread line or her family going on down the road, leaving her there.

"Somebody'll take her in," her mother had said, "feed her. Folks do feed a stray dog that comes up in the yard."

"Not if they a Gypsy and they got one green eye and one blue one," her father had grunted, never once taking his eyes off the road in front of them; you could barely hear him over the rattling of the falling down car going so slowly over the ruts the dust could wind up and around and catch up with them, engulfing them in their own leavings.

It took her family a long time to disappear, the road flat and off toward the horizon, straight as the edge of a well-honed axe, like something scratched in a sand dune with a stick, and when they dropped from view, almost like the sun going down, their noise went with them, until there was nothing left but a final little puff of dust. Soon that, too, settled back to the earth and left the air, the space, around Minnie silent, so quiet she wasn't sure there was any air about her at all, thought that maybe she had died and this was the hush of hell, the place that old crazy preacher talked about, scaring her and her brothers and sisters. Her father didn't believe in the white folks' hell, nor their heaven either; he was mad at God and everybody else. Her mother was scared of their God and everybody else. She made them pray to the Gypsy God. She whipped them often, and screamed at them. She wasn't somebody you could like very much.

Minnie stood very still. There was a chill in the air and she could feel it through the thin cotton dress she wore, a hand-me-down from her older sisters, washed so threadbare the pattern of interlocking flowers was barely visible. She didn't have on anything else but her underpants. She had no coat. She was so skinny and bony she looked like a featherless little bird that had fallen from the nest. Nothing was moving, anywhere. She was eleven years old and she had never had a lick of schooling and had never felt the lack of it; her Gypsy familia were migrant fruit pick-ers, and all she remembered was moving from place to place in one old beat-up truck or car after another. There were too many fruit pickers now, and there wasn't enough work to keep grits on the table, so they had split off from their band in the hopes of finding something, anything. When they could find a shack to live in they were lucky, and they might stay in one place for more than a day or two. But mostly they just camped and moved. "A Gypsy's life is moving, always moving," her father said, "to stay in one place is to die." There would have been something strange going on if her family had known beforehand what they were having for their next meal: fatback or plain biscuits, dried beans or canned sourdeens and soda crackers, a loaf of white bread dipped in somebody else's leftover bacon grease, whatever the few pennies of the day's labor would buy in whatever unpainted country store was nearby to where they were camping for the night. She would look with thirsty longing at the tin advertise-ments for RC Cola and Nehi orange drink tacked up all over the rough outside walls of the store, knowing that one day she would walk in there and buy all she wanted. As it was, her brother and her sisters would just take what they wanted—and extra food for the table, too—while their father distracted the store owner by bargaining about the price of a can of lard or a pound of bacon.

Minnie started walking down the side of the road, going in the direc-tion her family's car had gone. She tried to pick out the ruts of their car, but she couldn't tell one rut from another. She just put one foot before the other, gliding along like she was walking in some dream she was having, not even a nightmare because there were no scary animals or ghosts or tsinivari, or anything that she could see. There was just nothing. She did not register the tangled live oaks beside the road, nor the palmettos, nor the sawgrass, because they were so much a part of her young environment she would have noticed them only if they had not been there.

She walked for a long time, aware only of the padding of her bare feet in the sandy soil. The sun was moving down the sky to her left. She figured when night came she would just curl up in a nest of grass and pray that a snake or an alligator didn't find her there, and the next day she would go on, because there was nothing else to do. As long as she kept moving, like her father said, she was all right. That was the extent of her plans.

Presently the woods to her right began to thin, and she came to a clearing with an old house set back from the road, a narrow sagging front porch, the house a kind of faded patchy pink from the red it had once been painted. She stopped and looked at the house, at the two black, blank windows on either side of the front door that was standing open, windows that—if the door were a mouth—would be two blind, empty eyes. She could smell the ashes of last night's fire, rank and sour, so the house was lived in, occupied, and she remembered what her mother had said, that they would feed her like they would a stray dog. She would approach the house and ask for food. They couldn't do more than turn her away, could they? She started across the sandy yard and a mangy hound came out from under the porch and growled at her. The hound was splotched light and dark gray and its ribs stuck out on both sides. She was not normally afraid of dogs, but she was afraid of this one. He looked like he was nigh on to starved to death. And he didn't yap, but growled from way down inside him, like the growl was coming from his whole wasted body and not just from his lips and throat and his yellow teeth showing on both sides.

"Nora Lee, hush up," she heard a voice say, "git your scrawny ass back under that porch." She had not seen the old man come out onto the porch, because she wouldn't take her eyes off the dog. He had on what looked like a long john top and overalls and a grizzly gray beard. He grinned at her and his snaggled teeth were stained with tobacco, snuff she figured. His thinning gray hair was wild and sleep-mussed, as though he'd been napping. The old hound whined and went back under the porch, where Minnie could see his eyes, still watching her. She came on into the yard.

"You got any spare leftovers?" she said.

"Say what?" he said, cupping his hand behind his ear like he was going deaf.

"Somethin to give a person to eat," she said, louder.

The old man scratched inside his whiskers with one finger. He peered at her as though she were standing in fog. "I ain't never had a pretty little girl hobo come by here lookin for a handout," he said. "What you doin way off out here?"

"I'm headed to Tallahassee," she said.

He looked out at the road, all around the yard. "Walkin?" he asked.

"Yes, sir," she said.

"Well, you got a hell of a long way to go," he said. He was looking her over. "You ain't colored, are you?" he asked.

"No, sir," she said.

He seemed to chew the inside of his lip. "You just a little darker than the average little white girl," he said, "is why I asked."

Minnie heard a low growl from the dog under the porch. "Ain't I told you, Nora Lee?" the old man said harshly. He stomped his foot on the floor. "Goddam old dog," he said, "ought to shoot her, is what." He kept looking at Minnie, his jaw working slightly like he had a small chaw of tobacco in there.

"Well?" she said impatiently. "You gonna give me somethin to eat, or what?"

"You feisty, ain't you?" he said. "What's your name, girl?"

"Minnie Francis," she said. She knew better than to tell him her Gypsy name. She hardly ever used it, anyway, except in the familia.

"Well," he said, "come on into the house then."

"SHE'S SLOW, IS WHY," her mother had said to her father. "She ain't like the other girls."

"Ain't a thing wrong with her except them eyes," her father had said.

"She'll poison whoever's around her. She's the handmaiden of Beng, is what I'm tellin you. And anyway we can't afford to feed her."

"Gypsies don't do that to their own," he said.

"They do if they starvin to death. People are so poor they ain't even got any chickens or pigs to pick up. We can't find work."

"We'll take her on to Tallahassee," her father said.

"Ain't nobody in Tallahassee gonna want her, not long as she's got the smell of hell on her."

Minnie had known that her mother hated her, for some time, ever since she was old enough to notice. She would catch her mother watching her, the look on her face like she smelled something bad. Minnie didn't know exactly why, other than what her mother said about the Devil, or Beng as the Gypsies called him, which she doubted was so, since she'd never seen the Devil in her life. She could not know, except somewhere in her soul's silent memory, that she had almost killed her mother when she'd been born. She had been a breech and all the long night when her mother had screamed in pain and begged God to go on and take her, she had lingered there inside her mother's body as though she refused to be born. As though it were a willful thing on her part, and her mother had been sure it was. Lying in the cold room, after the intense misery of a living hell, the old worn sheets stained with blood, her mother had looked at the baby, another girl, not even another boy like they'd wanted, needed, but another girl. The baby looked like a dressed squirrel, ugly and deformed in the face, eyes and nose and mouth all scrooched up like one of those little devils you see in pictures, squatting and looking at you like they know some secret, like they know when you're going to die. She wanted the baby taken from her, but she had to feed her. Better the baby starve to death. But she couldn't do it. Not then, anyway. She wanted Big Ralph—as opposed to Ralph-Son, her third oldest—to take the baby outside and smash its brains out upside a hickory nut tree, so she would never have to look at her. But she couldn't ask him to do that, and she couldn't bring herself to do it. So she had watched the girl grow, skulking around, not able to pick even half the fruit—strawberries, peaches, apples or oranges, depending on the season and whatever state they were in, and sometimes cotton, too—couldn't pick half the fruit her four sisters did, two of them younger than her, too, not able to keep her mind on anything for more than a minute, not even when she sat the girls down and read to them out of the ancient stories, like the devil had already taken half her brain, maybe while she was still in the womb.

"She ain't right," she said to Big Ralph. Minnie could hear her from where she lay in the bed, under the thin quilt, her four sisters breathing raggedly and not at all in unison on both sides of her, her eyes almost closed so that she could see only the glow of the fire, sense more than see the orb of the coal oil lamp through her almost closed lashes.

"Hush up about that," her father said. "She can hear you."

"Don't nothin register with her, Big Ralph," her mother said. Minnie was a freak, and she knew it. And maybe even the part about the devil was true, too. But there was nothing she could do about it. When she looked at herself in the shard of a mirror that one of the girls had found in a junk heap, she saw a slight girl with a narrow face, pitch black thick hair, the only thing odd about her those mismatched eyes, one the color of a dandelion leaf, the other the color of a Milk of Magnesia bottle. Her sisters were pretty, the oldest one already getting her titties, but Minnie's body was like a stick figure, gaunt with lack of flesh, arms like twigs. Her hands were too big; half the time she didn't know what to do with them, so they fluttered around her like startled butterflies.

One day it came to her like a splash of cold water in the face that she looked exactly like her mother. Her mother was skinny, too, but with black hair streaked with gray, pulled back in a loose bun at the back of her neck, wearing the same shapeless dresses as her daughters. But it was the same face, lean and constricted, narrow mouth, sharp cheekbones. Her mother's eyes were both black, and she had dark circles under her eyes, where Minnie didn't, and she was always tired and complaining that the girls didn't help her enough, especially Minnie. Minnie saw her in the washtub, her titties flat and sagging like empty tobacco sacks. Big old black bushy hair between her slender legs. Minnie knew she would grow up to look just like that, except for the eyes. But because of her eyes, she would be a monster that nobody would ever love. Somebody hard and flinty as stone.

THE OLD MAN'S CABIN—ONE room, sparsely furnished—reeked of coal oil, sour ashes and his unwashed body. And old bacon grease that smelled rancid, and the fecal smell of boiling greens. And another slightly sweet smell that she knew was liquor, though her parents did not drink alcohol. She knew instinctively what it was; it was the devil's brew that the old preacher talked about. She sat down at a three-legged table, one corner propped on a chair whose back was just the right height. The table was covered with crumbs and bits of food, several dirty dishes. The old man rummaged around over at the wood stove. It was hot in the closed house, oppressive with all its old-man odors and the dim, fading sunlight that seeped between the boards that now covered the windows. He had closed them when they came in, along with the door that creaked on old rusty hinges.

He came over to the table with a tin plate and fork. On the plate were a serving of turnip greens and a wedge of cornbread.

"Let us pray," he said, "dear Jesus, this girl thanks you for her food. She's lost on your earth, dear Jesus. Help her find her way. Amen. Eat," he said. He set a glass of water next to it. "Sorry I ain't got no sweet milk," he said. She bit into the crumbling cornbread and chewed. The greens were only lukewarm but good, swimming in fatback grease. She could see his eyes watching her in the duskiness.

"You cook this?" she asked after she swallowed. The cornbread was dry and she drank some of the water, fresh well water that was cool and sweet.

"Who you think cooked it?" he said. "You don't see nobody else around here, do you?"

"No," she said.

"Well then, you know who cooked it then. Alexander Mossback Frill cooked it. At your service, ma'am."

She heard the chair squeak under his weight as he sat down at the table. He just watched her as she chewed the greens. The only sounds were the scraping of her fork on the plate and the old man's breathing, that seemed labored, like he'd just run around the yard.

"Did you know your eyes don't go together?" he asked suddenly.

"No, I didn't know that," she said.

"You ought to get a job in a circus," he said. "Folks would pay good money to see a girl with one blue eye and one green un."

"I doubt it," she said.

"Take my word for it," Alexander Mossback Frill said. "I could take you down to Sarasota and sell you for a hunnert dollars."

"Nobody's sellin me, mister," she said. She was gripping the fork tightly in her fist.

"Whoa, now," Alexander Mossback Frill said. "I's justa woofin you."

She settled back and continued eating, aware of his eyes watching her, never leaving her. "Ain't you gonna eat?" she asked.

"I done eat my supper," he said.

She finished the food and pushed the plate away. "I reckon you want me to wash that up," she said.

"Naw," he said. She heard a scratch and a match spurted into flame; he lit a lamp on the table as the sulphur scent of the match drifted by her nose. He had a broad, flat face. The growth on his face was more whiskers than beard. The buttons were missing from the top of his undershirt. He was fishing around in a top pocket of his overalls and he came out with a wilted-looking cigarette. "You want to share this here funny cigarette with me?" he asked.

"No," she said. She had no idea what he was talking about. She didn't know why he called it a "funny" cigarette; it didn't look funny to her, but sad and drooping. She just knew she didn't want to share much of anything with him. His breath smelled like old hay that had been rained on and then left out in the sun.

"I'm sorry I ain't got no pie nor nothin," he said. He grinned. His eyes were watery and gray.

"That's all right," she said. She pushed her chair back and stood up.

"Where you goin?" he said quickly.

"I best be on my way," she said. "I thank you for the food."

"Hold on, now. It's almost dark. You can't be settin off through that swamp in the dark."

"Swamp? I aim to stay on the road."

"Well, the road runs right through the swamp. There's quicksand and alligators out there, water moccasins and no tellin what all."

Minnie knew what he was up to. She knew about it. She had seen most everything in the migrant camps. She had even seen her oldest sister doing it in the bushes with a boy. She knew he wanted to put his thing in her. She wasn't going to let him.

"I ain't gone hurt you, girl," he said. "Set back down there. Talk to a old man. Talk to Alexander Mossback Frill. I ain't doin nothin out here but just settin around waitin on Jesus."

She sat back down but she said nothing. He peered at her. "You think

I want to fuck you, don't you?" he asked. "Dried up little pussy cat like you."

"You better leave me alone," she said.

"I ain't studyin you, girl," he said. It had hit her all at once what danger she was in. He was a big man, even if he was old. And she didn't have any idea how far down that road was another house or a town. She guessed that she could outrun him. But it wouldn't do much good to just run, not knowing where you were running to. "And here I was gonna offer you my own bed for the night. I was gonna sleep over yonder in that chair by the fire."

"You can't get in the bed with me," she said, and he grinned. "I'll kill you if you do," she said. The grin faded from his face.

"You a mean little ol scrawny thing, ain't you?" he said. "How you aim to kill me?"

"I don't know, but I will." She had no doubt of it. Somehow, she would. He just sat looking at her, shaking his head like he was seeing something he could hardly believe.

"Huh," he said. "All right, then, go on out there and get et by a alligator, then."

"I'll sleep in the chair by the fire," she said.

"Naw, you'll sleep in the bed or in the swamp. Take your pick."

"You ain't somebody that can tell me what to do," she said. They stared at each other. Suddenly she spit on the floor. His face was a mixture of puzzlement and anger, mystification and indignation. He looked at her, wide-eyed.

"Who the hell you think you are, Missy Cross-eyed?" he said, almost a whisper.

"I ain't cross-eyed," she said.

"Worse," he said. "Cross-eyes can pop back right. You marked for life." He sat back in the chair with a sigh of satisfaction at his own pronouncement. He put the wilted cigarette between his lips and lit it with another of the wooden matches. He inhaled deeply, held his breath. Then the smoke came out in a whoosh. "You know what this here is? This here is what the colored folks call reefer. Makes you feel good. Here," he held out the cigarette to her.

"No, thank you," she said.

"I reckon you'd prefer a drink of corn likker, huh? A cocktail?" He held the cigarette with his pinky finger cocked outward, a parody of someone with manners.

"No," she said. She stood up again. "I better be goin."

"You ain't goin nowhere," he said. He had a sly, crooked grin on his face. His missing teeth were like holes in a picket fence that needed painting. His gray eyes, milky and oyster-like, were fixed on her. "I got that door locked, and them windows, too," he said, "and I got the only keys." He patted the side of his loosely fitted overalls. She looked around. She could see the shiny new padlocks on the two windows and the door, glistening in the flickering light of the lamp. He must have done that when she was gobbling down the food. She was trapped. A gnaw of panic ate at her stomach.

"I . . . I got to pee," she said.

"Over yonder. They's a thunder mug by the bed."

"Ain't you got a privy?" she asked. She tried to keep her voice from shaking.

"Fergit it," he said. "You ain't goin outside."

She could see the white chamber pot sitting on the floor across the room. She imagined that there was some of his leavings in there. Maybe what she'd been smelling was not just the turnip greens cooking. She felt her stomach shiver. Bile rose in her throat and burned the back of her mouth. She thought she was going to vomit. She stood very still, willing the nausea to go away. Finally, it did. At least for a while, she thought.

"I ain't squattin on that chamber pot with you lookin," she said.

"Why not? Don't you want me to look at your little coozie?"

She ignored his question. He was still sitting at the table. She took a step or two toward the chamber pot. He was now sitting with his back toward her, looking at her over his shoulder. He was grinning. Her bladder was about to burst. She knew if she didn't pee soon she'd wet herself. "Turn your back," she said, "and don't peek."

"Awwww, I want to see your little—"

"Turn your back!" she yelled, her voice like an unexpected rifle shot. He jumped like somebody'd poked him with a stick. "I swear, if you don't turn around and close your eyes, I'm gonna piss all over this house. Wet it down real good."

"You do that and I'll whup you good with a belt," he said.

"That won't get the piss up off the floor, will it? Nor the smell."

He paused, as though he were thinking the situation over. "What'd you say your name was?"

"Minnie. Now turn around."

"All right. But you better not try to run. You can't get out of this cabin noway." He turned himself toward the table. She walked lightly and carefully toward the chamber pot, her eyes darting here and there like a hungry hawk's. She spied a stained and rusty wooden-handled butcher knife on a small work table. It had crumbs of cornbread clinging to it. She quickly picked it up and held it close to her body. She pulled her underpants down and sat on the chamber pot. It was clammy against her buttocks. She knew she had to hurry, because she knew he would turn around, to try to get a look at her. She slipped the knife under the quilt on the bed. He turned so quickly she thought he might have seen her, but he didn't react if he did. He just stood up and walked two or three steps toward her. "Look at that, would you, little Miss Cross-eyes settin on the thunder mug." She could hear her pee draining into the pot.

"Don't come any closer," she growled.

"Damn," he said, "you could teach old Nora Lee a thing or two." He took another step. The overalls fit him like a clown suit. "Do you bite like her, honey?" he asked.

"I'm warnin you," she said.

"Come on," he said, "let me see it. I'll let you see mine."

"I don't want to see nothin you've got," she spat at him.

He unbuckled his overalls at the shoulders and let them drop around his ankles. His long johns, once white, looked like mottled cream. He pulled open the flap and let his thing out. It was long and straight and pale white as a lizard's belly. Her stomach lurched. He was shuffling toward her. She felt it coming, hot and determined, no way to damn it up, and she leaned forward and puked the turnip greens and half-digested lumps of cornbread, spewed it all out onto the rough boards of the floor.

She heaved, still sitting on the pot. He jumped back, kicking his overalls away from her vomit.

"Goddam, girl," he said. "You gonna clean that up. What the hell ails you?"

"I told you," she said, when she could stop gasping, could get her breath back. "Stay away from me!"

"You done done it now," he said. "Git up off'n that pot and git that dress off and git on that bed. Do like I'm tellin you now, and I won't hafta hurt you."

She sat for a long time, her head down. She could hear him breathing, rasping. She could smell him, rancid and acidulous. Smell the decay of her own vomit, from the floor and her own mouth. She felt dirty, filthy. She needed a dipper of water. To rinse her mouth. To wash the muck and the grime from her mouth. She tried to spit again, but her mouth was dry.

All her sad, sorry life came down to this moment, her sitting in the sallow yellow of the lamp, on a grubby chamber pot, Alexander Mossback Frill standing there pumping his hand up and down on his thing. The old man was someone she had never even seen before an hour ago, never even known of his existence, and now it seemed like he held her life and whatever future she had in his grip. Well, he didn't. She wouldn't let him have that. She had the power to deny him that. To deny him everything.

"All right," she said.

"Say what?"

"I said, 'all right.'" She pulled her underpants from around her feet and stood up. She pulled the frayed dress over her head and stood there, naked. Then she fell backwards on the bed, spreading her legs like she'd seen her sister Evalene do in the bushes with the boy. The old man's eyes were wide and heated. He stepped out of the overalls and yanked the bottoms of his long johns down his legs, his thing wobbling, and Minnie let her hand snake beneath the quilt and grip the knife. All right. She was the Devil's handmaiden, her mother said. She was a freak, a monster, and maybe this old man was the Devil. Maybe that was it. Well, she had an answer to it, whatever it was.

He had one knee on the bed, leaning over her. He was trying to arrange himself, get between her legs, and she couldn't see his face. She pulled the butcher knife out, at the same time pulling him forward, off balance, and let his own weight impale him on the knife. He grunted, then screamed. He straightened up. The knife was in his chest; it had gone precisely between two of his ribs. He screamed again. He was looking at her with shocked disbelief, with a kind of incredulous disappointment. She reached up and with the heel of her hand hit the butt of the knife hard, pushing it further in. The old man looked down at it and then back up at her. His mouth was open and she saw blood welling up there, and it ran down his chin and his neck, dripping on her, burning her skin. Then his eyes rolled back in his head so that she saw only red-veined gray. He slumped, crumpled, fell heavily backward and lay flat on the floor with the knife protruding from his chest, his old thing flopped to the side, his wrinkled skin ashen and pasty like a plucked turkey. His body was as hairless as an infant's.

Minnie lay there, very still, afraid to move, watching the old man twitch and gasp for a minute and then grow still. She could see the life going out of him, his soul—if he had one—leaving him. He was the first dead person she'd ever seen. She did not even let herself ponder the fact that she had killed him, had robbed him of whatever desperate, hardscrabble living was left to him. Not much, she thought. Not much at all.

She used the quilt to wipe the blood from her chest and belly, then got up from the bed, being careful not to touch him or step in the blood or her vomit. The old man had landed square in the middle of it, and his bright blood was seeping into it, making little rivulets in the gray-green, thicker ooze. She wrinkled her nose. The whole pile smelled to almighty hell, like the old man had already started to rot. She found her underpants on the bed, stepped into them and pulled them up over her scrawny, little-girl's butt. She held the too large, loose-fitting dress over her head and let it drape down over her. It struck her mid-calf and turned a skinny child into a bony old woman. She stood looking down at Alexander Mossback Frill; he lay with his mouth open, his head tilted to the side, his eyes wide open and staring fixedly at something high over her head. Maybe he was looking at Jesus. Maybe Jesus had finally come for him.

She looked around the room. There was half a pone of cornbread left in a cast-iron skillet, so she got it and shoved it into an empty flour sack she found on the floor. She had nothing to put the greens in, and, anyway, when she looked into the pot at the congealed grease on the surface of the pot liquor her stomach fluttered mightily and she had to look quickly away. There was a pie safe with nothing in it. A pan with four Irish potatoes and an orange, which she crammed in with the cornbread. She put the sack next to the door.

She had to find the keys. She guessed they were in the bib of his overalls, and they were, three little brass keys on a string. The first one she tried opened the padlock on the door, and she pulled it open, hearing the old boards scrape on the floor. At the sound the hound under the stoop growled. She stepped back inside and found a stick of firewood about two feet long. She put it next to the sack. Then she found a can of kerosene and one of coal oil. She took the quilt off the bed and threw it over the old man. She doused the mattress—ticking about gone, clouds of cotton poking out here and there—and the quilt covering the old man. Then she shook both cans all around the inside of the cabin until they were empty, then flung them one by one against the wall, which set the old hound to barking. The smell of the kerosene and oil made her lightheaded and dizzy. She got the box of wooden matches off the table. She got the stick of firewood and her sack and went out onto the porch.

The night was a great dome of stars overhead. She scratched a match and threw it through the door. Immediately the flames began to lick across the floor, spreading outwardly, toward the old man and the bed. She stepped down off the narrow porch. The hound came out, growling, showing her teeth, and she hit her in the ribs with the firewood as hard as she could; the hound let out a yelp, wheeled and limped off toward the woods, whining like a baby crying.

Minnie stood across the road, watching the old cabin being consumed by the fire. The words "a cleansing fire" came to her from somewhere, maybe from the preacher back at the migrants' camp, maybe from the collected wisdom of her memory, maybe from the accumulated experience of her own soul. The fire hissed and crackled and roared with a ferocious purpose, the flames devouring the old tinderbox cabin as though it were made of paper. She watched bright red and orange sparks shooting toward the sky, rising and mingling with the silver sparks of the stars already there.

Minnie set out walking down the sandy shoulder of the road. It had turned cold, and she shivered in the thin dress. She would walk all night. She would keep walking for the rest of her life if she had to.

2

PIPER, FLORIDA

JUNE 1964

In the small town of Piper, Florida, there lived a young man—or boy, though it would not be entirely accurate to call him a boy, since he was mature before his time, having endured the first fourteen years of his life in the same rundown house with a drunken father, who beat the boy regularly for the first ten years and then got his due from the boy for the last four—tall and muscular, handsome, appealing to women of all ages but choosing to spend that portion of his time he spent with the female sex with an eighty-three-year-old woman suffering from advanced senility.

It was not that he was not attracted to girls his own age; he was. But once he was close enough to see behind the rouge and lipstick and be-ribboned hair he found them silly, unserious to a fault. They represented the type of people who populated the world, or at least as much of the world as he knew, with their babblings and petty arguments and insincere compliments, and he rejected them and rejected their world as well. He was more than content to walk alone.

Piper was a town of two thousand people, in the western Panhandle, on one of the main routes to the Gulf beaches. It was the type of place that people only passed through going elsewhere, stopping maybe for gas or at the numerous fruit stands lining the highway north toward the Alabama border, oranges and grapefruit mostly, melons, none of which was any fresher really than they could buy in their grocery stores in Birmingham or Atlanta or Chattanooga, since Piper was two hundred miles from the fruit-growing region down in the central part of the state, the fruit stand owners relying on the motorists' sudden awareness that soon they would leave Florida and their realization that they hadn't bought enough fruit to take home with them. Piper had little in common with the beach towns with their gaudy pretensions to happiness and escape—the broken promises and the desperation. Piper didn't even have a single motel, only an ancient tourist home sitting in stoic defiance of the obvious illogic of stopping when you're a mere two hours from the beach. Nobody ever stopped there.

It was a perfect early summer evening, not too hot, and the boy, whose name was Lester Ray Holsomback, walked along a dirt road—actually a street of the town—that ran along the river. He wore tight jeans and a white T-shirt, with a package of Camels rolled up in the sleeve. He was clearly visible in the bright moonlight, would have been even if he had not had on the T-shirt. He was just under six feet tall, with shoulders so wide they strained the T-shirt in the back. His hair was silky black, short, cut about half an inch all over, not so much cut as just there. He had a birthmark on the left side of his crown, white hairs in a misshapen V, as though some God or Fate had reached down and said thoughtfully, "Hmmmm, okay, him," and put a check mark there. His eyes were a light blue, sometimes in certain lights almost gray, providing a contrast with the sun-darkened skin of his face. The only odd thing about him this night was that he wore on his face a Frank Sinatra mask, made of rubber, fastened with elastic bands in the back. He came around toward the end of the road, a turn-around at the river, behind the city dump, paused in the moon shadows, and stood looking at the car parked there.

It was an old Chevrolet coupe, black with a red top. He knew whose it was: Billy Blankenship, a senior next year at the high school, whose father ran a business supply store downtown. Lester Ray stood in the shadows and lit a cigarette. He was not concerned about being seen. He knew he wouldn't be, because the occupants of the car would be too busy. He could not see them, but he knew they were in there. He had watched them come down here before, had seen them pass by his house earlier on this night, Billy and his girl friend, named Lucy Hatter, nicknamed "Lucy Goosey." A fat girl. Giggled all the time.

Lester Ray had quit school in the sixth grade. He did not know this couple very well personally, since he spent most of his time hanging out with Mrs. McCrory and doing yard work for her, or working in the pool room—sweeping out the place, racking balls—and, with whatever money he could put together, drinking beer at Saddler's Lounge, on the edge of town. He was not likely to see either one of them in one of those places. He just knew who they were. He moved out into the clearing of the turn-around, took a last drag on the cigarette and flipped it out into the road, the butt making a little golden rocket arch before it hit the sand. He walked up closer to the car. He peered into the open window. They were in the back seat.

He could see Billy Blankenship's plump ass pumping up and down, the girl's knees sticking up on each side. There was complete silence, not even any heavy breathing, much less moaning or whispering or crying out. Lester Ray fingered the switchblade knife in his pocket. He straightened the Frank Sinatra mask, made sure it was tight. He reached into the window and tapped Billy Blankenship on his ass; the boy froze.

"What's the matter?" Lucy Hatter said.

Billy still did not move. After a few moments he said, "Awww, now, Bubba, is that you? You crazy son-of-a-bitch."

"What is it?" the girl said.

"Somebody playin a trick," the boy said.

"Somebody's here? Git up offa me!"

They scrambled up, struggling in the narrow space. They were both buck naked. Lester Ray could see the girl's big meaty breasts waggling. They were both trying to see out the car window.

"Ain't no Bubba here," Lester Ray said.

"What the fuck?" Billy Blankenship said, gaping at the Frank Sinatra mask outside in the moonlight.

"Frankie boy is here," Lester Ray said, "get out of the car."

"What the fuck?" Billy said again.

"Get outta the car," Lester Ray said, "I ain't gonna tell you a second time." Lester Ray pulled out the knife and snapped it open. He held the blade up, letting it glint in the moonlight.

"Jesus," Billy Blankenship said.

"No, just old Frankie Sinatra," Lester Ray said, and laughed.

Billy Blankenship cocked his head to the side, trying to get a better look at him. "Who in the fuck are you?" he said. "Fuck, this ain't Halloween!"

"Get outta the car, hand me your pants and her purse. Now."

"Wait. Let her get her clothes on," Billy said.

"Hell no. Out!"

Billy clambered out, naked, his pecker still about half hard, drooping, pointing to the ground. The girl followed, heavy hipped, bulbous breasts wallowing. Lester Ray checked out her big bush of black hair under the hand that she tried to shield herself with. She was standing pigeon-toed, with her other arm across her breasts.

"What do you want?" the girl asked, in a high whine.

"I told you," Lester Ray said, "I want your money. Give me your pants and your purse, and don't try nothin or I'll cut your balls and tits off."

"Give it to him, Billy, for God's sakes," Lucy said.

Billy was rummaging around behind him in the car. "If this is a damn trick, I'm gonna . . ."

"Believe me, this ain't no trick," Lester Ray said. He was wary of him, poised, in case he came out with a tire iron or something. But Lester Ray was a head taller than Billy and fifty pounds heavier, and he would have bet good money that the boy would do nothing to defend himself or the girl.

The boy pulled his pants out and handed them toward Lester Ray. "Give me the wallet and all your change," Lester Ray said, motioning with the knife. Billy held out a handful of change and Lester Ray took it and put it in his pocket. He reached into the proffered wallet and slid the bills out; he could see that there were ones and fives. And some tens. Billy's folks were well-off. He flung the wallet out into the road. "Now your purse, lady," he said. She was shaking all over. She got the purse and handed it to him. He snapped it open with one hand, holding the knife on them. There was a red, plastic billfold in there with nothing in it but a one-dollar bill. He took that and flung the purse after Billy's billfold. "Give me your car keys," Lester Ray said.

"What the fuck?" Billy said. Lester Ray waved the knife. "Okay, okay." He reached in and snatched the keys out of the dash. Lester Ray took them and pegged them toward the river, into a stand of twisted live oaks along the bank. "Shit, man," Billy said. "You not even gonna steal my car?"

"No. Now reach in there, real easy, and hand me all your clothes. Underwear, all of it."

"Come on, man," Billy said. "What the hell you doin this for then?"

"Because I don't like you," Lester Ray said.

Neither of them moved. "Now!" Lester Ray said. Both of them scrambled around in the car, gathering up their clothes. They handed the bundle to Lester Ray.

"Now get back into the car. Go back to fuckin if you want to. But don't get out for another half an hour. You understand that, don't you?"

"Yes, sir," the girl said, climbing back into the car.

"Shit," Billy said. "If I find out . . ."

"You ain't gonna do nothin, piss-ant," Lester Ray said. "And if you report this to the police, I'm gonna come lookin for you."

After they were back in the car, Lester Ray walked back up the road toward his house. He passed a place where some old tires were burning and he tossed their clothes onto the fire. He laughed out loud.

HE WOULD NEVER FEEL sorry for himself again. Not since those days when he didn't know any better, when he was a little boy and thought his mother had run off because of him, and he would never see her again and there was nothing he could do about it. Maybe she had. Run off because of him. But now he knew it didn't really matter why she had left but simply that she had. His daddy had told him a thousand stories, all different, about what she was like, who she was and where she must have gone—Key West, Mobile, a whorehouse in Memphis, on and on—and his daddy would cry and moan and cuss her for the sorry bitch he said she was until he passed out, sometimes face down on the old secondhand Formica table with his arms flayed out to the side, like he was trying to fly down through the surface of the table.

His daddy's name was Earl Holsomback, and the two of them lived on that same sandy unpaved street that Lester Ray had walked down on his way to the turn-around on the river. It was a rented house, unpainted, two rooms and a kitchen, with a narrow falling down porch, little more than a stoop, on the front. There was paltry furniture; Lester Ray slept on a settee in what they called the living room, while his father had the bedroom where there was an ancient iron bed that had once been painted a gold color, to look like brass, with a mattress that they had found in the city dump where it had been discarded, probably by some rich man in town who had not even gotten the good out of it. Lester Ray did not sleep in the bed on any of his father's many long absences—when Lester Ray had no knowledge at all of his father's whereabouts, nor what he might be doing—because his father had pissed the mattress and the dingy sheets so often and so thoroughly that Lester Ray could hardly stand to walk into the bedroom, it stank so much. He was content with the settee, anyway, though it was almost too short for him. He was content with a lot of things, because he knew he was just biding his time until he could leave, until he could get some kind of car or motorcycle, anything, and go in search of his mother. That was the driving force of his young life: finding his mother.

His father was at home when he got there. He sat at the kitchen table in a shabby sleeveless undershirt, Pabst Blue Ribbon cans scattered all over the tabletop.

"Where the shit have you been?" his father said.

"I might say the same thing to you," Lester Ray said. His father had been gone for two months. He would do that, just suddenly pop up and act like he'd been down to the store for a loaf of bread when he had just disappeared without a word one day to stay away months at a time.

"Don't get smart with me, boy," he said. "You got any cigarettes?"

"No," Lester Ray said, though he knew his father could plainly see the package of Camels rolled up in his T-shirt sleeve. But his father didn't see them; he was so drunk that his eyes were opaque and watery, and he just sat there, staring at the beer can in his hand. Looking at it like he was surprised to see it, that he had never seen it before. Maybe he was so blind drunk that he hadn't even known he was holding it until he caught sight of it. What was the use of drinking it if you didn't even know you were doing it?

"Git yourself a beer," his father said, and Lester Ray crossed over to the ice box and pulled out a Pabst. He popped the top and sat down, taking a long sip. The beer was ice cold.

"You didn't tell me where you been," his father said.

"Like it's any of your business," Lester Ray said.

"I'm your daddy, boy," he said.

"You ain't nothin but a fuckin drunk," Lester Ray said.

"No, I'm a fuckin drunk and your daddy," his father said.

"You think that makes any difference?"

"Not a whole lot, no."

He didn't know how old his father was, but he looked like a very old man. He was losing his hair, the bald spot spreading outward from his crown, and he only had a few teeth left, one on the bottom in the front, so that his cheeks caved in and his lips formed a single narrow line above his chin. He was so thin he looked like a skeleton. "Git me another one, will you?" he said, and Lester Ray went back over to the ice box and pulled out another Pabst and opened it. He handed it to his father.

"Where you been?" Lester Ray asked.

"Down to Panama City," his father said, "had me a job cuttin grass on a golf course."

"And you got fired for drinkin on the job."

"Story of my life, ain't it?" his father said. He leaned back and drained about half the beer. Then he looked at Lester Ray. "I'm headin over to Crestview when I sleep this here off," he said. "Know a feller over there."

"Well, I might not be here when you get back," Lester Ray said. "This time."

His father laughed. It was a low chuckle, deep down in his throat, and he seemed to choke on it, losing his breath. When he righted himself he hacked and coughed up a wad of phlegm, which he spit onto the floor. "Still think you're goin lookin for your mama, huh? Boy, you better just give that up."

"Never," Lester Ray said.

"I've done told you, she was a whore, hooked up with a bunch of gypsies come through, ain't no tellin where in the hell she's at now. She had road dust in her veins. Couldn't set still. She's halfway round the world, far as I know."

"I don't care," Lester Ray said. "If you'd just tell me her name . . ."

"She didn't have no name. She was . . . what you say? . . . unusual. She was unusual. She wasn't born outta no woman, I'll tell you that."

"You're full of shit," Lester Ray said.

"Naw, now, she was . . . peculiar. Is all I'm sayin."

"You been tellin me this shit since I was old enough to understand what you were sayin," Lester Ray said. "You're so full of shit you need a bucket to tote it around in."

"That ain't no way to talk to your daddy, son," his father said.

"Fuck you," Lester Ray said.

His father shrugged. He drank down the rest of the beer. "Listen here," he said, "you got any money?"

"No," Lester Ray said. He unrolled his pack of Camels and shook one out. He stuck it between his lips and lit it with his Zippo. There was no way he would ever let himself get like his father, he thought. His father was like a piece of driftwood that had washed up behind a dam and was just bobbing there. His life had no direction at all, never had, as far as Lester Ray knew. Lester Ray wondered if that was why his mother had left him, or if he had gotten that way because she left him.

"I thought you said you didn't have no cigarettes," his father said.

"I did say that," he said. He tossed the pack onto the table, and his father took one. Lester Ray lit it for him. He watched his father suck the smoke deeply into his lungs. He stood there watching his father smoke.

Lester Ray was antsy, anxious. He could feel the days of his youth piling up, like blown leaves up against a fence. He didn't want to get as old and worn down as his father before he found his mother. He had thought of just going, sticking his thumb out, taking off in whatever direction the first ride took him. He was not frightened of being off on his own, not knowing where he was nor where he was going nor what he would eat when he got hungry. In a way it would be a comfort, a new kind of freedom. Except that he knew he would never find her if he just took off, with no plan, no idea whatsoever where she might be. He kept thinking that sooner or later he was going to get a handle on it, that his father would slip up and tell him something that would help him find her.

All he knew was that she had just left one day, without a word to his father, when Lester Ray was almost a year old. He had only the vaguest memory of her: her hands, soft, smelling of Jergens lotion. Maybe it wasn't a memory at all, just a sense of her that had lodged itself inside his mind and stayed there. His father told him that a Gypsy caravan came through Piper, on the way to one of their burying places down near Fort Myers, camping outside town out in a field behind Saddler's Lounge, and his father figured she had gone with them. "She was a Gypsy anyhow, that's where she come from," Earl has said.

"How do you know that?" Lester Ray had asked, "you don't know that. Tell me. How you know she was a Gypsy?"

"I just know," his father said.

"Did she look like a Gypsy?"

"I don't know," his father said, "look in a mirror and see." His father, even though he stayed drunk for a solid year—and had been drunk most every day since—and cried in the night and moaned about how much he missed her, had never tried to find out where she'd gone. Or at least to Lester Ray's knowledge he hadn't. Lester Ray could not understand that; he would have followed her and brought her back, even if he'd had to hogtie her.

He had known, when he got six or seven, that his father knew a lot more than he was telling, though how he knew it Lester Ray didn't know. He suspected that his father knew exactly where his mother was. It was maddening to him. He had searched through everything his father had: an old coming-apart cardboard suitcase that contained a few old yellowed bills that had never been paid, two or three pieces of hard candy in the bottom; his clothes, a few pairs of pants and shirts, most of them torn and put up dirty, underwear with the elastic stretched out of them. One day he had hit the jackpot, or as close to a jackpot, he had decided, as he was likely to hit: he had found a picture of his mother, in an old Bible with an imitation leather cover that was cracked and peeling. Or a picture of a woman that he was sure was his mother, even though his father swore that it wasn't. It was a black and white photograph, faded, with a checked border around it. The woman was sitting on the fender of a dark automobile, her elbow on her knee and her chin propped on her fist. She had on a light colored dress, maybe white, and her skirt draped around her legs. She was looking straight into the camera and smiling. Her dark hair was long and straight, parted in the middle of her forehead.

It was impossible to tell from the picture whether she was a Gypsy, but she was beautiful. Her eyes were squinted, as though the sunlight was high and bright.

"That's my sister," Earl had said when Lester Ray showed it to him. "Where'd you get that?"

"In the Bible, where you ain't looked in twenty years," Lester Ray said. "Nor me either, ever."

"My sister," his father said again.

"What's her name?"

Earl, drunk, hesitated just long enough for Lester Ray to know for sure he was lying and said, "Daisy. She died of the polio."

"You're lyin. That's my mama, I know it is."

"No it ain't, boy," Earl said, "give it here." He reached for it and Lester Ray snatched it away.

"No, it's mine now," Lester Ray said.

"Maybe Daisy was your mama. Maybe your mama died of the polio, and I been just tryin to spare you."

"All right," Lester Ray said, "my mother's name was Daisy, then."

"I ain't said that."

"Yes you did. You just did."

"My sister's name was Daisy. She died of the polio, I'm tellin you."

"Awww, fuck it, then," Lester Ray said, and he stormed out of the house, letting the rattly old screen door slam to behind him. He sat down by the river for a long time, looking at the picture. He waited until his daddy was passed out and then hid the picture in a Prince Albert can behind a loose brick under the house.

MRS. McCRORY, FROM BEHIND the thick tangle of wisteria vines draping her back porch—ancient vines, several of them as big around as a man's thigh—watched Mrs. Wrinstine's old tomcat cross her backyard. The cat crawled close to the ground, wary, suspicious; it seemed to know it was only a matter of time before the jay struck. Mrs. McCrory had heard the jay squawking earlier, raucous and shrill, but it was silent now. It was playing possum to trap the dumb cat. The cat scooted forward a few feet, then was still. The heavy wisteria blossoms hung like bright lavender-red

Japanese lanterns, and bumblebees floated indolently around them. The wisteria showered a fine perfume down upon Mrs. McCrory. She watched eagerly, anticipating the moment when the jay would strike. It would serve the old cat right. The old cat would sometimes come up on her porch during the night and puke on the floor. Leaving Mrs. McCrory a surprise. Mrs. McCrory was put out with all of Mrs. Wrinstine's animals. Just that morning she had seen the woman's milk cow flying over the fence, flying as though it had wings, up and away toward the river and beyond. It was not the first time she had seen the cow fly, but she could not immediately recall when the other time had been.

Mrs. McCrory never left her house any more. The boy went and bought her groceries, and in the winter he carted in the coal scuttles from the shed in back for the Warm Morning heater in her kitchen. Her son Orville had bought and installed the heater for her. Before that, for many years, she had relied on narrow coal fireplaces; there was one in every room of the old house, but she used only two or three of the rooms. Her son Orville had liked pronouncing the name of the heater: Warm Morning, he would say, like it was something out of the Bible, something you couldn't say like normal things, stove or fireplace or table or something like that. She was supposed to be very grateful to him for buying her a Warm Morning and not just some ordinary heater. She only had to run it about two months out of the year, anyway, and she didn't see how it was that big a deal. The boy cut her grass and raked her leaves, and he swept up for her, too, and dusted the house, and washed up whatever few dishes she used; she mostly ate her meager meals off a folded newspaper. She liked canned peaches and canned mandarin orange slices, Vienna sausages and potted meat.

Orville hardly ever visited her. He lived in Atlanta and was very busy. He was a traveling salesman for International Harvester. She couldn't remember if he was married or not, or the name of his wife and children if he was. Her grandchildren. She couldn't even remember her own grandchildren, or even if she had any. "I get older and stupider," she would say to the boy. "You ain't stupid," the boy would say, "you're eighty-three years old."

"Am I?" she said.

"That's what you said," he answered her.

"When did I say that?"

"One day."

"One day when?"

"Can I have some Kool-Aid?" he asked.

She had known the boy for years, since he was a little old bitty thing and she had watched him playing in her backyard and asked him to come up on the porch for some Kool-Aid. He had told her right off the bat that his mother had left, run off, leaving him with just his father. He was just a baby when she left, so he didn't remember his mother. He was a good boy, strong and willing to work when he was not more than six years old. And he had grown into a strapping, good-looking young man at fourteen, who seemed to be able to do most anything he set his mind to. His daddy was the town drunk, and they lived in a battered little house on the next street down toward the river, near the city dump. He was at her house all the time. She gave him books to read, books that had belonged to her husband. The boy liked reading about the Greeks, the myths and legends and gods.

Mrs. McCrory was a big woman, not fat, tall with the figure of a much younger woman. Sinking breasts, a narrow waist, a widening behind that looked more like middle age than eighty-three. The skin of her face was smooth, with plump rounded cheeks and deep-set dark brown eyes. Her hair was completely gray, but curly and springy and thick. She was still a handsome woman, and sometimes when she caught sight of herself in a mirror she thought she was someone else. She watched the cat; it seemed to be searching in the grass for bugs, its ears cocked. It had forgotten the jay. Mrs. McCrory caught a flash of blue out of the corner of her eye at the top of a pine tree, then watched the jay dart down like a dive bomber and peck the cat on top of his head, then caterwaul off, wings flapping, squawking, while the cat hissed and rolled over and swatted at empty air with its paws. Mrs. McCrory cackled with glee. She laughed and laughed. "That'll teach you, you mangy pussy," she shouted at the cat, as the cat scrambled back across the yard and disappeared under Mrs. Wrinstine's garage. The jay was preening, back in the top of the pine, pleased with itself.

Mrs. McCrory stood there a long time, gazing into the now empty backyard. She knew Orville was going to try to get her into a nursing home as soon as he could. An old folks' home. He said that was best for her. He wanted the house, to sell it. She didn't think it was worth very much. She remembered her Aunt Clara being in a nursing home in De Quincy Springs; she remembered the attendants asking her Aunt Clara if she "wanted to go potty." Mrs. McCrory didn't want to be anywhere where grown people asked other grown people if they "wanted to go potty." That must have been what they did all the time at that nursing home, go potty, because the whole place smelled like one gigantic old person's fart. Now who, exactly, was my Aunt Clara, Mrs. McCrory thought. What was her name, anyway?

Everything was suddenly gone from her mind, like the blue jay sweeping upward. Her thoughts were empty, a blank. Her head was like the inside of a child's balloon. She tried to recall what she had been looking at in the backyard, but she couldn't. She just stood there. She peered out at the world through gray eyes going blear. As though she were trying hard to see whatever she was looking at, even though she had no idea what it might be. She had been a widow for twenty years, but sometimes she thought it was only one or two years; sometimes she even talked to Winston, her husband, over the kitchen table or in the bed at night. She could feel the bed sagging when he got in and stretched his big frame out. No time had passed at all since she was a girl, being courted by the nice-looking young man she would marry, would spend thirty years with, would share everything with: their house, the many holidays, their triumphant days and their sad days, their son that neither one of them particularly liked as he grew up, Orville, with his sneaky eyes and greasy hair, and wherever in the world he got those eyes and that hair she did not know, could not imagine. She thought maybe that God had sent her this other boy, what was his name? Lester Ray. That God had sent her Lester Ray to make up for Orville, to be the son she should have had all along.

He was a good boy. She smelled beer on him sometimes, but it was many a good man's failing. Winston drank, too. He drank a lot, for a long time: moonshine, bootleg, good dark whiskey in a sealed bottle, it didn't matter to him. She didn't know what Lester Ray drank, and she wasn't going to ask him, all she knew was that he was a good boy. When she had showed Lester Ray the almost five thousand dollars she had saved out of her husband's pension check and kept in a shoebox in the pantry, he had insisted that she put it in the bank where it would be safe. But she wouldn't do that; she didn't want anybody to know she had it, especially Orville. Lester Ray, for a while, had taken to sleeping on the glider on her back porch, to protect her, he said, from somebody breaking in and stealing her money. And maybe harming her. She made him come inside and sleep on the sun porch. Which he did for a while, until Orville found out and pitched a fit.

She remembered that day. Orville had been on the way to a sales meeting in Jacksonville and had stopped by to see her. She hadn't known he was coming, and Lester Ray was asleep on the sun porch when he got there.

"Well, la do dah, what do we have here?" Orville said. His voice woke Lester Ray up and the boy sat straight up in the bed, a startled look on his face. "What the hell do you think you're doin, boy?" Orville said.

"He's my friend, son," Mrs. McCrory said. She was standing in the doorway, looking around her son.

"Your friend? Whattaya mean, your friend?"

"I invited him to sleep here, Orville, is what I mean. It ain't any of your business anyway."

"Mama, you can't be invitin every white trash boy that comes along into the house to sleep, for Christ's sakes."

"I can do whatever I want," Mrs. McCrory said. She pushed her way into the sun porch.

"Your mind's goin, Mama," Orville said, a whine in his voice that had been there since he was a child. "If this don't prove it I don't know what would." Though it was still fairly early in the morning, Orville's white shirt was splotched with sweat, his tie loose and hanging onto his copious belly that strained the buttons in front. His hair was slicked back with Vitalis, the scent of it permeating the room.

"I don't even know who you are, come bustin in here like this," she said.

"There, you see?" He looked at Lester Ray as if for confirmation. "Don't even know her own son."

"You ain't called me in three months," she said. "Like I care."

"I've tried, for Christ's sakes," he said, "your damn phone's out of order."

"I had it took out," she said, "didn't nobody else but you ever call me, so I figured it wasn't worth the money."

"Well fine, then, I can't call you," he said.

"That's right," she said, "who are you, anyhow?"

"Jesus, Mama," he said.

"That's right," she said, "that boy there is Jesus."

"Oh, for shit's sakes," he said. He went over to the bed and pulled Lester Ray by the arm. "Git up, boy, and git your ass outta here. You hear me?" Lester Ray rolled out of the bed and stood up. All he had on was a pair of white jockey shorts. Orville seemed momentarily startled at that, and how tall and big he was.

Mrs. McCrory saw it plain as day. He was! He was Jesus, only he didn't have a beard, and, anyway, Mrs. McCrory had always wondered how all those people knew Jesus had a beard anyway, and what he looked like with that long hair like a girl and all.

"I'm gonna call the sheriff on you, boy," Orville said, "breakin into an old lady's house, standin around half naked. What are you up to, anyway?!"

"I've seen tallywhackers before, Orville," Mrs. McCrory said, "it ain't like I ain't cleaned yours plenty of times."

"All right, that's it! That's it! Where's the phone?" He looked around. "Rape, is what it is. Or attempted rape. Whatever you want to call it. Where's the phone?" He looked around. "Well, shit, there ain't no phone," he said.

"Don't be stupid, Orville," Mrs. McCrory said. "You call the law, I'll tell em you broke in, that I don't know who you are."

"They know me, Mama. I grew up here, remember? No, I don't guess you do."

"Mr. McCrory," Lester Ray said. Both of them looked at him. He was pulling on his blue jeans. "I'll leave."

"No, you won't" she said, "he ain't runnin Jesus off."

"I'm not Jesus, Mrs. McCrory," Lester Ray said.

"You are, too. Don't I know who you are?"

"Apparently not," said Orville under his breath.

"Look, I don't want any trouble," Lester Ray said, slipping his T-shirt over his head. He didn't want any trouble—not for himself; he wasn't afraid of Orville McCrory—but he was concerned for Mrs. McCrory. He figured the man had caused her enough heartache. He was familiar with that kind of heartbreak, of course, except from the other direction, his own pain being caused mother to son and not the other way around, and Lester Ray could not understand what Orville was doing. He hated it, because he knew that if he just had one minute with his mother, could even just see her for the briefest moment, even if it had to be just a glimpse, he would give anything he had or ever hoped to have. And so he could not comprehend Orville McCrory's obvious disdain and lack of feeling for his mother. If that's what it was. Lester Ray would be the first to admit that he didn't comprehend Orville; the man just seemed to dislike his mother intensely, for no reason that Lester Ray could see. Else he wouldn't talk to her the way he did and make her go to an old folks' home when she so desperately didn't want to.

"I don't guess you do want to cause trouble, hot shot," Orville said.

Lester Ray was fighting the rage that had begun to seep into him. He knew that his remark about not wanting any trouble had emboldened Orville, had made him almost cocky. He wanted badly to smack the smug look off of his face, to flatten his already wide and flat nose even more. He wondered if the man was a success as a salesman; he wouldn't buy anything from him. Maybe you had to be a complete asshole to make it in the business world. That wouldn't surprise Lester Ray.

"You go on downstairs, Lester Ray," Mrs. McCrory said, "I'll fix you some breakfast."

"Awwww, Mama, you gonna fix him some breakfast? What is this, anyway?"

"I've told you, Orville, it's not your concern."

Lester Ray walked out the door and walked slowly down the stairs, the old boards creaking as he went.

"And I've told you, Mama," Orville said, after he was gone, "I've got the authority to put you in a home if you can't take care of yourself, and here I find you takin in a boy off the street that you don't know from Adam's house cat, and let me tell you somethin, there ain't a judge in this world that wouldn't see that exactly the way I see it, dangerous and irresponsible, crazy as hell is what it is, not able worth a damn to take care of yourself. That boy could knock you in the head and take everything in this house, and he would, too, in a minute."

"What's he gonna take? You already hauled off the silver and my good China."

"That's family stuff, Mama—valuable antiques—and you ain't in any shape to be responsible for it, and if you need proof of that he's down there in the kitchen right this minute, waitin to be served breakfast like some prince."

"Orville," she said, interrupting him, "you break my heart."

"What?" he said. He was startled. He could see tears rising in her eyes, glistening. He was momentarily taken aback; what she said was like a kick in the chest. He was suddenly aware of the room they were in; it was the sun porch, and it had been his old room. The same massive old live oak outside the window that he used to climb down, the branches evenly spaced like a well-planned ladder. The bed was his bed. He felt a jolt of nostalgia that moistened his eyes, at the same time a sharp, bitter resentment that his old room had been desecrated. The warring emotions froze his tongue, confused his mind, and he stood looking helplessly at his mother. The depth of his feelings astonished him. He felt vulnerable, naked and open, frightened. Tears were running down his mother's weathered cheeks, that looked chapped and rough, not smooth the way he remembered them from his childhood. He had to protect himself.

"Don't pull that on me, Mama," he heard himself say, "I can see right through it."

His mother just stared at him. She did not bother to wipe the tears from her face. They just looked at each other for a long time. Then, she said, "You're a sad man, Orville. Very sad."

"Yeah, well," he said, "I know my responsibility. Don't think I don't."

LESTER RAY AND MRS. McCRORY sat at the table for a long while after

Orville had left, drinking black coffee. It was already hot and stuffy in the kitchen, the sun higher in the sky, moving toward mid-morning. "He said two or three weeks," Mrs. McCrory said. "I'm on a waiting list." Her mind seemed particularly sharp this morning; possibly it was seeing her son, being mentally jerked back into a time when her thinking was clear.

"Yes, ma'am," Lester Ray said. Maybe there was something he could do. If there were, he would do it. In a minute. He was well aware that Mrs. McCrory was his only friend, unless you counted the several guys that hung out at Saddler's Lounge, and he didn't consider them friends at all. He only just stopped in to pick up a six-pack now and then. She was the only person in the world he felt comfortable with, could relax around, the only person who, even in her sometimes addled way, seemed to understand him.

"Maybe you could fix Mr. McCrory's old car," she said, "and we could just take off."

It was a thought that Lester Ray had had before. He had no idea if the old car would ever run again. It was an Oldsmobile, a 1939 model sedan, and it had been sitting in her sagging garage for as long as Lester Ray could remember. She had once told him that it had never been driven one time since her husband had died, twenty years ago, so it had been there that long. And she did not remember how to drive it if she ever knew. It was black and had a huge back seat, the kind of old hump-backed car that would be noticed anywhere it went, Lester Ray was sure, not an ideal car for a getaway. Lester Ray had spent a few nights sleeping in the back seat, when his daddy had come home drunk and mean and wanting to beat him up, the old rough upholstery smelling sharply of ancient dust and dully of vintage, out-of-date motor oil. It had a tall gear shift lever for the transmission and a choke on the dash. It was covered with dust and cobwebs and there was a dirt dauber nest in the tailpipe. He figured the thing had long since rusted through.

He had once raised the hood and looked at the motor. He knew little about cars, but he could see the rust and the spider webs, an old rat's nest atop the engine. He knew enough to know it would be a long shot to get it to run again. But it was sure as hell worth a try.

"I'll see if I can find somebody to help me fix the thing," Lester Ray said. "But I'll need some money."

"Don't you worry about that, Lester Ray, honey," she said, "and I know you can do just about anything you set your mind to."

"Yes, ma'am," he said.

He could see the open road stretching out in front of them, fading into the distance, beyond the horizon a vast, mysterious cloud that hid his mother and contained all the secrets of his life and his world. He knew, had no doubt, that it was within his reach. If only he had the means to go there, and maybe now he did. If they could get the car fixed.

3

Central Florida

November 1932

At a crossroads, Minnie sat against a sandy bank, across a shallow ditch, waiting for the sun to chase away the chill of the morning. She shivered in the thin dress, but she had not wanted to stay in the woods a minute longer. She had found ample downed wood—pine branches and a couple of wind-destroyed oaks from some old hurricane or tornado—and she had kept a good fire going all night, for the warmth and to keep the alligators and snakes away. And the panthers and black bears, too, for all she knew. The linings of her nose still held the stench of burning coal oil and kerosene so that the smoke from her own fire smelled that way, too, a constant reminder of the old man's body being consumed by the fire, her fire. She had slept very little, dozing off only to be jarred awake by a vision of the old man's face, grinning at her and then bursting into flames. The woods were haunted; she heard owls and frogs and scurrying creatures all night long.

The land was flat as a griddle, and she could see at least a mile down the roads in two directions, where the woods thinned and marsh grass took over. She did not know which road her family had taken, and she amused herself for a little while playing eenie, meenie, miney, moe. She wondered if they were already in Tallahassee. She didn't know how far away it was, nor how long it would take to get there. A lot longer walking than in the ramshackle car, she knew that.

Once the sun was over the tops of the live oaks it warmed her through. She felt her eyelids begin to droop over her scratchy eyes. She forced them open; she didn't want to fall asleep in the daytime out here in the middle of God knows where. The sky was cloudless, so vast a blue that it made her feel even more diminutive and insignificant, since to a hawk in the sky searching for rabbits, much less to God, she would appear as little more than a tiny speck sitting in the center of a huge wheel, the roads the wheel's spokes. She sat in the sun for a long time, not knowing which road to take, knowing that as long as she stayed right there she didn't have to make a decision. She didn't really think it would be very important, anyway, which road she finally took.

As she reclined against the sandy bank, very gradually she began to hear a metallic jingling that grew louder as it got closer to her and she knew someone was coming along the road that crossed the one she had come up, traveling west she knew, away from the sun, toward the Gulf of Mexico (though she did not know this fact, since her young life had been defined so thoroughly by travel, constant movement from place to place, that she was always unaware of where she was in relation to anywhere else, only that she was where she was, her understanding of the geography of the state of Florida, and even of the United States, nonexistent). Her instinctive reaction to the sound was to tense in fear, her immediate consternation that it was the old man himself who had somehow come back to life, or perhaps even escaped the flames, who was coming along in the wagon (she could now hear the hooves, and knew the jangling to be harness) but even with her lack of knowledge of geography, her sense of direction was good enough to know that the wagon was not coming from the old man's direction but perpendicular to it.

The mule came into view first, a pale gray bony creature, its ears flopped forward, its harness whose noise had preceded it and announced its coming pieced together from ancient leather and cotton rope in an elaborate rig that seemed ready, at any moment, to fall apart. On the seat, the cotton rope bridle draped across his lap, was an old Negro man, sound asleep. He had on a worn denim coat and wore a brown felt hat; the hat was too big for his head and fell to the tops of his ears and bent them downward. His head lolled on his chest and bumped up and down with the movement of the wagon over the ruts. The wagon's wheels had been repaired with planks nailed on in an X, and they wobbled and left squiggly trails in the sand. A brown coon hound trotted underneath the wagon. When the mule reached the crossroads it stopped and the old man's head jerked up and he said, "Hey up, Maylu!" The hound dropped into the dust of the road immediately and seemed to go right to sleep. Then the old man spied Minnie and he jerked on the reins—even though the mule had not moved at all—and said, "Whoa, there, Maylu, hold on there, gal."

He sat there peering curiously at Minnie. She sat on the bank hugging her knees. She just stared back. Finally, the old man said,

"Who you?" He shifted on the seat and it creaked. Then there was only silence. She didn't know whether to tell him her name or not. She was cautious, especially after her experience with the old man yesterday. "I don't reckon she heered me, Maylu," he said, "I done axed her who she is and she don't answer, so I reckon she deef and dumb."

"I heard you," she said.

"Uh-huh," the old man said. After a minute, he asked, "Where you headin?"

"I ain't headin nowhere," she said.

"Uh-huh," he said, "you done took up residence in a ditch?"

"No," she said, "I'm restin."

"Restin," he said, "uh-huh."

"Where are you headed?" Minnie asked.

"Rosewood, honey," he said, grinning widely, "I'se headed home!"

"I didn't figure you were goin to Tallahassee," she said.

"No, ma'am, I ain't goin to no Tallahassee. I reckon that's where you goin, when you get through restin?"

"I might be," she said.

"Thass a long way to walk, honey," he said.

"I ain't got much choice, do I?"

He shook his head. He rolled his tongue around in his mouth. "How'd you get off out here by yourself?" he asked.

"My familia put me out," she said.

"Yore what put you out?"

"My familia . . . my family."

"Lord Jesus," the old man said. "They just put you out longside the road?

What they do that for?" She didn't answer him. "When?" he asked.

"Yesterday," she said.

"And you just slept out here in the cold last night?"

"I ain't slept none, I don't reckon," she said.

He shook his head again and clucked his tongue. "Well, come on here, then," he said, "ride on into Rosewood with me. Ruby fix us somethin to eat."

"Who's Ruby?" she asked. She made no move to stand up and leave the ditch.

"My wife. She ain't gonna hurt you. Lord, you like a little wild thing, ain't you? Skitterish as a doe."

She did not want to be as trusting and gullible as she'd been yesterday with old Alexander Mossback Frill. But she felt herself giving in. The man was old, harmless-looking. He seemed gentle. She realized in retrospect that Frill had not seemed innocent and harmless at all. She had been a fool, and she didn't want to be one again. But she wanted to trust this man. She had to trust someone. "What's your name?" she asked, still not moving toward the wagon.

"My name Silas," the old man said. He removed the hat from his head, put it over his chest and bowed toward her. His smile was as wide as his face. "Silas Frost."

She stood up and brushed the back of her dress off with both hands. She had been wearing the dress over a week and it smelled bad; it was covered with dirt and it still reeked of smoke, whether her fire last night or old Frill's house. She skipped down through the dry ditch and crossed the road to the wagon. She climbed up onto the seat, and it wobbled and she almost fell.

"Look out, now," he said. When she was settled he looked curiously into her face. "What ails your eyes?" he asked. She just stared back at him, levelly, her eyes narrowed to slits. Finally he looked away and said, "All right, now you better ride back in the back there, on that pile of sacks." She did not hesitate nor question, just climbed over the seat into the back and settled against the tailgate. He shook the cotton reins over the mule's rump. "Hey up, mule, hey up, Maylu!" he said. The old wagon creaked ahead, squeaking like a nest of mice, and the coon hound stood and shook himself and began to amble along underneath them.

RUBY FROST WAS A light-skinned woman; she was as old as her husband but looked much younger, her skin as smooth and unwrinkled as a baby's. She was tiny, with a hint of a stoop, just a little taller than Minnie, and her black hair was limply wavy and oily. She was the daughter of a Seminole Indian and an ex-slave woman, and she and her husband Silas had lived in Rosewood—an all-Negro town in the west of central Florida—for many years. They had lived through the notorious race riot, the massacre and burning of 1923, in which they lost their home and their son Carl, but they had eventually returned and continued to make Rosewood their home, rebuilding. Silas replanted his kitchen garden in which he grew corn, watermelons, tomatoes, peas, and turnip greens— and in the fall pumpkins—for their own larder and to be sold. Indeed, Silas had been returning from carrying a wagon load of pumpkins to a farmers' market in Gainesville when he had come upon Minnie resting on the bank that morning.

They had a milk cow, several hogs and a chicken yard, so they were self-sufficient, and they felt relatively safe, existing as they did on high ground—or what passed for high ground in that part of Florida— surrounded on three sides by salt marshes, and they no longer feared the white people. "They always doin somethin," Ruby would say, "but maybe they done got their devilment at us out they system."

When the wagon pulled into the yard that morning Ruby was on the porch churning. The dogs under the porch heard them first and came boiling out, barking and yapping. When she looked up she saw Silas guiding their old mule Maylu around the house, a little white girl sitting in the very back of the wagon, as far away from Silas as he could get her and her still be in the wagon with him. "Sweet Jesus above," Ruby muttered, keeping the pumping rhythm of the churn going. Though it was twelve years ago she couldn't help flashing back to that New Year's day in 1923 when that white girl Fanny Taylor claimed she'd been raped by a colored man, a man whose name she did not know, a man she couldn't even describe, even as to how old he was, how tall, anything, just that he was colored, and Ruby supposed that it really didn't matter finally if she was telling the truth because it set off the massacre anyhow, two hundred killed and almost every house in Rosewood burned to the ground, the rampage going on for seven days. She and Silas had escaped on the train to Gainesville that the governor finally sent on January fourth, but their son Carl had already died by then, shot down in the street and then hung from a tree, doused with gasoline and burned. Ruby and Silas had finally returned to Rosewood because they had no place else to go, and, besides, as Ruby would say, it was their home. And their history, too, like it or not.

And now here comes Silas with a white girl propped up in the back of his wagon big as you please. "Sweet Jesus above," said Ruby again. At least Silas had sense enough not to let her ride up there on the seat with him, but he probably would have done better to let her drive the wagon and him sit back there on that pile of croker sacks, in case they met some white folks on the road and she could say, "I'm givin this poor ol colored man a ride." Ruby kept the churn going, feeling the thickening under the plunger, smelling the clean butter smell of the clotting milk. Where in the world Silas had found a little white girl out here she could not imagine. Maybe he had brought her all the way from Gainesville, in which case he was dumber than Ruby had thought or he had lost his mind, one of the two. Of course, Silas would have an explanation. There would be some logical reason, but Ruby, for the life of herself, could not imagine what it might be. She kept churning, not missing a beat, her wiry arms like steel cables.

THE GIRL'S COMPLEXION WAS not all that much lighter than Ruby's. Her hair was so black it reflected dark blue in the sunlight coming in the window, but it was straight, not a kink nor a curl in it. She sat at the table with Silas, both of them shoveling in the grits and chewing away on biscuits. When Silas finished and brought his plate to the sink and pumped water to rinse it, Ruby whispered to him, "She dusky, but she ain't colored."

"She say she a Gypsy," Silas said. "Say her people put her out on the side of the road."

"Put her out? Lord Jesus."

"What you make of them eyes?" Silas said.

"They ain't right," Ruby said. "I never seen that before."

"Me neither," Silas said.

"Well, I do know this," said Ruby, "a Gypsy is a lot more white than colored. That's a fact. What we gonna do with her?"

"I don't know," Silas said. "I couldn't just go on off and leave her out there."

"No, you couldn't do that." Ruby touched his hand gently then walked over to the table and sat down across from the girl. The girl looked up and put her fork down quickly, almost guiltily. "You know where you are?" Ruby asked her.

"No, ma'am," the girl said.

"You in Rosewood. It's an all-colored town."

"Yes, ma'am," the girl said.

Ruby glanced over at Silas, who was still holding the dish towel he had dried his hands with. "Don't no white peoples live here," Ruby said.

"Gaje," the girl said. "I'm gonna be gettin on towards Tallahassee soon as I rest up a little bit. I thank you for the food."

"What's 'gaje'?"

"Folks that ain't Gypsies."

"What you say your name was again?"

"Minnie Francis," Minnie said.

"I reckon we gaje, then," Ruby said.

"Yes, ma'am."

"Dark gaje," Silas said, and he and Ruby laughed, so the girl laughed, too.

"My gypsy name is Anna Maria Spirosko," Minnie said.

"You got two names?" Ruby asked.

"Yes, ma'am."

"How come you're not Anna Maria Francis?" Silas asked.

"My mama let me pick it out," Minnie said.

Ruby could see that the girl's dress was filthy, ground-in dirt and brown pine needles clinging to the back of it. She would have to heat some water and get Silas to bring in the wash tub from the backyard. The girl's hair was matted and sticky, greasy looking, and there was a smear of red dirt down her left cheek. She was a pretty girl, except for those eyes, which were startling and kept you from looking anywhere else. They were wide, too, and staring, which made the contrasting colors even more shocking. For the rest of her life, they would be the first thing anybody would look at when they faced her, and Ruby figured okay, it wasn't so bad, sure enough better than a harelip or something like that. But you would wonder how come they were like that, you couldn't help it.

"You can stay here with us for a while," Ruby said, and she didn't even know she was about to say it, and when she blurted it out she thought surely the girl would protest, but she just nodded and sat there as though she was where she had been expecting to be at that very minute in her life and was not at all surprised to find herself there.

4

PIPER, FLORIDA

JULY 1964

The man Lester Ray found to work on the car was named Lyman Duck. He found him in Saddler's Lounge. Lyman Duck was a little, extremely slim man with thin black hair cut vaguely—as near as he could manage, probably—in an Elvis cut, with long sideburns and greasy ducktails in back. He had showed up at Saddler's Lounge a couple of years ago, and he always sat at the same table and nursed a six-pack of Falstaff (Saddler's was a package store as well as a bar, and beer was slightly cheaper by the six-pack on the package store side, so Lyman Duck would buy his over there and bring it in, which Gerald Saddler allowed, since it was his beer sold either way, and if somebody wanted to drink their last four beers lukewarm it was all right with him). Lyman Duck always brought along his ugly daughter, a diminutive, dwarf-like girl not much more than three feet tall, in a faded red dress, which she must have washed out at night—when, if ever, she washed it out and hung it up to dry—because she always had it on. She was buck-toothed, with hair the color of a boiled carrot, cut ragged and shoulder-length like somebody had chopped it off with a hatchet. She sat at the table with him, drinking Dr Pepper and gnawing on a plate of pickled pig's feet. Nobody ever sat down with them, because they stank, and nobody knew where they lived. Gerald Saddler, the owner and bartender, a big man with a bullet head and thick neck and elephantine shoulders, said—laughing—that he bet they lived in a culvert under the railroad tracks outside town. One that raw sewage leaked through.

Lyman Duck claimed to be a mechanic who could fix anything. He was always bragging about it. He claimed to have worked on Patton's tanks in France back during the war, but nobody much believed him. He was a blowhard, and he might be a challenge to keep quiet, but he seemed to be Lester's and Mrs. McCrory's only choice, short of pushing the car into one of the local garages, who would probably get all suspicious and notify Orville McCrory that Lester Ray was stealing his mother's car. Lester Ray knew virtually nothing about cars, just enough to worry that the old car would need parts that might not still be available, but Lyman Duck had winked at that and told Lester Ray not to fret, that he knew where to find any part he needed. Lester Ray offered him fifty dollars to get the car up and running, and keep it a secret, and Lyman's daughter chimed in and said, "Seventy-five!" Lester Ray agreed.

The two of them showed up at Mrs. McCrory's garage the next morning, Lyman toting a rusty tool box. "What'd you bring her for?" Lester Ray asked him.

"She's my helper," Duck said.

"What of it?" the girl said, glaring at Lester Ray. Her eyes were such a pale green they almost disappeared, and her nose was flat, as though it had been broken some time in the past.

"Nothin," Lester Ray said. "I was just askin."

"Curiosity killed the fuckin cat," she said. She spat on the ground and wiped her mouth with the back of her hand.

"Yeah, well," Lester Ray said, "y'all better get started, then."

Lyman Duck raised the hood and peered inside. "Yes, sir," he muttered. "Where's the key at?" Lester Ray handed it to him. It was on a chain with an old yellowed rabbit's foot. "I ain't superstitious," Lyman said, wiggling the rabbit's foot in the air, "but we are gonna need some luck." He tinkered around under the hood, tapping at the engine with a wrench. "You tried to start this sucker?" he asked.

"Yeah, it won't turn over."

"Battery's dead as a doornail," Duck said, "sucker's three days older than God. We gonna need a new one. And some new spark plugs. And ain't no tellin what all else."

"No problem," Lester Ray said. "Whatever you need."

"Where you gettin all this cash, if you don't mind if I ask."

"I do mind," Lester Ray said. "Now shut the hell up and get to work. And remember, this gets out, I'll beat the shit outta both of you!"

THEY WORKED ON THE car for three days. When they needed a part or something, Lester Ray would go to the auto parts store out on the highway and buy it. When they didn't stock it any more—the parts manager turned the rusted generator over and over in his hands; "Where in the hell did you get this damn antique thang," he asked—then Lyman would send his daughter somewhere to fetch it; she might be gone two or three hours, but she'd come back with whatever they needed.

"Where you gettin this stuff?" Lester Ray asked.

"That's for us to know and you to find out, buddy," the girl said.

"Stealin it, I reckon," Lester Ray said.

The girl glared.

"Well," Lester Ray said, "they better be good parts, cause I'm gettin my money back if it don't run."

"It will," Lyman Duck said.

Lester Ray stayed in the garage with them, to see that they kept working and to make sure they didn't make off with anything. The girl mostly watched. The two of them sat on a couple of stacks of old National Geographics that had belonged to Mrs. McCrory's husband. Lyman was on his back under the car, banging away on something. Then it was quiet again.

"What's your name, anyway?" Lester Ray asked the girl.

"What's it to you, son?" she asked, cutting her eyes at him. She was flirting with him. He hadn't thought she was the flirting kind. For the first time he noticed she had pretty big breasts. It looked strange seeing breasts on a girl no bigger than an eight- or nine-year-old. If you could just get by her face she might be all right.

"I was just wonderin," he said.

"My name is Virgin Mary Duck," she said.

"You're shittin me," he said.

"No, I ain't. My mama was a religious Catholic nutcase. She named me that, and don't say anything about it or laugh at it because I like it."

"Okay, I won't," he said. "Virgin Mary Duck," he repeated. "Is that what they call you? The whole thing?"

"Don't nobody ever call me anything, cept sweet Daddy under there, and he calls me V. M."

"All right," he said, "V. M. How old are you?"

"Old enough to know better," she said. She cut her blanched-looking eyes at him again. "I'm fifteen," she said, "sweet fifteen." She smiled at him. About a quarter-inch of pink gum showed when she smiled.

They sat there for a while, listening to the metallic sound of Lyman tinkering underneath the car. Then Lester Ray asked, "Where do y'all live? You and your sweet daddy, as you call him."

"In a tent, out in the Flatwoods," she said.

"A tent?"

"Hell yes. Ain't you ever heard of a tent before?"

"Yeah, I've heard of a tent," he said.

"Well, what of it?"

"Nothin. You can live wherever the hell you want to live," he said. "I was just wonderin."

"Why?" she said, batting her eyes at him, "you think you might want to come see me sometime?"

Not likely, he thought. For one thing, the garage was close and hot, and he could smell her strong. For another, she was about the ugliest girl he'd ever seen.

"I might have some beer for you," she said, "and somethin else, too, if you know what I mean."

Maybe you could put a paper sack over your head, he thought, but then how would he get by the stink of her? He was amazed that such a little body could smell that rank. "I ain't got time to go visitin," he said.

"Where you and that ol lady goin in this thing, when Daddy gets it fixed?" she asked.

"Well," he said, "she just wants me to drive her around, you know, of a Sunday afternoon."

"Shit," she said. "You ain't got no driving license. You ain't old enough."

"How the hell do you know how old I am?" he said.

"Cause I'm older'n you. You ain't even old as I am."

"How old I am ain't got a thing to do with anything," he said, "so shut up about it."

"I bet I could teach you a thing or two," she said. She winked at him.

He laughed. "I doubt it," he said.

Lyman Duck came out from under the car and got in under the steering wheel. The hood was still up, like the car had its mouth wide open. He pressed the starter button with his thumb. The motor sounded at first like somebody rubbing two sheets of sandpaper together, then it sputtered. The car shook. The motor roared into life. Lester Ray felt lifted into the air, liberated. He could hardly believe what this would finally mean. He stood up and jabbed his fist into the air. Virgin Mary Duck jumped up, too, and started dancing around. She tried to hug Lester Ray, but he pushed her away. "Quit it," he said. "Git away from me." He went around to the driver's side. It was difficult for Lester Ray to believe the car was actually running. He realized he had doubted all along that Lyman would ever fix it, and now he was as surprised as he was thrilled.

"You ever drove a car before?" Lyman shouted over the rumbling of the engine.

"No," Lester Ray said.

"Well, look here now. This here is the accelerator pedal, see? You give her the gas with this. This here is the choke. You got to choke her some at first, to get the juices flowin. Same as you got to do to a woman, you know?" He laughed, and Lester Ray recoiled from his yellowed, rotting teeth. "You press this here button. This is the starter, and give it some gas at the same time. Once she gets to idlin good, you can let off on the choke. Oh, and you got to have the clutch down while you doin all that, I forgot to tell you." He leaned down. There were three pedals, and Lyman had the left one pressed to the floor. "The other pedal is the brake. You use that to stop, all right? And this here is the gear shift." He jammed it around here and there, "reverse, low, second gear, third. Got to have the clutch down when you doin that, too. Got it?" He shoved it into reverse. "Slam that hood down and get out the way," he said. Lester Ray went around and closed the hood.

"Look out, now," Lyman shouted. The car jerked and bucked, then slowly began to back out of the garage. Lyman backed out into the street and drove off down to the end of the block, the car backfiring a couple of times like cherry bombs going off, and turned right.

"Where's he goin?" Lester Ray asked.

"Around the block," V. M. said. "He'll be back, don't worry."

Lester Ray stood with a stupid grin on his face, shaking his head back and forth. "Well, I'll be fucked," he said.

"I will if you want me to," V. M. said.

"WE CAN GO ANYTIME you're ready," Lester Ray said to Mrs. McCrory.

"Go where?" she asked.

"We got that old car fixed," he said. "We can hit the road."

"What old car?"

She was looking at him as though she didn't know who he was, much less remember anything about their plans. "We got to get that alligator out of the house," she said, "the one that was in the front hall this morning."

"Yes, ma'am," he said, "I'll take care of it." He was not alarmed. He knew she snapped back and forth, in and out. It was Orville he was worried about; they had two weeks left, according to what he had told his mother, but there was nothing fixed about it, nothing guaranteed. He might show up anytime ready to cart her off to the old folks' home. As far as Lester Ray was concerned, he was not going to let that happen to her.

He had a plan, but they needed a running start. The West Florida State Fair was going on in Pensacola, and there would be a carnival with rides there, and Lester Ray knew that Gypsies usually traveled with carnivals, even ran them, he'd seen that himself with the smaller carnivals that came to Piper, and he planned to get a job with them and travel with them, wherever they were going, travel with them for the rest of his life if he had to, until he eventually met up with his mother. Who knew? His mother might even be traveling with that carnival. He knew that Mrs. McCrory didn't care, as long as he kept her away from Orville and out of the nursing home. He had spent a little over two hundred and fifty dollars on the car out of the box in the pantry (the car had a 1944 Florida tag on it, and they were going to be conspicuous enough without being stopped for an expired tag; he'd had to give Lyman Duck ten dollars extra for a new tag, and V. M. had come back with a current 1964 Rhode Island tag, wherever it came from Lester Ray did not know or care and well knew better than to inquire) and that left them enough—roughly forty seven hundred dollars—for a good long while of wandering, even a longer while if he got a good-paying job with the carnival. He was not afraid of hard work, and he was as big and strong as most men; he could pass himself off as a lot older than he was without too much trouble.

"Your wife," Mrs. McCrory said, "broke into the house and stole my panties."

"Mrs. Mack," he said, "I ain't got a wife. And once we get on the road, you can buy all the underwear you need."

"But I want my panties!"

"All right. I'll tell her to bring them back, okay?" He knew she'd find her underwear in a drawer in her room.

"Lester Ray!" she exclaimed suddenly, "what are you doing here?"

"I came to let you know we got the car fixed. We can leave any time you want. I just got to go home and get some clothes and stuff." He was praying that his father would not be there to make a scene. Not that his father cared where he went, or even that he was leaving, but he would not want him to go, because it was Lester Ray leaving and not him. Lester Ray might even have skipped the clothes, but he had to retrieve the picture of his mother from where he'd hidden it. He would never leave without that.

"Can you pack your suitcase?" Lester Ray asked.

"Of course I can, young man, I'm not a moron," she said.

ON THE WAY DOWN the sandy street to his house Lester Ray met Baby John on his mule, and the sight gave him a surprising stab of sadness. He would not miss much in Piper, but he realized with a jolt that he would miss Baby John, and he would not have thought he would since he rarely thought of him when he didn't see him. Baby John had been riding his mule up and down Commissioners Street ever since Lester Ray could remember. That's all he did all day, ride the mule up and down the street with no apparent purpose other than to do it. He was forty years old, and he lived with his elderly parents in a little white house up the road from Lester Ray, the third one, if you were counting, from the city dump.

"Evenin, Baby John," Lester Ray said. Baby John was barefoot and wore faded, patched overalls without a shirt. There was no saddle on the mule, not even a blanket, and the bridle was cotton rope.

"Evenin," Baby John said. "I'm gonna sang in church." He held his index finger in the air and waved it around as though he were keeping time to music that only he could hear. He would always say that same thing if anyone spoke to him. He rode his mule to all the little country churches around Piper, whichever ones were having dinner on the ground that day, and he would get up during the service and sing. Nobody could understand what he was singing, could not tell if it were a religious song or not, maybe something popular he'd heard on the radio. Lester Ray had wondered if maybe what he was singing was something nasty or blasphemous, but he guessed that as long as the people couldn't understand it they didn't care.

It's strange how you can sometimes tell if someone is home—is in the house—just by looking at it from the outside. Not chimney smoke or a car in front or lights on: it just looks different, like the presence of a live, warm body inside causes the outside appearance to subtly change, to undergo some chemical alteration. When Lester Ray looked at their house he knew his father was at home for the first time in over three weeks. He knew without a doubt that when he opened the door and went inside he would find his father either on the settee in the living room, at the kitchen table, or sprawled across his fetid bed, knew it so veraciously that it would have been cheating to have bet somebody money on it.

Earl Holsomback was at the kitchen table, a can of Pabst Blue Ribbon in his hand. There was a woman with him. She was at least as old as Earl was but she had on a kittenish, frilly pink dress, with ruffles all over it, like some little girl would wear. She had smeared her lipstick all around her mouth, outside her lips; Lester Ray supposed it was to make her lips look larger and more inviting, but she had failed miserably in the effort. His father was wearing a green mechanic's coverall jumpsuit with ROGER stitched over the front top pocket in orange thread.

"Hey, boy," his father said, "pull up a chair."

"I ain't got time," Lester Ray said.

"Hoo-de-do, what you got to do thass so important you can't set down here and meet Sherry."

"I got somewhere to be," Lester Ray said. He went over to a small chifferobe, missing one leg and propped on a brick, and began to stuff his few clothes into a pillowcase.

"What you doin, boy?" his father asked.

"Mrs. McCrory's gonna wash my clothes for me. She's got an automatic washer."

His father turned to the woman and said, chuckling, "This here Mrs. McCrory's his girl friend."

"Hmmm, I'd be his girl friend anytime," she said.

"He ain't but fourteen years old, he's just a boy," Earl said. "Shut that shit up!"

"Uh-huh, I know he's a boy! Hey, sugar, you wanna be my boy-friend?"

"Cut it out, Sherry," Earl said. "Lester Ray, you fuckin that old woman yet?"

Lester Ray whirled on his heel. He stared at his father, at the two of them. They were both drunk. Their eyes were swimmy, and it was an effort for them to focus on him. The woman had flat circles of rouge on her cheeks, uneven and smudged, her face like that of some plump baby doll that had been discarded, thrown away in the trash. Her hair was an unnatural white, like a cloud around her head. He looked at his father, at his caved-in mouth that was framed in a crooked, self-satisfied mock.

"You ever say anything like that again," Lester Ray said, "and I'll ram that goddamed beer can down your fuckin throat."

"Awww, come on," Earl said. "I's just makin a joke. Can't I make a joke?"

Lester Ray's disgust and anger bristled inside him. He could feel it, a physical thing, like a fist shaking inside his chest. He had most of his clothes in the pillowcase now. He almost forgot his red nylon jacket. He went over and took it down from a nail in the wall behind the door. He shoved it down into the pillowcase.

"Wait a minute, now," his father said, "I want to talk to you."

"Well, I don't want to talk to you," he said.

"No, listen now. There's jobs for us over there at Crestview, at a new paper mill they're buildin."

"Fuck your jobs, and fuck you," Lester Ray said. He started to move toward the door.

"Goddam you, boy, you can't talk to your daddy like that," Earl said, getting to his feet. He moved with surprising quickness to between Lester Ray and the door. "You better apologize, and do it now."

"Apologize to you?! Don't make me laugh."

They were close together and Lester Ray could smell him, the biting stink of his body, the soiled jumpsuit he must have been wearing for days, the beer stale on his breath. His smells were coming out of his pores like sweat and mingling all over him until the rancid odor was simply him. It would be hard to know where his smell ended and he began. Lester Ray suddenly knew—it felt as though the fist that had been trembling inside his chest had abruptly dropped into his belly—that to him this was the smell of fatherhood, all the fathering and parenting he had ever known. It was a huge void that was only partially filled by Mrs. McCrory, who had nurtured him for his entire young life even though she was not blood kin, was not his mother and never could be. She was not obligated to do it, but she did. And he would pay her back and try to care for her in the only way he knew.

"I said, 'apologize,' boy," his father snarled, "say you're sorry."

"Why don't you apologize to me?" Lester Ray said.

"For what?"

"For every goddamed thing in my entire goddamed life."

"Now fellas . . ." the woman Sherry interjected.

"Shut the fuck up," Earl snapped at her, "this ain't any of your business." He peered at Lester Ray, his eyes narrowed to slits. Lester Ray knew his father was showing off, that he didn't want to lose face in front of Sherry. Sherry, or whatever whore his father might be with at the time, was far more important than his own son. "You think you're owed, don't you, boy? You think the world, that I, owe you somethin because your mother was a fuckin whore, ran off and left her own little boy."

"Leave my mother out of this," Lester Ray said. He felt the burning of tears behind his eyes, and he did not want to cry. He would not cry. He had vowed he would never let his father see him cry, or anybody else if he could help it. He hoped they were tears of rage. Not the tears of the immense sadness that choked inside him, always.

"Shit," his father said. "Well, I want to tell you somethin, boy, that I shoulda told you a long time ago. I ain't your father. I wasn't nothin but a dumbass boy, myself, stupid enough to take in a pregnant little old Gypsy girl, half colored is what she was. You didn't know that, did you, Lester Ray? You're part nigger, boy."

"You're lyin," Lester Ray said. His father was inventing, making it up as he went. It was pathetic how desperately he was trying to justify himself.

"And soon as she got back on her feet good she was gone, leavin me with you, her part-nigger little love child."

"You ought to be ashamed of yourself, Earl, tellin that boy somethin like that," Sherry said.

"Didn't I tell you to shut up, woman?!" He turned and cocked his fist at her.

"I'll tell you this," Lester Ray said tightly, "if what you say is true, then I'm relieved! I'm glad as hell you're not my father. You're nothin but a fuckin drunk."

"I warned you, boy," Earl said, whirling back around to Lester Ray. He was practically in the boy's face. Lester Ray was taller than him by an inch, and they were looking eye to eye. His father's face was flushed flame-red, sweat beading on his forehead and his upper lip. His eyes were wide and knifelike, stabbing at Lester Ray's own. He reached out and shoved Lester Ray in the chest, causing him to stagger back half a step. The boy righted himself quickly.

It was something as unplanned and instinctual as a sneeze, so quick that it was over before he even knew he was doing it. The boy's fist caught Earl on the mouth and nose and blood splattered as he went backwards, crashing against the wall. He slid down the wall and lay propped there, his head lolling to the side. Lester Ray had split his lip, and there was a lot of blood. His nose was probably broken as well. The front of the green jumpsuit was quickly covered with blood.

Earl did not move, his eyes closed. The woman let out a shriek. Then she stood next to the boy looking down at Earl. "You've kilt him," she said.

Lester Ray was rubbing his knuckles, trying to massage away the stinging. "No," he said, "he's just passed out. I only helped him along a little."

They stood there side by side for a few moments, gazing down at the inert, bleeding man on the floor. Then she looked at Lester Ray. Her face was broad and chubby, with her powder caked around her eyes and at the corners of her mouth. She smelled of flat beer and talcum powder and strawberry shampoo. She winked at him, an expansive gesture that she, in her drunkenness, probably thought was subtle. "Less you and me, sugar, git somethin goin while he's dead to the world, whatayasay?"

It flashed into Lester Ray's mind that this might be the very picture of his mother, that this would be the woman his father would choose, the whore, his mother; it was unbearable to think that he, Lester Ray Holsomback, had sprung from the loins of something this hideous. He stood looking into her tired face, at her flat yet yearning eyes. His mother could not be anything like this. It was impossible. No. "No," he said aloud.

"Why not, baby?" she said, completely misunderstanding his negative.

And it took him a few seconds to fully comprehend her question. "Because," he said, "you make me sick to my stomach."

MRS. MCCRORY FOUND HER suitcase, but she didn't know what to put in it. She put in a doily that had been knitted by her mother, yellowed and limp, and then she took it out. "What would I do with that old thing?" she asked aloud, as though a companion were in the room with her. She picked up a fly swat and inspected it closely, trying to decide what it was. She tossed that in. She decided she'd best put in some clothes; all she had were the cotton house dresses, so she scooped a batch of them in her arms directly from the closet, with the hangers still dangling from them, and shoved them in. Her underwear. The boy's wife had stolen all her panties. She didn't wear brassieres anymore, nor corsets nor stock-ings, garter belts, things like that. She opened the drawer expecting it to be empty and saw all her panties there, most of them washed thin with sagging elastic. "She must have snuck in and put em back," she said. "I would've given em to her if she'd asked." She folded all the panties in with the dresses.

She found an extra pair of shoes, exactly like the ones she had on, black and chunky and comfortable. She put them in, along with a pair of her husband's old bedroom slippers that she happened to spy in the closet when she retrieved her long cotton nightgown. Then she remembered her medicine. She found a brown paper sack and went into the bathroom and dumped all the medicines, the ones she was supposed to be taking now and some as old as six or seven years ago, into the sack. She put in a jar of Vicks VapoRub and a bottle of Jergens lotion. She grabbed a box of Carter's Little Liver Pills, a box of Bayer Aspirin, and a bottle of Hadacol and put those in, too. She stood looking around for a minute. "Well then," she said, "I'm ready."

She lugged her suitcase into the kitchen and put it beside the door. She got the shoebox of money out of the pantry and set it on top of the suitcase. Then she took a long, last stroll around the house. There were lots of antiques, no telling what they were worth, but she reckoned Orville would find out soon enough. Her eye landed on something she didn't think she'd ever seen before, a little polished mahogany box with a tiny figure of a ballet dancer in a pink tutu on the top of it. The dancer was standing on one toe, with the other leg stretched straight out. Her arms were raised gracefully over her head. Mrs. McCrory picked it up, and when she did there was a little "ting" sound. She turned it around, discovering a key in one side. It was a music box! She wound it and re-leased the key, and the dancer began whirling around and around, while the music box tinkled out a song she'd never heard before. Until it came to her precipitately and without warning what the song was. It was "Let me call you sweetheart, I'm in love with you." "Well, ain't that the pret-tiest little thing," she said, as the dancer went round and round, and she decided she would take it with her. She must have seen it before because she knew there was something significant about it, but she couldn't recall what it was; sort of like when you wake up from a dream and you can't remember what it was about but you know it was a nice, pleasant dream and you'd like to go back to it but you can't.

She sat down in one of the kitchen chairs to wait for Lester Ray. She felt confident the boy would be able to drive an automobile safely, because he said he could. He told her he had taken it around the block a couple of times, after dark. He didn't want anybody to see the car and get suspicious why it was all of a sudden up and running again. He had told her they were going to Pensacola, to the West Florida State Fair. She remembered going to the fair when she was a little girl, when it wasn't much but some cattle and some prize hogs and some women's pies and canned figs and such as that. There was always a barbecue contest. You could go around to the various pits and have a sample of the meat, or a little cup of Brunswick stew. The men would be sitting around the pit, passing a bottle of whiskey around, their cigarette smoke rising up to mix with the sweet-smelling smoke from the pit. She had loved barbequed pork, but she hadn't had any for God knows how long. She and Lester Ray would stop at a restaurant and she would treat him to a barbecue sandwich or a slab of ribs.

She suddenly remembered something, so she got up and went into the hallway. She opened the coat closet and got her hat from the shelf. It was a dark blue straw hat with a tiny little cluster of red wooden cherries on the brim. It had been her church hat back before she'd stopped going. She laughed, thinking about the church: she supposed she'd lived too long, because all the preachers just kept saying the same things over and over again. She'd already heard everything ten times over. She figured she knew more than they did, anyhow. Most of them too young to blow their own nose.

She stood there in the hallway, holding the hat, looking curiously at it, because she could not understand what it was nor why she had it in her hand. Then she realized it was a hat. "Now whose hat do you suppose this is?" she asked the empty air. She put it on her head and looked in the mirror in the hall; she turned her head this way and then that way. She smiled at herself in the mirror. "Well, finders keepers, I always say," she said. She went back into the kitchen and sat down again. She crossed her still shapely legs and folded her hands in her lap. She felt dressed to go on a trip with the hat on her head.

IT HAD GROWN VERY dark as Lester Ray was crossing the backyard with his pillow slip of clothes—he had gotten his mother's picture from where he had hidden it and put that in as well—when he heard someone. "Hey," a voice said, barely above a whisper. It was a moonless night and very dark, and he could see nothing.

"Who's there?" he said.

A willow bush started to shake. And someone stepped out from behind it. Even in the dimness Lester Ray could see the red dress. The girl just stood there quietly. "What you want?" he said.

"Where you goin?" Virgin Mary Duck asked.

"Is it any of your business?" Lester Ray replied.

"It might be," she said. Her voice had a coquettish lilt to it, a flirtatious trill.

"You're trespassin," he said.

"So're you."

"What the hell do you want, girl?" he said, more harshly. "I ain't got time to stand out here in the dark and argue with you."

"I been watchin y'all," she said, "you and that old lady. Y'all are fixin to go off somewhere in that car, ain't you?"

"What's it to you?"

"I want to go with you," she said.

"Shit, don't even think about it."

"Listen here," she said, coming closer to him. "I'll be real good to you. I'll suck your dick."

"There ain't any way you're comin with us, so you might as well get on home," Lester Ray said. She was making it tempting, with her last proposition, though she was far from the sexiest girl he'd ever seen, with those buck teeth and that pale red hair. But he couldn't take any risks. He couldn't, and he wouldn't at this point even if she was the sexiest girl he'd ever seen, because he was focused on finding his mother and he wanted nothing to distract him from it.

"Listen, Lester Ray," she said, coming even closer, "you got to hear me. I got to get away from him. He's mean to me. Beats me. And he's been fuckin me since I was six years old. Probably before that, only I can't remember no further back than that."

"Fuckin you? His own daughter?"

"Don't make any difference to him. He's a mean sumbitch, I'm tellin you."

He could smell her now, her unwashed body. The cruelty that a man could inflict on his own children still amazed him, in spite of all he'd seen and experienced in his life. His own daughter! And her a halfwit midget to boot.

"Listen to me, V. M.," Lester Ray said, "we ain't got room . . ."

"I ain't got no bag or nothin," she interjected.

" . . . and it'd be kidnappin. Your daddy would come lookin after us. Or send the law after us. We can't have that."

"Please, Lester Ray," she said. "Please! I got to get away!"

"No, I said."

"Look here," she said, holding something out toward him. "Look what I got." It was a bottle in a wrinkled paper sack. He pulled it out. He couldn't read the label, but he knew it was whiskey, and from the weight of it the bottle was full.

"Who's that out there in the yard," came a voice from the back porch, from the deep shadows behind the wisteria. "Lester Ray?"

"Yes, ma'am, it's me," he said.

"That your wife with you?" Mrs. McCrory asked.

"No, ma'am, it's not," Lester Ray said.

The girl grabbed Lester Ray's arm and he jerked it free. "Please," she said, "just take me a little way down the road."

"No," he said. He handed her back the bottle of whiskey.

"You'd be savin my life, Lester Ray," she said. "You would. Just like you was snatchin me from a fiery pit."

"I got to go," he said. He left her standing in the yard. He knew she wouldn't leave. He was softening toward her in spite of himself and against his better judgment. Maybe they could take her as far as Pensacola, and then she'd be on her own. If they did take her, she'd have to understand that.

"Who you talkin to out there, then?" Mrs. McCrory said, when he came up on the porch, "if it's not your wife."

"Some little dwarf girl," he said. "She's beggin to go with us."

"How'd she know we were goin anywhere? You didn't tell her?"

"No, ma'am," he said, "she figured it out. It was her daddy fixed the car."

"Where's her daddy now?" she asked.

"I don't know. Probably laid up drunk somewhere." He paused a minute. "He beats her," he said.

"Well, let's take her with us, then," Mrs. McCrory said.

"It's risky," Lester Ray said.

"If she acts up and doesn't behave, we'll just put her out," she said.

"I wasn't talkin about that. The more people we got, the more folks might come lookin for us." He and Mrs. McCrory stood gazing out into the dark yard. They could barely make out the reddish form. "And she stinks to high heaven," he said.

"Well, bathe her."

"Her clothes are nasty," he said.

"Well, we'll give her some of mine."

"One of your dresses wouldn't even come close to fittin her," he said, "she's a lot shorter than you."

"You talk like she's a midget or somethin."

"Yes, ma'am," he said, "she is." He looked at the girl out in the yard. She seemed pitiful and alone. A small, lost child. But she wasn't a child. She was a woman. He walked back down onto the grass.

"Y'all gonna take me with you?" she said anxiously.

"We're gonna take you as far as Pensacola. Then you're on your own. Now you got to get that clear, all right?"

"All right!" she said, and she tried to hug him, but she had the bottle in her hand and he skipped quickly away.

"Come on," he said, "we're gonna bathe you."

"Bathe me? Why?"

"Cause you stink."

"You gonna bathe me, honey?"

"No." She followed him up onto the porch.

"Mrs. Mack," he said, "this is Virgin Mary Duck."

"I'm pleased to meet you, Virgin," Mrs. McCrory said. "I'm gonna get one of my dresses for you to put on. Come on this way."

"What's wrong with my dress?" V. M. asked petulantly.

"It's dirty, child," Mrs. McCrory said.

V. M. followed Mrs. McCrory down the hall and into the bathroom. Mrs. McCrory turned on the hot water and the tub began to fill. "Is it a red dress?" Virgin Mary asked.

"I don't think I have a red one. Maybe a nice pink one."

"Shit. I don't want no pink one."

"Well, a blue one, maybe. I'll let you pick it out." They stood there while the tub filled up. Why, this is just a child, Mrs. McCrory thought. Lester Ray wants to take along a child, running away from home. I reckon he knows what he's doing. The girl pulled her dress over her head and tossed it into the corner. Mrs. McCrory was startled. The girl had breasts, and a big bush of bright reddish hair down there. It was like seeing a full growth of pubic hair on an eight-year-old, with breasts to match. And the girl wasn't much more than three and a half feet tall. She had a nice figure, but she was unfortunately ugly in the face. Well, Mrs. McCrory thought, she'll probably grow out of it. Well, hell, what am I thinking? The girl is grown.

The girl climbed into the tub and sank into the water with a contented sigh.

"SHE AIN'T NO LITTLE girl," Mrs. Mack said, when she returned to the kitchen. Lester Ray was drinking a cup of instant coffee.

"No, she's not," he said. "I told you, she's a dwarf."

"I thought you meant just little."

"We'll let her ride along as far as Pensacola, and then that's it," he said. "Whatever happens then, happens without her."

"Why does she want to go with us?" Mrs. McCrory asked.

"I don't know," Lester Ray answered, "she just does."

"All right," Mrs. McCrory said.

The girl finished bathing and Mrs. McCrory helped her dry herself off. Virgin Mary picked out a green dress with little yellow flowers on it. It hung on her like she was a little girl playing dress up. They had to tie a big knot in the skirt up around her waist to keep it from dragging the ground. They were finally ready to go, and Lester Ray put his pillow case and Mrs. McCrory's suitcase in the tiny trunk. He kept the bottle on the floorboard next to the driver's seat. V. M. climbed into the back seat. She settled back. "All right, good lookin," she said, "haul our asses off to Pensacola."

5

CEDAR KEY, FLORIDA

1936

Minnie washed glasses and dishes, swept up, dusted, made beds, did anything Miss Ida Hooten needed her to do. It was not much different from what she'd been doing for Ruby Frost for the last four years, except that she no longer had to milk the cow and churn. Miss Ida Hooten ran the old Coronado Hotel in Cedar Key, that dated back to the middle of the nineteenth century and had withstood several bankruptcies and countless hurricanes, and still stood in the same spot where it had originally been built, turning its weathered-board walls in a kind of stubborn, passive defiance to the Gulf of Mexico, the source of the storms and the very reason and justification for the hotel's existence in the first place.

Since its inception, the Coronado Hotel had changed its emphasis and its clientele several times. In its early days it was a boarding house for the commercial fishermen on the island who manned the fish and shrimp boats that plied the shallow waters of the Gulf, supplying the cities of Gainesville and Tallahassee with fresh seafood; for a couple of decades, after the lovely little island was discovered by wealthy vacationers from those same cities, as well as ones from further north like Atlanta and Birmingham, the hotel became a fashionable resort and was remodeled and expanded. Around the turn of the century, the railroad bypassed the key, choosing a route further inland, that took those same rich sun-and-sand seekers to areas further down the peninsula—Crystal River, Tarpon Springs, Tampa, Sarasota and Fort Myers—and during the first years of the Great Depression the Coronado stood vacant, battered by sea winds and inhabited only by sand crabs, until the arrival of Miss Ida Hooten. She refurbished the hotel and made it a house of prostitution, servicing the sons and grandsons of those original commercial fishermen who had once boarded there; by the time of Minnie's arrival, the Coronado was thriving and had become the most widely known and most highly recommended brothel on the Florida Gulf coast.

Miss Ida Hooten (she insisted on the appellation) was born in Houma, Louisiana, and grew up there before she went to New Orleans to seek her fortune. She landed in the notorious Storyville district, where she gradually worked herself up to Madam in a house on the Rue Toulouse. When the Depression hit, she had quite a sizable fortune in cash, so she went looking for an investment on the Gulf Coast, making her way from Biloxi to Mobile, from Pensacola to Panama City, around the armpit until she came to Cedar Key, where she bought the Coronado Hotel. She recruited her girls from all over Florida; they were all beautiful, and none were over twenty-two or younger than eighteen, though the minimum age was open to speculation and, according to the Cedar County Vice Squad, was violated on a regular basis.

Miss Ida Hooten gradually learned Minnie's story, as she was certain from the start that there was one. A beautiful young girl with one blue eye and one green eye simply turning up one day had to be rich with understory, and Miss Hooten patiently got it out of her. She observed Minnie (or Anna Maria; Minnie confided her Gypsy name to Miss Hooten) closely, watching her every move, talking with her, judging her. Minnie had an incorruptible goodness and innocence about her, in spite of her eagerness to commence her career as one of the Coronado's prostitutes. Her parents must have believed that someone would care for her, that she would somehow be better off for having been left all alone in the wilderness, which she was, though in ways that her parents likely would never have dreamed. Or they might have thought she would die, starve to death, or be killed by wild animals in the swamps. They must not have seen what was in her (Minnie, herself, told Miss Hooten that she had been a skinny, ugly little girl, a "freak," she called her younger self), must not have remarked her intelligence, or her sensitivity, or else they did recognize it and it frightened them terribly. "It's history,"

Minnie told Miss Hooten, "I quit crying about it a long time ago."

Cedar Key was accessible only by water, separated as it was from the mainland by salt marshes and the Cedar River, a wide stream that began nowhere and went nowhere and was prowled by several giant manatees. There was a ferry that ran four times a day, from the foot of Race Street across to where the straight sandy dirt road that ran through Rosewood, twelve miles to the east, ended abruptly at the water's edge, this the self-same road that Minnie had taken four years before, along with Silas Frost in his wagon, from the anonymous crossroads where he had found her to the Frost household in Rosewood. From which, after four uneventful years of milking cows, washing clothes, and helping with the cooking, she had eventually found her way to Cedar Key and Miss Ida Hooten.

Minnie had to content herself for the present with only being a maid for the older woman. It was not that Miss Ida Hooten did not see the potential in Minnie; she was pretty, and she was shaping out nicely, and those eyes were a definite advantage. Miss Ida Hooten herself was a tall woman, slim, with high proud breasts and a crown of curly red hair. Her face had numerous moles on it, as though it had been splattered with brown paint. She smoked roll-your-own cigarettes and rarely left the confines of the hotel, instead sending Minnie to the grocer's market down the street or to the liquor store. The other girls saw Minnie's potential as a whore as well.

"Them eyes," said Margaret Hilton to the girl, "they gonna do you right."

"Yeah," said Clare. "And you gettin yourself a nice rack of boobs, too."

The biggest problem, as Minnie perceived it, was that she did not look as old as she was. She spent hours studying her face and her eyes in the mirror. Even with the filling out, she still looked like a child. Miss Ida Hooten did not consider that a problem at all. Her plan was to begin selling Minnie, in her own little frilly room upstairs, as a virgin being deflowered over and over again. It was a trick she had picked up in Storyville, using animal blood after the real first time. With that gimmick, and the mismatched eyes, Minnie was sure to be popular and certain to generate a lot of cash.

"But Miss Hooten," Minnie said, "suppose the man comes back? You know . . ."

"Oh, they don't care, dear. It's the fantasy of it. Some men will deflower you several times themselves and be the happier for it."

The older girls had piqued Minnie's curiosity about what went on in the upstairs rooms.

"It's a great way to make a living," a girl named Barbara told her, "especially if you like to fuck."

"I don't know if I do or not," Minnie said.

"Chances are you will," Barbara said. "The only ones here who don't like it are the dykes. But they manage to put on a pretty good act."

By 1939, Cedar Key had become a mecca for the sport of deep sea fishing. With the waning of the depression and the new monetary feasibility of it, the sport was becoming popular again, and men and groups of men came from all over the Southeast to fish in the Gulf. Where once the harbor had been crowded only with fishing boats and shrimp boats, they now had to share with sleek charter boats. These men—salesmen, professional men, sportsmen, along with the men who worked the local fishing industry—made up the clientele of the Coronado. Much to Minnie's surprise, even some women came to the hotel to purchase the wares of the prostitutes. Even though she had been raised early on in migrant camps and had slept nightly in the same room with her parents, and had, indeed, observed her sister fucking in the bushes with a boy, Minnie was virtually a naif in these areas.

One spring afternoon, as Minnie was putting clean glasses in their places in the downstairs lounge, there was a charter boat captain named Donohue Taylor Sledge drinking rum at the bar. Captain Sledge was middle-aged, with a flat belly and broad shoulders, and his head was completely bald and glistened in the dim lights of the lounge. "How much for that one?" Captain Sledge asked Miss Ida Hooten, indicating Minnie with a toss of his head.

Miss Hooten was perched on her stool behind the cash register at the end of the bar. "That one ain't for sale," she said.

"Why not?" asked Captain Sledge.

"I'm savin that package," she said. "The man that opens that one is gonna pay well for the privilege."

It made Minnie uneasy to hear them discussing her as though she couldn't hear them, or as though she wasn't even in the room. It annoyed her. She slammed a glass a little too heavily into its place and it broke. "I'm sorry," she mumbled, her head down, as she raked the broken glass into a waste can.

"Don't cut your hand, dear," Miss Hooten said.

"I'll pay for it," Minnie said, "you can take it out of my wages."

"Don't be silly," Miss Hooten said, "forget about it."

"Here, let me pay for it," Captain Sledge said. He slid some coins across the bar toward Minnie. Minnie looked up at him and their eyes met. "Hey," he said, "this girl's got a green eye and a blue eye! I'll be damned."

"That's not all that's unusual about her," Miss Hooten said.

"Whattaya mean?"

"Think about it for six months and I might let you see," Miss Hooten said.

"Six months! Shit."

"Anything worth havin is worth waitin for," Miss Hooten said.

"Hell, in six months I might be in Tim-buc-too."

"She'll be here when you get back." Miss Hooten lit one of her wrinkled cigarettes and blew the smoke at the ceiling. She took another drag and inhaled deeply.

Captain Sledge was looking Minnie up and down. He smiled at her. She was wearing a thin white cotton blouse and khaki slacks. She knew her breasts looked good in the shirt. "I liked the way you looked when you bent over to pick up that broken glass," he said. "Bend over like that again." She looked at Miss Hooten. Miss Hooten smiled and nodded. Minnie bent over, her rump toward Captain Sledge. A sudden rush of warmth washed through her. It aroused her to have him looking at her like that. "That is fine," he said, "really fine."

"Isn't it?" Miss Hooten said.

"She'll fetch a pretty penny, that one," the captain said.

"Indeed," Miss Hooten replied.

A GIRL NAMED PAULA, who was from Orlando, a little town in the middle of the state, offered to let Minnie hide in the closet in her room and watch. Minnie thought that would help her not be self-conscious and nervous when she started turning tricks, which Miss Hooten had told her would be very soon. She was anxious to get started.

As she sat in the dark in the closet, she thought about her family. She wondered where they were and what they were doing. Whether her father had found work, and whether they were hungry. She missed them, but the truth was she did not think she could have had better mothers than Ruby Frost had been or Miss Ida Hooten was. Ruby Frost was gentle and kind, and life there had been unhurried and pleasant; Silas puttered in his truck garden, Ruby (with Minnie's help) cooked their food, and they spent a good deal of their leisure time sitting on their front porch and rocking. It was the first time in her life that Minnie had known there was such a thing as leisure time. She had thought that everyone lived and worked and traveled at the hectic pace kept up by her family and the rest of the migrants. They were Gypsies, yes, but Minnie didn't really know what that meant, other than the times her mother or her father lapsed into a language she didn't understand, or used strange words to refer to something she knew was called something else, like "diklo" for scarf or "glata" for the younger kids. They were no different from the other migrant families, and Minnie, in retrospect, supposed that they were all Gypsies, too. Her mother and her father had told them their family were Gypsies, so there was no reason to question it or to wonder. They had been told that their ancestors had come to America from Romania, in the old country of Europe. She supposed that it was simply like Ruby and Silas being colored, and their ancestors coming from Africa. But Minnie's people were not colored people, were they? She could see, in the mirror, that she was dark-complexioned, that her hair was black and thick. And she remembered the old man, Alexander Mossback Frill (she forced the image of him burning up in the fire from her mind), had asked her, "You ain't a colored girl, are you?" She had asked Miss Hooten, right after she had first arrived on the key, if she was colored.

"Lord no, child," Miss Hooten had said, "you are . . . exotic."

"I'm a Gypsy," she had said, and Miss Hooten's eyebrows had shot up her forehead. She pursed her lips in surprise, regarding Minnie as if she had just that very second appeared out of thin air, had materialized without warning right there in front of her. And Miss Hooten had said,

"Why yes . . . yes you are!" The revelation, which if she had just paid the girl a little more attention she would have known, made her eyes glisten.

Minnie heard Paula and her man ("Do not call them 'johns,'" Miss Ida Hooten said. "They register in this hotel under their own names or they do not register at all.") enter the room, Paula giggling, probably at some lame joke her man had made. Minnie put her eye to the crack of the not-quite shut door. She watched Paula remove her dressing gown and drape it across a chair. Then she pulled her nightgown over her head and stood naked in front of the man. Minnie inspected the man: he was short and plump, with graying hair. She could see the front of his britches poking out with his erection. "Get undressed, honey," Paula said. She sat on the bed. Then she lay back and stretched out. The man fumbled with the buttons on his shirt and yanked it off. He undid his belt and let his britches drop, pulling down his underwear. His thing popped out (she still thought of them as "things," though she had learned numerous other names for them) and waved in the air, as stiff and straight as a metal pipe. "Nice," Paula murmured, "you got a nice one, honey." The man approached the bed and Minnie expected him to climb up and assume the position in which she saw the Mexican boy with her sister, but to her surprise he didn't. He sort of crawled up between her legs and put his mouth on her down there and started licking and kissing and munching on her, right in amongst her tangled black hairs. "Oh, oh, baby," Paula said. She moved her hips and moaned. After a few minutes of this, she pulled at his shoulders. "Come on, honey, you're drivin me crazy, come on up and fuck me good." Then the man slid up and Paula opened her legs wide and then locked her heels over his back. Minnie could see his thing go into Paula, sliding in easy and quick, and they began to buck against each other, both of them groaning now. They went on like that for a while, until Minnie saw the man's back stiffen, and he let out a long moan and then collapsed on top of Paula. He looked like he would be heavy. They were very still, except that Paula was running her hands up and down his back. Then the man sat up on the edge of the bed and Minnie could see his thing, not so stiff now but dangling down and gleaming wetly in the light from the lamp. The man sat there for a while, then stood up and began to put his clothes back on. "Come back, honey, okay?" Paula said. She was still reclining naked on the bed. The man did not answer her. When he got his clothes back on he left, without a word, pushing the door to behind him.

"Come on out, Minnie," Paula said. Minnie pushed the closet door open and stepped into the room; Paula made no attempt to cover herself. "Well, what'd ya think?"

"That's it?" Minnie asked.

"That's it," Paula answered.

THE DAY WAS FAST approaching, and Miss Ida Hooten put blue and green crepe paper streamers all around the lounge. She devised a raffle, with the winner getting to deflower Minnie. Tickets were ten bucks apiece, and most of the men on the Key at the time bought one. For the winner, the visit to Minnie's room would be an extra cost, of course, the standard twenty-five-dollar fee, which, as was her custom, Miss Ida Hooten would collect and deposit in the drawer of her cash register in the lounge before the lucky man could mount the stairs. The raffle was so unusual and provocative that word of it spread over all that part of Florida, and men were driving in from Gainesville and Tampa and other cities to get in on the fun. Many charter boats with home ports elsewhere along the Gulf coast put in temporarily at Cedar Key.

AND OF COURSE THERE was no way that Silas and Ruby Frost could not hear of it in nearby Rosewood. They had heard rumors of where Minnie was, ever since she had climbed out the window that night and struck off walking somewhere.

"Where she goin, you suppose?" Silas had asked.

"I don't reckon it makes any difference to her, long as she's goin," Ruby answered.

Ruby had known that it was only a matter of time before the girl moved on, but she was with them long enough for them to grow attached to her. She was a sweet girl, but she had itchy feet, and itchy other parts of her body, too, if Ruby's intuition was correct, and she would have bet that it was, and I suppose that the truth of my intuition is borne out now, proved, Ruby thought. The image in Ruby's mind of the girl sitting in the ditch beside the road, just sitting there minding her own business like it was the most normal thing in the world for an eleven-year-old girl to be out there all by herself not knowing where she was nor where she was going, that image seemed to Ruby to define Minnie: that maybe that was her place, her home, alongside the road, and any other place she lit for more than a few days would soon start to get old to her. She had that Gypsy blood in her, all right, and she had told them right off that's what she was, a Gypsy. So it was no real surprise to Ruby and maybe not even to Silas when one morning they found her room vacant, the window propped open with a stick of stove wood, and her gone, like she'd just turned to vapor and blown away. Like she just appeared out of nowhere, lingered, and then vanished, so that their little cabin was no more to her than the sandy ditch Silas had found her in.

Ruby and Silas had both known that it was dangerous to grow as fond of someone as they had the girl, someone you don't have any firm ties to, either legal or blood or even race. Still, she had seemed close to kin almost from the start, moving into the little lean-to room off the kitchen, wearing one of Ruby's house dresses that had been cut down for her, them watching her grow from a half-starved, skeletal child into a healthy young woman, Ruby herself the mother instructress when the girl's first blood came, the nurturer when the girl was sick, putting cold rags on her forehead when she was feverish. Answering her questions, and some of her questions about what men and women did together were very specific, indicating to Ruby that she already knew the answers. She was extremely curious about all that. Only four years, but I knew you, Ruby thought, maybe even better than I knew my own child if that is possible, since he was a boy and then a man, with that core of mystery that is always there in someone of a different gender, even between mother and son. And I knew, could have predicted, that you would wind up right where you are now, before you have even lived out your fifteenth year. I'm just glad you didn't mess with Silas, as some would have, and him an old man with a dilly that ain't good for anything anymore except running water through it.

IN THE END THERE were forty-one chances sold, which gave Miss Hooten a quick profit of $410 before any merchandise had changed hands, so to speak. She promised to split it with Minnie, right down the middle, half and half, though her usual split was forty-sixty, so that every time one of her girls turned a trick she pocketed fifteen dollars and Miss Hooten kept ten, out of which came Miss Hooten's profit, all the expenses of the hotel, and a bribe for the local police department. It was an arrangement that was fine with the girls, since in other houses they had worked they made less than half, and those who had worked with pimps had gotten much less than that. Miss Hooten believed in keeping her girls happy.

Minnie was excited. Just this once would net her $235. But she was thrilled just to finally get to do it and find out what it was like, and she was pleased that forty-one men had forked over ten bucks apiece just for the chance of going to bed with her. They had been looking longingly at her ever since her plump little breasts had made their first appearance at the Coronado Hotel.

"They weren't all men," Paula told her. They were talking about the forty-one who had bought chances.

"They weren't?" Minnie asked.

"Three of them are women," Paula said.

"How's a woman gonna deflower me?"

"Oh, they'd find a way," Paula said.

That information bothered Minnie only moderately, since she had heard the other girls talking and she knew they considered that being with a woman was only different from being with a man, not any less pleasurable and certainly not unnatural, as Minnie was inclined to feel it was, since somewhere in her past she had been told that it was strange and not right. She supposed, though, that she would get used to it. She was not locked into anything she had learned in her previous young life, since this was a new life with all new rules and possibilities. She was just anxious to get on with everything and she didn't really care who her partner was as long as he wasn't some pervert who wanted to knock her around and hurt her.

The day finally came. The lounge was crowded with men, and when Minnie came in there was wild cheering and applauding and stomping. The smoke from their cigarettes and pipes hovered against the ceiling. She became nervous and started having second thoughts when she saw the men's eyes; they looked like wild animals' eyes must look just as they are about to be released from a cage. Miss Hooten had dressed her in a frilly blue dress, with white lace at the collar and at her wrists and around the hem of the skirt. The bodice was tight, so her breasts were shown to good advantage.

I must be pretty, Minnie thought. Since so much had been made over her, she had lain awake at night trying—and failing—to see herself as men saw her. Up until now she had been shy and extremely self-conscious about her eyes, her eyes that had got her rejected by her own family and that everybody she came in contact with felt the need to comment on, as though when they looked at her that's all they saw, a pitiful little girl with mismatched eyes. The eyes had provided a buffer for her shyness, though, when she was a little girl; nobody ever saw Minnie, they just saw a blue eye and a green eye, so the real Minnie was shielded from them as surely as if she had on a suit of armor painted blue and green. Her deviant contrasting eyes may have made her ugly, but they protected her. They allowed her to withdraw into herself as a counter to anyone who might want to reject her again, as she was convinced everybody wanted to do. Because of her eyes, she was alone in the world, cut off from everybody normal.

It would take Minnie a long time before she stopped thinking of herself as a freak. Her family had branded her, as certainly as if they'd pressed red-hot steel to her flesh. She didn't think about her family much any more. The pictures of them in her mind had grown faint, vague, like photographs wasting in sunlight. Her father's misshapen felt hat, jammed down on his head, and her mother's cotton dresses, worn everywhere she went because they were all she had, were two of the few details that stuck in her mind. She couldn't even remember what her sisters looked like, as though all that had happened to her, starting with old Alexander Moss-back Frill, had erased a part of her mind, the part given over to memory, the part that assures us all that we are alive and that we have been living a life, accumulating remembrances of events and people that shaped us and that add up to who we are. That part of Minnie was fragmented, almost gone, had been since the moment they put her out of the car, so that when she lived with the Frosts she began being somebody new. She did not decide to do it; it seemed to be already decided for her. And she just was. The crawling through the window in the middle of the night (something she did not have to do and knew she didn't; she could have left anytime she wanted to) was like being reborn into a new Minnie. She reinvented herself. She even found herself creating memories to fit who she had become, though those memories proved to be ephemeral and were soon replaced by others that were equally fictitious and vaporous. So her life was like a series of dreams that you wake up from and can never recall again.

It was Captain Donohue Taylor Sledge whose name was called. Immediately Minnie looked at Miss Hooten, who gave her the slightest wink. Of course it was a put-up job. She didn't care; it was not her business, though she didn't know that Captain Sledge had paid Miss Hooten an extra fifty dollars to win the raffle. (Later it would occur to her that Captain Sledge had probably paid extra to win the raffle, and Miss Hooten never made any effort to share that money with Minnie.) Everybody cheered and clapped him on the back. Captain Sledge was muscular, of just under medium height, with wide shoulders made bulky from years of working on his boat. His completely bald head was sun-burned, along with his face, and he had a little black Van Dyke beard around his mouth. His skin was ruddy, weather-beaten. His legs beneath his shorts were covered with wiry black hairs, and he wore a thin off-white linen shirt that tied at the neck. He had soft brown eyes. He was forty-six years old. That is: exactly twenty-nine years older than Minnie.

He escorted her up the stairs to wild cheers from the lounge. The old wide floorboards were so uneven they squeaked, even squawked like you were stepping on a small bird, when you walked on them, and you could stump your toe even under the fake oriental rugs that covered the floors. They went down the hall to the room that Miss Hooten had fixed up for the occasion, lacy green curtains, a matching spread on the bed. If

Minnie was nervous she didn't show it. Captain Sledge sat in a straight chair and watched Minnie take her clothes off. She was all that he had expected, compact, smooth, shaped as though with the fine hand of a master sculptor. Her erect little nipples stuck straight out. The hair at the bottom of her stomach was as thick and rich as the hair on her head.

"Take your clothes off," she said, a slight trembling of her voice threatening to betray her. Minnie stretched out on the bed and opened her legs, the way Paula had done it that day. She could hear the faint male voices from the lounge below, occasionally punctuated with a laugh or a bellow, smell the high bitter cigarette smoke mixed with the thick, sweet cigar and pipe smoke that seeped upward through the cracks between the wide boards of the floor. She watched Captain Sledge remove his clothes. She marveled at the size of his dick (she might as well begin to employ the words for it that she had learned since she'd arrived there): it was much longer and thicker than the one Paula's client had had. Captain Sledge approached the bed, and like Paula's client, he, too, dropped to his knees and buried his face between her legs; Minnie tensed, then threw her head back and relaxed into the warm manipulations of his tongue.

THERE WAS NO BLOOD, no blood at all. Minnie wondered if somewhere, in some time beyond and away from what she could remember, she had already given up her virginity, but the difficulty that Captain Sledge had had in inserting himself into her would seem to belie that.

He was not disturbed at the absence of blood. "Some girls don't bleed," he said.

"But . . ."

"Don't worry about it, Minnie," Captain Sledge said.

It was painful; it had not been fun. Captain Sledge had seemed to enjoy it, however, moaning and grunting and jerking on top of her as she tried to lock her ankles over his back, not being able to reach, realizing that Paula was much taller than she was. She had felt awkward, worrying that she was not doing the right things. Or doing them in the wrong way.

In the coming months and years, she would come to understand that she need not have worried at all.

6

THE PANHANDLE, FLORIDA

JULY 1964

They were on Highway 98, a few miles west of Grayton Beach, when Lester Ray saw the police lights flashing behind him. "Oh, shit," he said.

"Oh, shit," Mrs. McCrory parroted.

Lester Ray coasted to a stop on the edge of the highway, as with one hand he shoved the bottle under the seat. He had been feeling warm and mellow with his occasional nips of the whiskey. He had kept it on a steady fifty miles per hour, so it couldn't be speeding. He thought, Orville! But how could the man know his mother was gone that soon? Unless he came to get her in the middle of the night and she wasn't there, which seemed unlikely. And he didn't think Lyman Duck would ever call the police for any reason. It was one in the morning, and there was no traffic to speak of. He peered into the rearview mirror, his throat tightening. He had already decided what he would say about not having a license if they were stopped, but he had not discussed it with the women. "Just go along with what I say," he said, putting two Sen-Sens on his tongue.

"Why should we?" Virgin Mary said from the back seat.

"Because I'll put your ass out beside the road if you don't."

"Yes, sir, captain," she said.

The cop stood just outside the open window, peering into the car. He was a tall, thin man with a blond mustache. He wore his hat on the back of his head. He had a flashlight in his hand, resting on the sill of the window, his face mostly in moon-shadow. The insects were loud outside;

coupled love bugs drifted in both cars' headlights. At least a minute went by before he asked,

"Where in the world did you get this heap of junk?"

"At home," Lester Ray said.

"You drive this antique all the way from Rhode Island?"

"Yes, sir," Lester Ray said.

"A little hot for you snowbirds this time a year, ain't it?" he said. "Lemme see your license, boy."

"Well, sir, I don't have one," Lester Ray said.

"You don't have one?" the cop exclaimed. "He don't have one," he said, as though to someone else outside the car, but as far as Lester Ray could see he was alone. "Don't you know it's against the law, son, to drive without a license?"

"Yes, sir, I do. But, you see, I'm taking my grandmother there home. She wants to go home to Pensacola to die."

"To die?"

"Yes, sir, and, you see, we got robbed in Chattanooga, Tennessee, and they took my billfold with all our money and my drivers' license and everything."

"I see," the trooper said, "what ails her?"

"Sir?"

"You said she's goin home to die. Is she sick, or what?"

"Yes, sir, she has the cancer," Lester Ray said. He detected a snicker from the back seat. The cop must have heard it, too, because he switched on the flashlight and shined it into the back seat.

"Who's that?" the cop asked.

"My little sister," Lester Ray said quickly, hoping to cut V. M. off, or at least drown her out, but she said at the same time, "Virgin Mary Duck."

"Huh?" he said. He shined the flashlight on her for a long while, then all around the car, on the floorboards, on Mrs. McCrory. Then he looked Lester in the eye. His eyes were pale yellow. "That ain't funny," he said.

"She didn't go to be funny," Mrs. McCrory said. "That's her name."

He shined the flashlight on Mrs. McCrory's face. "Well," he said, "it still ain't funny. Where'd you say y'all'r headed?"

"Pensacola," Lester Ray said.

"Y'all don't talk like you from any Rhode Island," the cop said.

"I was born and raised in Pensacola," Mrs. McCrory said.

"If you let us go, I'll suck your dick," V. M. said from the back seat. Lester Ray reached back over the seat and squeezed her leg.

"What'd she say?" the cop asked.

"She said she was sick," Lester Ray said. "She's sick, too." He squeezed harder.

"Oh," V. M. cried out. "Stop that, you asshole." He squeezed so hard he thought his fingers were going to meet in the middle of her leg. "Ohhhh," she moaned.

"She's hurtin," Lester Ray said. "I'm in a hurry to get em there, but I ain't been speedin. No, sir. Not over fifty miles an hour."

"I seen that," the policeman said, "you wasn't speedin. Get out of the car, please."

"Huh?"

"You understand English, don't you? I said, get out of the car."

"Why?"

"Now don't go gettin smart-ass on me, son. We been doin okay up to now." He yanked open the driver's-side door. Lester Ray got out. He figured the cop had smelled the whiskey. He was not as tall as the cop, but he was bulkier, heavier. The cop made him put his hands on top of the car and he started to pat him down. "Hey, what's this?" he said, pulling some bills from Lester Ray's pocket. There were three twenties, a five and a one. "I thought you said you got robbed." The cop put the bills in his pocket.

"We had that hid under the floor mat," Lester Ray said.

"You shoulda hid your drivers' license under there, too," the policeman said. "I'm gonna have to take you in."

When Lester Ray had stepped out of the car he'd noticed the policeman's riot stick dangling from his belt. He spun quickly, catching the cop's nose and forehead with the back of his fist. The cop dropped to his knees, trying to grab Lester Ray, but the boy was too quick for him. He got the night stick and brought it down heavily on the back of the cop's head. The man went down on his face by the side of the road.

"Come on, help me," Lester Ray said. V. M. scrambled out. Lester Ray was holding both arms, dragging the policeman toward his car. V. M. grabbed his belt and helped him along.

"You shoulda let me suck his dick," she said.

"Shut the fuck up!" Lester Ray said.

"Is he dead?" she asked.

"No! He's not dead. He's just out cold."

They dragged the cop around on the ditch side of his car. The lights were still whirling around and around, flashing red on them every half-second. A car went by, but they were out of its headlights and it didn't stop. Better them than me, the driver was probably thinking, better them than me. Lester Ray got the man's handcuffs and fastened them onto his wrist and onto the underside of the car's bumper. He fished in the man's pockets and got his keys and the bills; he tossed the keys across the ditch into the weeds and jammed the money back in his pocket. Then he and V. M. hustled back to the car and got in. The engine roared, Lester Ray floorboarded it, and the old car fishtailed its way back onto the highway.

Nobody said anything for a long time. The love bugs danced two by two in the headlights and spun by, whirling and blundering, occasionally splatting on the windshield. Then, on down the road, V. M. said, "Them bugs are fuckin."

"I said shut up," Lester Ray said.

UP AHEAD, AS THOUGH waiting for the travelers, (though there was, of course, no way they could have known they were coming) were two men drinking sweet red wine in an Airstream trailer parked among others like it behind the J. F. Freeman Traveling Rides and Shows, the carnival portion of the West Florida State Fair in Pensacola. One of the men was Emil Kirova, the general manager of the Freeman carnival, a dark, handsome, brooding man in his late forties; the other was Xillarmet Yak, a "little person" in his thirties (billed as a midget in the show, though most knew not to refer to him as such in his presence), perched on the edge of the built-in sofa, dressed in a tuxedo, his legs dangling above the floor by six or so inches. Everybody called him simply Yak, since they didn't want to go to the trouble to try to correctly say his first name, which annoyed Yak, since the name was simple and easy to pronounce: "Yarmay."

"Are we going to make the movie or not?" Yak asked. He wore his brownish hair oiled and swept straight back; his face looked as though some giant (there was one of those, too, in the show) had put one hand on his head and the other under his chin and squeezed, so that his features were flattened and squished together. His little eyes were like silver BBs.

"The plans are still in place," Emil said. His hair was black and curly, his skin ruddy, his teeth startlingly white against his swarthy skin. He wore a metallic blue shirt, unbuttoned down the front revealing thick black, kinky chest hairs, a pair of purple bell-bottomed trousers, and high-heeled cowboy boots. He wore a bright red scarf around his neck. Emil was the Big Mick, or King, of the kumpaniy, or union, of Romani Gypsies that traveled with and operated the carnival.

The J. F. Freeman Traveling Rides and Shows was constantly on the move, traveling from town to town all over the southeastern United States from March through October every year. The winter months they spent near Fort Myers in south Florida, which was convenient, since Fort Myers was the site of one of the biggest Gypsy burying grounds in the entire country, and the destination for many Gypsy pilgrimages. The carnival consisted of numerous rides—a Tilt-A-Whirl, two Ferris wheels, bumper cars, two carousels, some other children's rides, and a small roller coaster, along with booths of chance, food and drink stalls, fortune telling tents, and the shows: THE FANTASTIC ODDITIES OF THE WORLD and THE STREETS OF PARIS, a girly show featuring varying degrees of nudity, depending upon whether or not the local law enforcement agencies were open to bribery. Most were.

"I need a 'little woman,'" Yak said.

"We all need a woman," Emil said.

"You know what I mean," Yak said.

They had made several stag films, using the girls from THE STREETS OF PARIS show and various men they had recruited (Emil himself had starred in one of the movies, with the lead dancer whose name was Sheila Serena), which they sold in the Annex in the back of THE STREETS OF PARIS tent, which cost extra to enter and featured some moves by the girls that they couldn't do out front, even with the police suitably bribed. Yak had had the idea of making a film with two "little people." "It'll be a curiosity, we'll sell hundreds of them," he said. "People will like a movie with two midgets fuckin in it."

"I thought you didn't like the word 'midget,'" Emil said.

"Listen, this is show biz. I'm a midget out there on that banner-line, and the Talker calls me a midget. On the label of that movie, I'll be a midget. But," he said, "I'm not a midget, and don't you ever forget it." He drank down the rest of his wine and poured himself another glass; it was Mogen David, and they were drinking it out of juice glasses.

Emil leaned back in his chair and propped his boots on an ottoman. He sighed. "We had a good crowd tonight," he said.

"That we did," Yak said.

People were bused in from all over the Panhandle to come to the West Florida State Fair. There had been an inordinate number of school-age children in attendance that particular night, which had caused a near riot in the Oddities tent. There was a lot of angry pushing and shoving when the crowd learned that you had to pay extra to get into the Annex to see Joe-Josephine and the dead two-headed baby preserved in a large jar, and you had to be at least eighteen years old. Joe-Josephine was billed as a half-man, half-woman, and she (she preferred that gender designation) was a true hermaphrodite, with two sets of genitals between her legs, male and female. She gave those who had paid the extra quarter a quick peek by spreading her legs and lifting her skirt for a moment; it was never really a good enough or long enough look for them to be sure they had actually seen what they had seen. She had breasts, but she strapped the right one down beneath her costume, so that it appeared she had only one. Emil and Yak had tried to persuade Joe-Josephine to star in one of their movies, but she steadfastly, even angrily, refused. Unlike the true authenticity of Joe-Josephine's genitals, the two-headed baby was a fake made of rubber.

Xillarmet Yak had been born in Stolpen, Germany, and had come to America with his immigrant parents in 1921, when he was a baby and it was not yet apparent that he would not grow beyond three feet, four inches tall. They had settled in Helen, in north Georgia, near family members who had come over earlier. When the child was old enough for them to perceive his stunted growth, his parents were disappointed, then horrified, that they had spawned a deformed child. They were uneducated, superstitious people, and they kept little Xillarmet locked away in a closet in the house until he was fifteen years old, when a cousin convinced the parents that they were sitting on a money-making proposition. When Ringling Brothers Circus came to Atlanta, they hired the teenager out to the show, and he traveled with Ringling Brothers for the next ten years, learning to dance, to cavort with the other midgets and crack jokes, even to sing. J. F. Freeman Traveling Rides and Shows offered him equal money, so he broke his contract with Ringling, thus cutting his parents out of their share of his earnings, and he had been with Freeman ever since. He had not seen his parents or any other members of his family for more than thirty years.

Emil Kirova had been traveling with this same band of Gypsies all his life. His parents had died when he was twelve, and he had become a child of the vitsa, or extended family, which included all the families of the kumpaniy. Early on in his life they had traveled around picking fruit or tarring roofs and building porches, picking up auto body work when they could, the women telling fortunes and selling plastic flowers. When Emil was in his early thirties the kumpaniy had hooked on with J. F. Freeman, first as gazonies, or laborers—the lowest-ranking workers—and worked their way up. Emil had become a Talker outside the ODDITIES tent and THE STREETS OF PARIS show until he eventually took over as general manager of the carnival.

"A good crowd translates into money," Yak said. "How many loops did we sell?" He was referring to the stag reels.

"Nineteen," Emil said.

"You know," Yak said, musing, "I believe pornography's gonna become a big business someday."

VIRGIN MARY DUCK DISCOVERED cotton candy. She shivered with delight and pleasure as the finely spun sugar—with its intense sweetness—melted in her mouth, on her tongue. It seemed to her the perfect culmination of her lifelong unfulfilled yearning for candy, so much so that she didn't even have to chew it. All the effort it required was parting with a dime. At first she found it hard to believe that the essence of candy could be so easily achieved, that the joy of sweet could be so readily distilled into one handful that seemed to simply dissolve and disperse itself throughout her body by the simple action of her beating heart and her circulating blood, so that she, herself, became a pillar of sugar. A walking all-day sucker. It was the kind of ecstasy she had never experienced in her sad, severely deprived life.

But she had a new life now. She had put her old daddy behind her. She was already in love with Lester Ray, and she didn't mind admitting it to herself. She wouldn't tell anybody else. Not the old lady, though the old lady was nice to her. Mrs. McCrory didn't treat her like trash. At first V. M. was suspicious of the way the old lady was so sweet to her; now she took it for granted. They had all three slept in the car last night, when they finally got to the Fairgrounds, which they had a difficult time finding. Neither she nor Lester Ray knew anything about Pensacola, and they had kept going down streets that ended at water they couldn't even see across.

"That's the bay," she had observed.

"No kiddin," Lester Ray had sneered.

She knew it was the bay because she and her father had come through there once, staying two or three weeks. Her father had been working for a company that was resurfacing the highway. He stood all day with a sign that had STOP on one side and SLOW on the other, letting cars take turns using the one lane that was open. They had pitched their tent inland from Pensacola and had never ventured into the city, but she heard people talking about "the bay."

Lester Ray had drunk nearly half the bottle of whiskey by the time they found the Fairgrounds, and he passed out as soon as he got the car parked. He didn't offer the bottle around. V. M. would have liked some, but she didn't say anything. Mrs. McCrory had been asleep since right after that cop had pulled them over, sitting upright with her hat askew on her head, the little cherries jiggling with the motion of the car, and she didn't wake up when they stopped. V. M. got out of the car and poked around a little bit, but everything was dark, all closed down, and the huge parking lot was mostly empty. So she went back to the car, but she was too excited to sleep. She had the back seat to herself, the only one who could lie down, and she was the one who couldn't sleep. She lay there thinking about her daddy, snoring away in their tent back in Piper. He was going to be mad as a hornet when he found out she was gone. Especially when he realized that she had taken the whiskey and the money, about twenty dollars in small bills and change hidden in a Tube Rose Snuff can underneath her father's cot. (She didn't know what he had done with the rest of the money from fixing Mrs. McCrory's car.)

It was the scent that led her to it, as though it had reached out and grabbed her by the nose and forced her to the cotton candy stand. She stood there watching the man roll the little paper cone around and around in the machine, picking up the spun pink sugar. There were other people standing around, and she was aware that they were all looking at her, probably, she thought, because they knew she was an ignorant redneck who didn't know what the cotton candy was. Or because she was ugly. Those were true, but it was mainly the overlarge dress, with the skirt oddly tied up around her waist so that it ballooned out around her bare knees.

"You want a sample?" the man in the booth said, after she'd been standing there watching him for a long time.

"Say what?" she asked. She looked around to make sure he was talking to her.

"A bite. See. Here." He held out a small fluff of the stuff, like a pink cotton boll.

She took it and put it in her mouth and in two seconds it was gone, leaving her mouth as sticky sweet and as unsatisfied as she had ever experienced. "How much?" she asked eagerly.

"A dime," he said.

MRS. MCCRORY WAS SITTING in an aluminum folding chair that the boy had found for her somewhere. She was watching little children and some of their mothers lining up to ride the merry-go-round. They were happy, and Mrs. McCrory smiled. She had no idea where she was. It could be heaven, she thought, but it was too noisy for that. Surely it wasn't hell. God wouldn't let little children ride a merry-go-round in hell, would he?

She had totally forgotten her house, and her son Orville, and everything else about Piper. As far as she was concerned, her life had begun this morning when she opened her eyes. She had no history that she knew and it did not bother her in the least. The only thing that nagged at her was that she was hungry. She had had no breakfast this morning. She had waked up in somebody's car, stiff and sore from sitting up to sleep. The first things she was aware of were the smells of dust, parking-lot tar, and whiskey. She had straightened the hat on her head and sat there by herself for a while (she didn't know how long) until the boy came up to the car with the chair and helped her out and led her into the carnival. She knew what a carnival was, though she hadn't seen one since she was a little girl. It was enough, she supposed, that she knew it was a carnival. And it made people happy.

LESTER RAY WALKED ALL over, looking at the rides, standing out in front of the shows. He saw a number of people that he was almost certain were Gypsies: slightly darker people with skin like parchment and coal-black hair, joking and laughing among themselves, an occasional flash of gold from their teeth. They seemed other-worldly, as if they existed in a country of their own devising, not this country but a different country within this country, foreign and enchanting. Not a part of this life at all, as though they were just passing through it. He envied them their identity, which was a not-identity, a refusal to be a part of anything but themselves and what they were: constantly moving, never putting down roots that would hold them in a specific place and define them, stifle them, confine them within a set of rules and mores and customs that were not their own. Lester Ray felt an affinity with them, a tug and a pull toward them, and he supposed that that was his mother in him, that part of him that was her and not him, Earl Holsomback. It was whatever it was inside her that had made her have to go off and leave him—made her, he knew that now, so that she had no choice. She had to go, but that did not stop him from hating her and resenting her and missing her and loving her all at the same time. He knew that he did not yet fully understand, and he was not sure he ever would.

He approached a man sitting outside the bumper cars tent. He was swarthy, his black hair thick and speckled with gray, as though some-one had taken a watercolor brush and dipped it in white and dotted here and there, and he wore a gold earring in his left ear. He wore an open-collared blue work shirt, with a heavy gold chain visible behind it, blue jeans stuffed into shiny cowboy boots with high heels and sharp, pointed toes.

"Hi," Lester Ray said, and the man looked up and fixed him with an inquiring gaze. His eyes were pools of motor oil.

"Hi," he said. He had a day or two's worth of growth on his cheeks and chin; it looked as though his face had been dipped in tiny iron filings and they'd stuck all over his lower face.

"I'm lookin for a job," Lester Ray said.

"A job?" the man said, "you're mighty young, ain't you?"

"Seventeen," Lester Ray lied. "But I can do the work of any man."

The man smiled. He, too, had a gold tooth. "You can, can you?" he said.

"Yeah," Lester Ray said.

"Just while we're here in Pensacola? Or you want to get on perma-nent?"

"I want to travel with you," Lester Ray said. "I've got my own car."

The man took out a pack of Camels. He offered Lester Ray one, and Lester Ray took it. The man lit both with a wooden match. Then he settled back and blew his first cloud of smoke toward the sky. He stuck out his hand. "I'm Malik," he said.

Lester Ray shook his hand. "Lester Ray Holsomback," he said.

"Most of the gazonies we get are winos or people runnin from the law," Malik said.

"The what?"

"Gazonies! Gazonies. Laborers. Guys who do the dirty work, you know? The grunt work."

"I'll do anything," Lester Ray said.

"You ain't a wino. I can tell that by lookin at you. You a junkie?"

"No, I'm not any junkie."

"All right," Malik said. "I guess you runnin away, ain't you?" Lester Ray just stood there, not knowing what to say. "Don't worry about it," Malik said, "everybody in this fuckin outfit's runnin away from something or other." He stood up. "Come on, I'll take you back to Emil. He's our Big Mick, he has to okay any gaje we take on." Lester Ray fell in stride beside him. He was not understanding all that Malik was saying, but he didn't want to interrupt him to ask. "Most of the gazonies are gaje, and they come and go," Malik said and laughed. "They spend their time fightin and drinkin when they're not workin. We usually leave three or four of em in the jailhouse in every town we stop in. There's a real turnover problem with the gazonies."

They went around behind the show tents, where there were several silver-colored Airstream trailers and other house trailers of various colors and sizes, and a number of big eighteen-wheeler trucks. They stopped in front of one of the Airstreams that was hitched to a long, red Cadillac, and Malik knocked on the metal door.

A man opened the door. When he did the door scraped a noise, metal on metal, which could have been an audible rip in the fabric of Lester Ray's universe. He somehow knew—from that second on—his life was altered, thrown off track. The man was of medium height, in a red shirt, his skin the color of cream with several tablespoons of coffee in it. It was not really dark; he could have been one of the vacationers passing back through Piper on their way home after a week of lying out on the beach. His eyes were chocolate, soft and calm, settled and confident, charged with an energetic self-awareness. They were full of an almost-feminine kindness. This is the way Jesus's eyes would have looked, Lester Ray thought. The man just stood there for a moment, contemplating Lester Ray, then he stepped back and said, "Come in." It was as though Malik didn't need to tell him what the boy wanted, as if Emil knew everything about him just by looking at him: his history, what he was doing there, everything.

The inside of the trailer was dark and hot, with just two weak twenty watt bulbs burning in sconces on the wall, which was covered with vari-colored scarves and hanging beads of all colors and sizes. There were icons, too, many of them exquisitely painted on wood, Madonna and child, Jesus, the Sacred Heart, the Saints. Emil had been raised in the church. Up until the time his mother died, no matter where they were camped, she would find the nearest Roman Catholic Church and take him to Mass. The Roman Mass was very close to the Eastern Orthodox ritual, the church she'd grown up with in Bulgaria and Romania, the countries in which her familia had journeyed. Emil had quit going to Mass a long time ago, right after his mother had died. His trailer was crowded with furniture; there was a bedroom on one end and a kitchen on the other. There was a faint hint of rose perfume in the air, along with the scents of spices: rosemary and curry and garlic.

Emil motioned the boy to a chair, and he sat. Emil sat down across from him, on the built-in sofa. "What can I do for you?" he said.

The boy glanced at the closed door, where Malik had been only seconds ago, then back at Emil. "Well," he said, "I want a job. And Ma ...Ma ..."

"Malik."

"Yeah, Malik told me I need to speak to you. Since I'm a whatcha-callit."

The man smiled. "Gajo," he said, "it means a non-Gypsy."

"Yeah. So. Here I am."

"What's your name?"

"Oh, Lester Ray Holsombeck," Lester Ray said.

"I am Emil Kirova," Emil said, "what kind of job do you want?"

"I'll do anything. Even ..." He could not remember the word. "... even grunt work."

"How old are you?" Emil asked.

"I'm seventeen, almost eighteen," Lester Ray said.

"I hope you're not lying to me. We have to be extra careful, you know." The man smiled broadly again. He winked. "We kidnap little white children, and we eat them."

"Well, I'm no child, and ain't nobody kidnappin me!" Lester Ray said.

"I suppose not," he said, "you look like you could take care of yourself. What about school?"

"I quit school a couple of years ago. Ain't missed it yet."

"All right," Emil said, "you can help me on shows. Helping put the tops and the banner-line up and take them down, fillin in with ticket sales, just anything I need you to do. It's a full-time job, and I do mean full-time. Thirty dollars a week. Okay?"

"Okay," Lester Ray said. "There's just one other thing."

Emil lifted one eyebrow. "Yes?" he asked.

"See, I'm travelin with my grandmother. She comes along with us."

"You have your own truck?"

"Yes. Car."

"Fine, then," Emil said, and he stood up to indicate the end of the interview.

Outside the trailer Lester Ray felt the summer sun burning down on his head. He would have to get a hat. He was excited to have his first job, but troubled by what he had felt when he'd first seen Emil Kirova. Off balance. Maybe what he was sensing was a warning; he didn't know. He just knew that when he had first looked at Emil something had crawled through him like little electric sparks. It stimulated and cautioned him at the same time. It was unfamiliar, like the inside of Emil's trailer, which resembled something from an old movie. Something he had seen some-where before, maybe in that movie, maybe in some dream long forgotten. And Emil himself: it was as if Lester Ray had seen him, had known him, even before he opened the door, as if he knew who would be there and what he would look like. Not like an old friend or relative, but like a glimpsed photograph from some old time that Lester Ray had lived, a time faded from memory but not quite erased.

MALIK INTRODUCED LESTER RAY to a man named Artago, who had a small Airstream trailer for sale for five hundred dollars. It was old and ragged and smelly inside, dusty and mildewed, but it had two bunk beds and a kitchen, plus a small sitting area, and the tires were in good shape. Artago was fat, with greasy skin and hair, and two teeth missing in the front. "You can pay me by the month," Artago said, "fifty dollars a month, okay? For another fifty I'll weld a trailer hitch on your car for you."

"Okay," Lester Ray said. He could have taken the entire five hundred fifty out of the money they had, but he didn't want anybody to know they had a large amount of cash, so he could simply take what they needed every month from the stash to make up for the payment on the trailer that would come out of his wages. As soon as the West Florida State Fair was over they would be ready to move on with the carnival, which Malik had told him was headed to Mobile, Alabama, next.

The three of them had slept in the car for the last two nights. Lester Ray knew that sooner or later he was going to have to dump Virgin Mary; he had told her emphatically that he would bring her this far, but then she would be on her own. There was no room for her in the Airstream, which he had been cleaning with bleach and airing out. And he was tired of her constant carrying on. She had found a store somewhere near the fairgrounds and bought her some clothes, some pants and a shirt. (Where she got the money he did not know and did not plan to ask. But he did get the shoebox out of the trunk and count Mrs. McCrory's money, just to be sure.) They were obviously boy's clothes, buckle-butt khaki pants that zipped up the front, a blue, button-down short-sleeved shirt. Some black tennis shoes.

"You're gonna walk around lookin like a little boy," Mrs. McCrory said.

"You think I give a shit?" V. M. said.

"Maybe you ought not to talk like that around Mrs. McCrory," Lester Ray said.

"Maybe you think I give a shit about that, too?"

They were sitting around in straight chairs in front of their new Airstream. It was not yet attached to the Oldsmobile, which Malik had assured Lester Ray would pull the trailer with no problems.

"Well," Lester Ray said, "what are you gonna do, V. M.?"

"Whattaya mean, what am I gonna do?"

"This was as far as I agreed to carry you. You're on your own, now. That's what I mean."

"If you think you're just gonna go off and leave me in Pensacola, you got another think comin," she said. With her carrot red hair chopped off short, she really did look like a little buck-toothed boy. She was better looking as a boy than as a girl. She was going to rot all her teeth out with all that cotton candy if she didn't watch out. That was all she ate, day and night. ("That ain't healthy," Mrs. McCrory had said. "You think I give a shit?" V. M. had shot back.)

Virgin Mary sat there glaring at Lester Ray. She figured he didn't have sense enough to know that she loved him. He was just sitting there, puffing on a cigarette, thinking he was going to get rid of her that easy. No way in hell. "You desert me here I'm gonna put the law on you so fast it'll make your head swim," she said. "Drivin a stolen car, assaultin a policeman, kidnappin me and haulin me off to Pensacola for immoral purposes . . ."

"Immoral purposes!?" he exclaimed. "It's immoral to let you loose on other folks! You ought to be kept in a cage!"

"Do you think it'll rain today?" Mrs. McCrory asked. She was looking off at the sky, at something way on the other side of the sun.

"Hah, you'd like it if I was in a cage, wouldn't you, sugar," V. M. said, "cause then you could get at me any time you wanted."

"When have I 'got at you?'" Lester Ray exclaimed.

"That don't mean you don't want to," she said. "I can see it in your eyes."

"If you see that in my eyes, girl, then you're a blind damn fool."

"See there," she said, "flirtin with me!"

"Shit," Lester Ray said, throwing down the cigarette butt and grinding it under the heel of his shoe. He got up and walked off, leaving them sitting there.

So HE SHOULD HAVE known, should have foreseen, that he would be no match for her, back there in Piper in that yard in the dark of night when he relented to her begging and agreed to take her with them. Or maybe he should have known from even the first time Lyman Duck brought her into Saddler's Lounge to sit there drinking a Dr Pepper through a straw. But he didn't. He knew little enough about girls and women, hadn't known that they played by a different set of rules, but he should have, he reasoned, he should have known from whatever of his mother she had left in him when she ran away. He might want to choke the girl and dump her body off a bridge into a bayou, but he couldn't do that, could never do that. In spite of her foul mouth and foul ways, there was something innocent about her, unless he was confusing innocence with plain ignorance. But there was that woman thing again, that mystery that had been a plague on men since Adam, and he knew that he did not know Virgin Mary Duck very well at all, not even enough to know innocence from ignorance. The only significant woman in his life up to now had been Mrs. McCrory, and her mind was such that she was absent half the time or more, and even if she'd been sane all the time he doubted that an eighty-three-year-old woman was what he needed to teach him, a fourteen-year-old boy, what he needed to know about women. And the sloppy, dumb whores that his father brought home were no help at all. Lester Ray already knew about sex. There was Mrs. Nijim, of course. When he was in the seventh grade there had been a high school girl named Lacy Limm, a dirt-poor girl from out in the piney woods, that all the boys called Lacy Limburger, who would do it with anybody, and Lester Ray had jumped at the chance. Lucy Limm turned out to be a nice girl who just liked sex as much as boys did, and Lester Ray had ended up beating up a couple of the older boys for taunting her. Then, just after he turned thirteen, there had been a waitress at Saddler's Lounge named Maude, who was in her forties, blonde and heavily made up, very curvy, who took him to bed a few times and taught him a lot of things. Maude eventually moved on to another dead-end job in another deadbeat town, but she left an indelible impression on Lester Ray.

So his mind was already there when he first saw Sheila. One of his morning chores was to clean up the tents (or "tops," as everybody around there called them), picking up trash—napkins and paper cups and candy wrappers, popcorn bags and other debris—off the ground and stuffing it into a canvas trash bag he dragged around. Then he would dump it onto a growing pile out behind the trailer village, which he figured the city of Pensacola would have to deal with when they were gone.

Sheila Serenas was a tall, lean brunette, a beautiful face with high, sharp cheekbones and a little pointed nose. She was the lead dancer in THE STREETS OF PARIS show and she had a natural smile that seemed to be always there. She had long slim legs, tanned and sleek, and her breasts, though not particularly large, were well-shaped and firm.

So it was in the morning, when Lester Ray was cleaning the top, that he first saw her, walking out from behind the curtains that closed off the backstage area. She wore tiny white short shorts that Lester Ray at first thought with a shock were just panties, and a navy blue T-shirt, and she had a cup of coffee in her hand. She stopped and looked at him, and he stared at her. She was certainly the best-looking woman he had ever seen. She looked stunning, as though she had just stepped out of a perfume ad in a magazine. Until that moment he had not known women like that actually existed. He had thought women like that were like the underwear models in the Sears Roebuck catalogue. The items—first the toys when he was little and then the shotguns and rifles and motorbikes when he got older—were things to be looked at and admired and longed for but were forever out of his reach, that never actually took form and became real.

"Did you fix the loose board in the stage floor?" she asked him, her eyes sparkling even in the dim light of the tent. He just stood there, gripping the neck of the trash sack.

"Ma'am?" he asked. His tongue felt swollen in his mouth.

She was smiling as though he had cracked a joke, said something funny. Her lips were bright red, shiny. She came to the edge of the stage, which was about a foot off the ground, and looked down at him. "Oh," she said, "you're not Mahmoud."

"No, ma'am," he said. He knew exactly who she must be and what she must do. The idea that he might be allowed to see her naked made his hands tremble and caused a tingling in his pants.

"You're new," she said, "what's your name?"

"Lester Ray Holsomback," he said, without stammering, and she said, "I'm Sheila." She knelt down and extended her hand toward him. He took it, a petite hand, delicate bones under soft skin like he was holding an unfeathered baby bird that had fallen from the nest, held it until she initiated the shake. "Glad to meet you, Lester Ray Holsomback," she said. Her teeth were even and astonishingly white. He felt more than smelled her perfume: lavender, lilac. It seemed to surround his head like rising steam. It pulled him forward, jerked him so quickly and so firmly that he almost lost his balance, even as he realized that he had not moved at all.

"Good to meet you, too," he said, and he had no idea where that nicety came from, as he didn't think he had ever said it before. The occasions in his life when he had felt moved to be polite were few, maybe even nonexistent.

"When did you join us, Lester Ray?" she asked.

"Day before yesterday," he said.

"Well, welcome to the Freeman shows, such as they are." She drained the last of her coffee from the cup. She was still kneeling on the edge of the stage, her face not three feet from his. He could feel her heat. "Want to come back for a cup of coffee?" she asked.

"I . . . I better finish cleanin up the tops," he said. Somehow he knew he had better be careful. He sensed he might be in a lot of trouble if he jumped in where he had no business being. And he had no business sitting and drinking coffee with her.

"Okay," she said, "some other time. You have a rain check." She stood up then, and turned and walked back toward the curtains, sashaying, for his benefit he knew. He knew she knew he was looking at her ass, the crack of it plainly outlined, the bottom fourth of each cheek bulging out of the brief shorts. She disappeared behind the curtain, exactly as she must in her show, he thought, though he had never seen a girly show before. Only in his imagination.

MRS. McCRORY LAY ON the narrow bunk in the house trailer. She didn't think she'd ever slept in a house trailer before, but she couldn't be absolutely sure. The boy was good to her, making sure she was comfortable. But that little buck-toothed boy, where did he come from? The boy—not the buck-toothed one but the good-looking one—had told her that they had gotten yet another license plate, this one a Mississippi one, because he was afraid somebody had seen them in the car with the Rhode Island plate. He told her he might have the car painted, and asked her what color she wanted it to be. Why should she care? It wasn't her car. She told him to paint it chartreuse or heliotrope if he wanted to. She knew they were running away, but she couldn't remember who they were running from. But she was glad to get out of that old house and go somewhere. He told her they were in Pensacola, but it didn't look like Pensacola to her. It looked like a carnival. Pensacola was on the beach, with the waves rolling in. Why would somebody want to fool her like that? Lester Ray.

That was the good-looking boy's name. Of course. How had she forgotten that? She hoped his name didn't leak out of her brain the next time she saw him. Lester Ray. Lester Ray. She would remember, then the minute his face popped up in her sight the name was gone. Gone with the wind. Hah. He might as well be called Rhett Butler. Now who in the world is that? No sooner had she thought of that name than it too was gone. She lay there taking inventory, as she had done every night of her life while waiting for sleep; it was like a child's prayer: . . . and bless mama, and papa, and grandma, and Aunt Silvia. She thought of Winston, her husband of so many years, and allowed herself to miss him for a few moments. She wouldn't dwell on it. She thought of Orville: but she thought of him as a little boy, and not the person who became a teenager and then never emerged from the grotesquery of that, as though he had somehow been arrested in a perpetual post-adolescence, had not survived beyond his thirteenth year except as a person she did not know and did not like. She blamed herself and Winston for that, though she had tried to be firm when she was supposed to be and lax when it was best, but she had never fully known which was which. And Lester Ray, who seemed to have outgrown and gone beyond that ugly phase before he was ten years old and had become a man beyond his years, under her watchful eye and perhaps her guidance, too, though she had already failed once and so was hesitant to take any credit at all. All of this began to drift away, like smoke on the horizon that was disappearing even as it was observed.

So finally she slept, her demented mind a mixture of fear and pride and vanity and hope. Seasoned with love, and with terror. She slept profoundly and peacefully.

7

NEW YORK CITY

DECEMBER 1942

innie stood on the sidewalk in front of Lackey's Tavern on Seventh Avenue, a little north of Times Square. The traffic ground by, its steady growling punctuated by car horns. The neon lights danced in the air all around her. She wore dark wool slacks and a heavy blue jacket, both of which she had bought at a used clothing store. It was cold and she was hungry. She still had a little of the money she'd left Cedar Key with, but it was dwindling fast. She had sworn when she left the Coronado Hotel that her days of turning tricks were over, that she would no longer allow herself to be for sale to any man who nodded in her direction. She was tired of that phase of her life and she was moving on.

There were Christmas lights on the street and in the shop windows, and carols blared from speakers in the cafes and taverns onto the sidewalk, which was crowded with soldiers, boys shipping out to the west coast to train before going off to fight the Germans in Europe or the Japanese in the South Pacific. They poured up the avenues during their layovers, a thick, khaki flood, surging up from the huge, gray stone Penn Station, a night on the town before reboarding their train for California. They jammed the bars and clubs, their noise swelling, their laughter and their yelling a cacophony with the recorded carols and the jazz bands and singers stretching to be heard above the crowd. Most of the soldiers were concentrated in Times Square with its flood of bright, jerky lights, its bars and cut-rate movie houses. It all had a frantic, hurried tone, a desperation, as though each one of them knew that he would not return from the vicious conflict in the Pacific.

Minnie was twenty-one years old, just about the same age as most of these boys who were going off to die. Whereas most of them were a young twenty-one, Minnie was an old twenty-one. She had lived three lifetimes to each one of theirs.

"I want to see me some things," Minnie'd said to Miss Ida Hooten, before she left for Tallahassee with an insurance salesman named Buster Willingham, where she halfway expected to run into her family on the streets. But then she didn't really expect it, actually dreaded the possibility, though she knew it was unlikely that it would happen. She was certain that they had forgotten all about her. She had trouble visualizing their faces, and besides, it was virtually certain that they would not still be in Tallahassee, anyway, but would long since have continued their never-ending journey to wherever the long road led them. Which, Minnie realized, was exactly where she was now: on the road to nowhere and everywhere. She didn't care where it eventually took her.

Her immediate history was a long string of faces, men's faces, more recently the smooth young faces of soldiers and sailors, the faces stretching away into the past, merging and dissolving together, becoming first one man and then another, always coming back to the terrible face of old Alexander Mossback Frill. Her parents' and her sisters' faces were vague, even blank, but old Frill's was still sharp and focused; even Silas and Ruby Frost's visages had faded, but not Frill's, and Minnie now knew that it never would. The other men, the long ranks, were interchangeable, lacking substance and identity, though on the surface their connection to Minnie was as physically intimate as a man and a woman could be, yet her connection to old Frill seemed to her more intimate; it was the intimacy of the shared moment of death, the look in his eyes as he must have known that she was the last person, the last thing, he would ever see on this earth, at the same time her watching, observing, with fear and loathing, with neither sadness nor compassion, the departing of his soul (if he had one, if not, simply his life) from his body. His eyes, lit however dimly with the surge of living in one moment, in the very next going empty and blank forever in the nothingness of death. All the other men were as insignificant as flies around a fruit bowl.

"They think they are dominating you," Miss Ida Hooten had told her, "but they are not. You are always in control, and something in them knows this but they won't allow it to emerge into their consciousnesses. You are like the master, putting food out for the dog; you could withhold it, starve him, pen him up and starve him, and something in him knows this but then his nature won't allow him to really believe it, and he will be there each time you open the door, panting with eager and confident anticipation. You are the illusion that reassures men that they are, after all, really men, in control of their own lives and of you, while all the time you know they are just dogs slobbering at the bowl."

SHE HAD MANAGED TO save over four hundred dollars—a fortune, she thought—with which to leave Cedar Key, so she could have afforded her own hotel room in Tallahassee, which she had planned to get, but she wound up staying with Buster Willingham in his room, paying her share with a blow job and then a quick fuck the next morning before she walked to the downtown Greyhound bus station, carrying her carpetbag with her few clothes and belongings stuffed inside, to buy a ticket to Jacksonville. She did not know why she was going to Jacksonville; she knew nobody there, had never been there as far as she knew, though it was entirely likely that she had passed close by with her family, in a caravan going north from the orange groves of Florida to the apple orchards of North Carolina, but she would not have remembered it because it would have been just another nameless and faceless city marked only by water towers and some tall smokestacks belching white clouds into the otherwise empty and pale Florida sky.

She stayed in Jacksonville a week, making no attempt to locate anyone, not even inquiring if there might be a Gypsy caravan camped somewhere in the vicinity, because, she understood, that was not her purpose. She needed no reason to be there. She walked the streets, ate in little cafes, visited the zoo. Jacksonville had a large naval base, and there were many sailors in town every night, and she had many opportunities to turn a few tricks, but she didn't. She drank beer with them, sang Andrews Sisters' songs with them, but she did not go to bed with them. They nicknamed her "Speckled-eyes" and she laughed with them, coyly let some of them kiss her once or twice, but otherwise kept her distance. She was free and totally her own person.

At the end of the week she bought a ticket to Charleston, stayed a few days, spending her time there walking on the waterfront and gazing out across the harbor, then went on to Atlanta. Atlanta was the first real city she'd ever been in, and she got a room at the Cox-Carlton Hotel downtown; she sat at the window and watched the thick, heavy traffic on the street below. She felt like some kind of queen, looking down on her subjects from high above. She felt as though she were finally real, and not somebody else's creation, not some fantasy that had been invented for a quick moment of sensual frenzy and then discarded. For the first time in her life she felt whole and vital. It was then that she turned her sights on New York, the biggest of the big cities.

In the night, in her dreams, the faces returned, marking a monotonous succession of days and nights on Cedar Key, some of the faces, she knew, of boys she could have loved, might have loved under different circumstances. Sometimes her fantasy had been that they were all the same man, a mocking parody of marriage, with all its securities and its sameness, and the very idea made her cringe. That kind of rootedness was against her nature, violated something so deeply inbred in her that it made her momentarily nauseated, reminding her that she had been there too long, that staying in one place too long was an unnatural and conflicted state of being that made her feel unsettled and out of sync. It was the same thing she had felt, but was too young to articulate, when she knew she had to leave Silas and Ruby Frost's welcoming and warm house: it was as though she feared getting stuck there, as firmly as if she stood in slowly drying cement, that there would be a moment when it was too late and she was bound and trapped and unable to ever move again. That general, unspecified fearfulness had started to plague her, day in and day out, as she helped Ruby around the house. Like a constant hunger, it was always there, growing larger with the passing of time, hanging in the back of her mind like a persistent shadow that would not go away. And she had known she was leaving without ever having consciously decided it. As she made her way toward Cedar Key, in that dense predawn darkness, she thought there must have been a moment when she said to herself, "It's time," but she didn't remember it. It just was.

THE SOLDIERS, SOME MARINES, milled around her on the sidewalk, some stopping up short to appraise her, stare, some of them speaking, smiling: "Hey, you want a beer?" "Come go with me, baby!" "Right on in here, okay?" She stayed entrenched to the spot, not moving, simply smiling and nodding back at them when they propositioned her. She did not know why she continued to stand there, other than that she enjoyed seeing them, the tanned, lean faces, the cropped haircuts, their smells of sweat and shaving lotion. She was not looking to be picked up. She just relished the frantic motion, the noise, the simple and eagerly innocent excitement. It was like some pageant being staged for her benefit. She was content to be outside it all, as distant as she could be in the center of such a maelstrom.

And then she heard it, her name, Minnie, spoken shyly and hesitantly, a tentative question: Minnie? Barely audible above the buzz of the crowd, Anna Maria Spiroski? so that she thought at first that she had imagined it, that it was an echo of her own thoughts, a projection from her imagination of her own identity in this throng of anonymous and nameless khaki: I am Minnie. She turned her head, looked over her shoulder.

He was thin and slight, with a narrow face crowned by a premature widow's peak, and he was looking at her inquisitively, as though he were not quite sure it was her. When he looked into her eyes, he smiled and nodded his head. There was something very familiar about him. It hit her suddenly, and without warning, that he was one of her brothers. She was struck dumb. It couldn't be, could it?

"Hello, Minnie," he said. She just looked at him. "You don't know me, do you?"

"N . . . no," she stammered.

"It's me," he said, "Shon."

"Shon?"

"Your brother," he said. "You are Minnie Francis, aren't you? Anna Maria Spiroski?"

"Yes," she said. She hesitated. "But I have no brother," she said. She stepped back away from him, and he reached out to her. He grabbed her lightly by the arm.

"Wait," he said, "wait a minute."

"I'm afraid I must . . . that I've got to go," she said.

"Listen," he said, "I'm sorry, about what happened. But it wasn't me! I cried all the way to Tallahassee that day, and cried myself to sleep every night for a month. It was Mama, fuckin stupid bitch."

She might as well have been all alone again, on that sandy road between the live oaks and the sawgrass. Before old Frill, before Silas and Ruby, before Miss Ida Hooten, in another life before this one. She felt that same sense of aloneness descend on her, envelop her, as though she were on an empty sidewalk in a deserted city. She did not know this skinny boy, indistinguishable from all the other khaki-clad soldiers crowding the sidewalk. Then, abruptly, she could see him, in the car that day, huddled against Evalene, wearing shorts even though it was November and chilly, already crying before she got out of the car, stepped out into that shock of disbelief in what was happening to her, unaware at that moment of all she would have to endure to survive. And she had done it: she had survived.

"You . . . you're not old enough to be in the army," Minnie said.

He leaned toward her, grinning. "I lied," he said, "Evalene signed for me."

THEY SAT ACROSS THE table from each other in a diner tucked away up 41st Street, almost away from the teeming humanity of Times Square. They could still hear the noise, but it was muffled now. The uniformed men in the diner were quieter, earnestly eating their hamburgers, sipping their beer, talking softly among themselves. Shon ordered a beer. "Don't you want one?" he asked.

"No," Minnie said. "I've never taken it up." She ordered coffee.

He took out a package of Lucky Strikes and shook one out and lit it. He put the package on the table, turned it so the open end was facing her.

"Nor that either," she said.

"Not like a true Gypsy," he said, smiling. One of his front teeth was gold, reflecting the harsh overhead fluorescent lighting.

"Am I a true Gypsy?" she asked.

"I don't know," he answered, "are you?" He sipped his beer from the bottle. "I knew it was you when I saw your eyes," he said, "still green and blue, huh?"

She laughed. "I don't expect them to change," she said.

"Goddam," he said, "you sure did turn into a good-lookin woman."

"Well, thank you."

"Whatcha been doin all these years?"

"I've been working in a hotel, on Cedar Key down in Florida," she said. "At first I lived with some people, an old couple."

"Took you in, huh?" Shon said. "Just like Mama said, the bitch."

"What about you?" she asked. "What about y'all?" The coloration of his face made it look as if it were in shadow, even in the bright lights of the diner. He had a heavy beard that turned the lower half of his face even darker, as though he needed to shave again.

"I don't know where they are, except Evalene. She lives in Henderson, North Carolina. She quit the road and then I did, too. Pap said we were bein untrue to who we were. Maybe so. But it ain't like it used to be. The familias are breakin up."

"So you don't know where Pap and Mama are? And the rest?"

"No idea," he said. "What the hell are you doin in New York?"

"I don't know."

He laughed.

"No, I really don't. I've been just travelin around. All of a sudden I found myself here. So I'm here." She sipped her coffee, not taking her eyes from his. "So," she said, "you're shipping out."

"Yeah. My outfit's headed to San Diego, then we'll ship out to . . . wherever. I don't know."

Something that had been buried so deeply within her she had forgotten she had it began to pain her. He was her brother, and he was headed to war. She had gotten so used to the idea that she had no family, no obligation to anyone, that it surprised her to learn she had a brother, that he was real and not a vague memory, that he was sitting there across from her now, looking out the window, turning the beer bottle up and draining it. It was a curious feeling, even bizarre, as though some dream she had had as a child had suddenly come true, and she was not sure she wanted it to. Why should she hurt for him? For anybody? Where was he when she was enduring all her fears and uncertainties, that she still struggled to pull through? Here he is, like some stranger, darting in and touching her heart before flying away again and leaving her to deal with the burning and the stinging of it.

"I have forgotten them all," she said. "You, too. I have forgotten you."

"Huh?"

"I suppose you thought, that you all thought, I would carry that day around with me for the rest of my life, like some stinkin sack of shit on my back. Well, I won't."

"I don't know what you're talkin about," he said.

"I don't guess you do. I don't even know if I want you to."

"It wasn't my idea, Minnie, it was ..."

"But you went along with it."

"I was just a little boy."

"And I was just a little girl!"

They were quiet for a minute as the waitress set another beer before Shon. "More coffee, hon?" she said to Minnie, and Minnie shook her head. When she was gone, Shon said, "You're obviously still mad as hell about it."

"Wouldn't you be?"

"Hell yes. I just thought you said ..."

"Look," Minnie said, and she started to stand up, "I've really got to go."

"Where you got to go that's so important?"

"I don't think that's any of your business," she snapped.

"Okay, okay. I just thought ... Well, I've got a couple of hours before my train leaves. I thought we could visit."

"Visit?"

"Yeah, visit. You've heard of it?"

She was half standing. She sighed and sat back down and motioned to the waitress for more coffee.

"I'LL LEAVE YOU HERE," she said. They were in the lobby of the massive, crowded, noisily echoing Penn Station.

"You don't want to walk me to the train?" he asked, smiling.

"No," she said.

"Okey-doke," he said. "Well . . ." He leaned forward and kissed her on the cheek. She remained stiff, unbending. She couldn't help it. During their long talk, in the diner, walking, she had felt nothing toward him, nothing even remotely like what a sister should feel for her brother, especially one she has not seen in years. Minnie had no idea what that feeling should be or might be. She just knew that it was missing. She was not angry with Shon, she didn't blame him. She just felt frozen inside, locked, as though nothing would move, could move. All the time they were talking, a dawning awareness of Shon emerged in her mind: he was like the others, the hundreds represented by the faces in her dreams, and she had no doubt in her mind that he—maybe even that very night, earlier—would eagerly buy a girl and root around on her for a few sweaty minutes and pay her and then forget her as soon as he walked out the door. No, sooner, as soon as he pulled himself out of her and reached for his clothes.

She watched him move away, fading into the mass of men just like him, mirror images; they closed around him like water restoring its wholeness after you throw a rock into it, so that in a matter of seconds the rock might never have existed and you might never have thrown it. He was absorbed. The familias were breaking up, he had said, things were not the way they used to be: the Gypsies were disappearing, were being absorbed into the culture they had existed alongside, that they were not a part of until they began to melt like a sugar cube dropped into tea. They slowly disappeared into that which surrounded them and ceased to be any more. So it was with Shon, she thought, still standing on the marble floor of the terminal, its chaos vibrating loudly around her. He ceased to be, was as absent from her as he had been three hours ago before she ever saw him, before she ever even knew he was still alive and breathing.

She did not care. It was a relief to see him gone. She had felt as if she had been picked up and then plopped down somewhere foreign, where the history and the customs and even the language were alien and exotic. She had been lost, flailing around, reaching, trying to come to some comfort in the situation. That she and Shon were connected by blood was impossible. She did not know him. She did not care about him. He was a total stranger. She had found it difficult to reply to his most inane remark. There had been an invisible, but solid, wall between them, so that whatever he said bounced back to him and whatever she said bounced back to her. She could almost hear the sound the ricochet made.

She left the terminal, went back out into the cold. She began to walk up Eighth Avenue, her hands jammed into the pockets of the old jacket. She met streams of soldiers—streams of Shons—making their way back to their trains, some of them staggering, most of them loud and profane, their voices reverberating in the otherwise empty street, into the silence of the December midnight. "Hey, baby, wanna fuck?" they said. "Wanna suck my dick?" She smiled, even laughed. They could not really touch her, not in any significant way. She was a part of the flood, and separate from it, too, like a sapling that bends with the current and then pops right back up.

Seen from above, with her black hair and blue jacket, she would have looked like a housefly floating on a river of cocoa. Making her way idly and slowly, without any haste whatsoever, almost as if she were drifting, she strolled back up toward midtown, debating with herself whether or not to go on home to sleep. She had rented a room in an old hotel on 50th Street that had once been a proper place for young ladies come to town to find their careers but had long since given in to hard times and was cheap. It was in midtown, good for walking everywhere. Her landlady was an elderly widow and the other roomers were an assortment of taxi drivers and construction workers that she rarely saw. At Cedar Key, she had gotten used to being active at night and then sleeping most of the day, a habit she was trying without much success to break. She loved walking at night in the city, much to the consternation of her landlady, Mrs. Cabelas, who had been managing the place for many years. "Somebody's gonna knock you in the head and rob you and take advantage of you," she told Minnie; Minnie supposed she couldn't bring herself to pronounce the word "rape."

"Lord if your eyes ain't different colors," Mrs. Cabelas had exclaimed when Minnie had rented the room.

"Really?" Minnie replied. "I hadn't noticed."

"Pshaw," the old lady said, and went into her room and closed the door.

It took her over an hour, but Minnie was now back uptown in Times Square. The various clubs were still full to overflowing. She spotted the boy standing off by himself, leaning against the side of a building, smoking. He was young. His uniform hung on him like he was a child playing dress-up. He smoked as though he were looking in a mirror, teaching himself how. He was shy, unable to join in with the other soldiers, unable to relax. He was frightened and nervous. Minnie approached him.

"Hey, soldier," she said, and his eyes darted to her and away. He looked as though he wanted to run. "Hey," she said, "I'm not gonna hurt you."

"I . . . I know that," he said. He took a deep breath, and then he looked at her. She could see the expression on his face alter subtly when he noticed her eyes. He took a drag on his cigarette and inhaled deeply. He looked off down Broadway as though he were looking for something or someone, expecting them. He wore a light jacket, and she could almost see him shivering.

"I'm Minnie," she said, "what's your name?"

"Jim," he mumbled, still looking away from her.

"Jim?"

"Yeah."

"Nice to meet you, Jim," she said. "What are you doing standin here all by yourself?"

He didn't answer for a moment. He turned back to her, his eyes brushing back and forth across her face. Then he said, "I'm just people-watching. I like to people-watch."

"Hey, you do that, too?" she exclaimed. She smiled. A hesitant smile flickered on his face. He was unsure of himself, unsure of her. He was confused. And he was sad. Minnie could see sadness in his eyes, and loneliness. She had no trouble at all in understanding how he could be lonely amid such bustle. He did not fit. He had not yet begun to understand who he was. He had been snatched up from some comfortable home, yanked away from his family, and here he was, cold in a strange city, waiting to be shipped off to the war. The smile momentarily faded from her face as she had a sudden premonition that he would not come home; she could see him clearly in her mind's eye sprawled in mud on a Pacific Island, his eyes wide open and staring at nothing, blood dripping from his mouth. She shook her head to clear it. She knew her vision was true, and she couldn't bear to see it any more. She remembered the Gypsy women in the camps who told fortunes; their predictions came true. Always. She smiled again, looking into his eyes. The color of slate. Melancholy, dispirited slate-gray eyes.

"Look," she said, "you want to get a beer? Or coffee, or something?"

"No," he said.

"Oh, come on."

"Well, okay," he said. "But I guess I ought to tell you, I don't have any money."

"My treat," she said, tucking her arm under his, turning him.

"Wait," he said. He held back. "I don't mean that. I mean, you know, I can't afford to pay you."

"Like I said," she murmured, "my treat."

THEY WERE SITTING IN the same diner, at the same table, where she and Shon had sat earlier. She had chosen the diner and the table without questioning why because it seemed correct and appropriate, almost a birthright. The boy, Jim, ordered a beer; she ordered coffee. Jim would not meet her eyes with his; he stared off out the window as though he had discovered something of riveting interest out there. He did not even seem to notice when the waitress brought their order. It was awkward, but Minnie didn't want to push him.

"Look, Jim," she finally said. He didn't turn around. "Jim?" He turned to look at her. The skin of his face was smooth and pink. He probably didn't even have to shave more than once a week, if that. "I want you to know that I'm not a prostitute."

"You're not?"

"No, I'm not. I'm just a lonely girl."

"You? Somebody that looks like you? Lonely? Shit."

"Really. I saw you there, and I said to myself, I want to take that boy home with me."

"Don't kid me like that."

"I'm not kiddin you, Jim. How long do you have before your train leaves?"

"Coupla hours," he said. "But I don't know."

"Well, think about it," she said. "I'm not used to being turned down."

"I'll bet you're not," he said.

They sat there then in silence for a few minutes. She finished her coffee, and he had drunk about half his beer. He didn't look as though he was going to finish it. She folded her hands in front of her on the table. He was staring down at the table top.

"Well?" she said. He didn't answer. "Look, Jim, I don't want to make you do something you don't want to do, okay?"

"Oh, I want to, all right," he said. "But, I just don't know."

She knew what was going on in his mind. He knew that she was much more experienced than him; he might even be a virgin. And he didn't want her to know that. He was afraid of her finding out, of embarrassing himself with her. If he only knew how little all that mattered. But she had known a great many men in her life, and she knew the consternation was real. It had to do with the fear of being unmanly. It was something that she knew she would never fully understand, because she was not a man. She, herself, remembered being anxious that she would not know what to do, but her nervousness had had little to do with her identity as a woman. Or she didn't think it did. This kind of thing went so much deeper than that with men. Especially shy and sensitive men.

She sat there looking at him. She could not get her earlier vision out of her mind. It troubled her. He might even die a virgin. And it would be her fault. He was a good-looking boy, but his face was too thin and his nose was way too small and pointed, like an owl's beak. His eyes were weak-looking and she was sure he wore glasses but just didn't have them on.

"Well, listen," she said, "you can at least walk me home, okay?"

"Where do you live?" he asked.

"Not far."

"Okay," he said, "sure."

IN THE LOBBY SHE said, "You sure you don't want to come up?"

"Well . . ." he said, hesitating. "I guess, for a little while."

She always left one dim bedside lamp on. He was standing in the middle of the room. It was a small, corner room on the sixth floor, overlooking 10th Avenue. A sagging iron bed, a table. A wooden straight chair. A closet that she didn't really need, as she could carry all her clothes, all she needed, in her carpetbag. She took off the coat and draped it over the chair. She began to unbutton her shirt, a faded blue denim work shirt, also from the used clothing store, as were the heavy woolen pants.

"What are you doin?" he said, a note of alarm in his voice.

"I'm just getting comfortable," she said.

"Shit," he said, but he didn't take his eyes off her as she removed the shirt, reached behind her and unsnapped her brassiere, letting her breasts fall free. She tossed the shirt and bra on the chair with her coat. He had not moved. She could see him plainly in the light from the street lamp out on the corner. His eyes glistened, whether with lust or tears she didn't know. She unbuttoned the pants and let them fall around her ankles, then stepped out of them. She wore only a pair of white cotton panties. She reached into her carpetbag by the bed and took out some condoms and put them on the bedside table next to the lamp.

"Why don't you . . ."

"Ungodly whore!" he said bitterly, interrupting her. She was stunned into silence at the abrupt change in him. She just stood there, watching him tear frantically at his clothes, ripping buttons, throwing articles aside onto the floor. He was erect, ready, moving toward her.

"Wait a minute," she said. "What do you mean . . . ?"

But he was upon her. She could hear his breath snorting, whispering gutturally through his nose, like some starving animal at its prey. He ripped the panties down her legs, his fingernails scratching her as he did, and pushed her onto the bed.

"Put on a rubber," she spat at him. "At least put on a rubber!"

She tried to fight him off but he was wiry and strong, and in some insane, hysterical state. He was between her legs. "Fuckin whore," he muttered, "goddamed fuckin whore." She felt him penetrate her. He was looking down into her face, his eyes squinted, as though in pain, and he began to move frenziedly, violently on her and in her. She raked her fingernails across his back, drawing blood she hoped; she tried to pull her arms in and get them between him and her, but he now held them on each side of her. "You asshole," she said, and he raised up with one hand, arm, and slapped her hard across the face with the other.

"Shut up, you whore of Babylon!" he said, panting, gasping. Then he shuddered and stiffened. He was coming.

"Not inside me, you crazy son-of-a-bitch!" she screamed.

But he did not even pause. He kept moving until he gave a few final, long thrusts and then lay still, a dead weight on top of her. She pounded his back with her fists. "Get off me, asshole!" she said.

He rolled over, then sat on the edge of the bed. She saw with some satisfaction that she had drawn blood on his back, several long red streaks. Then he stood up and moved away a couple of feet and turned and stared down at her.

"What the fuck did you think you were doin?" she said. "Comin inside me like that?" But it was done. She had no douche bag, nothing. "Are you crazy!?"

"God will punish you, you whore of Babylon," he said. She almost laughed at him standing there with his dick drooping, come still dripping from the head, telling her how evil she was. "You will rot in hell for eternity."

"I noticed you didn't worry too much about all that sin business until you got your pussy, did you?" she said. She lay back on the pillow and pulled the covers up over her.

"Evil, evil," he muttered. "Sinful."

"Get out!" she screamed. "Get out! Leave me alone!"

He began to dress, hurriedly. She saw that he was buttoning his shirt crookedly. She turned her face to the wall. After a few minutes, he said, "I'm not sure I know how to get back to the train station."

"Well then," she said, "you're just shit out of luck, ain't you?"

"But . . ."

"Wander around. You'll find it. Get a fuckin taxi. What do you want me to do, draw you a map or somethin?"

She heard him shuffle across the room. His voice came from the doorway. "Listen," he said, "I lied to you. I've got plenty of money. How much do you want?"

"I don't want your fuckin money, asshole," she said. "Didn't I tell you to get out?"

She heard him close the door. She heard his footsteps going down the hall, then down the stairs, his footsteps fading as he reached the lower floors. She lay there listening to the drone of traffic down on 10th Avenue. She could taste the blood on her lower lip, where he had slapped her. She closed her eyes, longing for sleep to come.

All night long crowded trains left Penn Station, headed west.

8

SOUTH ALABAMA STATE FAIR

SEPTEMBER 1964

Malik was looking at the picture that Lester Ray thought was his mother. "I don't know. Maybe I've seen her. I've seen a lot of women that look like that." He held it away from him and narrowed his eyes, studying the old photograph. It was early morning, long before the gates were to open, and there was even a teasing hint of autumn in the air, a brief cooling that would quickly disappear as the sun got higher.

"Is she a Gypsy, do you think?" Lester Ray asked.

"Hard to say. Could be. Damned if she don't look like one." He brought it closer to his face again and squinted at it. "Who you say she is?"

"My mother," Lester Ray said.

"Your mother?" Malik exclaimed. "She don't look old enough."

"It's an old picture."

"Oh. Yeah. Could be I've seen her. Could be I never laid eyes on her."

Lester Ray took the picture back and looked at it. He put it back into the Prince Albert can.

"Say she's your mother, and you think she's a Gypsy, then you must be a Gypsy, too."

"I aim to find out," Lester Ray said. "I'm gonna find her, I know that."

"Well, good luck to you. Ain't no real tellin where she is, even if she is a Gypsy," Malik said. "It don't mean all that much any more, bein a

Gypsy, to tell you the truth. Things ain't like they used to be. There's buryin grounds around. There's one in Mississippi where the old queen is buried, and there are still pilgrimages to visit her grave, but not nearly as many as there used to be. There's a big buryin ground outside Fort Myers, where the carnival Gypsies spend the winters. So many of the old ways are gone, a lot of the familias splittin up, those that ain't bunched up around a carnival or somethin like that, anyway. Young people want to be like everybody else, dance to the rock and roll, Elvis, all that shit, they ain't interested in the old ways. They want to get out. So even if you knew what band she used to be in don't mean she'd still be there. Even if you could locate it. Was she with a familia when you were born?"

"I don't know."

"Used to be, bein a Gypsy was like livin in a small town, everybody knew everybody else, and knew everybody else's business, too. Maybe you ought to talk to some of the older people. Old Saartjie would be a good one to talk to." Saartjie was a fortune teller. She was ancient; she looked like a brightly colored bag of sticks, with her full skirts and scarves. She had a thin, dark face with a hook nose and sunken cheeks. Her tent was on the midway: REV. SAARTJIE, HEALER AND SPIRITUAL ADVISER.

"I'll do that," Lester Ray said.

THEY HAD BEEN IN Mobile a week and a half. V. M. had been sleeping on the floor on a pile of quilts, though some nights she didn't come home. Lester Ray would think All right, she's gone, we're rid of her, but then she would show up the next morning and sleep all day. Even with them letting her stay in the trailer, she still complained. "That old lady farts all the time," she told Lester Ray. "Shut up," he growled, lest Mrs. McCrory hear her. Lester Ray didn't know what V. M. did at night, other than ramble around the fair. One afternoon she told him she was getting a job.

"Doin what?" he exclaimed.

"Dancin in THE STREETS OF PARIS show."

"You? Don't make me laugh. What they gonna do, put a paper sack over your head?"

"Never you mind," she said. "There's somebody thinks I'm beautiful."

"And who might this moron be?" he asked.

"Never you mind."

Mrs. McCrory did all their cooking for them. She fried up a lot of eggs and a lot of bacon. It was what they all liked. That and French toast with a lot of syrup. She made biscuits and they poured syrup on them, too, hot out of the little oven in the Airstream. Lester Ray thought they were like some bizarre family, with him and Mrs. McCrory as the parents and V. M. as the child. Not that he had ever lived in a normal family. He didn't even know what that might be like, and he didn't really care. Early on he had realized that you had to live with your situation, whatever it was, and make the best of it, and it was a waste of time sitting around wishing for something else, because you weren't ever going to get it anyway. Even if your situation changed you were still going to be you. There was not much you could do about that.

V. M. HAD TAKEN UP with Yak, who was an inch or two shorter than she was and forty or so years older, but she thought he was cute. He talked intelligently, like he'd been all the way through school. He wore a tuxedo to perform in, and he was teaching V. M. to waltz.

"We'll get you a pretty dress, and you and I can dance on the stage," he told her. "People like to see two midgets dancing."

"I ain't no midget," she said.

"Neither am I, dear, except to the rubes out there. We are just different. People don't know what to make of us so they make up a name for us: 'midgets.' We're simply little people, you and I."

"Folks sometimes call me a dwarf," she said.

"That's even worse, dear," he said, "but we just have to put up with it."

They were in Yak's house trailer. It was smaller than the others, built on a smaller scale to accommodate his stature (he could sit in any of its chairs without having his feet dangle above the floor) and was painted a bright tomato red. He was sitting in his favorite chair, a mahogany rocker, wearing a dark maroon silk dressing gown he'd had made especially for him. Mostly he wore little boys' clothes, even the tuxedo, which he'd found in a formal bride's shop; the clerk had told him it was designed for a ring bearer. But all little boy's robes were cotton or terry cloth or chenille, very ordinary, the kind of thing he wouldn't even wear alone in his trailer, so he'd had to have the dressing gown tailored. He could tell that V. M. was impressed with it.

"Stand up and let me look at you," he said, and V. M. stood up. The girl had an extraordinary body; it was hard to believe her claim that she was only fourteen years old. It would be easy to pass her off as eighteen, which they would have to do if they used her in a movie. Her face, however, was unfortunate, with its extreme over-bite protruding from between her thin, usually chapped, lips. Her eyes were the color of dirty motor oil, her hair the most hideous carrot red he'd ever seen. That could be taken care of, of course. Her hair could be any color they wanted it to be. But there was little to be done with her face. Perhaps make-up would help. "Turn around," he said, and she turned slowly, cat-like, and he appraised her ass again, which was perfectly shaped, as were her legs. Her breasts were about the size of cupcakes, but on her short, slight stature they looked like melon halves. "Take off your clothes," he said, and without hesitation she began to remove the little boy's shirt, quickly letting her cupcake breasts jiggle unrestrained in the air, as she wore no brassiere (where would she find one to fit her? Obviously a training bra would not do. He would have to ask when they encountered some of his female little people friends); the nipples were like pennies, even to the faint hint of copper glow. She kicked off her tennis shoes (she wore no socks) unzipped the pants, pulled them off each leg, rolled her panties down her legs (they were actually, he noted, little boys' jockey shorts, which, he had to admit, added something extra and rather delicious) and stood there naked. Her nether hair was also red and there was a great deal of it, quite a bush. She would do quite nicely. They could cut away from her face, edit it out after the filming was done, though close-ups of fellatio might be something of a problem.

He was quite aroused. He opened his dressing gown and let his erection rise into the air, the same air that caressed her naked body. She was on him in a split second, on her knees, gulping his penis into her mouth and halfway down her throat. She was very good at it, using her tongue a lot, and he wondered where in heaven she had learned such a technique. She worked with a determined, concentrated purpose, obviously immensely enjoying what she was doing. He relaxed in the rocker and let her feast. When it came to the big moment she did not hesitate but quickened her oral manipulation and he shot off into her mouth, where with remarkable skill she continued with her lips and tongue while swallowing at the same time. Yes, she would do quite nicely.

She still knelt between his knees, looking up at him, smiling. "Your dong is as big as a normal man's," she said. "I want it in my pussy."

"In good time, dear, in good time," he said.

THE OLD WOMAN SAARTJIE was sitting outside her fortune-telling tent, drinking tea with Margie, "The World's Fattest Woman." The little lawn chair that Margie was sitting on disappeared beneath her expansive body, which bulged off in every direction. She had six—"Count Em"—double chins; her legs were like the legs of a giant piano, and her upper arms were almost as big around as her legs. Her breasts looked like over-inflated basketballs that were about to explode. She was wearing a blue cotton house dress that was made of eighteen yards of material, and even it tightly hugged her body, the seams looking dangerously close to bursting. The cup she was holding looked like a child's play teacup in her large, swollen hand. She weighed six hundred and seventy-two pounds, "before breakfast this morning," she was fond of saying. She did not say it as a joke. She only put on the "jolly fat woman" act for the rubes. She had a specially built house trailer and a broad wagon with large, bicycle-type wheels that her assistant, a heavy-set, brooding man named Careem, pushed her around on. A light blonde, her skin was a puffy pinkish white, her face heavily made up with dark red lipstick and disks of rouge on her cheeks. Margie was originally from Carlisle, Pennsylvania, where she had been raised in a strict Presbyterian family; her mother had drummed into her head every day, from the day she could understand, that they—her family—were among the Elect, that when their time came God would swoop down and take them bodily to heaven. She still fervently believed that. (Once she had made the mistake of telling Emil Kirova about her belief, and he had looked at her in some astonishment and said, "Man, that's gonna be some heavy-duty chariot!")

"Them whores in the skin show think he's about the best-lookin boy they've ever seen," Margie was saying. They were talking about Lester Ray Holsomback. "They got a bet which one of em's gonna get in his jeans first."

"I heard he ain't but fourteen years old," Saartjie said. "They will be driven from the garden."

"Amen," Margie said. "Like the Lord ain't gonna already punish em plenty for displayin their naked bodies to anybody wants to look at em. I reckon they figure they're already goin to the bad place anyhow."

"They are," Saartjie said. "No doubt about that."

Saartjie was eighty-seven years old. Her clothes were a myriad of colors: orange and green and bright red; she had on a sleeveless bright blue vest pinned with a gold brooch over her thin, fallen breasts. She wore high-heeled, gold patent leather sandals and long hoop earrings that hung down to her shoulders. She was a Romanian Gypsy who had come to the United States with her family when she was a baby, and she was the last of her family still living. She had always made her living as a fortune teller, even in the old days when her familia went from small town to small town, stealing chickens, helping themselves to peaches, pecans and figs, whatever they found growing that they could eat. Even an occasional pig or goat. She still carried the old ways, the old stories, with her, and she would often launch into Romani, the old language, which very few people understood any more. She often told this story:

"After Jesus was arrested and was going to be crucified, a Gypsy black-smith was ordered to make four nails, three for his hands and feet, the fourth for his heart. The Gypsy stalled and stalled, but he was whipped repeatedly, so finally he made the four nails. He was so bothered by this that he asked God's help. God cried, and the Gypsy blacksmith cried. When the time came for him to deliver the nails, he swallowed the one for Jesus's heart and told the soldiers that he had lost it. He was severely whipped again, so badly that he almost died. When God saw this, he said: Gypsy, you are free to go and travel anywhere in the world and you can help yourself to any food in my kingdom, no matter who thinks they may own it, and you can freely take whatever else you need to live, wherever you might find it. And that is why Gypsies travel and why they steal."

Margie had heard old Saartjie tell this story many times. It was her experience, though, that Gypsies were hardly the kind of people that God spoke to. They were irresponsible, and, however many excuses they made or stories they told, they were still thieves if they took something belonging to someone else, and that clearly was a sin. When she was growing up she had heard stories of how they kidnapped little children when they came through a town, but in the years she'd been traveling with them she had never seen that happen. Unless maybe that ugly little boy who hung around with Lester Ray Holsomback and his grandmother had been kidnapped from somewhere. But it seemed unlikely even for Gypsies that they would steal a child that unsightly.

"God is a stern judge," Margie said. "He can't stand no mendacity." She had recently learned that word from a crossword puzzle. "I can think of a whole lot of people gonna be punished when the time comes."

The morning was warming, the sun moving up in the sky. It would be another hot day, cloudless, the Gulf Coast sun unmerciful. Before long the string of yellow school buses would begin rolling in with their happy, excited youngsters and their sullen teenagers. Today was Margie's day to sit outside on the stage under a sun-umbrella beneath the long oddities bannerline; the younger kids and the girls would gape at her in disbelief and the teenage boys would mostly ignore her as they focused on faking their way into THE STREETS OF PARIS show. The townspeople—housewives, young sports taking the afternoon off, the elderly—would begin filtering in after lunchtime. By nightfall the fair would be jam-packed with noisy people, brimful and crawling like a lambently lighted and brazenly colorful anthill.

Margie finished her tea and Careem helped her slide onto the wagon so that he could push her back to her trailer to eat her lunch—six cheese-burgers, four hotdogs, two bags of potato chips and three Snickers bars, washed down with two large chocolate milkshakes—to sustain her during the long afternoon on the platform under the bannerline.

OLD SAARTJIE LOOKED FOR a long time at the photograph, her lips moving almost imperceptibly as though she were saying a prayer to herself, or automatically reciting some mystical formula from some primordial and obscure Transylvanian ritual. She held her head cocked slightly forward, very still, like an old hen getting ready to peck. Lester Ray watched her, as patient as he could be, yet anxious, and the longer she was silent the more convinced he became that she knew the woman in the picture, knew who she was, had perhaps known her well in the past, even that she knew her now, knew where she was. He did not want to speak, to urge her aloud, did not want to break whatever spell she seemed to be under or disturb whatever vision she might be having of the woman—his mother—whatever prescience the old woman might have regarding her, and somewhere in the encumbered quietude he passed the point where he no longer wanted her to speak at all, because the possibility that she knew what he so desperately needed to know was so unbearably sweet that he was willing to forego the real truth and accept in its stead the anticipation. Perhaps it would be better not to know either way, never to know, since not knowing had been his life and the minute, the second, he learned the truth a part of him would die.

"Yes," she said, "I knew her," and he had known it all along, ever since the day that Emil Kirova had opened that metal door. Lester Ray had so strongly sensed that his life would change, maybe had already changed the minute the harsh, metallic grinding of the door began fading from his hearing, maybe even while the discordant, grating timbre still lay gnashing against his eardrums before it dissipated back into the soundlessness of the air.

"When?" he asked. "Where?" The words seemed to come from somewhere behind him, passing by his head, his consciousness, like an echo. They were spoken by the person he had been before he heard them. They seemed to reverberate somewhere outside and beyond his skull.

"She may or may not be the person you seek," the old woman said.

Her words startled him into awareness. "What?" he said. He said it harshly, impatiently.

"She is a shade, a spirit," she said.

He was numb now. Suspended somewhere above the ground. "Do you mean she's dead?" he asked.

"No, I do not mean that," Saartjie said. The old woman had not looked at him. She still held the photograph, but she was no longer looking at it. The skin of her face was like worn, scarred leather.

"What do you mean then?" he said.

"Do not speak in anger," she said.

"I'm not angry!" he said, and he knew he was sounding that way, too loud, too impatient. "I'm sorry," he said, "it's just that this is so important to me. She's my mother." Saartjie looked him in the eyes for the first time. Her eyes were a pale gray, bloodshot. "This woman is not your mother," she said.

"How . . . how do you know?"

"Because I know."

"How'd the picture get in my house, then?" he said. "I found it there. Who is she?"

"Pictures are not people," she said. "A picture of a woman is not a woman. A picture of a mother is not a mother."

"Well, hell, I know that," he said.

"Do not curse in my presence," she said.

"Okay, okay," he said. "But you said you knew her? The woman in the picture?"

"I feel her reaching out to me, yes. I feel her hands caressing my heart. She is a lonely person. Her heart is broken."

"Well, where is she?" Lester Ray said.

"I'm afraid I don't know that," the old woman said.

His earliest memory was of being carried in someone's arms, he didn't know whose, into a mostly empty house, the air smelling closed in and musty, the odor of mildew. He didn't remember being put down or what happened after that, only the moment of entry. Perhaps the reason that instant stuck in his mind was that even at not yet one year old he knew that a house was supposed to have lots of furniture, even though he would not have been able to articulate furniture or house or even put a mental label on them. No doubt he knew what they were, as he knew what the air was, or birds, or grass, took them for granted the way a newborn, after the first initial shock, must take for granted the world into which he has been ejected. Maybe in his child's mind this was his first experience of the reversal of expectations, the first tiny step toward maturity, toward all the disappointment and heartbreak that awaited him in his life.

Then came the first Christmas he could recall, when he had wanted a BB gun and had naively expected to get it, expected it because he talked about it with his classmates, who always got what they asked for. They could not have been called his friends because they made fun of him at school, made fun of his ragged clothes and his shaggy hair, taunted him because his father was a drunk. Even then he was becoming aware that they played together outside school, always without him, that they attended each other's birthday parties, went to Sunday school and church together, so that what he overheard them saying to one another sounded in his ears like some secret shorthand or some foreign language that was beyond his understanding. As though they existed in some parallel world that was totally different from his.

He did not understand this and it made him feel outside and disparate, less than they were, because they treated him as less. It made him sad, made him cry, and at that time he was still crying for his mother, too, still clinging to the belief, fostered by his father, that she was just away, had gone on a trip, that she would return eventually and they would all be together and he would be like the others, finally be able to understand their covert language because he had come to believe that the only thing that separated him from them was the fact that he had no mother living at home with him.

As he got older, he got bigger, and the taunting faded in frequency, especially after he beat up several boys who were older than him and bigger than him. He fought with a fury and an abandon that they did not expect; sometimes it took three or four boys to hold him down on the hard-packed sandy playground and make him quit swinging his fists, his jaw clenched, his face so red it looked aflame, the sweat pouring down his face so thick that it mixed easily with his tears so that they were never sure if he was crying, though he was, and on two occasions they had to borrow some girl's jump rope to bind his hands behind his back before they could leap safely free. He would lie there cursing them, his lip bloodied, his faded shirt, already full of holes, ripped even worse.

The principal's name was Mrs. Martin, a slight, petite lady who always wore dark clothes, whose hair was blueish gray (her nickname among the students was "Old Blue").

"We do not settle our differences by fighting, young man," she said to Lester Ray.

"Yes, ma'am," he answered. He touched his lip with the Kleenex she had given him.

"Only crude barbarians fight," she said.

"Yes, ma'am," thinking well then I am a barbarian then, and I do appreciate you telling me what I am, because I sure need to know.

"What church does your family go to?" she asked. Of course she knew the answer. Piper was a small town, little more than a village, and everybody knew about him and his father, the town drunk, living in that old rundown house that was not even up to being called a house but was more a shack.

"We don't go to no church," Lester Ray said.

"My husband and I would be happy to pick you up on Sunday morning and take you with us to ours," she said. "We go to Community Baptist." Mrs. Martin and her husband, a local contractor, were childless ("All my students are my children," she was fond of saying with a smile). With that desperation of a woman in middle age who had longed for a child of her own—who had prayed for one constantly while watching her child-bearing years slip inevitably and relentlessly away—she dreamed of actually adopting and giving a good and decent home to one of her students, had dreamed it so long that she had actually come to believe that it was really possible, even probable.

"No, ma'am, I don't reckon so," Lester Ray said.

"Please," she said. Lester Ray was shocked to see tears welling up in her eyes. Everybody said Mrs. Martin would cry at the drop of a hat, but he had never seen it. He was not even sure if he truly believed that grown people, that adults, ever cried except when they were drunk, like his father did sometimes. "Please, Lester Ray, go with us," she said. Her voice cracked on his name.

"I ain't ever been to a church in my life," he said. "Don't you have to dress up to go?"

"No," she said, "well, not really."

"Is that my punishment for fightin?" he asked.

"No, no," she said, "of course not. It's just that you are not happy at home, and I thought ..."

"Who said I'm not happy at home?"

"Well, nobody really, I guess. It's just that I ... that everybody ... knows about your father and his drinking. That's not a healthy environment for a young boy. And a home without a mother, well ..."

"I've got a mother!" he said sharply, interrupting her.

"Yes, I know, but ..."

"She's comin home," he said.

Her eyes popped open wider. She didn't say anything for a long time. Then, "She is?" she asked.

"Yeah," he said, "what'd you think?"

"Well, I'm sorry, I just ...." she trailed off. She'd had her eye on Lester Ray Holsomback since he had entered first grade, a dirty little ragamuffin with a crude, home-administered haircut that left his hair patchy, in varying lengths around his head, who brought either a cold sweet potato or a Moon Pie to eat at lunch every day, and who, according to Miss Fanny Brasfield, the first-grade teacher, learned to read faster than any other child in first grade (faster than any other child Mrs. Martin had ever known of, though her experience with first graders was limited since she taught fifth grade and not first grade, in addition to being the principal) but who along in the spring of that first year, according to Miss Fanny, suddenly flatly refused to read anything at all and would not budge in spite of threats of punishment or failure of the grade. Lester Ray would not say why he didn't want to read. He simply refused.

Mrs. Martin didn't think he could have advanced up to the third grade, where he was when she called him in for fighting, without reading something. Billie Billings, the third grade teacher, pronounced that "he just knows things." He could do simple math before they ever got around to it in class, and Miss Billings let him do art, which he liked, while the other children were struggling with addition. He painted brightly colored splotches—red, yellow, green and blue—in tempera on yellowed, blank newsprint paper, and once, when Miss Billings asked him what the subject of a particular painting was, he replied, "Colors."

ONE DAY IN THE late spring, when he was still in the third grade, he returned home and his father was not there. His father did not return that night nor the next day. Lester Ray went searching for him, to the poolroom where his father sometimes hung out, to Saddler's Lounge on the edge of town where his father drank, but he was not in either place. The poolroom, smelling of dust and chalk, was empty on the weekday afternoon except for Mr. Roy Webster, the owner, who told Lester Ray that he had not seen his father for a couple of weeks. Saddler's Lounge was a dark, forbidding place for the boy. Several men were drinking beer at the bar, men that Lester Ray had never seen before. Gerald Saddler, the owner and bartender, a big, completely bald man, stared at Lester Ray when he came in. The boy just stood there until his eyes grew accustomed to the dark.

"What you want, boy?" Gerald Saddler asked him.

"I'm lookin for my daddy," Lester Ray said.

"Who's your daddy?"

"Earl Holsomback."

There was a silence then, and Gerald Saddler was looking at him peculiarly, as though he were trying to puzzle him out. He slowly shook his head. Lester Ray thought he looked sad. Then one of the men at the bar laughed real loud. They were all staring at Lester Ray. Then another one of the men said, "I heard he's done took a job, paintin houses up in De Quincy Springs."

So he had left, too, and Lester Ray should have known it was coming, that it would happen sooner or later. His sense of loss now was dry, though, an unfamiliar kind of sadness that was lighter, that was tempered with relief. So his father had left, too, and Lester Ray had not yet had time to be afraid, so he fastened on the knowledge that he would have a moratorium from the whippings, from the drunken babblings, from the screams when his father had the D.T.'s. The men turned back to their beers. The big bartender disappeared into a back room. Lester Ray stood there next to the cash register. There was a basket of cellophane-wrapped sticks of dried beef jerky on the bar. He took four of them and crammed them into his pocket. There was a cardboard display of narrow bags of beer nuts, and he grabbed six of the bags and headed for the door. Nobody saw him. Nobody said a word.

Outside the sun blinded him. It was easy to forget the sun inside the dim, cool lounge, but it was always there, hurling its blistering rays earthward. That he was now alone in the world strangely did not bother him. He thought, I can go looking for my mother now. When he got home he sat for a long time on the settee where he slept. The little house was quiet. He wants me to take care of myself, and I will. As dusk settled in, that pale time between the stringency of the sun and the cooling relief of darkness, Lester Ray went into the kitchen and looked in the icebox. There was only a small block of ice left, melting fast. Half a quart of milk and an opened package of bologna. He had almost a full box of cornflakes on a shelf above the stove. He looked on that same shelf and found a snuff can; inside were three wrinkled dollar bills that he had seen his father put there. He could buy some more ice. He had Mrs. McCrory to depend on. He could survive. He ate the dried beef jerky with water from the tap in a jelly glass, and then as the night deepened and the insects around the house chorused, closing in, protecting him with their familiarity, their sameness, he slept. He slept soundly. He did not even dream.

His father did not return home for three weeks. Each morning Lester Ray dressed himself and went to school; about every third day he bathed himself in their cold shower. He learned to wear a loose shirt, so he could hide things beneath it, and he prowled the A&P and McNeil's Store in the afternoons and made off with whatever items he could get without being detected: packages of wieners, candy bars, cans of pork and beans and Vienna sausages and potted meat, sardines, a loaf or two of bread, peanut butter. He stole rolls of Life Savers and an occasional handful of bubble gum from the drugstore. He stole cigarettes, even though he did not smoke, stockpiled them for his father.

When his father came home Lester Ray was not surprised. He was just there one day when Lester Ray came home from school, sitting at the kitchen table, drinking beer. "Where your books, boy?" he asked, as though he had not been away at all, had sent Lester Ray off that very morning for school, an ordinary day no different from any other. "Ain't you got any homework?"

"They don't give homework in the third grade," Lester Ray said.

"Oh, yeah, that's right," he said. "Where'd all them cigarettes in yonder in the cabinet come from? You ain't already took up smokin, have you?"

"I got em for you," Lester Ray said, unconsciously wanting his father's approval, at the same time shrinking from him, knowing in his bones that in so many ways at the age of eight he had already surpassed his father. It was like his father was going in the other direction, drifting backwards, like he had already started to die just as Lester Ray was starting to live.

His father grinned. He had lost another front tooth since Lester Ray had last seen him. The boy wondered if it had been knocked out in a fight or had just rotted out on its own, like several of his others. His snaggled, stained teeth made him look older, even like an old man. He looked like the men who had been drinking that day in Saddler's Lounge, as though they all belonged to some degraded, perverse fraternity or social club. Lester Ray had no idea what the future held, but he knew he didn't want to be like that: ugly, drunk all the time, seeing and feeling spiders crawling all over him when there was nothing there at all.

HIS FATHER'S ABSENCES BECAME more frequent, usually a week or two but sometimes longer. There came a time when his father was gone, with no word from him, for six months, and that was when Lester Ray began spending more and more time with Mrs. McCrory. He had known her since he was five years old, when she had spied him playing in her back-yard and invited him up to the porch for Kool-Aid. She would prepare him food from time to time, insisting that he take some home with him. He would cut her grass and trim her hedges and run errands for her in return. He did not tell her about his father's absences, but of course she could tell by looking at him that they were poor and did not eat regularly (he came to realize that she was probably the only person in Piper who didn't know about his father's drinking) and she was simply a kind person who would respond warmly to someone in need. Sometimes, to get away from his father, he would sleep the night in the back seat of the old car in the garage; she didn't know about that, either.

So he existed on Mrs. McCrory's food and her caring and the little money he made at his job of racking balls at the poolroom after school and on Saturdays, for which he was paid nine dollars a week, and whatever he might steal around town (he never once got caught). He and Mrs. McCrory dined on filet mignon that he lifted and slipped under his shirt when the butcher turned his back. He stole a turkey at Thanksgiving and a ham at Christmas. He would wait until the people at the cash registers were occupied with someone else and simply walk out. Any time Mrs. McCrory needed something repaired around her house (something Lester Ray did with ease, though he had no idea where he might have learned how a faucet worked or what to use to fix a squeaking door hinge or how to saw away a rotting board on the porch and replace it with a new one) he went to the hardware store or the lumber yard and helped himself to whatever tools and wood he needed. He burglarized the hardware store one night by breaking through a back window when he needed a saw and couldn't figure out how to get it out of the store without being seen, and he got the lumber he needed late at night, right under the nose of old Carter Richardson, the night watchman, who was snoozing away, his chair propped against the side of the office building.

When Lester Ray was thirteen years old, at the beginning of the seventh grade (in what was to be his last year in school, but he didn't know it then) he had a new teacher who had just come to teach in Piper. Molly Nijim was thirty-two years old, married with two children: a little boy in the first grade and a little girl in the second. Her husband Wayne Nijim worked as a lineman for Florida Light and Power. Molly Nijim was not really very attractive, but she was not what you would call unattractive either. She was ordinary, somewhat plain: her hair was brownish blonde, she was short and chunky, but with what all the boys considered a good figure. Her breasts were large and her ass would jiggle when she turned and wrote on the board, eliciting groans and giggles which she ignored. The class assumed that she did not know what they were giggling at, but of course she did, and she enjoyed every minute of it.

Molly Nijim had received her teacher's degree from a college called Florida Temple, a strict fundamentalist school in Tampa run by the Assemblies of God. She had met her husband there; he was studying to be a teacher, but he was having difficulties with the course work so Molly had become his tutor and had wound up writing all his papers for him and helping him cheat on the tests. By the time they graduated, he had lost all interest in teaching and had worked at a variety of jobs while Molly taught, first at a school in Tampa, then at one in Crystal River, and finally—when Wayne Nijim took a job with Florida Power at their regional facility in De Quincy Springs—at Piper Middle School.

Molly Nijim did not understand what was happening to her. Nothing in her past life—her education, her spiritual development, her marriage, motherhood—had prepared her for the overpowering feelings she felt for Lester Ray Holsomback, ever since the first time she had laid eyes on him, the first day of school that fall when she spied him sitting halfwayback, looking off out the window almost like he was posing for one of those Greek statues you saw in the history books. She couldn't see anything else; he could have been alone in the room. She knew it was the work of the devil, because he was almost a child, but then he was not a child, either, and she immediately assumed that he was grown, that he had failed several grades and should have been a senior in high school or something like that, but when she checked she discovered that he belonged in the class, that he was thirteen years old, even though he made the other boys in the class look like little kindergartners next to him.

As the year progressed, when she would turn to write on the board she did it just for him. She would contrive to touch him any chance she got, laying her hand on his arm or his shoulder, and when she did it was like touching a flame, one of the flames that were growing around her, darting and dancing and consuming her, destroying her soul (she had no doubt of that, but she did not care), casting her into eternal damnation, devouring her with her own lust, because she knew from the start that what she was feeling had nothing at all to do with love. She did not attempt to fool herself, to deny. She knew what this was about, and she knew she had to have him. Every day after school she would close and lock the door and go back and lay her face on the seat of his desk, still warm from his body, resting her cheek against whatever heat was left until it faded.

Lester Ray was well aware of what was taking place in Mrs. Nijim's mind. He had already had his experience with Maude, a forty-five-year-old waitress at Saddler's Lounge, and he could read everything about Mrs. Nijim in her eyes, the way they darted away from him and then back, away and then back, as though she were fighting with herself. She asked him to stay after school and beat the chalk out of the erasers, and she sat on the steps and watched him while he did it. The principal of the school would get very angry when students beat the erasers against the dark brick outside wall of the school, leaving white, eraser size blotches that had to be hosed off, but when Lester Ray did it right in front of Mrs. Nijim she didn't say a word. She offered to tutor him in math, even though he was having no trouble with it and had an A+ in the class. She invented occasions to pull him aside and whisper confidentially to him about something unimportant, like whether he thought it was warm enough (or cool enough) in the classroom. So close that he could feel her hot breath on his cheek as she gripped his bicep as though she wanted to rip it out of his arm.

Then one day in early November she asked him if he wanted to do some work around her house after school, and he agreed. He could always use some extra money, but of course he knew something else was being offered, too. She told him to come at four, and he walked across town to their little brick house and went up and rang the doorbell. She answered the door in a filmy negligee, which was jolting not only for what it was but also because he had never seen her in anything other than the severe dark suits and dresses she wore to teach in. He could see her large nipples and her triangle of dark hair through the diaphanous cloth. She took him by the arm and pulled him into the house and down the hall to her bedroom, talking all the while, nervously and excitedly, the words tumbling out crazily one on top of another, something about her husband being gone with the children to a doctor in De Quincy Springs, they had time but must hurry, please, please, please. She kept repeating please all the time she was helping him undress, throwing off her negligee and pulling him down on top of her on the double bed.

They saw each other as often as she could arrange it: in her car, on a little hidden-away sandy beach that he knew of on the river, in his house on the settee, and at her house when she knew she would be alone. She would not let him use a condom—she told him it was because she had had an operation so she couldn't have any more children, but it was really because she wanted to have his child. She was insatiable, and she blindly wanted something that was a part of him that she could keep for the rest of her life. She prayed for hours every night, on her knees on the hardwood floor, but she knew she was flinging her words of contrition into a void where they would not be heard and the absolution she longed for would never be hers. She had turned her back on God and continued to every time she could manage to get Lester Ray alone, and she did not think God could love her beyond that betrayal. But she couldn't help it. She was an addict who would give up eternity for a few minutes of ecstasy.

To Lester Ray it was little more than a diversion. It was what men did with women, and it didn't have to mean anything beyond what they were doing with their bodies, and women had taught him that. She gave him money, sometimes as much as twenty dollars a week, and it did not occur to him that he was a kept boy, her plaything, and it would not have mattered to him if it had. He never thought about her when he wasn't with her. He suspected that other people knew about them, but that didn't matter to him, either. He was totally bored with school, with his life, and he was becoming bored with Mrs. Nijim. The only thing in his life that had come to mean anything to him was his mother, finding her. He was becoming convinced that that was what he'd been born for, that his whole life was shaped by it, that by that simple but momentous act of walking out of his life his mother had set in motion the direction of all his days and months and years on this earth.

One day, on a Monday morning in late February, there was a new teacher in Mrs. Nijim's classroom. The family had moved away over the weekend, suddenly, giving no reason, not even to the pastor and the people at the Assembly of God church that they regularly attended, and not to the school board. The superintendent of schools in Panellas County got a telegram late on the preceding Friday, in which Mrs. Molly Nijim resigned her position without explanation.

Lester Ray felt that his life had been precipitately simplified. There was no one he was connected to now but Mrs. McCrory and the elusive, phantom-like existence of his mother. A week later he quit school.

9

In Northern Virginia

April 1943

The girl driving the blue Pontiac convertible picked Minnie up alongside the highway where she was hitching. She told Minnie her name was Penelope Sapp Simmons, that she was on the way home from her college, Smith, to Bon Air, which was, according to her, both a part of Richmond and not a part of Richmond at the same time. "Everybody calls me Penny," she said.

"I'm Minnie Lou Hinson," Minnie said. She had started the practice of giving herself different names in different circumstances, using whatever name might pop into her head. She had a Social Security card in the name of Mary Lou Williams that she'd stolen in the women's room at a downtown YWCA. She had a District of Columbia drivers' license in the name of Sally Ann Warneke that she'd simply pocketed and walked away with one day while she had a temporary job working the cash register in a gas station, when Mrs. Warneke, who was at least sixty years old (sixty-one, Minnie discovered later, when she had a chance to inspect the license) paid for her gas by check and had to show it for identification. Minnie had no family, no home town, no home state. She was a nonperson. She had no nationality and no ethnic identity, except that she was a Gypsy, and she couldn't figure out any real significance to that, (except that it seemed to make her not Caucasian and not Negro, either) especially after the soldier who was posing as her brother Shon had told her that Gypsies were dying out, that her old familia had basically broken up. Which, as far as she was concerned, was okay. She had no loyalties to Gypsies, or to anyone else. She was free.

"Did you take somethin to make em do like that?" Penny Sapp Simmons asked her.

"What?"

"Your eyes," she said. "Some kinda medicine or somethin?"

"No, I was born that way," Minnie said.

Penny Simmons drove very fast. They were on a highway numbered U.S. 301, and there was a lot of traffic, many heavy trucks. Penny had the top down on the convertible and when they passed one of the trucks going the other way it would create a vacuum that would make their hair stand straight up before it went back to whipping in the wind. "Cause my Uncle Howard, he's a doctor, and I could get him to get me some."

"What's that?" Minnie said, having to practically shout over the roar.

"You know, my eyes. Somethin to take to make one of em a different color. I don't like the color of my eyes anyhow."

Minnie had not noticed the color of Penny's eyes, and she made no effort to lean around and look. Penny looked to be in her early twenties; she was extremely thin, with sandy hair, and she was flat-chested, with long skinny legs. Her skirt was bunched up in her lap to free her legs for driving. Her face was gaunt to the point of sickly. She kept flicking on the radio to music they couldn't really hear and then flipping it off again. She was either nervous or a person who was wound so tight she couldn't be still for a moment.

"So where you headed?" Penny Simmons asked Minnie. She pulled out a long Pall Mall and stuck it between her lips.

"I don't know," Minnie said, "just travelin."

Penny was thumbing her Zippo lighter frantically, trying to light the cigarette, but she couldn't; the wind whipped the lighter silent as soon as it sputtered.

"You got to be goin somewhere," Penny said, the cigarette bouncing up and down in the loose grip of her lips. "If you're goin, you're goin somewhere. You can't just wind up in thin air. Shit," she said and flung the cigarette out into the highway, where it bounced and rolled under the wheels of a northbound pickup truck.

Maybe Minnie was going somewhere specific. She was like a wounded animal, trying to find someplace safe to die, or maybe to curl up to live. Maybe that was where she was going. But she felt unaccountably safe and protected, secure. When she thought of the large empty void that was her immediate future she felt comforted and warm rather than afraid, because she was confident that in the course of existing through that vacuous nothingness she would be becoming what she was supposed to become, that it was in that way that she would learn what and who she was, and this would be true not just in that imminent slice of vacant time just ahead but for the rest of her life, like the sculptor looking at the plain block of granite and knowing that the ideal form of the piece of art he is to make of it has already been determined somewhere outside and beyond himself and he only has to discover what that ideal form is by the process of creating it.

Penelope Sapp Simmons picked up another hitchhiker. He was a slight young man who said his name was Edgar Cassavetes. He had an army duffel which he tossed into the back seat on top of Minnie's carpetbag before he squeezed back there himself. Penelope took off with a great squealing of tires accompanied by the terrible prolonged honk of a heavy truck that was bearing down on them, and Penny gave the driver, who continued to lean on his horn, the finger, which was easy to do in the open car. The truck veered out and went around them, the horn still blaring, so loud that it seemed to be practically in the car with them.

"Jesus!" Edgar Cassavetes said from the back seat when the truck gained space in front of them and its noise began to subside.

"Are you prayin or cussin?" Penelope shouted above the wind noise.

"Cussin!" Edgar shouted back. He had both arms stretched out on the back of the seat. He looked like he had made himself completely at home. He was older than he'd looked standing by the highway, maybe because of his slim stature. He had on blue jeans and a plaid cotton shirt, red and light blue, that looked like it had been carefully chosen to go with the jeans. "So," Penny said, looking at him in the rearview mirror, "are you a deserter, or what? AWOL?"

"How'd you know?" the boy asked, grinning broadly, his brown hair flapping in the breeze.

"No kiddin?" Minnie said. "Really?"

"You think I want to get my ass shot off? No thank you," he said. Minnie thought about the boy who had knocked her around and maybe raped her, though she didn't know if you could call it rape or not since she was naked on the bed inviting him to come and fuck her. She had taken him home with her for that purpose, and she doubted that the law would allow you to change your mind at that point.

"And where are you two fine-lookin girls goin?" Edgar asked.

"Down the road a piece," Penny said.

"That right?" he said.

"Where're you headed?" Penny asked.

"Satsuma, Alabama," he said, "home, where I belong."

"Satsuma?" Minnie asked. "There's really a Satsuma in Alabama?"

"There's lots of satsumas in Alabama, but only one town named that that I know of," he said. "Down near Mobile. Right square in the swamp. The way I like it."

Penny turned off the main highway onto a secondary road that she said was a short cut. They were going through foothills brushed with the new green of fresh growth. The air was brand-new and fragrant. Penny continued to fiddle with the radio. Everything that came through it was absorbed by the wind: what sounded like war news, a weather forecast, swing music, all became static and was whipped away. They came into the outskirts of a small town and Penny pulled into a gas station. The attendant came out, a stooped old man with a rag in his hand. "Fill er up," Penny said, "and, hey, do you sell beer in there?"

"No beer," the old man said, "this here is a dry county."

Penny and Minnie went to the ladies room, which was large but filthy. A single toilet sat almost in the middle of the floor. Penny began to line the toilet seat with toilet paper. "He's kinda cute, ain't he?" Penny asked.

"Who?" Minnie said, "oh, the boy in the car."

"Yeah, who'd you think I meant, old grampaw?"

"No, just ... my mind's just wandering. I can't keep it focused on anything."

"You think we ought to fuck him?" Penny asked.

"I don't think so," Minnie said, "but you go ahead. I mean, if you want to, do it, don't let me stop you."

"Why would you want to stop me?" She pulled up her skirt, tugged her panties down below her knees and sat down. Immediately Minnie heard her trickling.

"No, I don't mean that. I just meant that I don't particularly want to fuck him, but don't not do it because of that. Okay?" Penny was looking up at her. Minnie noted that her eyes were a pale brown. Her lips were thin in her skeletal face. She looked unhealthy, starved half to death. Minnie pulled a coin out of her baggy khaki pants and shoved it into the rubber machine on the wall. When the little cellophane-wrapped condom came out, she handed it to Penny. "Here," she said, "be my guest."

Penny wiped and stood up and flushed. She took the condom. "Maybe I don't want to fuck him," she said.

"Then save it for next time," Minnie said. She hurriedly sat down. She hadn't realized how badly she needed to go. It was a great release.

Penny stood there watching her. "You ain't gonna shit, are you?" she said.

Minnie laughed. "No," she said. The girl was weird. She looked like some starved child. She drove like a child, too, not halfway paying any attention to what she was doing. Minnie was tempted to get her bag and get out here. Catch another ride. But the girl was going all the way into Richmond, and she had learned that in this part of the country long-range rides were hard to come by, especially now that they were on the less-traveled highway. She had gotten into Virginia, south from D.C., with a series of short rides: an old man in a pickup truck going to the next town, a family on their way to church, two fishermen headed to the Chickahominy River.

When they came back around front, the boy Edgar Cassavetes was not in the car, so they assumed he was around back at the men's room. The old man finished filling up the car. They watched him half-heartedly wash and wipe the windshield, leaving mostly new smears. He headed back to the station without a word and they followed him. It was a rundown place, practically leaning to the side, and the screen door rattled behind them. There were signs on the wall for RC Cola and Nehi drinks, Baby Ruth candy bars, Dubble Bubble, AC Spark Plugs. A big sign with Uncle Sam in a top hat pointing right toward you saying UNCLE SAM WANTS YOU. The place reeked with the odor of stale, scalded coffee. Penny went over to a cigarette machine and dropped a quarter in and got a fresh pack of Pall Malls, and at the same time the old man waddled behind the counter and opened the register with a tinkling ring. "Two seventy-five," he said. "Plus stamps. You got em, ain't you?"

"Sure," Penny said, and pulled out a book of ration stamps.

Just then Edgar Cassavetes stepped out from behind a rack of potato chips with a pistol in his hand. It was an army-issue .45. "I want all the money in that cash register, pops," Edgar said. The old man froze, his hand hovering over the drawer. It took the two girls several seconds to realize what was going on. Neither could move. Then Penny said, "What the hell are you doing?"

"What does it look like I'm doin?" he said. "Hurry!" he yelled at the old man.

Then things began to move so fast, happen so quickly, that neither of them knew or had a clear idea of what was happening. It all transpired within the scope of a few seconds. It was more an eruption than anything else. The old man suddenly raised a pistol, a big, clumsy revolver, from underneath the counter and fired, hitting Edgar Cassavetes squarely in the chest, and just as the boy rocketed back with the force of the shot he fired, too, in nothing more than a reflex because he was dead before he pulled the trigger. The shot hit a big jar of pickled eggs and shattered it, splashing vinegar and hardboiled eggs everywhere. The roar of the almost simultaneous shots was intense and deafening. The boy crashed back into the rack of potato chips and turned over a display of spark plugs and motor oil. The old man turned the pistol on Penny, who was standing there flat-footed. The smell of burnt gunpowder was overpowering.

"You little thievin bitch," he said, "y'all think you can get the better of me, don't you? Well, you can't."

Just then Minnie looked down and spied Edgar Cassavetes's pistol on the floor, a few inches from her foot.

"Now I'm gonna shoot both you bitches, and laugh while I watch you die!" He aimed the pistol right at Penny's chest.

Minnie dropped to the floor and grabbed the pistol and came up firing blindly toward the old man. She pulled the trigger and the automatic fired three times before it jumped out of her hand. The old man spun around and dropped behind the counter. The sudden quiet was further unnerving, an abrupt return to normalcy, as though nothing had happened, had possibly had the time to happen, as though anything that might have occurred had been quickly consumed by the silence. Minnie slumped to the floor, exhausted. Penny still stood in the same spot, the same posture, as though her shoes were glued to the floor. She had been paralyzed with fear and shock. There was no way she could believe what had just transpired. It was all impossible to take in. Things like this did not happen to Judge Simmons's daughter.

"We better get out of here," she said, but she did not move.

Minnie still lay flat on the floor. "Is he dead?" she asked in a quivering voice.

Penny tiptoed over and looked behind the counter. "He sure as hell looks it," she said, "looks like you got him twice, once in the chest and once between the eyes. And Edgar is dead, too. No doubt about it. We better leave."

Minnie did not ever want to get up from the rough, splintery floor that smelled of dust and spilled vinegar, of mud and gas and oil. She did not have the strength or the energy to pull herself upright, so she surrendered to the tug of the grimy floor. It was as though she were about to be consumed in some punitive fire and she had to succumb, to give in, her mind shooting inevitably back to old Alexander Mossback Frill and the fire of her escape, her redemption, the reek of coal oil that day and the fierce and terrible heat of the flames, that moment when she ceased to be a child forever. I have killed twice now, she thought, in these few years I have already killed twice. And she had no more planned to or wanted to than she would scheme to jump off a twenty-story building, but she knew she could do that, too. She knew because if she could she would, and she shivered, imagining finding herself in that situation, seeing clearly her toes over the edge, looking down to the traffic below, yielding to some demanding and powerful impulse to suddenly and without any forethought at all destroy herself finally and completely.

THE SIMMONS MANSION SAT solidly and majestically on the ridge of a mountain, as if it had been carved out of the granite of the mountain itself. Its gray stone walls were marked by splotches and streaks of the greenest ivy, like green paint applied by the brush strokes of a painter in a hurry. The imposing house was shaded by huge oak and hickory trees on its sloping lawn, and in the center of the circular driveway was a soaring magnolia tree, heavy with spring buds the size of dinner plates. Judge Simmons was a tiny man with a great, bushy shock of white hair that made him look like a top-heavy sapling, and Mrs. Simmons looked like a bale of cotton with two stubby legs and two sausage arms. Her head gave the impression that it was that of another person entirely who was hiding inside her squat, squared-off body, her head and face sticking out and sitting flat on the top as though she had no neck at all, or else it was still sunk below the surface and had not yet emerged along with the head. Penelope Sapp Simmons called them Boo-Boo and Tay-Tay.

"You have to stay, at least one night. We have room. God, I don't even know how many bedrooms that place has!" Penny had insisted, when they began to pass into the outskirts of Richmond.

They had left the gas station in a hurry. The station was isolated on the edge of a town, with no houses or other businesses near it, and apparently no one had heard the shots. Penny began to drive very fast again, recklessly, and Minnie cautioned her. "We don't want to look like we're runnin from somethin," she said, "and we sure as hell don't want to be stopped for speeding." Once they got through the little town, and there were no other cars coming from either direction, they slowed down and Minnie hurled Edgar Cassavetes's duffel bag into a grassy ditch, where it disappeared under a tangle of vines. "So much for Edgar," Minnie said, trying to sound light, but it was not convincing.

They were both still in a state of suspended incredulity. They had left the men there in pools of blood, with more blood splattered on the

counter and the wall behind it and all over a display of candy bars that
had been behind Edgar. Unless someone had seen them, and evidently
no one had, they figured that nobody could tie them to what happened
in the gas station. They had no real connection to either one of the dead
men. The two pistols were there, one behind the counter with the old
man, still in his hand, and the other dropped beside Edgar, who lay on
his back with his eyes wide open, staring, as if he were scrupulously
searching the low-hanging ceiling for a leak or a blemish. They were
certain that both men were dead. The front of the old man's skull was
shot away and they could see a bloody, grayish mass from which they
quickly averted their eyes.

"How the hell did all that happen?" Penny kept muttering, her hand
gripping the steering wheel so tightly her knuckles were white. "How
the hell . . .?"

"It just did, out of the blue," Minnie said. "It didn't have anything to
do with us."

"You shot that old son-of-a-bitch," Penny said, "you killed him."

"Only because he was about to kill you," Minnie said.

"Oh, I know! I didn't mean . . . Anyway, thanks for that. I owe you."

"No you don't. The ride's enough."

"It's not."

"Listen, Penny," Minnie said, "he woulda shot me next. It was all in
self-defense."

"Okay," she said. "But I want you to stay a night or two with us."

"I really need to get on down the road," Minnie said. She dreaded
staying with Penelope's family. With anyone's family. It made her nervous
and anxious to be around people she didn't know, people who were so
vastly different from her, and she knew full well that these would be.

"No, I insist," Penny said. "You can rest up. Eat some good food."

Minnie could feel it happening, feel herself being sucked in. It was
going to be difficult to escape going along with what Penny wanted.
Penny would not hesitate to make it as awkward as possible. And she had
to admit the thought of a home-cooked meal sounded appealing. And a
comfortable bed. Penny had said her father was a judge, that they lived in
the most exclusive part of Richmond. No doubt they were rich. Minnie

had never been around rich people before, and she was willing to concede some curiosity. But next to Penny, with her new little college-girl dress, Minnie—in her baggy pants and sweatshirt, her black chopped-off hair, the hint of an odor clinging to her skin that had last been washed in cold water in the lavatory of a gas station rest room, everything she owned crammed into a canvas-sided bag—would provide quite a contrast, and there was a possibility that Penny's parents would want to throw her out into the street. Which would make Minnie very angry, and she was not sure what she would say or do in such a circumstance, but it wouldn't be pretty. So it was a situation she would normally have avoided.

As it turned out, Penny's parents seemed welcoming enough, if somewhat cold. Her mother looked at the way Minnie was dressed and sniffed but she said nothing. Her father, holding a glass of Scotch, peered for a long time into Minnie's face before saying, in a guttural voice that was surprisingly loud coming from such a slight figure, "By Christ, you've one eye a different color from the other! Did you notice that, Tay-Tay?"

"I did," the dumpy woman said shortly.

"Well, then," the judge said, turning back to Minnie, "would you like a cocktail?"

"Maybe a Coke?" Minnie said.

Penny had already retrieved a beer from the kitchen, bringing one for Minnie that sat untouched on the coffee table in front of her.

"You are going to get as fat as a pig," her mother said to her.

"You ought to know," Penny said. The judge laughed heartily. Mrs. Simmons's face was grim, her lips clenched in a narrow straight line.

"Why don't you take your friend upstairs and get her settled, Penny?" Mrs. Simmons said tightly.

When the two girls ascended the winding staircase and were out of sight and out of earshot, Mrs. Simmons said, "I think she's a Mexican."

"No, no, no, my dear," the judge said. "Octoroon. I'll bet you ten dollars she's from New Orleans. That hair is as black as a crow's wing."

"I believe those eyes are a symptom of some serious dysfunction of the brain," Mrs. Simmons said. "Eyes like that are often a sign of insanity. I wonder how she got admitted to Smith, especially with all that nigra blood in her."

"If she is a lunatic, she's a beautiful one," he said.

"You leave her alone, Austin," Mrs. Simmons said sharply. The judge had a habit of going after many of Penny's friends that she brought home with her, sometimes with surprising success. There were so few young men around these days that it was a field day for old lechers like him. Mrs. Simmons always watched him with great zealousness, trying not to let him out of her sight in those circumstances, but, as Mrs. Simmons was fond of saying, he was a wily old bastard.

Upstairs, Penny took Minnie to a room across the hall from hers. "This is my brother's room," she said, "he's stationed in England now." The room had finely detailed model airplanes hanging from the ceiling on threads, and along one wall was a long table with what looked like radio equipment on it. "He's a ham," Penny said when she noticed Minnie inspecting it. Minnie had no idea what she was talking about. But she didn't care to ask. There were army insignias all over the walls, stuck to the wall paper. A big double bed that looked soft and inviting, and Minnie could have sunk herself into it at that moment and slept until tomorrow. She put her bag on a footlocker at the foot of the bed.

"Nice," she said. It was unlike any room she'd ever seen. She could have been in a foreign country. Just being in the house itself had gotten her off balance, out of sync, disconnected to anything around her. The solidity of the huge house reminded her of her own lack of ties to anything as substantial as it was, as permanent, but she knew she preferred it that way. The house was such an imposingly established place that it would have shackled her, tied her down, held her back. You could never escape such a home. It would follow you everywhere for the rest of your life. To her, it would have been a prison.

"We'll have supper in about an hour," Penny said. "You want to take a bath?"

"Oh yeah," Minnie said. Just the thought of it was relaxing to her, soothing.

Penny went into the adjoining bathroom and turned on the water in the large tub. She went to her room and came back with some bath salts and fragrant soap. She sat on the closed toilet lid. She established herself there. She was going to stay there while Minnie bathed. All right.

Minnie stripped down, and when she was naked she climbed in and let herself sink into the hot water with a long sigh. "I'll get Gertrude to wash all your clothes for you tonight, okay?" Penny said. All right. The hot water, softened and tingling from the bath salts, was almost unbearably pleasurable, caressing away the road grime of days, tingling into her pores as though it were entering the very centermost parts of her body. She put her head back, closed her eyes. Penny sat on the closed toilet and watched her. "Good, huh?" the girl said.

"Oh yeah," Minnie murmured. The soap smelled of lavender and roses. It seemed to wash away the memories of the day, the blood, the horror. I have killed a second time now already but it is over and there is nothing now to be done about it. She stretched out her legs and felt the tension going out of them, the dull tightness being absorbed out into the soapy water, the muscles of her back and neck relaxing and easing. She had bathed like this often at the Coronado Hotel, but that was a long time ago. She had forgotten the delight of it. It could get to be a habit if you weren't careful.

THE SPREAD AT SUPPER was lavish by Minnie's standards, served by a Negro woman in a white uniform: boiled shrimp, roast beef, mashed potatoes, green beans, fluffy biscuits, all accompanied by red wine which the Simmonses seemed to virtually inhale, including Penny, and winding up with pecan pie and ice cream, coffee, and more alcohol for the Simmonses, this time snifters of brandy. Judge Simmons was one of those men who was not going to allow the scarcity of various items and the necessity for ration stamps to cripple his enjoyment of good food and drink, and he used his friendship and influence with various government people and agencies to get all the ration stamps he wanted, so that he could buy good beef, bacon, real butter, all the gas they needed, new tires, and anything else that was rationed to everyone else.

By way of explanation, as he noted Minnie's surprise at the feast that was put on the table, he said to Minnie, "It's the duty of the wealthy to keep the economy going during war times, to keep the money circulating." He savored his warm pecan pie with melting vanilla ice cream puddling around it. All three of the Simmonses drank glass after glass of wine and, after they retired to the parlor to allow the servant to clear the table, several snifters of brandy each. Minnie drank four or five cups of coffee; she lost count. Judge Simmons lit a large cigar, and Penny one of her Pall Malls.

"So where is your home, Minnie?" Mrs. Simmons asked, settling into a heavily overstuffed chair.

"She's from Florida," Penny said.

"Oh?" Mrs. Simmons said.

"Yes, ma'am, a small town. Cedar Key," said Minnie.

"Oh, heavens, I know Cedar Key," Judge Simmons said, "I've been there deep-sea fishing. Marlin. Wonderful. Forty-one pounder. Tay-Tay, where is that picture?"

"I have no earthly idea," Mrs. Simmons said, to Minnie's relief dismissing the entire subject with a wave of her hand. "How did you come to enroll at Smith?"

"I'm not enrolled there," Minnie said. "I don't go to college."

"Oh, really?" Mrs. Simmons said, arching her eyebrows. "Then how did you meet Penny?"

"By Christ," Judge Simmons said, "I would have sworn you were from New Orleans."

"That's enough of that, Boo-Boo," Mrs. Simmons said. "I assume," she turned back to Minnie, "that you are of Spanish descent, though you have a most un-Spanish name. Is that right?"

"Yes, ma'am," Minnie said. "My parents came to Florida from Madrid."

"Wow," Penny said, "you didn't tell me that. Wow."

"So how did you two meet?" Mrs. Simmons asked. She was like a persistent dog at a rabbit hole. Her little eyes jumped back and forth between the two girls.

"I was hitch-hiking," Minnie said, "Penny picked me up and gave me a ride."

"Hitch-hiking?!" Mrs. Simmons exclaimed. "Oh, my."

"She's jokin," Penny said, "she's a friend of Martha Sue's roommate."

"Indeed."

"She goes to Martha Sue's roommate's church in New York. River-side."

"Well, it's not a funny joke. With all the drunk soldiers and drunk Negroes you see these days. I wouldn't be surprised if Penny picked some of them up."

"How do you know I haven't?" Penny asked.

"I just said it, dear," Mrs. Simmons said, "you probably have!"

"Now girls," Judge Simmons said, "not in front of our guest." He smiled at Minnie. Minnie knew the look in his eyes. She had seen the identical look in the eyes of thousands of men. He believed the hitch-hiking, and it aroused his interest even more. He would be even more pleased if he knew Minnie's whole story. She realized she was going to have to fight him off later, anyway, even if he knew no more about her than that she was there, because he would have already invented in his imagination, in his fantasy, a sordid and exciting past for her that had delivered her to his opulent mansion solely for his enjoyment. It would be his entitlement. He may have already visited her, at Cedar Key, on one of his fishing trips, visited her bed at the Coronado Hotel, though she doubted it, because she knew if he had he probably would remember it, if only because of her eyes. He didn't appear to be a subtle enough person to have covered his recognition of her when he commented on her eyes earlier, but it was certainly possible that he was.

"I'm going to bed," Mrs. Simmons said abruptly, struggling up out of the soft cushions of the chair, staggering slightly as she stood up.

"We're tired, too," Penny said. "Aren't you tired, Minnie?"

"Yes," Minnie said, imagining the feel of the cool, clean, ironed sheets as she slid between them. Mrs. Simmons disappeared down a hallway, without wishing them good night; apparently their (her?) bedroom was on the first floor.

"Good night, ladies," the judge said, bowing to them.

Minnie and Penny mounted the stairs. The door to the room Minnie was staying in was open, and she could see all her clothes folded neatly at the foot of the bed. Cleaned, and pressed, too, probably. For the first time since she'd stayed at a hotel—she thought it had been in Providence.

"You want to borrow a nightgown?" Penny asked.

"No, thank you," Minnie said. "My T-shirt'll do. I probably couldn't sleep in anything else."

"Okay," Penny said. She started to turn toward her door.

"Penny," Minnie said. Penny turned back. "Listen. I really appreciate all this, I really do."

"Sure," Penny said, "Okay." She was suddenly close to Minnie. She grabbed Minnie by the shoulders and kissed her on the cheek. Minnie returned the kiss, then stepped back. They were chaste, sisterly kisses, but the air around them was as thick as warm, heavy fog. "Okay," Penny said again, "good night."

Minnie went into the room and closed the door. She stood there for a moment, staring at the door. Okay, she thought, okay. Maybe she was the only one who felt the warmth and not Penny, too, but she knew that was not so because she was always right about things like that. She felt it as clearly from Penny as she'd felt it from the old judge. She undressed, dropping a clean T-shirt over her head. Then she slid under the smooth sheets, under the light blanket on top. She lay her head back on the soft pillow, large and fluffy, giving. She clicked off the bedside lamp. The room was full of silver moonlight—a full moon, she knew. There would be moon-shadows on the lawn. The room was almost as light as day.

So she could see Penny plainly when she slipped in the door and padded quietly across to the bed. She watched her come, and Penny, in a short nightgown, sat on the edge of the bed; their eyes met. Penny's face was narrow, spare and angular, her eyes over-large in such skinniness. They looked at each other for more than a minute, neither speaking. Finally, "I'm in love with you," Penny said.

"Penny, you've only known me for a few hours," Minnie said.

"But I feel like we've been through so much together that that doesn't matter. And I know I love you."

"Penny . . ."

"I do! I know I do," she said.

Minnie slid across the bed and threw the covers back to let her get in. When Penny crawled in she snuggled against the girl's slight body, light and feathery, all the while Penny tugging at her shoulders, pulling her to turn so that they were facing each other. Penny kissed her forcefully, thrusting her tongue. Minnie felt her hands on her breasts. Suddenly Penny pulled back, gazing at her. "I've never done this before," she said, "have you?"

"Yes," Minnie said, pulling the girl back toward her, planting her lips on her open mouth. She let her hands run up and down the girl's body, felt her breath catch and quicken. "Yes," Minnie said again, "just relax."

WHEN JUDGE SIMMONS, JUST as Minnie had thought he would, tapped softly on the door and slipped silently into the room, he found them there, asleep, naked, their arms around each other, washed in the lustrous moonlight—transfigured, commuted—like some misplaced and youthful and erotic Florentine sculpture.

10

Gwinnett County, Georgia

October 1964

Bellarmine Fagafoot, the giant, was eight feet, eleven inches tall and weighed four hundred and ninety pounds. He had an especially made ten-gallon (or perhaps twenty- or thirty-gallon) hat that was as big as a beach umbrella. He was thirty-seven years old, and he had quit school in the sixth grade, before he would have gone on to junior high, because he was already six feet three inches and he did not fit into the desks in the school rooms. All the way through he had had to sit at a table in the back. Even though the basketball coach at the high school begged him to stay in school and come out for the team (his name was Lloyd Parsley, and he guaranteed Bellarmine a starting position even in the seventh grade), Bellarmine's mind was made up. He was not interested in school anyway, because he was not very bright. He had trouble with even the most elementary math problems (he could barely make change, and people who found out about that would sometimes try to cheat him; if he caught on, however, he made them sorry) and he couldn't spell very well. For example, even as he approached middle age, he still thought water was spelled "warter," walk was spelled "wawk," and cereal was spelled "sereal."

Bellarmine was from Bowling Green, Kentucky. He had been born to normal parents (his father was five foot nine, his mother five foot two) and he had two sisters and a brother who were of average height. By the time he was sixteen years old he had to have specially made beds, and everything else cramped him. Like Xillarmet Yak had an undersized Airstream with undersized furniture, Bellarmine lived in the trailer of

155

an eighteen-wheeler that was outfitted with oversized chairs and tables and a bed ten feet long and six feet wide. He enjoyed all the attention he got from certain kinds of women, like the dancers in THE STREETS OF PARIS tent, who assumed his penis must be gigantic to match the rest of him, but he discouraged them in the end because he did not want them to find out his secret: his penis was actually tiny, so little and short that he had to be extra careful when urinating not to pee on the inside of his pants. He never let anyone else see it, if he could help it. On those occasions when he was in a public men's room, stooped over and practically squatting, and he had seen someone at a nearby urinal glance at it, they would look from it to his face with a startled, puzzled expression. When they saw the fierce look on his face they would hurriedly finish and fly out the door as fast as they could, sometimes still zipping up as they went out the door.

Bellarmine Fagafoot was not a "gentle giant." Anyone who ever had the effrontery to laugh at or make fun of his name found that out in a hurry. Bellarmine had broken arms and legs, had given quite a few concussions, had thrown people through plate glass windows, had been known to smash to splinters all the furniture in an entire barroom. He had not killed anyone yet, which was something of a miracle, because he liked to drink and was often drunk, and when provoked would sometimes lose all control. As a result, all the people who knew him knew to leave him alone to sit and brood over his drink, but there were always, in every town, one or two tough guys who wanted to prove something by challenging him, inevitably coming all too quickly to regret it, with bloodied lips and noses from his huge fists, which hung from his arms, his wrists, like bloated country hams.

Bellarmine, drunk or sober, was always the first to respond to a "Hey, Rube!," the shouted alarm that went out when there was an especially difficult troublemaker at the show, (which would sometimes happen when the troublemaker found out he had to pay extra to see Joe-Josephine, the hermaphrodite, or when he happened to get too close and friendly with his hands at THE STREETS OF PARIS show) and Bellarmine usually simply had to show up next to him to send the character fleeing. Emil relied on him for that. There were two girls besides Sheila, and they all, including

Sheila, subtly and sometimes not so subtly invited the marks to cop a feel and most of the marks were content with that. But occasionally there was one who had to go further and would make a grab for one of the naked girls. Some of them were only showing off for the other men, but some of them were crazy and could be dangerous. It was usually Sheila who yelled—screamed—the "Hey, Rube!"

The boy, Lester Ray, was always quick to respond, too. The first time there was a "Hey, Rube" in THE STREETS OF PARIS tent after the boy was hired, Emil rushed in at the same time as Lester Ray. The girls were still on the stage, giggling now, and Bellarmine had the offending mark immobilized, both his arms clasped behind his back in one of the giant's hands. Emil saw how Lester Ray looked at Sheila. The boy already had it bad. All the other men in the audience were shrunk back against the tent walls. Sheila was completely naked, the other two in various stages of undress. Emil saw Lester Ray's eyes grow wide, almost bulging out of his head. He couldn't blame the boy. Sheila, naked, was something to see. What bothered Emil was the way Sheila looked at Lester Ray. Like he was some delicious pastry she was about to devour. She stood unselfconsciously on the stage, and while the boy was staring at her, his mouth slightly agape, she made a delicate little bump with her pelvis, a barely visible movement, or it would have been from one of the other girls, but from Sheila it was as noticeable as a cartwheel.

Lester Ray could not have shifted his eyes away from her even if an angry bear had growled right behind him. He would have tensed, waiting for the piercing, burning claws, the knifelike, gnawing teeth, but he would not have moved his eyes away from Sheila's body. It was the most glorious, most heavenly gorgeous body he had ever seen. Admittedly, he had not seen that many naked women—some of his father's fat whores who sometimes walked around the house with no clothes on, Lacy Limm, Maude, Molly Nijim—that was about it, and none of them had looked the way Sheila did. Her skin was smooth, unblemished, very white under the lights. Her waist was narrow, her small breasts firm and alive, the hair at the bottom of her flat belly as rich and black as the hair on her head. Her eyes were black, too, or very dark brown, eyes that reached out and grabbed him and yanked his head toward her.

"Okay, let's go," Emil said, "so they can finish the show." Bellarmine began shoving the mark out between the flaps of the tent. "You, too," Emil said, looking at Lester Ray.

Lester Ray could not find his voice to answer. He was uncomfortably aware that he had a tight erection. He hoped it was not showing too much through his blue jeans. He followed Bellarmine and the mark to the outside. He watched Bellarmine give the man a shove in the back that sent him sprawling. It was like watching a normal-sized man push a puppet. "Don't come back," the giant said. The man scrambled to his feet, dusting himself off, and sprinted off out into the carnival. He disappeared into the crowd. Lester Ray looked up at the immense man. He had been told that Bellarmine had once been cast as a giant in a picture show being made out in Hollywood but had lost his job because of his drinking and because he had beat up one of the other actors. It was easy to imagine Bellarmine being a giant in a picture show.

"You'd better be careful," Emil said to Lester Ray, "she's like a hot stove. Get too close and she'll burn you."

"All right," Lester Ray said. He already knew that. He wanted to be burned. Like sinking into too-hot water in the tub at Mrs. Mack's house, the sensual peace that comes when your body realizes it's not too hot after all, but just right, and it goes through you like a soothing salve. He had come to see Emil to show him the picture of his mother. But Emil wanted to talk about Sheila.

"She's way older than you are, even if you are eighteen, which you told me, but which you ain't. She's almost thirty years old. She's been around the block a time or two."

"All right," Lester Ray said. "Is she your girl friend?"

"My girl friend? No way. I mean, I fuck her now and again, but I wouldn't call her my girl friend, no."

They were in Emil's trailer. Emil had his hands clasped behind his neck, leaning back in his swivel chair, a desk piled high with papers behind him. It was not like he cared that Emil and Sheila were making it, Lester Ray was thinking, insisting to himself. They lived in a different world from his. A world he was determined to enter, though, mainly because it was not his world, his life. His was a world of rootlessness and uncertainty and he was anxious to escape.

Emil had a heavy gold chain around his neck, his shirt opened down the front almost to his waist. The skin of his chest was brown, covered with dense, wiry black hairs. He wore a tiny gold earring that Lester Ray had not noticed before. He smoked a cigarette, thrusting his head back even further to blow the smoke in a thick stream toward the ceiling.

"Is she a Gypsy?" Lester Ray asked.

"She's part Gypsy," Emil said, "the best part." He grinned, his teeth remarkably white against his skin. His hair was intensely black, curly and shiny. It reminded Lester Ray of Sheila's hair down below. It was Emil's lined face, his tired eyes, that gave him away. In Lester Ray's fourteen-year-old mind, the man was close to being old, like everyone who passes out of the turbulent fields of youth into that mysterious, unknown sphere of adulthood where time and living begin to take their toll. It was difficult for Lester Ray to imagine him being with Sheila. Lester Ray would not even have guessed how old she was, and it had surprised him that she was almost thirty, that is, if Emil was telling the truth. To Lester Ray she existed in some timeless, ageless realm, not adulthood at all but an unvarying paradise of beauty, of woman. She was not touched at all by her earthly years, however many or few there had been.

Emil was leaning back so far it looked as though he would tip over any minute. "I know you're just dyin to get into some of that," Emil said, "but why don't you try it with one of the other girls? That little blonde, Judy. She ain't but nineteen. Officially she's twenty-one, but she's really nineteen."

"Okay. Sure," Lester Ray said. He held the picture out toward Emil.

"What's this?" he asked, taking it.

"It's a picture of my mother. I think it's my mother. She was a Gypsy, and I want to know if you've ever seen her. Or knew her."

Emil held the picture close to his face, studying it intently. He looked at it for a long time. Lester Ray could read nothing in his expression. He remembered what old Saartjie had said, that she had known her but that she was a spirit, whatever that meant, and he had decided that she was just giving him the mumbo jumbo she gave people who paid her to tell them their fortunes. But she had spontaneously blurted that she knew her, maybe before she thought, and then had seemed to want to cover that up with the crap. Why, he didn't know. She would not talk to him about it again.

"Well?" he said. When Emil didn't reply, he said, "Old Saartjie said she knew her."

"Oh?" Emil said, still inspecting the picture. "What'd she tell you about her?"

"Nothing. Nothing that made any sense."

"Uh-huh," Emil said. He looked up then. "Why do you think this is your mother?"

"Because I found the picture in my house. It's an old picture, look at that automobile. She lived there with me and my father after I was born, I don't know how long, and then she left. She was a Gypsy."

"Because she deserted you?"

"No, because she couldn't stay in one place too long at a time. She didn't want a home. Like you."

Emil gestured around him. "This is my home," he said.

"Exactly," Lester Ray said, "on wheels."

"That don't make it any less a home, does it?"

"I don't guess so," Lester Ray said.

"Everybody needs a home," Emil said.

"All right." Lester Ray was focused on the photograph in Emil's hand. He wanted to know, but then he didn't want to know. He was afraid of what Emil might tell him. He had put off asking him about it, delayed showing him the picture. He had been so single-minded about it, about the mystery of it, for so long that he didn't know if he could bear to have it end. One way or the other. He did not know why he was so sure that Emil would be the one to know the truth. He was basing that only on the feeling he'd had when he'd first seen him. But he was sure.

"Tell me," Emil said, "did she have one blue eye and one green eye?"

"What?" Lester Ray said.

"Just what I said. Did she have one green eye and one blue eye?"

"I don't know. I don't remember. My father never told me anything like that."

"Well, it would help if you knew," Emil said.

"Why?"

"There's not too many people with that characteristic."

Lester Ray took the photo back and studied it. It was impossible to tell. "Anyway," Lester Ray said, "do you think you knew her? Know her?"

"Maybe. I don't know."

"Either you do or you don't!" Lester Ray said.

"Things are rarely that simple, my young friend," Emil said.

"I'm gettin kinda tired of all these fuckin riddles!" Lester Ray said.

"Well, nothin's keepin you here. You can leave any time you want."

"No. I'll find her. I'll find my mother."

"You might be lookin in the wrong place entirely. Did that ever occur to you?"

"I might be. But I don't think so." These were her people. Eventually he would find her or find her grave if she was dead, which was a possibility that had occurred to him. Either way, he did not plan to give up.

Emil looked at him curiously. "Where is your father, anyway?" he asked.

"Back home, I guess," Lester Ray said. "He's a drunk."

"Where's home?"

"A little town. You never heard of it."

"Okay," Emil said, "I see." He held his hands up, palms out toward Lester Ray. "I don't want to know your business, man." He sat for a long time, looking at the boy. "Let me give you some good advice, Lester Ray," he said.

"All right."

"Stay away from Sheila. If you know what's good for you, you'll stay away from Sheila." Emil looked suddenly angry, his teeth clenched. "One thing's for sure, she's not your mama!"

THEY PUT UP A small tent next to old Saartjie's MADAME SAARTJIE, FAITH HEALER AND FORTUNES TOLD for Mrs. McCrory, and gave her one of Saartjie's long, colorful dresses to wear, a red headband, two dangling hoop earrings. Emil didn't think it would take business away from old Saartjie, simply double the fortune telling business, but old Saartjie wasn't too sure. She complained, in her strained, scratchy voice.

"What she says don't make sense," she said to Emil.

"And what you say does?" he answered. "She's different than you. She don't read the future." He promised Saartjie that her money would remain the same. Any extra was gravy. And the old woman, Mrs. McCrory, didn't know the difference.

Lester Ray did, though. "Listen," he said to Emil, "you can't make fun of her. Use her. I ain't gonna let you do that."

"I'm not making fun of her. She's here, she might as well work. The rubes don't care. The weirder she talks the more they'll think she's in tune with the beyond, or whatever."

Mrs. Mack wanted to do it. "Come on, Lester Ray, I don't ever get to have any fun," she said. "Let me do this." She seemed to really want to, so he relented.

She had a sign: HOUSE OF PRAYERS. The next lines read: "God sent. God's Messenger," with a picture of Jesus underneath, and "Rev. Mother Pocahontas, Spiritual Healer and Adviser, Come see her in person. All prayers and healing to you."

"It's too much like mine," Saartjie complained.

"Goddamit, Saartjie," Emil said, "ain't you noticed that all these Southern redneck towns we set up in have got a fuckin church on every corner? And they all seem to do all right, okay?"

The sign continued: "Touch of her hand will heal you. Everyone welcome—White or Colored—to Rev. Mother Pocahontas's tent." Underneath that, in smaller letters: "Are you suffering? Do you need help? Do you have bad luck? Bring your problems to Mother Pocahontas now and be rid of them. She gives lucky days. She lifts you out of sorrow and darkness and starts you on the way to success and happiness. If you suffer from alcoholism and cannot find a cure, don't fail to see this gifted woman, who will help you. Rev. Mother Pocahontas guarantees to restore your lost nature."

Old Saartjie's tent had a crystal ball, cards, tea leaves, with various spicy incense burning all the time. Mrs. Mack's tent smelled only of motor oil and popcorn; that was the smell of the carnival, its identifying scent, one of its few constants, motor oil and popcorn, hovering like mist. Her tent only had two chairs and a little table with an empty coffee cup on it for the coins. Mrs. Mack liked the chairs. They had bought them in the furniture department in a nearby department store. They had arms and a soft cushioned seat covered in red and blue plaid. She was to charge fifty cents. She didn't know about that. It seemed a lot. But if she could cure somebody from being an alcoholic, she guessed it would be worth it. She had no idea how she had arrived at this juncture, but she guessed she must be qualified or she wouldn't be here. She didn't remember anything past today, yesterday at the outside. Every time she saw the handsome boy and the little ugly boy who seemed to live with her they were strangers to her. One night she had thought she was going even crazier when she noticed that the little ugly boy had grown titties! And she would swear the handsome boy had grown a couple of inches just in the little time after he had come in the door. He knew her name. "Mrs. Mack," he called her. The little ugly boy didn't call her anything. He hardly ever said anything at all. Last night she had said to the little ugly boy, "Cat got your tongue?"

"Fuckin aye, grandma," he'd said.

So she said it back to him: "Fuckin aye." He just laughed. Sometimes Mrs. McCrory blurted out the worst language she could imagine and she wouldn't even know it until she had already done it and even then she wasn't sure she'd actually said it or where she'd learned it, unless it was from the little ugly boy. She could always just hear an echo of the words, dying away, but she knew they'd come out of her mouth and she didn't even know them, didn't think she'd ever heard them before. It was like she had all of a sudden learned to speak in some foreign tongue, like a Dutchman or something, and didn't know what she was saying when she spoke it.

She remembered the most curious things. An old Raggedy Ann doll she'd had as a child, with button eyes, red stitched mouth, stuffed with raw cotton right out of her father's field. She even remembered who had made it for her: their old black cook, Punchy. She couldn't quite recall her brother and sister. She was almost sure her brother was Orville, who lived in a city and who, she thought, wanted to put her in a nursing home. She had a sister who had had the polio, but she couldn't recollect her name. Or maybe that had been her daughter. It made her head hurt to try to put all those things together. She wondered what was happening to her. She was dumb or crazy, one of the two, or both. She had said that to Lester Ray. Lester Ray! That was the good-looking boy's name. "No, ma'am, Mrs. Mack," he'd said, "you're not dumb nor crazy either, you're just old. Everybody gets old." He wasn't old, but he was wise, she could tell that. "Who are you?" she'd asked him. "I'm Lester Ray, Mrs. Mack," he'd said. She didn't know him. She'd never seen him before in her life.

A woman came into her tent. She was overweight, wearing a shapeless gray dress and a sunbonnet. She was missing several teeth in the front. Her face was round and wide and flat, like the bottom of a skillet. She dropped a fifty-cent piece into the cup. She sat down in the second chair, across from Mrs. McCrory. She wore high-topped, clodhopper shoes, the soles caked with dried mud. They were stiff and black and looked as though they'd been hammered out of cast iron. She just looked placidly at Mrs. McCrory, out of drooping eyes.

"Do I know you?" Mrs. McCrory asked.

"No, ma'am, not that I know of," the woman said. The corners of her mouth were stained brown with snuff. "I come from up near Rehobeth, brought the chaps to the fair. I seen your sign."

"Yes," Mrs. McCrory said. "What sign?"

"The one outside there. I need to talk to you bout my husband," the woman went on. "He's a mean un. He's bad to drink."

"All rivers flow back to the sea," Mrs. McCrory said.

The woman said nothing for a moment. Then she said, "That's from the Bible, ain't it?"

"Yes," Mrs. McCrory said, but she had no idea what she had just said. She did not even know she had said anything. Who was this fat faced woman looking at her like she was a monkey in the zoo? "Who are you?" Mrs. McCrory asked.

"I don't have to tell you my name, do I?" the woman inquired suspiciously.

"No, but who are you?"

The woman cocked her head to the side and peered at Mrs. McCrory for a moment. "That's Bible talk, too, ain't it?" she said.

"You're not my sister, are you, the one that had the polio?" Mrs. Mc-Crory asked.

"No, ma'am," she said, "I ain't never had the polio that I know of."

"Well then, who are you?"

The woman squinted her eyes. She looked down at her hands clasped in her ample lap, then back up at Mrs. McCrory. "Are you talkin bout my soul?" she asked. "Who I am inside my soul?"

"Yes," Mrs. McCrory said.

"I'm saved," she said.

"From what?" Mrs. McCrory asked.

"Saved. Saved! Like with Jesus, you know?"

Mrs. McCrory blinked her eyes and suddenly a woman appeared before her, sitting in the other chair. Where did she come from? Mrs. McCrory thought she'd seen her somewhere before. "Didn't I buy some fresh okra from you one time?" she asked.

The woman stared at her. Neither said anything for a minute. Then, "What ails you?" the woman asked.

"My brother Orville got sprayed with a shotgun one time. Old Mr. James Taylor Jones shot him for stealin watermelons out of his patch," Mrs. McCrory said. She laughed merrily.

"I don't know no Orville," the woman said. "I think you done excaped from the loony bin."

"I'm crazy, and dumb, too," Mrs. McCrory said. "But you got to remember, if you chop down a peach tree, it won't bear any fruit."

The woman wanted to be outraged, but she was cautiously puzzled. Confused. Jesus himself had talked in riddles, too, hadn't he? And a lot of it didn't make a whole lot more sense to her than what Rev. Mother Pocahontas was saying. This old woman was God's messenger, she'd been touched by the spirit. She claimed to have the Holy Ghost in her. Suppose it was true? The woman wanted to grab her fifty cents back and bolt from the tent, but she was scared to.

"I . . ." she said, "I . . . I reckon I can get my preacher to explain that to me, can't I? Bout the peach tree?"

"What?"

"About the peach tree." Maybe the old woman was kind of deaf.

"Yes. What preacher? I thought you said he was a drunk."

"No, ma'am, my husband. Not my preacher, my husband."

"Your husband?"

"Yes, ma'am."

"Your husband is a drunk?"

"Yes, ma'am."

"Well then," Mrs. McCrory said, "I think you ought to kill him."

"Say what?"

"Shoot the fucker. Kill him."

"Kill him?" She was incredulous. Mother Pocahontas must mean something else, like Jesus sometimes did. Jesus sometimes seemed to say just the opposite of what he meant. Or maybe she is crazy as a loon. As daft as a scarecrow.

"If you don't do it," Mrs. McCrory said, "then I'll come and kill him for you."

Mrs. McCrory had a sudden burst of clarity. The expression on this woman's face, whoever she was, made her laugh. She cackled. She could feel the heavy earrings dangling from her lobes. She looked down at her dress. It looked as though she were headed to a costume party. She looked at the strange woman again. She chuckled. She couldn't help it.

"How can you come there? You don't even know where I live," the woman said, "do you?" She asked it as though she were suspicious that Mrs. McCrory might know where she lived.

"Why should I know where you live?" Mrs. McCrory asked.

The woman looked angry now. Her full, oval face turned a bright red. Mrs. McCrory thought she was going to charge out of the chair any second and attack her. The woman didn't move, gripping the arms of the chair with her rough, chapped hands. She trembled slightly. She looked as solid and heavy as a pallet of bricks.

"You makin fun of me, ain't you?" the woman said. She stood up. "You gonna rot in hell, old lady, claimin you speak for God!"

Mrs. McCrory was shocked, taken aback. Who was this woman who was yelling in her face? The woman grabbed her coin from the cup and charged out through the curtain that hung over the door. Bright sunlight exploded briefly into the dim tent, then the curtain fell back into place. Mrs. McCrory looked around. She had no idea where she was or why she was sitting there in a tent with a Gypsy dress on. It didn't frighten her, though. She had no reason to suspect that there was anything out of the ordinary about it at all.

There are no seasons in Florida, except for a slight change in temperature between the hottest months of the summer and the coolest months of mid-winter. The only real seasons are on the calendar. October in Florida is still dull, dusty green and sand-shaded, not the showy splashes of color you see in the maples and hickories and sumacs of the hills further north. There may be a cooling breeze, promising November and then Christmas and then what passes for winter beyond, but the sun is still savage and cruel, broiling the delicate skins of the unwary, the unsuspecting rookie snowbirds from the north who will never again make the mistake of going out uncovered, thinking, "Well, it's December!"

Miss Millicent D. Roget was sweating beneath her clothes. She had expected it to be warm and pleasant, not hot like this. She was a representative of Boston Mutual Life Insurance Company, sent down to investigate a claim filed by one Orville McCrory in an attempt to collect on a fifteen-thousand-dollar policy on his mother.

"She's bound to be dead," the man was saying, "don't matter if somebody killed her or not, or if she died of natural causes, does it? Just so she's dead."

They were sitting in the stuffy office of the Sheriff of De Quincy County: Orville, Miss Roget, Sheriff Ralph Prudhomme, and Deputy Al Lister. An oscillating fan sat on the desk, whining like a deranged mosquito, giving little relief, only rearranging the heated air that came in through the screens in the open windows. All three men had been greatly surprised to discover that the representative was a woman, thrusting her card at each one in turn with an abrupt gesture that was obviously not designed to be friendly. Miss Roget was, the men assumed, making up for not being a man by acting like and dressing like one: she wore khaki pants and a man's shirt and tie. Her hair was chopped off short, much shorter than Deputy Al Lister's, who wore his in Elvis ducktails. The other two men were mostly bald.

"Just hold on a minute, Orville," the sheriff said. "We need to fill Miss Ro-git here in on all the details."

"Ro-jay," she corrected him.

"Okay," the sheriff said. "Anyhow, Mrs. McCrory was this senile old lady . . ."

"Is," she said. "There is no proof that she's dead, is there?"

"No, ma'am, not in the way that we've found her body, her corpse, or anything like that. Anyhow, she disappeared. Just vanished. Didn't nobody know when nor how. She hardly ever left that old house she lived in, Orville here's house now, I reckon, so nobody missed her for a while. Orville seen her sometime in April or May, he couldn't remember exactly . . ."

"And that boy was there," Orville interrupted. "Livin in the house with her! It was that boy . . ."

"Hold on, Orville, let me tell it. Anyhow, it musta been after that that they left. Some time in the early summer, probably, because we found this fellow, name of Duck, claims he fixed up that old car of Orville's daddy's, got it to runnin so that the boy he's talkin about, Lester Ray Holsomback, could take Mrs. McCrory on a trip or somethin. The boy paid him seventy-five dollars to fix it. It ain't clear where he might of got the money . . ."

"Hah!" Orville said.

"It was an Oldsmobile, a 1939 model, but we couldn't find no papers on it or nothin so we had to track it down through the courthouse over in De Quincy Springs. Got the number of the last tag it was issued. And damned if we didn't find the tag itself, out at this fellow Duck's tent, son-of-a-bitch lives in a . . . pardon me, ma'am, I forgot myself." Miss Roget waved him on with an impatient wave of her hand. "He lives in a tent, or he sleeps in one, spends his days drinkin beer in Saddler's Lounge. We found the tag in his tent. He claimed he didn't have any idea how it got there, but he finally admitted he found another tag for the car before they left . . ."

"That right there tells you he stole it," Orville interrupted.

"Anyhow," the sheriff went on, "he then claimed that that boy, Lester Ray Holsomback, kidnapped his fourteen-year-old daughter and took her along. The boy ain't but fourteen hisself, by the way. She was gone, no doubt about it, cause she used to set in Saddler's Lounge with her daddy all day and watch him drink beer. All the regulars there said one day she was just gone. Duck didn't report her missin. I reckon he was too busy drinkin up that seventy-five dollars. So we put out a bulletin with the Highway Patrol. Good description of the car, but it had different license plates, we didn't know what. They set up road blocks, checked out every Oldsmobile between here and Chattanooga. Near as we can tell they just vanished into thin air."

"No one vanishes into thin air," Miss Roget said. She took out a Camel cigarette, thumped it against her thumbnail, then lit it with a Zippo. "What makes you think they would have stopped at Chattanooga?" she asked around a cloud of exhaled smoke. They were all three watching her smoke, which she did like a man, too, and they were beginning to get the picture, at least the two older men were. Deputy Lister was just mystified. "They may be in Canada by now, or California," she said. "What about this boy's family?" The fan turned in her direction and scattered the smoke up toward the ceiling.

"Oh. He lived with his daddy. Old Earl Holsomback is a drunk, gone all the time. Never took care of the boy. He was gone, too, and for a while we figured he'd gone with em, but then he turned up in about a month, didn't even know the boy had left home."

"So we've just assumed she was dead," Orville said. "How long do we have to wait before . . . ?"

"I don't deal in assumptions," Miss Roget interrupted.

"But if the highway patrol in six states can't find em, what makes you think . . ." Orville said.

"I'm not the redneck highway patrol," she interrupted him again. "I'll find them. If they exist."

"What the hell do you mean by that, if they exist?" Orville asked angrily. Miss Roget ignored him.

"I'd be careful about throwin that 'redneck' language around in these parts, Miz Ro-git," said the sheriff.

"Why? Are you saying that you three are rednecks?" she asked, blowing a stream of smoke across the desk right at his face.

"No, ma'am. I'm sayin that you seem to think we are."

"You got to find that boy and arrest him, goddamit," Orville said. "Do your job, Ralph."

"The problem, Orville," the sheriff said, leaning back in his chair, it creaking under him, "is that we can't determine that any crime has been committed here."

"What?! No crime?!"

"No, not lessen you want to count that boy drivin without a license, and we would have to catch him while he was doin that. I mean, Mrs. McCrory coulda just decided she wanted to go somewhere with the boy. She could have give him the car, for all we know."

"He stole it, sheriff," Orville said. "And what about that patrolman they almost killed, over there near Pensacola?"

"We don't know that they had a damn thing to do with that," the sheriff said. He turned to Miss Roget. "Highway patrolman, musta stopped somebody, he don't recall a thing about it. On July the tenth it was. They musta hit him in the back of the neck with a tire iron or somethin, paralyzed him from the neck down. He can't even remember the make of the car he stopped, if that was what it was. They arrested one of these beatniks, you know? Hitchhikin. Figured he musta done it, but they couldn't pin it on him. Had to let him go. And we got nothing at all to connect our runaways with that incident."

"Runaways, my ass!" Orville said. "Jesus Christ Amighty, what's the law for if it ain't to protect innocent citizens?"

Millicent jammed her cigarette out in a heavy glass ashtray on the desk. These bozos just didn't get it. She had two jobs, as she saw it: first, find out if this Mrs. McCrory actually existed and was still alive at least when this creep son of hers took out the policy on her, and second, find her to ascertain whether she was at this moment still alive or actually dead. Millicent Roget was Boston Mutual's prime investigator of insurance fraud, and this one smelled terrible. Of course, Orville McCrory had no real claim unless he could prove that his mother was deceased and he had an official death certificate, but he could bring suit and you never knew how judges in these countrified states would rule, especially against northern, big-city insurance companies. She stood up. She'd about had enough of these yahoos.

"Where can I find the boy's father?" she asked.

"Well," the sheriff said, "go down Commissioners Street toward the river. It's the last house before you get to the town dump. But likely he's not there, or if he is he's drunk. You can probably find the girl's daddy at Saddler's Lounge, out on the De Quincy highway. I don't know what they can tell you that they ain't already told us."

"I'll be the judge of that," she said. She hitched up her pants. The men were staring at her, curious, inquisitorial. She knew that to them she was a freak. Not so much that she was a lesbian—even the dumbest hick knew there were lesbians and had probably, at one time or another, encountered one—but that she so blatantly and proudly advertised it. Most little towns had a woman or two who was mannish, who even dressed as a man, who was "weird," but she went around with her head down, in the eyes of the community suitably ashamed of being who she was. Millicent enjoyed throwing it in their ignorant faces. "You have my card," she said, "I'll be in touch."

Her assistant and long-time lover, Cassandra Birmingham, was waiting in the car for her. Cassandra was short, stubby, where Millicent was tall and lean. Slightly older than Millicent, Cassandra had worked for Boston Mutual as a secretarial assistant in the insurance fraud division for fifteen years. The two women lived together in an apartment near the Harvard campus, and, as often as she could, Millicent took Cassandra along to assist on her investigations. They had flown into the Panama City, Florida, airport, the terminal hardly more than a Quonset hut-shaped hangar, and rented a car, a nondescript black Ford that smelled inside of urine and vomit. Cassandra had all the windows down and was fanning herself with a *Saturday Evening Post*. "Shit," she said, "I thought Florida was all beaches and palm trees and orange groves. Where the hell are we?"

"Florida," Millicent said.

"Well?" Cassandra asked. "What's the story?"

"We're on their trail, sweetheart, and I think we'll start with Pensacola," Millicent said, cranking the beat-up Ford.

11

NEAR EAST DUBLIN, GEORGIA

JUNE 1949

Before the completion of the interstate system, U.S. Highway 80 was a main east-west corridor that ran across the southern United States from Savannah, Georgia, to Los Angeles, California. On one rare and particularly pleasant late afternoon in June, three years after the end of World War II, there was a small Gypsy encampment alongside that highway near the small town of East Dublin, Georgia. It was a small familia: three automobiles with trailers, several pickup trucks with their beds covered to look like typical old-fashioned Gypsy wagons. Several tents. The kumpaniyi, along with others like it, all small because of the diminishing population of Gypsies in the late forties, was making its yearly pilgrimage to Meridian, Mississippi, to visit the grave of Kelly Mitchell, the last Queen of all the Romani Gypsies in North America. They had been making their way slowly westward, pausing to take brief jobs tarring roofs and driveways and painting barns and houses.

Kelly Mitchell had died in childbirth on January 31, 1915, at Coatopa, Alabama, and was brought to Meridian for burial by her husband Anton, the King. Her body lay in state for twelve days awaiting the arrival of Gypsies from all over America. Emil Kirova's grandfather had been there and had told him all about it. When Anton took her to Meridian, the first funeral home, a white one, refused to take her and directed them to the colored funeral home across town. They did not want her either. Finally a new mortician, who had just opened up there, came forward and agreed to handle the burial; his mortuary was in an old house next to a Methodist church, in a white residential section of town. She was laid out with jeweled combs in her hair and a necklace of priceless coins dating back to 1750, in a mahogany casket with a glass top that was brought in on the train from Memphis.

Soon there was a crowd of six or seven thousand Gypsies camping all over town, especially in the section where the funeral home was, setting up tents and parking their wagons in people's yards. There were many complaints, there were fights, there were threats by the police and the Ku Klux Klan. People's yards were trampled (and pissed in and shat in, sometimes in full view of the citizens, Emil's grandfather had told him, laughing—"Where else were we to relieve ourselves?" he said, "nobody would open up their own houses or their privies to us, not even the colored people, who were scared of us!") and countless chickens and hogs, even cows, went missing and wound up on spits over open fires in those same front yards, and dogs disappeared too, and the white citizens claimed that the Gypsies were roasting and eating dogs. The people of Meridian had never seen anything like it, and there were too many of the Gypsies, who kept arriving, more every day, for the authorities to do anything about it.

Things were especially chaotic in the area around the funeral home, as ritual processions were conducted every four hours, around the clock, when long lines of Gypsies, dancing and chanting, would pass through and view the Queen in her coffin, many of them splashing red wine on the coffin in tribute. Finally the day of burial came: February 15, 1915. A crowd of eight thousand people followed the hearse, drawn by six black horses, out 7th Street from 21st Avenue to Rose Hill Cemetery. The hearse had to stop every few minutes for more ritual anointing with wine. At the cemetery, much damage was done to other graves, stomped by the masses of people. Her vault was said to be concrete armored with steel, and there were numerous attempts in the intervening years to break into it and rob the grave. The cracks of the attempted robbers were still clearly visible in 1949. Anton, the King, was also eventually buried there, with other members of the family, and, as time passed, the graves were visited yearly by the few remaining Romani Gypsies and decorated with multi-colored beads, picturesque glass figurines (many of mythical animals), streamers of brightly colored cloth, bottles of whiskey and medicine, various good luck gewgaws, photographs, pictures and statues of saints, scraps of paper with prayers, petitions, and requested curses and even poems, original or copied by hand from books.

"WAIT, STOP, LET ME out here," Minnie said. The driver, an old man who had picked her up a couple of hours ago, coasted his rusty, rattling pickup to a stop on the shoulder.

"Here?" he said. He saw where she was looking. He shook his head. "Them are Gypsies," he said. "You don't want to stop here."

"Thanks," she said, opening the door, stepping onto the running board, reaching her old carpetbag out of the back. It was a Gypsy camp, a caravan, seven or eight cars of various vintages, trailers, a couple of tents, several late-afternoon cook fires going. The camp was in a field behind a filling station and small store. It was rare to see a Gypsy camp any more, and, in the past, when she'd seen them in her travels she'd avoided them. Minnie was lean and tan, wearing a green sleeveless blouse and jeans and sandals. She wore no makeup. Her black hair was long, parted in the middle, tied loosely at the back of her neck with a leather thong.

Two days ago she had left Beaufort, South Carolina, where she had been living for a couple of years, working behind the counter in a bookstore called the Old Bay Trading Company, living in a rooming house. Beaufort was a beautiful little town, and she enjoyed the quiet streets with their towering shade trees and old houses, the bay, the low-country salt marshes to the east of town with their haunting and rich smell of the sea. She enjoyed the men from the nearby Marine base. It was a comfortable town, one she wouldn't have minded settling down in, but the minute she started to think that way she had become anxious and uneasy, disquieted, and she had begun making plans to move on. As soon as she began envisioning the open road again she had felt that old sense of release, of freedom, of peaceful calm dropping slowly around her and soothing her.

Stopping at the Gypsy camp was simply an impulse. At twenty-seven years of age, in looking back over her brief life, she had realized that that was the way she had most often conducted that life: on impulse. It was the way she preferred it. Acting in the moment and of the moment. If somebody asked her what she did, she was likely to reply, "I'm a drifter," to curious stares or shrugs of dismissal, or sometimes glares of hostile disapproval. Recently she'd read an article in the paper about "displaced persons," war refugees from the countries of eastern Europe, from where, she knew, her family had originally come, though she still felt no fealty to her people, in either the smaller or the larger sense. She realized that from the beginning of their time on earth, Gypsies had been "displaced persons," not dislocated by war but by choice. Once, when passing through Hendersonville, North Carolina, where her brother Shon had said her sister had settled with a family, she had tried to find them, but could not. She had known at the time that it was a half-hearted effort. She had merely moved on to the next town, and, if she was out of money, to the next menial job—she had been a waitress, a short-order cook, had sold tickets at a movie theater, had clerked in stores, and from time to time, if she was really hard up, had turned some tricks. She supposed she qualified as a "displaced person," or DP as some people called them when they came to this country. If she was, it was certainly by choice. Dis-placed: place meant nothing to her, nothing more than somewhere you might stop for a while, to rest or replenish or linger only long enough to catch your breath. She now knew this about herself: all her life motion would be the comfortable norm for her. She could not be sedentary. It had always been true, but she had not always known it, had not been able to articulate it, had not been mature enough to learn it. She had feared that she was only aimless, without purpose or direction, but she now realized that her aimlessness was a direction and a purpose. She was not doomed to wander. She was free to wander. She had forever recognized that she was different from others (if only for her eyes, which for a while had threatened to define her totally, had indeed almost cost her her life, had changed that life eternally and set it on its seemingly random course) but it took her a long time to understand that that difference did not make her less than others but more.

She smelled the burning wood smoke, the spices that took her back to her childhood: garlic, cumin and ginger, rosemary. For a fleeting, stunning instant, she feared that she was walking right into her family, that she would recognize them and they her and it would be another of those crushing moments that would scar her deeply, a new scar refusing to go away, festering and hurting into perpetuity. She could still recall every detail of the day her family put her out on that desolate road (the road she was still traveling down, counting out her life not so much in minutes and hours and days but in miles): the slight chill in the air, the feel of the crushed shell surface of the road under her bare feet, the intuition of the vastness of eternity as she watched the old car sputter away and finally disappear and fade from sight and from her life, leaving her all alone and helpless in a world so immense that she could not take it in, could not even imagine it. So, like the child she was, she focused only on what she could see and feel and taste and hear, in that spot and in that moment, so she had already started to forget her family before the harsh, metallic chugging of the old motor died away.

She stood at the edge of the camp, realizing suddenly that she did not know what she was expecting, what she would say when someone spoke to her. It was like her to already be into something before she paused to ask herself why she was there and what she was doing. She heard guitar music, a song in a plaintive female voice. The smoke began to sting her eyes, so she moved away from its blowing direction. It was seeking her out, as acrid smoke from a campfire will do; she remembered that from her childhood, too.

"Hello, sister," she heard a man's voice say. The "sister" sounded like a generic term, nevertheless she was jolted by it. "Welcome," he said.

His look was a familiar one to her, though she had never seen him before, the particular mien indelible in her memory, a type ordinary and as common among Gypsies as blood. He was tall and slim, dark skin, black hair, black handlebar mustache. He wore a loose red cotton shirt with a blue neck-scarf (the name for which popped into her mind, diklo, from some shared history that was mostly long departed from her conscious mind), white flared trousers, a black belt with a large gold buckle, shiny cowboy boots. He was smiling at her. He was not one of her brothers, but he could easily have been.

"Have you eaten your supper?" he asked. "I have a beef stew. I'll be pleased if you have a bowl of it."

"Yes," she said, "yes, I'd like that."

"Good," he said. He stuck out his hand toward her. "My name is Emil Kirova," he said.

"Anna Maria Spirosko," she said, using her Gypsy name for the first time in as long as she could remember. He was looking at her eyes, appraising them, assessing her. She felt her oddly mismatched eyes pulling him in, capturing him. She had gotten accustomed to that effect on men. It was a way of taunting. And of control.

"SHE WAS THE LAST queen of the Gypsies," Emil said, sipping his coffee. The coals of the fire only glowed now, their red heat dulled. The sounds of the insects, frantic and random, surrounded them in the gathering darkness, the tree frogs chorusing back in the scrub woods. "If you are a Gypsy I'm surprised that you do not know of her."

"I was born a Gypsy. I was never raised as one," she said. "Even before I left my family, when I was eleven, she was never spoken of. I don't remember it, anyway."

"You were separated from your family at eleven?" he asked.

"Yes," she said. Her tone made him drop it, though he was naturally curious. She was an extremely attractive woman. Once he got a beautiful woman in his grasp he did not want to let her go. He sensed that this one did not want to go, did not want to escape him. She said she was not a Gypsy any more, but in Emil's opinion you couldn't stop being a Gypsy if you were one. She said she was just a "drifter," hitching around. Her skin was dark enough, her hair dense and lush. Her enigma, her mystery, drew him to her. Her eyes: one a royal blue, the other the green of a ripe grape, though neither color was a hue typical of the Gypsy people. But she radiated an alien quality that kept her separate from the culture in which she lived, or the culture she lived alongside, because she was not a part of it at all, not through any kind of conscious and intentional non-conformity but because her soul altered its shape and reformed itself in exotic ways without her even being aware of it, certainly not because of her planning of it or her designing of it. Mystery: a word that when applied to other women was too often a hollow and meaningless cliche but was her, distilled, her essence, tantalizingly ephemeral and elusive.

He sensed that she did not come from anywhere that was commonplace or ordinary but from some mythical place.

"Why don't you come along with us," he asked. "I've plenty of room in my Airstream."

"All right," she said.

She did not question him: who is the "us" that you speak of? She did not ask if he was married, if he was traveling alone, if he was inviting her to share his bed. Simply, all right, she said. It could have been the response to a casual offer of a cigarette or a drink of wine, or it could have been the voicing of a life-altering decision, which it was.

LIFE IN THE CAMP seemed as familiar to her as if she'd left it all only yesterday. The only major difference she could see was that there were no covered wagons mixed in with the other vehicles, no horses. There were a number of pickup and half-ton trucks that were rigged to look like the old wagons, with rounded canvas covers over the beds, and there were more car-drawn trailers. Some of them were flatbed for carrying trunks and tents and cooking equipment, some were small house trailers like Emil's. There were maybe forty people in the camp, all ages but most of them old, even elderly.

"So many of the young people are just droppin out," Emil told her. "Gettin jobs in the cities. They don't want to have anything to do with the old ways. They want to be like the gaje. Shit, they want to be gaje. The old people are mad about that. They still believe that settling down in one place leads to sickness and bad luck."

As soon as a new site was chosen and a new camp was being set up, the older women cooked stews, or gulyás, in large cast-iron pots over open fires. Minnie watched them cut up chickens or fish the men had caught in a nearby lake or creek and drop them into the boiling water, adding any vegetables they had—beans, chopped tomatoes, chopped potatoes, sometimes corn—and spices: tarragon, paprika, parsley, thyme, basil, hot red peppers and green poblano chilies. Into the mix would go chunks of smoked sausage and ham, sliced onion, olive oil and rice, whatever was on hand. It might have curry powder and chopped ripe olives, marjoram or butter. The gulyás would be served over chunks of bread the women had baked in ovens in the trailers, and accompanied by chiyo, a hot tea made with fresh fruits: oranges, lemons, apples, even bananas. The women would not allow Anna Maria to help with the cooking and would get angry and snap at her if she tried, so she kept her distance.

"They don't want you to touch the food," Emil told her. "They think you may be gadji. The old people won't eat anything a gadji has touched. Another reason they won't talk to you or be nice to you is they associate your blue jeans with the young people who've left. Besides, most of these old women don't speak anything but Roma."

Anna Maria remembered very little Roma. Her family had spoken mostly English, with a lot of Roma thrown in, words and phrases that came back to her from time to time. She was surprised at how quickly she felt at home otherwise. The people looked the same. Most of the older men were overweight and snaggletoothed, with lots of gold teeth, and some wore shiny and dusty old metallic blue or green, large-lapel nineteen-thirties style suits, even in camp. They sported gold rings, diamond tie clasps and diamond-studded gold belt buckles. Those not in suits, the younger men, wore brightly colored shirts with contrasting bell-bottom trousers.

The older women wore traditional Gypsy dress: long, colorful pleated skirts made from red chiffon or metallic or gold lame that hung well below the knee, a sleeveless blouse that buttoned in front and on top of that a loose overblouse that was a kind of sleeveless vest, pinned in front, between the breasts, with a gold brooch. There were younger women and a few girls in the camp, and their blouses were cut very low in front, re-vealing the tops of their breasts. They all wore a lot of jewelry, even when working around the camp: gold coins made into necklaces, brooches or pendants. Some of the younger girls wore gold teardrop necklaces, which Minnie remembered were symbols of being engaged to marry. All the women wore high-heeled sandals, gold or other patent leather colors, and long, dangling gold earrings. They wore their hair braided and pinned up, usually tied with a scarf.

"They think your hair hanging long like that means it hasn't been combed," Emil told her, laughing. "They think it's probably dirty!"

One of the old women who seemed especially hostile to Anna Maria wore an enormous necklace of huge gold balls that hung to her waist. Another wore a sheriff's star with a gold Indian head soldered into the middle of it, with little gold hearts hanging from each point of the star. Anna Maria knew they were midwives and doctors inside the camp, drabardi—or fortune tellers—outside. There was one pregnant girl in the camp, a small, dark and petite girl with an immense, swollen belly, who looked as if she might have her baby any minute. Finally at one camp the men erected a large tent where the girl was confined. Minnie remembered that pregnant women were considered unclean, that they couldn't touch any food or anything someone else might use.

"We'll stay in this camp until the baby is born," Emil said.

"I want to be there," Anna Maria said. "I want to see it."

"Well, just go then," he said. "Don't ask. They won't let you if you do. Just slip inside and watch."

The day came and Anna Maria saw the old midwives moving toward the tent, along with some of the other women, so she lingered a few minutes and then followed. She slipped through the tent flap and stood against the canvas wall. The girl was crying out in pain. The interior was lit with two coal oil lamps suspended from the ceiling, the air smoky and close. Strong smells hung in the air: human feces and blood, sweat on unwashed bodies, a startlingly sweet incense so thick it was almost palpable. The girl was stretched out on a cot, naked, her legs open, her head thrown back, mouth clenched with gritting teeth, eyes squinted shut. Several women knelt beside the cot with a pile of white cloths, like ripped up bed sheets, and someone was mumbling what sounded like prayers. From time to time the girl let loose with a wail that became a scream. She bucked on the cot. One of the old midwives had her hands on the tight belly, the other's buried between the girls thighs which were covered now in blood. The woman's hands and arms were bloody to the elbows. To Anna Maria it was a moving and emotional and shockingly primitive scene, and she marveled that she, herself, had likely come into the world in just such surroundings. Memory knew. She had come back to the beginning, to the end of a thousand savage and lonely highways that ran as one. The road ran north through Georgia, the Carolinas, Washington, New York, then back south through Virginia and Tennessee and Georgia again, here at this moment. The road was seventeen years long. She had been in turn waitress, prostitute, clerk, and prostitute again. She had begged and stolen and she had even killed two men, and this was the end and a beginning.

The girl gave one last scream and suddenly a purple, bloody mass was between her legs, in the arms of the old midwife, a bulk crusted with buttery discharge and slime, a vile and odious and beautiful and soul-rending thing. Tears of joy sprang to Anna Maria's eyes even though she did not even know the girl. She did not have to know her. She watched intently as the old woman cleaned the baby, saw the baby wiggle, heard the baby's first cry. A mysterious and new happiness surged in her chest, expanding it, inflaming her and calming her at the same time. In this moment she felt yoked to the girl, bound to her, her sister. She was enmeshed with these women: they were her people, her family.

THE CEMETERY WAS COOL, shaded from the summer sun by large oak and hickory trees, the sandy, red dirt paths and graves dotted around with stunted, dark green cedars, so dark as to be almost black in the shadows of the graveyard. The Queen's grave was brightly arrayed, decorated with a great assortment of items, many handmade. The beams of the sun that shafted through the leaves glittered on the display, which was gaudy, garish and excessive, but to Minnie it had a particular kind of beauty that she could not quite define. The King's resting place next to the Queen's was not nearly so cluttered with tributes and petitions. It was obviously the Queen who had reached transcendent status and was the reason for those who still undertook the old traditional pilgrimages to visit her shrine. Many of the decorations were old, rain-stained and shriveled, faded to only vague semblances of their original colors. Many were new and fresh, bright, testaments to the endurance of the Queen's lasting allure and enchantment even in death.

"The Last Queen of the Gypsies," Minnie said.

"Yes," Emil said.

"Did the people come here when she was alive?" Minnie asked.

"Oh, yes," Emil replied. "Not here to the cemetery, but to her home in Coatopa. Across the Alabama line."

"Kelly Mitchell. That's not a Gypsy name."

"No. She came from the old country. Her real name was Mara le Stevanosko. Mara, the daughter of Stevan."

The other members of the familia gathered around, the children putting charms they had made on the graves. Some of the older women chanted prayers, fingering rosaries. The cemetery was oddly peaceful, a place of refuge. Quiet and static. Permanent.

"She is gajo," the old woman said angrily. Her head was covered with a black wool scarf, even in the summer heat, and her two gold teeth glittered in the sunlight. "Tsinivari!"

"No," Emil said, "she is not gajo. She is Gypsy."

"Gajo whore!" the old woman said. She spat on the ground.

"She is wuzho," Emil said.

The old woman shook her crooked finger at Minnie. Then she turned and walked away, her long orange skirt dragging in the dirt. She was muttering to herself.

"What?" Minnie asked. "What's her problem? I mean, I got the 'whore' part."

"Nothing," Emil said.

"Come on. You said 'she is' what?"

"She says you're not a Gypsy. That you have evil spirits."

"Hah!" Minnie said, "I've heard that one before."

"I told her you were pure."

Minnie laughed.

"I told her you were unashamed."

"Well, you got the last part right," Minnie said.

They were camped outside the town of Quitman, Mississippi, on Highway 45 south of Meridian. It had turned exceptionally hot for June and they had stopped after only thirty-five miles because one of the cars, an old gray Pontiac pulling one of the Airstream trailers, had overheated. Emil and Minnie were sitting in the shade of an elm tree outside Emil's trailer. They sat in aluminum and plastic folding lawn chairs, the kind of chairs that had only become available after the conclusion of the war. Minnie's head was back, her eyes closed, fanning herself with an old copy of the *Meridian Star*. She wore tight white shorts, the style of shorts you rarely saw except in movie magazines and pin-up pictures. They were so short they made her legs look ten feet long. She wore a light cotton blouse, white, too, so thin that he could see the outline and darker shading of her nipples. She didn't wear bras, one thing that had prompted the old lady to complain, he knew. Minnie didn't seem to care about what anyone thought of anything she did, she just did it.

He sat appraising her as she leaned back in the chair, her chest rising and falling with her breathing. He had never seen a woman with eyes like that. He'd not known it was possible. She seemed easy with everything. She was not in a hurry to get anywhere. Her soul was Gypsy, if not her blood, but he knew it was that, too, he would have staked his life on it. He knew there was so much more there, beneath the surface, inside, something waiting to erupt when it got the right prompt. Whether it would be in passion or anger he didn't know, couldn't have predicted, but he knew it was there. He sensed that even in their lovemaking she was holding back, cautious, as if even she were wary of whatever it was and afraid to let go of it and free it. He wanted to tap into it, unleash the passion, but he was afraid of it, too, and he hoped he wouldn't come to regret having asked her to come along with him. He had poked through her belongings in the pack she carried and discovered a seven-inch switchblade knife. A woman on the road by herself needed protection, but that one struck him as an odd choice; it carried an aura of aggression, of something masculine and contentious. More than once it had crossed his mind that he could end up in a ditch somewhere, his throat sliced through.

The mechanic who came out to work on the car was named J. D. Pequad. He did not like the assignment and resented having to work on a Gypsy car, the same way he would have hated to have to make a special trip to work on a Negro car. To him, Gypsies were as bad as Negroes and should be run out of Mississippi as quickly as possible. When his boss at the Pontiac place in Quitman had told him he had to go he had seriously considered quitting right then and there. But he thought of his wife Maureen and their two school-aged children, and he sullenly agreed to go. He threw his toolbox and a paper sack full of spare parts into the back of his pickup and headed out to the Gypsy camp.

J. D. was the son of a sharecropper. He had spent his youthful years busting dirt that wasn't even owned by his family, working from bare daylight every morning until after first dark, breaking his back for a crop of scraggly cotton that barely came up to his knees. His family didn't own anything, not the falling down dog-trot shack the old rich man named Rufus Piha who owned the place called a house, heated by fireplaces in both rooms and cooled by whatever breezes they could coax through the open, screenless windows (the house in summer was always full of flies and mosquitoes), not even the tools they used, their plow, even their mule, not the clothes on their backs except for maybe a few days around the time their meager crop came in and they could settle up at old man Piha's store for another year, with maybe two or three dollars left over to buy oranges and apples with come Christmas time. It was a life not even fit for colored people. J. D. had fled that life as soon as he was old enough and had vowed that never again would he sharecrop another man's land, so he had learned to be a mechanic and had a good job and a small house for his family that he was paying for himself.

He fumed and stewed all the way out to the Gypsy camp. J. D. Pequad was a member of an organization called White People In Jesus Fellowship, and he wished all the other members of the group felt exactly the way he did about Gypsies, but only a few of them did, men like him who were willing to stand up against any nonwhites. Everybody in the Fellowship were all of the same mind about the sons of Ham, the coloreds, but they did not view Gypsies exactly as colored people. But they didn't view them as white, either. They were heathen foreigners, dark in color because they came from one of those Arab (J. D. would have pronounced it A-rab) countries, dark enough, in J. D.'s view, to qualify as coloreds, if not out-and-out Negroes. At any rate, they had no business in Quitman or in Mississippi; everybody knew they would steal you blind and, if they got a chance, would kidnap little white children and make slaves out of them, make them roam around the country with them begging and stealing.

J. D. had worked himself up into quite a state by the time he got to the camp and had the hood up on the Pontiac. "Just get the hell on out of here and give me room," he said to the few men who stood around watching him. They all looked dirty and greasy, and he would have hated to meet up with any one of them in a dark alley. It did not occur to him at first that being surrounded by them in their own camp was more than the equivalent of the dark alley. The situation he was in gradually dawned on him, and as he worked he became more and more nervous. He really didn't think they would have mettle enough to harm a white man in Mississippi, but you never knew when there might be a hotheaded one who would go off half-cocked, like some young Negro men insisted on doing from time to time only to end up weighted down with chains at the bottom of some farm pond. But that didn't prevent anything. By the time they were dead they had already done the harm they set out to do, and that left J. D. in a precarious position. He was wishing that he had some of his buddies from the White People In Jesus Fellowship with him.

He flushed out the radiator and replaced a couple of clogged hoses. (He'd brought a supply of hoses, because he figured that was what it would be, that and a rusty radiator.) He cranked the car and let it idle. He watched the heat gauge: the needle was on "cool" and it didn't move. "Who's the boss of this outfit?" he asked one of the men who were still watching him work, who had not even pretended to give him the space he requested.

"Emil," one of them said, as if he would know who this "Emil" was.

"He own this here car?" J. D. asked.

"No, Diego owns that car," the Gypsy said.

"Well, fetch em both here," J. D. said.

"I'm Diego," one of the other men said.

J. D. cocked his head and peered at the Gypsy. He was big. His belly hung out over his belt. His blue jeans looked so grimy and befouled they would've stood upright on their own. "You gonna pay this here bill, then?"

"Is the car fixed?" the big man said.

"What do you think? I'm gonna give you a bill for somthin that I ain't done?"

"I don't want to get twenty miles down the road and have this thing blow up on me again," Diego said.

"That ain't gonna happen," J. D. said.

"Well, suppose it does?"

"It ain't gonna happen. The car is fixed." J. D. handed him the bill that he'd written out. The man took it, but made no move to take out his wallet. J. D. looked around at the men. There were four or five now who'd gathered. "Who'd you say the boss is?"

"Big Mick," one of them said, "Emil is the Big Mick."

"Well, tell the 'Big Mick' to come here," J. D. said. He was not a big man, but he was thin and wiry. He was still strong, from hard work. He had come off out here without even a weapon, so he reached into the tool box and came out with a monkey wrench, hefting it in his hand. "I got to have this bill paid before I leave here," he said, "my boss ain't gonna like it atall if I show up without it, and the Quitman po-lice ain't gonna care for it neither." Besides, though he didn't say it, he knew his boss would make him pay it if he failed to get the money out here.

"Is there some kind of problem here?" a man, younger than the others, said. He walked up with a woman. He was dressed fancy; he looked like some kind of "Big Mick" all right.

"No, no problem," J. D. said. "I've just presented this here Diego (he pronounced it "Da-go") with a bill for repairin his car. I just need to collect and be on my way."

"All right," said the young man, who must be Emil. J. D.'s eyes fell on the woman, or girl, he realized. She looked so much lighter skinned than the others. There was something wrong with her eyes, but he couldn't immediately say what. He stared at her. He thought, Why this is a white woman! These heathens have kidnapped em a white woman! She was a good-looking one, too, with hardly any britches on and a shirt tied under her titties in the front letting her belly show to the world. He felt his simmering resentfulness returning, growing again, against them for taking her or against her for going with them, he couldn't separate the two. It was both. Swamp scum like these men didn't deserve any woman who looked like that, especially a white woman. They needed to be run out of town and she needed to be taught a lesson. Pachuta County, Mississippi, was the wrong place, if ever there was one, for a white woman to be messing around with coloreds.

The man called Emil was looking at the invoice. He took out a wad of cash and peeled off two ten-dollar bills. He handed them to J. D. "Will that cover it?" he asked.

"Just about," J. D. said. He was still eyeing the woman. He could not for the life of him figure out why such a beautiful white woman was traveling with these slimeballs. One answer would be that they were holding her against her will. But she sure didn't act like that. She stood real close to Emil. She stared at J. D. as though she were just getting ready to call him white trash or something. She was a little darker in complexion than your average white lady, but that was probably because she spent so much time outdoors. "Anything else you need?" he asked.

"No," Emil said.

J. D. stood there for a moment holding the bills. "This here is twenty dollars. The bill was for eighteen," he said.

"Keep the two for yourself, for your trouble," Emil said.

J. D. said nothing. He reached into his pocket and pulled out his cash, a few wrinkled and matted dollar bills and some change. He pulled out two of the limp bills, damp from his sweat in the heat. Then, "No thank you," he said, pushing the bills toward Emil.

Emil stared at him for a moment. The woman was looking narrow-eyed at him, too. Emil snatched the two dollars out of J. D.'s hand. He turned and walked away, the good-looking woman following him. J. D. took a good, long look at her ass in those shorts. Then he was aware of the four sets of eyes around him, all the same shade: as liquid and dark as a puddle of clean, fresh motor oil.

"Well, fellas," J. D. said, "it's been fun, but I guess I best be gettin on back." He climbed into his truck and hit the starter button. He let the truck idle for a moment while he took one last look out the open window at the Gypsies. Maybe it won't be my last look at all, he was thinking. He backed around and bumped across the pasture, then out onto the highway.

MINNIE HAD JUST RELAXED into sleep when she heard the loud banging on the metal door of the trailer. It was so loud in the cramped interior that it sounded like gun shots. She sat up just as Emil did. The bed was a narrow one and they slept tangled together, naked because the inside of the Airstream would be stifling until late, sometimes long after midnight, when the breezes through the small windows became cooler. The bed smelled of their bodies, musty and stale, the sheets moist and snarled. The banging came again, then a voice. "All right! Come on out here, now!" A harsh, country drawl.

Minnie could see through the window the beams of several flashlights and their glinting on the barrels of shotguns or rifles. There was a group of men crowding around the trailer outside.

"Shit," Emil said, "it's the fuckin Klan."

"What do they want?" Minnie whispered.

Emil rolled over and up and put on his pants. Then his boots. "Get somethin on," he said.

"They're not comin in here, are they?" she asked. Her mind was still bleary with sleep. Emil didn't answer.

"Get dressed!" he said.

She found her shorts and pulled them on. She couldn't locate her blouse. Her hands were shaking. She searched frantically for something to put on. Oh God, she was thinking, Oh God, have I come all this way, traveled all those miles, only to be raped and lynched in some Mississippi backwater by a bunch of ignorant rednecks? She found a T-shirt and slipped it over her head. It must have been Emil's because it swallowed her, drooped off her shoulders, but it covered her.

The beams of the flashlights darted through the window, around the tiny room. Emil was searching in a cardboard box he'd pulled from under the bed. He came up with a pistol, a heavy and awkward-looking snub-nosed revolver. "You better get your knife," he said.

"What knife?"

"The one in your pack. Hurry."

She spoke tightly, with great effort. "You went through my bag?" she asked. It was the last thing she expected of him, that kind of casual betrayal.

"Jesus, Anna Maria, this is no time to be . . ."

She interrupted him. "What makes you think you have the right to go through my things?!" she shouted at him.

"Get your fuckin knife!" he yelled back at her.

She did not move. The pounding on the door resumed. She knew Emil kept the door locked at night. Then the trailer started to rock back and forth, causing her to fall onto the bed. The little statues of saints, Emil's collection of icons on their narrow shelves, fell to the floor. The shouts from outside were taunting and bitter. She couldn't understand much of what they said, but she did hear "Whore!" and "Whore of Babylon!" For the first time she realized they were after her! They were hooting and laughing. She caught glimpses of them in the lights of their own flashlights. They were not wearing white sheets. It didn't matter. Emil was standing in front of the small window next to the door.

"What do you want?!" he shouted over their curses. Minnie's anger tempered; she admired Emil's courage, showing himself that way. Or maybe it was only foolhardiness. Conflicting emotions collided in her mind. Anger. Not hatred, not love. She was fond of Emil, but she didn't love him. She was beginning to pick up hints that he wanted to control her, own her, and she would not allow that. She was already starting to pull away from him, at least in her mind, before all this.

"We want the woman," a voice shouted. She recognized it. It was the mechanic from this afternoon. She remembered the way he had looked at her through his slitted pale gray eyes, the look of a mad dog about to pounce. Where were the other men in the familia?

"How many are there?" she hissed behind Emil's ear.

"A bunch," he said. "Maybe ten."

"Send her out," the voice shouted, "and we won't bother you any more."

"No way," Emil yelled.

"Shoot him!" somebody screamed, and Emil and Minnie rolled away from the window, Emil in one direction, Minnie in the other, just before there was a shotgun blast from a gun shoved through the window, the concussion not two feet from her. It seemed to go off inside her head, her ears ringing, her eardrums pounding and painful, the air full of the smell of sulfur and black gunpowder. The closeness of the explosion jolted her, and right after the concussion everything went silent, as if everything were suddenly sucked out of her head. She felt as if she were floating high in the air, suspended far enough above the earth that she could not hear the cacophony of noises that accompanied ordinary daily life on the ground, much less the chaotic rumblings of a bloodthirsty mob. Emil was saying something to her, something urgent by the look of strain on his face, but she couldn't hear him. She couldn't read his lips.

"What the hell's the matter with you?" Emil shouted at her. She was standing there with an uncomprehending, baffled look on her face. She pointed to her ears. The shot had momentarily deafened her. The trailer began to rock frantically then, the battering on the door even louder. Emil knew they must be using a sledge hammer or something equally as heavy.

"Anna Maria?" he said above the noise from outside. She obviously could not hear him. Her face was a mask of surprise and astonishment. He found her old carpetbag that she used as a pack at the foot of the bed, rummaged around and found the switchblade. Its handle was pearl colored plastic. He snapped it open. He could tell by looking at it, even in the dim light of the trailer, that the blade was honed to a perfect sharpness. He put it in her hand. She stared at it, open mouthed, as though she'd never seen it before.

They both stood with their feet wide apart for balance in the shaking trailer. Her hair was mussed, tangled around her head, one of his old T-shirts draped on her upper body, hanging to her thighs like a dress. In spite of her disarray, or perhaps because of it, she was the most beautiful woman he'd ever known. A hell of a time to be making that observation to himself, he knew, but he could not make it to her, and even had she been able to hear him she would have thought him insane to be saying such a thing in the midst of all this.

To Minnie, it was as though everything was happening in some drug-induced nightmare, some surreal vision from the remotest corners of hell. It was incomplete, only half an experience, something distorted and terrifying in its unreality. Maybe I've already crossed over into death, she thought, and this is what it feels like when you are a soul departing its body. But she was still in her body. She could see the knife trembling in her hand. Feel the sweat running between her breasts. She could smell herself, her woman smell, delicious and sharp, complete.

The door was about to give. A sledge hammer came partially through.

They were coming in. Her panic, then, gave way to calm. What was the worst thing they could do to her? She had already suffered through the most horrible thing that could happen to her all those years ago when she was eleven years old. She looked at the knife in her hand. I can kill again if I have to, she thought, I know what I'm capable of. Not many people know that about themselves, but I do.

The interior wooden trim on the steel door splintered. The hinges shrieked as the screws were pulled from the frame. Emil held the gun before him, ready to fire. The ragged door flew inward with a crash that startled Emil, pushed him back against the opposite wall. He realized that the force of the door had knocked the gun from his hand. The mechanic from this afternoon came through the now gaping opening, other men crowding behind him. Emil stepped toward him and the mechanic brought the barrel of the shotgun he was carrying down across Emil's head.

J. D. watched the fancy Gypsy fall to the floor. He had blood across his forehead, right at the hairline, and his eyes were closed. He was out cold. J. D. turned then to the woman. She was just standing there, in an old T-shirt or maybe a dress stretched all out of shape and none too clean either, a blank, inquisitive expression on her face. One of the other men shined a flashlight into her face and J. D. realized abruptly what was wrong with her eyes: they were two different colors! One blue, the other green. Blueberry blue, and green like the first tender leaves on an oak tree in the spring. She had a mean-looking knife in her hand. She made a menacing motion with it, a threatening gesture. He could tell by looking at her that she'd cut him just as soon as she'd look at him. He moved closer and she swiped out with the knife, missing his face by inches. Scared the shit out of him. He managed to grab her wrist and twist it and the knife fell out of her hand. She seemed to be in some kind of fog, high probably on some kind of Gypsy dope. He yanked her arm behind her back, forcing her to bend forward. "Easy there, Jezebel," J. D. said, "we're just gonna teach you a lesson."

For Minnie, everything was off center, out of focus, distorted, warped. She could feel nothing but the sharp pain in her shoulder. She could not hear anything but a tiny ringing in her ears. There was something so unnatural about the totally silent movements of the men in front of her that she could not believe they were real. The mechanic's mouth moved, but there was no sound. She had morphed into a different kind of organism, one that was missing half of what it once was, one that was without a vital part of its identity. She lost the sense of where she was, of what she was doing, because nothing was logical any more, the elements were all wrong, did not add up to what they were supposed to. She couldn't move; she wondered for a moment if she had forgotten how to walk.

The mechanic's pale eyes were wide, as though he were terrified by what he was doing. They were full of a kind of distorted, demented craving, displaying his confusion about the salvation that had been promised him and the real satisfaction of his own blood-lust. He was doing God's will, but he wanted to rip her clothes off and fuck her right there, and he was not sure if that were not God's will, too, His plan, since she had corrupted the order that God imposed on his people on earth and then said that is good. The Reverend Bobby Crouch, head of the White People In Jesus Fellowship, had said as much. "There can be no sin in serving as the hand of God in bringing about his will. Those who defy his will must be punished, in any way those of us who are washed clean of sin decide is right." Reverend Bobby Crouch had sent them on this mission to show this whore the fury of the wrath of God and turn her life around, to free her of her sinful lusts, to free her to find salvation, to save her life.

He reached out and with his free hand ripped the T-shirt from her body. She took a swing at his face with her free fist, but she missed. He got a good look at her perfectly formed little jiggling titties before she folded her arm across them and tried to step back away from him. He roughly twisted her arm harder and pulled her toward the door. "Get on out there and take your punishment," he said. "Go on now and get right with God!"

Minnie yanked free from the little man, surprising him. She punched him in the face and launched a kick at his privates, and two other men grabbed her, one on each side. She tried to resist but they were too strong and there was no place to run, to get away to, and together they pulled her through the door and out into the humid night. The mechanic was saying something to her again but she couldn't hear him. He was furious, his nose red where she had hit him, a streak of blood like red snot on his upper lip. There was some power in the fact that he didn't know she couldn't hear him. At least she could take some minute solace in that. Outside, as the heavy flashlights' powerful beams sprayed around she could see the rest of the familia, crowded into a group in the middle of the camp, three men guarding them with shotguns. She felt lightheaded, her legs unsteady. As the two men held her, another one pulled her shorts down so that she was naked. She could feel their eyes on her. They hustled her along. The stones and twigs on the ground hurt her bare feet. In the lights she could see the low limb of a tree, about four feet higher than her head, with a rope hanging from it, and she knew they were going to hang her, that she was going to die within minutes, and she was ready and she was not ready, she was resisting and surrendering at the same time. She could see them laughing, whooping, putting on an oddly comical dumb show, and she actually smiled because there was nothing else she could do.

They did not put a noose over her head, around her neck. Instead they tied the rope around her wrists and raised her arms over her head, pulling her up until she was standing on her toes. One of the men she had not seen before, whose hair was white, bleached she could tell because he was too young to be gray, approached her, holding a long bull whip. He spoke to her, his mouth moving soundlessly and uselessly, his words turning back into himself because he was the only one who could hear them. He had the cocky air of a leader. His eyes lingered on her breasts, on her exposed pubis. Then he disappeared around behind her, and when she felt the first lash her knees buckled from the burning intense pain, so terrible she almost fainted, her arms and wrists burning from the yanking of the rough rope, and she closed her eyes in anticipation of the next stroke which came with the same ferocity and strength, ripping her skin, the lashes moving lower and lower toward her buttocks, until she could no longer tell where on her body the biting strikes were falling and she lost count of them. She gritted her teeth. Her whole body was like one violent persistent flame, a fire that grew more and more out of control until she knew that she could not bear it any more. Then she was outside her body. She was perched on a high branch in the tree—it was a shagbark hickory—watching herself being whipped. Her body was beaming like newly polished silver. The pain lessened and then went away. She could see the men gathered around, shining their flashlights on her body, but the shafts of light no longer blinded her because she was not there any more.

Reverend Bob Crouch folded his whip and ceased. Her skin was cris-crossed with the red cuts, her blood leaking in narrow rivulets down her legs and onto the ground.

The flashlights of a semicircle of men still illuminated her from the front, her head slumped to the side, the front side of her body relatively unscathed. One of the men was J. D. Pequod, standing in the darkness behind his torch, his free hand down the front of his pants, finishing off his masturbation that had become increasingly more pleasurable as the whip lashes added up and he hungrily watched the naked woman writhe in her terrible agony.

12

COASTAL GEORGIA FAIRGROUNDS

NOVEMBER 1964

This would be the last stop for J. F. Freeman Traveling Rides and Shows before they returned to south Florida for their winter season. J. F. Freeman Shows used the southeastern United States as its territory, since the climate allowed them more months of good weather there. The last time they had toured outside the South had been before World War II, during which and right after which their traveling had been severely curtailed because of gas shortages. During those war years they had worked out a tight and satisfyingly lucrative schedule, playing one-week engagements in small towns and cities in Florida, Alabama, Tennessee, Georgia, and South Carolina, and longer stays at state fairs which began in the summer months and ran into late autumn, the last being the Coastal Georgia State Fair in Savannah. After their return to Florida they would set up adjacent to several amusement parks scattered around Fort Myers, West Palm Beach, and Miami, with limited travel for three and a half months, until the middle of March when they would begin the next year's touring season.

The weather had turned chilly and the girls were complaining.

"We ought to make that son-of-a-bitch get out there naked," said Maxine, speaking of Emil. "See how he likes it."

"Ummmm, I wouldn't mind seeing that," Judy said.

"Like you ain't already," Sheila said.

"Look who's talkin," Judy said.

They were in their dressing tent behind the stage. There were three collapsible dressers with lighted mirrors, the surfaces covered with jars of makeup and boxes of tissue. Three folding canvas chairs. Planks laid down for a floor. One three-hundred-watt bulb dangling in the center, and a portable electric space heater that didn't even get hot to the touch. The bulb provided more heat than the space heater did.

Sheila looked into her mirror and applied her lipstick, a dark blood-red. Her eyes looked tired. She could use a rest. She tilted her face to the side, inspecting her skin, which was still good, without blemish, not the sandpaper harshness of Maxine's nor the pale puffiness of Judy's. She did not look thirty-one years old, more like twenty, with plenty of healthy color in her face, plenty of the highly charged energy of youth that some people retain even into their forties or beyond. She intended to be one of those people. She didn't have a single wrinkle, and her teeth were even and straight, without a hint of grayness or of yellow. Her good looks were what she had, her possession, her fortune.

Sheila Serena (her real name was Betty Lou Willoby) had been born in Waco, Texas, to a Baptist preacher and his wife. She had two younger sisters, but she had neither seen nor heard from them or her parents either in fifteen years. Her father, the Reverend Thorne Willoby, was a secret drinker and a secret lecher, not only with the depressed and lonely housewives and the confused and desperate adolescent girls who sought him out for counsel but with his own daughters as well. Betty Lou's mother, Anita Willoby, was a shy and frightened creature, living in fear of her husband and of the vengeful God that he represented on earth. She rarely left the house except to attend church on Sunday mornings and Wednesday evenings, where she played the piano for the hymns with a too-slow, dragging rhythm that all but ignored the futile attempt of the congregation to sing along with her. (Betty Lou and her sisters said it was like listening to a 78-RPM record played at 45-RPM speed.) Mrs. Willoby never seemed to notice that half the congregation finished the hymn before she did, the other half struggling along half reciting and half singing, unable to maintain any sort of melody or establish any cadence before the hymn slowly died away, hesitant and ragged, fading into an unsatisfying, deficient silence.

Reverend Willoby began with each of the girls in the same way, holding them on his lap so they could feel his erection against their little butts. At first Betty Lou had had no way of knowing that that was in any way unnatural, had assumed that sitting on the lap of any man meant being aware of his tee-tee which, she also assumed, was always hard and stiff. Betty Lou, being the oldest and by far the prettiest, was the first to experience the progression of the man's twisted desires, first touching her all over her body clothed, then doing the same thing when she was naked, then forcing his finger into her tee-tee and into her butt hole. He would take out his stiff tee-tee and ask her to kiss it, and when she did greasy milk would spurt out of it.

When she was thirteen he told her that she was now old enough to perform as God had intended her to, and he put her on the bed and forced himself into her, hurting her and causing her to bleed. It was not long before she deduced, through conversations with those same classmates, that what her father was doing to her, and surely would soon do to her sisters, was wrong, a dreadful thing, a terrible sin. She told her mother, and her mother slapped her face and told her to shut up and never say such a thing again.

She endured it for three more years, until she was sixteen and had a boyfriend. Her father forbade her to date. One night the boy, Cal Cunningham, took her home after they had met for a Coke at a cafe and her father attempted to beat him up, but Cal was a big boy—a football player, a tight end—and Cal beat up Reverend Willoby pretty badly instead, causing a ruckus and a scandal in the church. Cal got put in jail and Betty Lou never told a soul about what her father had been doing to her. She left home on the next Greyhound bus headed east, using money she'd saved from working behind the candy and popcorn counter at a Ben Franklin five and dime. She was heartbroken about the boy, Cal, whom she had thought she loved. But she knew she could never look him in the eye again. It seemed to her so obvious that her father had acted out of a perverse, depraved jealousy that she couldn't imagine Cal, and others, not seeing, too. She knew she hated her father. That was clear to her. He was one big lie, and his God was a lie as well. If God existed at all, he wouldn't have let all that go on, so she just rejected all that she had learned in Sunday school and church along with her family. In later years she would wonder what had happened to her father and mother or her sisters; she didn't care about her parents, but she did think about her sisters from time to time, hoping they had gotten away, too, and that wherever they were they were doing okay.

She landed in New Orleans and got herself a job at a Woolworth's on Canal Street. It was the only thing she knew how to do. She met another girl, Katy Phillips, who worked there, too, who lived in a rooming house just off Magazine Street, and Katy invited her to move in with her. Katy, nineteen and from Pelehatchie, Mississippi, was a demure-looking blonde who was anything but. She drank a great deal and smoked "reefer," which she bought down in the Quarter, and soon Betty Lou was drinking and smoking the intoxicating "sweet tobacco," as Katy called it, as well. They brought home boys and Betty Lou discovered what sex was really about, not the heavy, gloomy sin-drenched gropings and manipulations of her father but something pleasurable and wild, still forbidden but delightful in the taking—liberating and guilt-free. And she was still only sixteen years old.

There was a strip club down on Bourbon Street that Katy was "dying" to work at, she told Betty Lou, called Barely Legal, that specialized in very young girls, as young as the people who ran the place could get away with, which was just about as young as they wanted since all they had to do was pay regular bribes to the New Orleans Police Department.

"I mean, come on, they're not gonna put some twelve-year-old up there, you know? But sixteen is plenty old enough," Katy Phillips told Betty Lou. "As long as you look like a woman when you're naked, you're okay. At least, that's what Donald told me." Donald was a friend of hers who danced in a female impersonation show up the street from Barely Legal. He was the first homosexual Betty Lou had ever met. She had never even heard that such people existed. "I think you been livin in a cave," Katy laughed.

"I don't think I could get naked in front of people. In front of men!" Betty Lou said.

"I ain't noticed you keepin your clothes on when you got a little party goin," Katy said.

"That's different."

"How is that different?" Katy asked, mocking the way Betty Lou said the word.

"At least I know his name," Betty Lou said.

"Shit," Katy said and laughed.

"Why is that funny?" Betty Lou asked.

"You can ask em to register their names when they come in, so you'll know who's out there poppin their eyes at you," Katy said. "Jesus."

So Betty Lou worked on the stage at Barely Legal until after she actually became legal. It was not only easy to do, it was fun. She had never learned to dance, but the other girls helped her and she taught herself, discovering that it consisted of little more than moving her pelvis to the beat of the music and allowing her body to shake in ways that it seemed to want to do. There were usually two or three girls dancing at one time, and the opposite wall was a huge mirror so they could watch themselves performing. Betty Lou made more money than she had ever thought possible. She was one of the most popular girls. Men stuffed dollar bills and sometimes even fives into the garter on her thigh, which was the only thing she wore. And she could do private dances in a back room, ten dollars for ten minutes, lap dances or what they called "bedroom dances," when the customer sat in a chair and, through a little window, watched her writhe on a bed simulating (and sometimes not just simulating) masturbation. She often got tipped a five, or sometimes even another ten, which she did not have to share with the house.

After Betty Lou had been five years at Barely Legal, a new place opened on the corner of Bourbon and Toulouse called the Café Risque, and Betty Lou Willoby changed her name to Sheila Serena and became their headliner, with a life-size picture of her mounted on a plywood cutout out front. In the picture she was completely naked, with two red stars painted over her nipples and a black star painted over her pubis. Her act became famous because of her willingness—no, eagerness—to "show pink." The price of her private dance rose to twenty-five dollars. She was renowned in New Orleans and all along the Gulf Coast, known as one of the best in the business. She only did one show a night and there was always a line out the door and snaking along Bourbon Street, the barkers at the other joints trying in vain to coax the waiting men into their own clubs.

Her dancing career prospered for five or six years (she lost count) and she was happy with her lot. She had many men, some that she lived with for months, some one-night stands, and she partied a great deal. She was even married for a few months to a man named Billy Bush. She often partied all night, and went without sleep for days at a time. She loved her life. Until one night she collapsed on the stage. She was just dancing, like every other night, looking over the heads of the customers, the music grinding and thumping away, when she began to feel dizzy. It had happened to her several times before, lately with more frequency. The blinding lights seemed to be dancing, too, cleaving her brain, mashing their bright gels into her eyes. The shouts and hoots of the men in the crowd pierced her ears painfully, washing over her like the lights were doing, all of the light and sound blending together like something palpably hot and liquid that someone was dashing onto her body in great heaving splashes.

She woke up in Charity Hospital. Her mouth was as dry as lint and she had IVs in both arms, the inside of her head swollen and threatening to burst through her skull and her skin. She could feel the pounding of her heart in her entire body, hear its furious throbbing in her ears. She had been brought in in an ambulance, unconscious and naked, without even a sheet covering her, several dollar bills still in her garter. They had treated her in the emergency room until she was stabilized, then she was taken to a room, a double room with a curtain down the middle. The other bed was occupied by an elderly woman, a stroke victim not expected to recover. In examining the contents of her stomach and in testing her blood, they determined the presence of large amounts of alcohol, cocaine, marijuana, an over-the-counter cold medication, aspirin, and librium. The doctors were surprised that she was not already dead.

In the audience at the Café Risque the night that Sheila fainted on stage was a dark-complected man with a handlebar moustache. He was handsome, spry, in his forties, dressed in a gaudy purple shirt, tight black pants, and spit-shined cowboy boots. His black and curly hair was brushed back from his forehead. His name was Emil Kirova. He had recently taken over the management of the freaks and skin show that traveled with the J. F. Freeman carnival, and he was in New Orleans looking for some girls to dance in his show, THE STREETS OF PARIS. The two women who were with the show when he agreed to take it over were old and washed out, two old whores that the former manager had picked up somewhere that not many men, apparently, were willing to pay to see naked, and Emil intended to make the strip show profitable, and the way to do that, he believed, was to hire two or three young, experienced, beautiful dancers who were not too particular about what they were required to do in addition to dancing. He had big plans.

SHEILA SAT ON THE edge of the stage, her long legs encased in tight beige slacks that came down to the middle of her calves. She had on a long-sleeved denim work shirt, several sizes too big for her, with the sleeves rolled up to her elbows. Her arms were propped behind her and she was leaning back on them, looking toward the door flap of the tent, when Lester Ray came in. He usually cleaned the tent at the same time every morning. He carried a canvas bag for the trash.

As soon as he saw her he knew she'd been waiting for him. He gave a quick, hardly noticeable jerk of his head. He stopped still, looking at her. "Mornin, Lester Ray," she said, sitting up, fumbling in the pocket of the shirt for her cigarettes. She took out a package of Chesterfields. She held the pack out, offering him one. He crossed the matted grass floor, took one.

"Good mornin," he said. He had never yet called her Sheila. He didn't call her anything. Certainly not Miz Serena. She took out a book of paper matches. He leaned forward and she lit both cigarettes with the same match. His eyes lingered on her mouth, her lips, as she took the cigarette out and exhaled the pure white smoke. His chest felt tight as he drew in his own smoke, let it warm and soothe his lungs. He looked up, half expecting her eyes to be of different colors. That image, that detail, had lodged itself in his thoughts, even in his dreams, ever since Emil had asked him that question. Sheila's eyes were dark brown, a rich liquid brown, almost black. Her eyes smiled all by themselves. They laughed, too, in the same way. She picked a bit of tobacco off the tip of her tongue and flicked it to the floor. The gesture made him catch his breath, look away, randomly twist the sack in his hands.

He had nothing at all to say to her. But everything, too. A river of unfamiliar emotions flowed through his head, bubbling and smashing over rocks, the noise of it a constant droning in his ears. He was afraid if he looked at her face he would be struck blind by some angry Zeus. She was Helen and he understood all that now, all that he had read in that book of Mrs. Mack's, knew clearly for the first time what the old poets were writing about, how men could fling themselves to horrible deaths because of a beautiful woman made by the gods, olympian perfection on earth. He allowed himself to look. She was human. But made in the image of all the beauty on the earth, or all the beauty he knew or had ever known.

"How are you this morning, Lester Ray?" she asked.

"Fine," he said before he could think not to, before he could imagine that he couldn't make words in any ordinary way but would have to speak in some ancient poetry, some higher form that mere everyday language could only aspire to.

"You seem to like your work here," she said.

"Yes, ma'am," he answered.

"Oh, please, Lester Ray, you make me sound like an old woman. Not 'ma'am' please."

"Okay," he said.

"You don't think of me as an old woman, do you?" She tilted her head in a questioning, almost pleading manner.

"No . . ." he said. He almost said "ma'am" again. He did not want to ever say "ma'am" again. She was hardly an old woman. She was new flesh, fresh warm living flesh that he wanted to touch. She was naked flesh that he had seen, could see again, any time he wanted to, simply by lifting the flap to the tent, from his post where he stood selling tickets to the show, like the one time she had seen him there and their eyes had fastened together and she had smiled—only at him, he knew—and his gaze had then relished her ivory body, watching her move totally naked under the lights in her maddeningly languid feline manner, oblivious to the snorts and vulgar catcalls of the men for whom she was dancing, removed from their gaping, he knew, by her sublime indifference to them, her willful denial that they even existed.

"Well," she said, "I'm glad you don't. It would hurt me if you did."

"Why do you care what I think?" he asked. It was a question that he wanted an answer to and a hopeful one at the same time because he knew what he wanted the answer to be.

"Why do you think I care?" she answered.

"I don't know."

"Yes, you do," she said. "I know you do."

"No," he said, "I don't." He knew what he hoped she meant but did not dare hope that she really did mean it.

"Because I like you, Lester Ray. You like me, too, don't you?"

"Sure," he said. No, he didn't like her. He loved her. Of that he was sure.

"I know you do. I've seen you watching me when I dance."

"You . . . you're beautiful," he blurted. He immediately felt foolish.

"Why, thank you, Lester Ray," she said. "A girl always likes to hear that. And you're a good-looking boy, too. Very handsome. I bet all the girls tell you that."

"No," he said. "I mean, I don't hang around with a lot of girls. Any girls, I mean."

"Then there are a lot of stupid girls in the world," she said.

"I reckon that's right," he said, and she laughed. It was a gay laugh, happiness bubbling up like a spring. He didn't think he'd ever laughed like that in his life. He could not remember ever hearing anyone laugh quite like that.

She actually was happy at that moment, which, she had learned, was the only kind of happiness available to her, the kind that only came in rapidly fleeting moments that departed almost as soon as they arrived. Like sex, making love. Exquisite and life-affirming, but tantalizing in its briefness. She quietly appraised the boy in a man's hard body, the way he stood: solid, balanced, immovable. Emil had told her he was only fourteen years old, told her she would be a monster if she seduced him. Warned her that he was jailbait, that it would be statutory rape. "I've never seen that stop you," she'd said to him, and he'd shot back, "Okay, fuck him if you want to, but don't say I didn't warn you." There had been other boys in the past, working around the carnival, and Emil had never said anything like that to her before, to any of the girls. It was clear that for some reason he didn't want her to have sex with this particular boy. This "man," she corrected herself, because years hardly mattered in his case. He was self-assured, strong, on his own, able to take care of himself and the old woman he traveled with, even the weird dwarf who came along with them and sometimes still slept in their Airstream when she was not with Yak, making their movies that Sheila, herself, had no desire to see, but she knew from experience that the world was full of all kinds of deviants who got their kicks in all kinds of ways. If watching midgets fuck was your preference, if watching women screw dogs and horses was your game (Emil and Yak actually had a reel of that that they'd ordered from somewhere in South America), if watching two women together or two men together got you off, just about anything you could think of, then Emil and Yak had the movie for you. She had even done a couple of girl on girls for them herself, with Judy. A body was just a body, right? Just like any other. She and Emil had filmed a threesome with Judy, with Judy pretending to be the baby sitter and Emil and Sheila the parents. It had been a lot of fun.

"Where did you come from?" she suddenly asked Lester Ray.

"Ma'am? I mean, what?"

"Where'd you come from, before you showed up here at the show?"

"A little old town in Florida that you never heard of," he said.

"I doubt that," she said. "I've probably played that town."

"No. No carnival ever comes to Piper. Not that I remember, anyway."

She took a drag off her cigarette, contemplating him, measuring him.

"Have you ever had a girl friend?" she asked, knowing at once that he wouldn't know what she really meant, which didn't matter because she already knew the answer to that question, too, she could tell by looking at him and talking to him. He was plenty experienced.

"Nope. There weren't no girls that I'd have anything to do with in Piper. I never met a girl like . . ." He stopped.

"Like? Like me?"

"Yeah. Like you."

"How like me?" He didn't answer, but he didn't look away from her face. His eyes were a pale, light blue, steady, not wavering at all, not even blinking. "I mean," she said, "I know there weren't any girls there who danced naked in front of men for a living, hah! But other than that?"

"Well, you . . ." He paused. "You're like somebody I dreamed one time that came true. And you're not a girl, you're a woman, and I don't mean that in any kind of age kind of way, but just that you ain't . . . well, silly! Seems like every girl I ever met was silly and flighty, downright feeble-minded." Once he started talking, the words just rushed out. "But you're not like that. You're somebody I would trust, somebody I could like, not just for . . . well, you know. I think we're alike, you and me, I mean, I've been hurt, hurt bad, and I think you have, too, and to me you're not any older than I am, I don't even want to know how old you are, because it doesn't matter at all. What difference does it make how old we are? I mean, I love you."

She was shocked at what he said at the last. "You . . . love me? Oh, no, Lester Ray, you don't."

"All right, then, I don't." He said it quickly, the abrupt, firm denial. The periwinkle blue eyes never faltered from her face. She could tell he was unsure of her, but not of himself. He seemed to know himself completely. Am I a monster? she thought. She remembered her father, recalled the anguish of her young life, the loneliness and terror, the helplessness, the pain. Lester Ray knew she'd been hurt, he said, he could intuit it without even really knowing her, because he was sensitive and perceptive, and where did that come from in a little country boy like him? What had his life been like, other than one of deprivation and hunger, and, according to what Emil had told her, a long and fruitless search for his long-gone mother, who had forsaken him as a child and abandoned him to a drunken and abusive father? And now he thinks love, he thinks I love, and that's it right there, that's what separates us, that's what it means him being younger and me being an older, half worn-out woman, because he doesn't yet know how complicated and impossible love is, he thinks it's a matter of feeling that tickle and that warmth and that sharp pain and then just saying it, saying I love. Maybe he is just a boy, then, and maybe I'm my father, maybe I am a monster, bringing pleasure that blinds—if not destroys—the soul.

"Would you like to come back to my trailer for a little while, Lester Ray?" she asked.

13

PIPER, FLORIDA

DECEMBER 1949

The lash marks were mostly all healed now, leaving raised, pinkish scars across Minnie's back and her buttocks. There were no open wounds any more, the stitches were all out, but the scars were still sore, so sore it was painful to sleep on her back, which was a problem because she was pregnant, about five months she would guess. The lounge where she was worked was decorated for Christmas with a string of colored lights draped behind the bar. Gerald Saddler, the owner and bartender, had been hesitant to hire her because of the hearing problem, which was really worse than she let on. She was actually stone deaf and a little scared because her hearing was not getting any better. She had learned to read lips a little bit, but not well enough to completely get by, so she carried a little ring notebook and a pencil for people to write down what they wanted to say to her. That's the way her customers placed their orders. Sometimes people asked her to write down what she said back to them. Apparently, since she couldn't hear herself talk, her own words were still hard to understand. The old doctor in Laurel, Mississippi, who had fixed up her back had told her she talked like a duck. A kind of squawk.

After her whipping, she had awakened in early morning, a crisp dawn, on a blood-stained blanket laid on the ground. At first she had not known where she was and was confused by the eerie silence that surrounded her. She could hear no birds singing, no insects. She had been in a deep, unconscious state. Disoriented, she had no recent memory, could not recall why she was on the ground, why her back pained her so terribly. There was a sheet over her, but otherwise she was naked, at the edge of some thick woods in an empty clearing, a clearing that seemed doubly empty because she sensed more than knew that it was supposed to have something else in it, as though she had blinked and whatever it was had simply disappeared, leaving a visible void in its place. There were the remains of several fires, ruts where vehicles had been. Only gradually did the images return, as if revealed by a lifting fog, vaporous and hazy at first, becoming sharper and more distinct, so that she slowly started to remember it all, the Gypsies, Emil, the trailer. The men who beat her, the white-haired, albino-looking one who had wielded the bullwhip, whose cruel, colorless face was indelibly etched in her mind.

They had left her. Emil. He had simply left her there. Unless he was gone to the nearest town to get a doctor for her and she knew simultaneously with thinking it that it was not true. The Airstream was gone. Its empty space spoke to her with a grinding finality. She looked around. There was a pile of her clothes on a corner of the blanket. Her worn carpet-covered pack sat next to them, open, probably emptied of anything of value, which wasn't much. Her knife. An ivory brooch that Miss Ida Hooten had given her. Maybe as much as thirty dollars. As she looked around she spied some money, bills folded neatly in half, lying on the blanket next to her so that they had been underneath the sheet that had covered her. She reached for them, picked them up, and even that simple movement caused her back to cramp with bitter pain, as though sections of her skin were splitting open, pulling apart, the hurt so severe that she almost passed out again. It was like someone cutting her with a rusty, dull knife, or marking her with a fiery-red branding iron. She grimaced and sweat popped out on her forehead. She held as still as she could. Gradually, the intensity subsided. She counted the money. Five ten-dollar bills. Thank you, Emil, she thought bitterly. Just another lesson in men, why am I surprised?

She recollected then the barrel of the shotgun coming through the narrow window, its violent and terrible detonation, louder than it could possibly be, the last thing she heard. Exploding inside her head, then the ringing like a far distant telephone, one that she would never find no matter how long or how far she looked. Surely this was temporary.

She would shake her head and her hearing would be restored and she would feel a little foolish for ever worrying otherwise. But she could hear nothing at all, as if all sounds had gone out of the world, and she could look out and the world was still normal except for that. She saw a bird, a breeze in the leaves of a persimmon tree, but no noise, no accompanying din, and she knew the woods were never quiet, always full of the sounds of myriad life, but it was all missing now and gone.

She said her name out loud. "Anna Marie Spiroski." The words drifted soundlessly from her lips and evaporated into the silent air. She could not even be sure what the words were, whether they were actually her name. Maybe she had merely thought them and had not said them aloud at all.

The old doctor in Laurel would not even look into her ears. "You need a specialist," he wrote on a piece of paper, "you need to go on to New Orleans and see a specialist. About all I could tell you is you are deaf and you already know that."

She had caught a ride into Laurel with a teenaged boy and his girlfriend. It had been sheer agony dressing, gathering her extra things and putting them into her bag. (At least her knife and the brooch were in there, but not the money.) It was excruciating just to stand up and then bend back down to pick them up. She left the bloodstained blanket and sheet. Let somebody come upon them and make of them what they will. She could feel the blood, cool on her back, seeping through the shirt she'd put on. The jeans rubbed against the raw slashes on her buttocks as she walked up to the highway and stuck out her thumb. The sun was high now, and hot, and there was very little breeze. The first car that came along, an old black Ford with the right front fender missing, was the boy and girl. They stopped and Minnie limped painfully up, catching them. The girl had to get out to let her into the back seat.

"My God, what happened to you?" the boy asked. He had a package of Lucky Strikes wedged under the sun visor and he took it down and passed it back to her.

"What?" Minnie said. She pointed to her ears and shook her head. She took one of the cigarettes and passed the pack back up. "I can't hear you. I'm deaf."

"You got blood all over your back," the girl shouted at her. She looked about fifteen, wearing a pale green sleeveless blouse and black shorts. Blonde and skinny, pretty in a country sort of way. Minnie read her lips, got the gist of what she said. But there was little she could do about it.

There were some schoolbooks on the back seat and a notebook. Minnie found a pencil. She wrote, "I had an accident," and passed the notebook and pencil to the girl. She drew hungrily on the cigarette.

"What kind of accident?" the boy asked when they had both read it. The boy was tall and thin, wearing a black T-shirt. Minnie pointed to her ears again. She pointed to the notebook. The girl wrote, "he said what kind of acident?"

"Me and my boyfriend, we had a wreck on his motorcycle. I skidded down the highway on my back." Why wasn't she just telling them the truth? She didn't know. She really didn't even have a clear idea of what she was saying. She knew what she thought she was saying, but she couldn't hear it even in her inner ear. She might as well have been just moving her lips.

"Where's he at?" the boy asked. The girl wrote that down and showed it to Minnie. "Don't get blood all over my back seat," he said. The girl didn't bother to write that last.

"I'm sorry to say he was killed," Minnie said.

"Killed?" the boy exclaimed. "Jesus Christ."

The girl wrote "when did this hapen?"

"Yesterday."

"Yesterday?!" the boy said.

"Look," she said, "could you drop me off at a doctor's office? I need to get all this looked at."

She saw the boy and girl look at each other. "Where's the body?" the girl wrote on the notebook. She had an awkward, looping, uneven penmanship.

"I left him back there in a ditch," Minnie said.

"Jesus Christ!" the boy said. He tapped the brake a couple of times as though he were going to stop and turn around and go look for him but then he kept going. He even picked up speed.

"I'll get somebody from this next town to go out there and get him,"

Minnie went on. "A funeral home or something," she said.

The girl wrote, "but he was your boyfrend."

"Yeah, but he was an asshole," Minnie said.

They did not react to that, at least not in any way she could see from the backs of their heads. They rode along in silence for a while, the boy and girl staring straight ahead. Then, turning around, the girl wrote, "why do you talk funy?"

"Do I talk funny?" Minnie asked. "How funny?"

The girl wrote, "not funy funy, just werd."

"Because I'm deaf, I guess. I haven't been deaf all that long."

The girl just peered at her over the back of the seat. Her eyes reflected her mystification. Minnie could tell she had a million questions she wanted to ask. Minnie wished they would hurry. Her back hurt terribly. "What's this next town?" she asked impatiently.

"Laurel," the girl wrote on the pad. Then, "did the acident make your eyes go like that?"

"Like what?" she asked.

"Diffirent colors," the girl wrote.

"My eyes are different colors? I didn't know that. I guess it must have, then."

The girl looked even more confused. The boy's neck and head were rigid, and he gripped the steering wheel with both hands. "She's nutty as a fruit cake," he said to the girl out of the corner of his mouth. Minnie looked out the window at the raw, naked red clay mounds, the stunted trees, the patches of wild sedge, yellow even in July. An occasional bony cow, chewing its cud, placidly watched them go by. She saw a filling station, then a general store. They were coming to a town. The prospect of more people, of the normal noises of a city that she wouldn't be able to hear, made her anxious. Sound was hovered around her like an invisible cloud of charged air. She knew it was there. She thought of it as a bright beam of light that was aimed elsewhere, going in a different direction, away from her. It was like reaching for something that she saw, something solid, and having her hand pass right through it even as she was looking at it. The car she was in seemed to be drifting along above the ground, the warm air rushing in the windows hushed and muffled. The only way she knew it was there was that she could feel it on her skin, feel it mussing her hair.

They let her out in front of a two-story brick house. There was a sign in the yard that read c. UNDERWOOD, M.D. Minnie went up the walk which was lined with wilted, sun-fried verbena, and up onto the porch. There were two doors, the one down on the right with a card mounted over a doorbell that read "Doctor's Office." Minnie rang the bell. After a minute the door was opened by a colored woman in a white dress. She was a little woman who reminded Minnie immediately of Ruby Frost and Minnie felt a prick of homesickness, wondering what had become of the Frosts. They had been good to her, had taken her in without hesitation and made her like family. The woman opened the door wide, motioning her in.

Her mouth moved. "Doctor Underwood will see you in a minute," Minnie guessed she said. The woman went off into another room. She was in a parlor, with chairs and sofas, but Minnie chose to stand. She didn't want the pain of sitting, and she was afraid she'd get blood all over the velvet chairs. Heavy maroon drapes covered the windows and there were marble-topped tables here and there with ceramic and glass knick-knacks and photographs in silver frames on them. The smell of rubbing alcohol, sharp and spicy, mingled with the scent of roast beef cooking with garlic and the winy smell of pine-scented furniture polish. She wondered if the colored woman was a nurse or a cook or a house-keeper. Or maybe all three.

The old doctor came into the room. He wore a three-piece gray suit that hung on his frame like he had recently lost a lot of weight. He was stooped. He wore little wire-framed glasses. He looked about ninety years old.

"I'm Doctor Underwood," he said, "folks don't normally come around botherin me on Sunday mornin." She read his lips enough to understand his name and deduce "Sunday morning."

"Is this Sunday?" Minnie asked.

The doctor squinted at her through the little glasses. "What seems to be the matter?" he asked. Minnie pointed to her ears. She rummaged in her bag and came out with some of the paper from the notebook and the pencil that she had lifted from the teenagers. She handed them to the doctor.

"I'm deaf right now," she said. "Write down what you want to say."

The old man wrote, "How can I help you?" and showed it to her.

Minnie removed her shirt. Just as she turned around she saw the old man glance at her breasts. There was not a man alive who wouldn't do that, even a doctor older than God.

"Thunderation," he exclaimed, "what happened here?" Her back was turned. She didn't answer. He reached for the paper and pencil and wrote, "How did this happen?" and held it around in front of her face.

"Somebody beat me with a bullwhip," she said. "It's still bleedin some and I'm afraid of the cuts getting infected."

He touched her back, pushing at the wounds with the tips of his fingers. "Your husband, I reckon," he said. She didn't answer, of course, because she couldn't see him and had no idea he'd said anything at all. There were deep slashes on her back, many of them beginning to scab over, swollen and red. He eased her blue jeans a little bit down her hips, noting that she wore no panties. When he did that he hurt her and she flinched and whimpered.

He wrote on the paper again and turned her around and showed it to her. "Who did this to you?"

"Some men I don't know their names," she said quickly, because she guessed what he would say next. "I don't know who they were."

"The police," he wrote.

"No, sir," she said. "Please."

He turned her back around. She flinched again at his poking. He went out of the room for a minute, then returned with the colored woman. She had a steel tray with some instruments on it and several jars of salve. They motioned her behind a screen in the corner of the room; there was a white, enamel table with a towel on it, and they indicated she should lie down on it, on her stomach. He folded the paper over and wrote, "A few stitches. Shot is going to sting." She felt the woman pulling her jeans down around her ankles. When she was naked she crawled onto the table. Where her bare skin touched the enamel it was icy cold. Two sets of hands jabbed at her buttocks. He wrote "Sting" and held it before her face. She felt the needle, then again in several more places. Then in a few minutes she could feel him stitching her up, but there was no pain. The woman rubbed salve all over her back. It had a clean, menthol smell. They put some small bandages on her here and there, then told her she could get up. They handed her her clothes.

When she was dressed and back out in the parlor the woman put a piece of newspaper on one of the chairs and told her to sit. The old doctor sat in the matching chair. He had already determined that she was a transient, a female hobo. She didn't look as though she came from anywhere around there. And he had noticed that she suffered from a condition of the eyes called heterochromia, as well as being deaf.

"What is your name?" Dr. Underwood wrote.

"Minnie Francis," she said.

"Where do you live?"

"Actually," she said, "I'm just passing through. How much do I owe you."

"I've never had a patient with both heterochromia and deafness," he wrote. "Heterochromia is unusual."

"What?"

He gestured to his eyes, then to hers.

"Oh," she said. "Well, my eyes have been like that all my life. I think I've just lost my hearing temporarily. A shotgun was fired right next to my head."

She sat and watched him scribbling on the paper. He wrote for a long time. Then he handed it to her. "This is sounding more and more like something I should call the police about. Shotguns and bullwhips. $10. No checks."

She pulled the bills from the pocket of her jeans and peeled off a ten. She handed it to him. "No, please don't call the police, that's all right." She was afraid dealing with the police would simply delay her in this place and nothing would ever be done about it, anyway. "One thing more. Will you look into my ears? Try to see what's going on?"

He wrote, "No. No ears." Then he took the paper back and wrote for a while. "You need to see a specialist. You should go on to New Orleans and see a specialist. I can't help you there. All I can tell you is that you are deaf, and you already know that."

"People say I talk funny," she said. "Is that because of my deafness?"

"Yes. You can't hear yourself. Sometimes the sounds get all garbled in your head. You squawk like a duck."

She crumbled the paper in her fist. "Thanks a lot, doc," she said, trying not to say it sarcastically and failing. She stood up. She walked to the door. Before she went out she turned and said, "Daisy Duck says no police, Doctor Underwood. Okay?"

He nodded in the affirmative, and she let the door close softly behind her.

SHE PASSED A CITY park where she went into the free-standing, concrete block women's room and changed out of the bloodstained clothes. She found a fresh blouse and clean jeans in her carpetbag. She washed her face in the stained sink and inspected herself in the cracked mirror. Her hair was dirty and coarse looking. Her eyes were tired. I look twenty years older than I am, she thought, but she didn't care. She was also beginning to realize that she didn't really care that she was deaf. In fact, she rather liked it. All her life she'd wished that she could just shut people up, just snap them off the way you could do somebody talking on the radio. Often when people would talk to her she'd longed to just cease hearing them, close her ears, but the best she could do was let her mind wander and not listen to what they were saying. But she could still hear them. She knew they were still yapping at her. She could still see them, see their mouths working—which actually was freakish looking and grotesquely comic, something she'd never noticed before when words and sentences and exclamations and proclamations would come out—but she didn't have to hear them.

She thought it would be pretty nice that people would have to write down what they wanted to say to her. They would have to go to more trouble than just opening their mouths and letting it flow. Maybe it would even make them think about what they wanted to say before they wrote it down and she would be free of all the inane, useless chatter of the world. Perhaps the little bits that people would write down for her would be like little poems, distilled thoughts without all the clutter of unnecessary words that had no real function other than to confuse or disguise. Her world—and her life—would be boiled down to its essentials, to the things that ultimately really mattered and she would not have to concern herself with the disorderly, messy lives of others. But even as she thought all this she knew it was only a fantasy. No one could walk through life without stumbling over the garbage of others. Even the hermit who has found the remotest refuge in the tops of unconquered mountains would eventually be rooted out and exposed to the curious probes of the prying masses. Because people owned you. ("They do own you," Miss Ida Hooten had told her, all those years ago in Cedar Key, "so you might as well make em pay for that right.") You could not get away from them even if you could shut them out completely.

In the past, some people had expressed surprise, even amazement, that she traveled alone—a girl, then a young woman—but to her it was the only way. She was not afraid, and aloneness wasn't lonely to her. It was sweet peace. She had known even when she had gone along with Emil and the Gypsies that it was only temporary, a brief side trip. The idea of permanence had never entered her mind. Apparently it had not been very fully lodged in his, either, though he had sung a different song. He had told her the day after they slept together for the first time that he wanted to marry her, and her alarm bells had gone off.

"You would be my queen," he'd said to her when they'd visited the grave in Meridian.

"Your queen?"

"Yes," he'd said.

"No thanks," she'd said.

Every time he brought something like that up she rejected it, firmly and totally. And it no doubt had hurt his feelings, injured his man-confidence. He had begun to act like she was his property as soon as she walked into the camp. That was his marker. That was who he was. He was his good looks. He was the cocky posture he assumed, his air that he pronounced to the world, and she could see that there was very little else behind it. It was what defined him, far more profoundly than the Gypsy blood he carried in his veins. She had not been surprised when he had left her that way, maybe even left her for dead. He had discarded her like a worn-thin tire, because she had not slid easily inside that periphery of masculine masquerade the way he was used to other women doing. She had butted up against it. That kind of stance—it proclaimed power: the meanest bull in the herd, the fiercest lion in the pack—was not something that invited her, but something that repelled her. She had known all the time they were journeying across Georgia and Alabama, camping in fields beside the highway, then during their more extended camping outside Meridian, near the Queen of the Gypsies' burying place, that it was only a matter of time, that soon she would snap and have to flee. She supposed that the White People for Jesus, or whatever they called themselves, had made up her mind for her, had saved her the trouble of a decision. She knew that one reason Emil had left her was fear, for himself and the people in his familia, because she was considered "white" by those Mississippi rednecks who had a strong propensity for violence, especially if they thought someone they considered "colored" had the audacity to have what they considered an inappropriate relationship with a "white woman." In truth, she was not "white." She was not Gypsy, either. She supposed—as long as her loss of hearing continued—she would be defined as "deaf." That would be her niche, her cubbyhole, what differentiated her from everybody else. It would make a neat category to put her in, so that people then would not have to bother with seeing the true her but could simply respond in their shallow way to an outward manifestation of her that they, in their lazy, ignorant way, could pretend to understand.

TEN DAYS LATER, ON the outskirts of Montgomery, Alabama, she caught a ride with a man carrying a load of watermelons to a little town in Florida. The man's name was Leon Lutenbacher, and he was driving an old International Harvester two-and-a-half-ton flatbed truck with high, slatted wooden sides. He drove slowly because the watermelons were piled precariously high.

She'd been standing in the parking lot of a restaurant when a man had come up to her. He was pale and puffy, with vague yellow eyes. He handed her a little pamphlet. She first thought it was one of those HAVE YOU BEEN SAVED tracts, then she read it. "HELLO!" it read. "Pardon me, please. I am a Deaf Person and I am selling these Mini-Booklets to Support My Family. Any Donation you wish! Thank you very much, and May God Bless You All." She opened it: it was filled with little pen-and-ink drawings of hands twisted in all manner of shapes. "Hand alphabet used by the Deaf throughout the world. Easy to Use," it read.

She looked into the man's eyes. They were passive and benign, already resigned to her refusal. The pamphlet had an odd, completely unexpected effect on her. She felt self-conscious and nauseated. The whole scene sickened her. She wanted to throw the pamphlet in the man's face, yet she felt connected to him, as if they were related by blood. He just slumped there, flatfooted, and she felt him pulling her into some bizarre communion: they shared the same affliction, were crippled in the same way. Up until then she had not thought about it, had not really realized that there were other deaf people in the world, that they formed some sort of freakish community, that they even had their own language. The fact that the first one she encountered was this pallid, pathetic creature jolted her. That he was a beggar shamed her. She felt not an ounce of compassion or empathy for him. All she wanted to do was get away from him.

She pulled her change from her pocket. Two dimes and a quarter. She dumped the coins into his outstretched hand. When her hand lightly touched his, it felt damp and warm. He continued to stare at her with his bloodless—dead—eyes as though he were looking into the darkest corners of her soul. She shivered. She backed away. She turned and walked quickly across the hot, tarred lot, the soles of her shoes sticky on it. Once she stopped and looked back and he was gone, as if he'd simply vanished. For a moment she wondered if she'd imagined him. But she had the little pamphlet in her hand.

The encounter shook her. She strode quickly up to a slender little man with a truck load of watermelons. "I don't care where you're going," she said, "but I'm going with you."

"Whoa, now," he said.

"Seriously," she said, "I need a ride." She handed the pamphlet to the man. He slowly read it.

"Feller give me one a these not five minutes ago," he said. She pointed to her ears. "Oh," he said. She handed him her little pad and the pencil.

He wrote "going down into Florida" on the pad. He started to fumble in his pocket and came up with some change.

"No, no," she said. "Just the ride."

He wrote "all right" on the pad.

"My wife knew I was pickin up a good-lookin woman like you, she'd have my head," he said, and climbed into his truck. Once they were under way he began to talk, rattling on, forgetting she was deaf. "The Panhandle's where I'm goin. The folks I'll deliver these here watermelons to will sell em alongside the roads leadin north out of Florida. Tourist'll think they was growed in Florida, but a course they weren't. These were growed in Cullman County, Alabama. You could put em alongside a road in Cullman County and wouldn't nobody stop even to look at em, but put em out in Florida and a stream a cars'll be stoppin all day long." Leon Lutenbacher kept a wrinkled, drooping cigarette in his lips constantly. He rolled his own, and he could roll one with one hand while holding the wheel with the other. With a gesture, as though he suddenly remembered her deafness, he offered to roll her one and she said "Sure" and he did, one handed, and licked it with the pink tip of his tongue protruding next to his cigarette.

He began to talk again and she didn't try to stop him. He couldn't have written on the pad anyhow while he was driving. "They don't grow doot in the Panhandle cept a little cotton ain't fit to pick," he said. "Even a voodoo doctor couldn't coax a watermelon out of that sand."

When she finished her cigarette she dozed off, her head against the back of the seat, the jiggling of the old truck rocking her to sleep. He didn't seem to mind at all that she was sleeping. When she woke up she had no idea how long she'd slept. She imagined that he had talked the whole time she slept.

They were both smoking his hand-rolled cigarettes when they crossed the Florida state line. Nothing was the same to her after they entered Florida. The air pressure seemed to change when they passed the WELCOME TO FLORIDA sign, a slight swelling inside her head. She kept staring out the window at the level, bleak landscape, and she didn't know if he was still chattering on since she couldn't see him. Her ears popped, like they were coming down a steep mountain, but they were on as flat a terrain as she had ever been on, exactly as she remembered it. It was the first time she'd been back in Florida since she'd departed Cedar Key. The image of the crushed-shell road where her parents had put her out, somewhere south of where she and Leon Lutenbacher were, popped into her mind, along with the still-terrifying face of old man Frill. She knew that as long as she lived she would never be free of those visions.

She rode along then in her newfound hushed stillness. Hot, humid July-in-Florida air poured through the open windows. They were headed to a warehouse in a town called Piper, Florida. Minnie was just about out of money; the fifty dollars that Emil had left for her had dwindled to five. She planned to get some kind of job in Piper, if it was large enough to have anything. After that, she didn't know.

She glanced over at Leon Lutenbacher. He was talking away. She smiled and looked back out the window, at a swampy pond with dead, black trees growing in it. She squinted her eyes, looking for an alligator. She was content to exist only inside her own mind, with nothing that she didn't invite in to disturb that isolation. She had invited the hidden, imaginary alligator in. Unless it was actually in the lake it was only in her fantasy, shut off from everything and everyone else, closed off even from the lake, which was probably really empty but for a couple of snakes and a few bullfrogs.

MINNIE FOUND A JOB waitressing in a place called Saddler's Lounge, a low-slung concrete block bar and grill on the edge of town, alongside the two-lane highway heading down to the Florida beaches. It was a job she knew and was comfortable in. She had lost count of the number of times she'd worked as a waitress, either in a bar or a cafe. Piper was a placid, faded town, the kind that if you were traveling through you would wonder why it was ever established there in the first place. It was not the vacation Florida that you read about. After the war, more and more tourist courts and vacation cottages had been springing up in places like Fort Walton Beach, Grayton Beach, Destin, and Panama City. She did not want those crowds, those joints with their echoing wooden dance floors and bubbly juke boxes playing Glenn Miller and Arty Shaw, still spewing "Bell Bottom Trousers, Coat of Navy Blue" and "Boogie Woogie Bugle Boy" because the war had been good for business and there were still lots of servicemen stationed down there. She took a room in a dowdy, timeworn two-story house that boasted a sign on the front porch that read PIPER TOURIST HOME, but there were no tourists there, only a couple of welders, a rural mail carrier, and Minnie. The home was run by a woman named Mae Clair Belvedere Bean, who was a poet. There was a copy of her book of poetry, *When God Planted His Garden*, in each of the guest rooms. Minnie read the first poem in the book: "Lilac Time." "When Angels flap their wings / On the breeze comes many things / The smell of lilacs in the spring / And honeysuckle." Minnie supposed that Mae Clair Belvedere Bean couldn't think of anything else to rhyme with "wings." She was a tall, spare woman with hair dyed a pinkish red.

Gerald Saddler was a thick-necked, broad-chested man with a completely bald head that was polished and shiny. It glittered, reflecting the lights of the beer signs behind the bar: Falstaff, Pabst Blue Ribbon, Schlitz, Jax. There was a roadside store attached to the lounge that sold Esso gasoline, soft drinks, potato chips, boiled peanuts, and packaged beer to people in a hurry to get to the beaches. There was a fat cook named Alex Hardey who grilled hamburgers and fixed up bacon and eggs in the mornings, but even then the lounge's customers mainly wanted beer. Gerald Saddler's wife, Pearly, worked the early shift and Minnie came on in mid-afternoon and worked until closing, sometimes as late as two or three in the morning.

"Why's a good-lookin woman like you wantin to work in a dump like this?" Gerald Saddler asked her when she came in. She pointed to her ears and slid the pad and pencil over to him. "Jesus, a deef mute," he said aloud, for the benefit of several men who were drinking beer at the bar. He wrote on the pad: "I can't hire no deef and dumb person."

"I'm not dumb," she said, "I can talk as good as you. I just can't hear."

"As good as me?" Saddler said. "I reckon there could be a argument there," and he laughed and the other men laughed, too. She frowned and pointed to the pad and pencil. He wrote, "you sound like a rusty door hinge."

"But you can understand me, can't you?" Minnie said. "I ain't speakin Chinese."

"No, you ain't speakin Chinese," he said, "I heard enough of that over there. I don't ever want to hear any more of it again." He was smiling at her. Then he caught himself and frowned. "You can't understand a word I'm sayin, can you?" She just looked at him. He was wearing a white T-shirt with a full-length, white cotton apron. There were grease smears on the front of the apron. He looked like a powerful man; the muscles in his upper arms bulged and there was a thin sheen of sweat across his forehead. He was a pink and white giant. The place was dim, lit by beer signs and a few low-wattage bulbs. It was exactly the kind of mildly depressing place that Minnie was looking for.

"Well?" she said. "The job?"

He wrote: "O. K. 50 cents a hour and tips."

"Dinner and supper?" she asked.

He grinned. He wrote, "O. K."

Her room was only four dollars a week, so she should do all right. But it was not good enough to tempt her to stay too long, and that was a good thing. She would save up a stake, hit the road again. This time maybe she would go west, somewhere out of the South again, maybe out of the South for good.

But when she first went to work at Saddler's Lounge, Minnie did not yet know she was pregnant. She could not have had any way of knowing, either, that—totally contrary to her nature—she would spend the next year in that shabby and seedy little town: Piper, Florida.

14

COASTAL GEORGIA FAIRGROUNDS

NOVEMBER 1964

Precisely at the moment that Lester Ray and Sheila Serena retired to Sheila's dressing room to be alone, Miss Millicent D. Roget and her partner, Cassandra Birmingham, were drinking coffee in a Stuckey's just outside Oxford, Alabama. There had been no trace of the runaways in Pensacola. In Mobile, an itinerant worker in a bar on the waterfront had told Miss Roget that a dwarf girl resembling Virgin Mary Duck had been traveling with a carnival that came through, that the carnival had a freak show and she was in it. The man had seen her dance with another midget.

"Funniest damn thing I ever saw," the man said, as Miss Roget bought him another drink.

"I'm sure," she said dryly.

That a carnival would have a freak show with a midget girl resembling one of the runaways did not strike Miss Roget as a significant clue. Every freak show in the country had a midget girl resembling the Duck girl. But it was something she filed away. It didn't change her plans to go on to New Orleans, and if nothing panned out there then they could double back and pick up the trail of that particular carnival.

Two weeks in New Orleans turned up nothing. It seemed likely that the old woman would need some sort of medical care sooner or later, but they could find no semblance of her as they checked hospitals and doctors, or of the youngsters, as they prowled through the unwashed runaway children that gathered near Jackson Square every day to beg.

They asked questions all over town, but no one knew them or had seen them. How could someone not notice an eighty-three-year-old woman traveling with a fourteen-year-old boy and a—at least according to Sheriff Ralph Prudhomme—very ugly fourteen-year-old dwarf?

So they doubled back to Mobile and picked up the trail of what they thought was the carnival, Cole Brothers Rides and Shows (which was, of course, the wrong carnival, having done a short engagement in Mobile after J. F. Freeman), finally catching up with it in Tuscaloosa. They interviewed everyone connected to the shows and rides, the mechanics and the show people, the freaks and the girls, and there was not a sign of their being there or ever having been there. "I think we're looking in the wrong places," Miss Roget said. They were now driving to Atlanta and had stopped for a break at a Stuckey's.

"But it would be the perfect cover," Cassandra Birmingham said, sipping her coffee. She still leaned toward the theory that they were traveling with a carnival. She and Milly had just been following the wrong one. They probably needed to go back to Mobile and start over, but Milly didn't want to. Draped on the wall behind their booth was a huge beach towel made like a Confederate Flag. The tag on it said, "$1.00."

"That's right. But they don't even know we're looking for them," Miss Roget said. "They probably think they've foxed the law, since they haven't been caught by now. We've got an advantage, since they don't even know they're running from us. We've got to think like them."

"That boy would know that Orville McCrory would want to find his elderly mother."

"You're right, of course. The boy would think the law would be after him for stealing the car and maybe for kidnapping the other two. But the highway patrols of six states haven't been able to turn up even a hint of that car, and it's one that ought to stand out like a sore thumb. They're smart. How do you suppose they're traveling? If they're traveling? They might be hunkered down right outside that dreadful Piper."

"Maybe they're in Atlanta," Cassandra said.

"If they are, I'll find em," Millicent D. Roget said. Well, you haven't found em yet, Cassandra thought.

SHEILA'S SKIN WAS SOFT as hot melted butter, inside like hot syrup. Lester Ray's fingers trembled when he touched her. He was afraid he would pull back stumps, burned to the first knuckle. Nothing in his life had quite prepared him for this. He felt that his entire body was being sucked into her, being absorbed into her heat, into her beating blood. He became the scent of her. He was no longer a separate being. His selfhood had been consumed by her essence, and together they were as formless and shapeless as a pool of molten lava. He didn't know where he was. He might as well have been on another planet, in another universe, and time became twisted back upon itself so that it raced frenziedly ahead and then did not move at all.

THE FAIRGROUNDS WERE NEAR the beach, on Tybee Island, and Virgin Mary Duck liked to prowl among the souvenir shops and the narrow, dark seafood places offering fried shrimp in wax-paper cones and beer in large paper cups. People stared at her. Little children pointed until their mothers raked their arms down and marched them away. Most of the people she met on the sidewalk, even the clerks who walked up to her in the shops, did a double take. She knew full well it was because she was a dwarf, and an ugly one to boot (she had been told that often enough, all her young life), but she liked to imagine it was because they had seen her in one of her movies and recognized her in the flesh and it surprised and startled them. She really hoped that one day somebody would stop her and ask for her autograph.

Actually, she had only made three movies and she wasn't even sure they had been put up for sale yet. One of them, called "Sixty-Nine Heaven," she had made with Yak. In it they started off dancing, doing a waltz, and Yak swept her all around the dance floor (the same waltz they did together out front, to help draw a crowd), and then they clench-danced, real close, and she could feel Yak's dick getting hard against her. (He had told her that it really turned him on to do it in front of the cameras, and she had found that true as well. She liked it that the cameraman and Emil, who was the director, barking out directions telling them what to do next and then next, were right there watching them.) They pretended to get carried away—they didn't have to do too much pretending, at least

V. M. didn't—and wound up on the floor ripping each other's clothes off, and they started doing it right there. Fucking like puppy dogs and then sixty-nining each other while the camera hovered right over them, so close she could hear it grinding and buzzing. Then they made one of the films in Yak's trailer, on his bed, called "Little Fuckers." She made one with one of the carnival workers, a tall, muscular guy named Ephusis, who had a dick so big it had frightened her a little bit, but then she'd had no trouble with it at all, except trying to get her mouth around it. That one was called "Even Ugly Midgets Like To Do It, Too." She wasn't too pleased with the title, but Yak told her they called it that to attract attention. "It'll make it stand out," he told her, "among all those other stag reels out there."

V. M. browsed down the aisle in the beach store. They had lots of plastic floats, all different bright colors, bins of different-sized sea shells, racks of bathing suits both male and female (none, obviously, that would fit her, except for little girls' suits that were frilly and kittenish and flat in the front, with no room for her tits. Yak had promised her that when they got to south Florida, where they were going next, he would have one made for her). Cases of soft drinks and beer in cans and bottles, some even in big quart bottles that she'd never seen before, lined the aisle along with different kinds of snacks, a whole rack of sun tan oil and lotion that smelled sweet like coconut. There were racks of post cards, beach towels, and T-shirts with palm trees on them, blowing in the breeze. V. M found a T-shirt that she liked. It was a little boy's shirt with a big, colorful alligator on the front, its mouth wide open, showing rows of sharp looking teeth. Written underneath the alligator was "Whoopee! Okefenokee Comes to the Beach!" She slipped it beneath the loose boy's shirt that she was wearing and continued sauntering down the aisle, looking at everything. She found a little plastic dolphin mounted on a tiny, shellacked wooden block that she stuck into the pocket of her khaki pants.

By the time she got back up to the door and started out she was weighted down with other stuff, all tucked away out of sight: a deck of cards, a Tybee Island paperweight, a *Movie Screen* magazine wedged into the waistband of her khakis along with the alligator T-shirt. She had started out the door when the man behind the counter yelled at her. "Hey, little boy, where the hell you think you goin?" He started around the counter toward her. "Goddamit, you . . ." he said, then as he approached her he stopped dead still. He stood staring at her, a bewildered expression on his face. Then, "Listen here . . .," he said. "Listen here . . ."

"You listen here," she said. "I ain't no little boy!"

"You . . . you got to pay for that," he blubbered.

"I ain't no little boy," she said. She reached up and quickly unbuttoned her shirt and let her tits pop out. A look of total amazement and disbelief came over the man's face. He seemed paralyzed with shock. Pulling her shirt together with her hand she turned and ran out onto the sidewalk. Immediately she ran into a heavy woman wearing flowered shorts and bounced off her hip, her hand releasing the shirt, and she continued running, darting in and out among people, folks exclaiming and jumping out of her way, her tits free and bouncing and jiggling as she sprinted. There were squeals and shouts. One little girl screamed, "Look, Mama, that girl's got no privacy!" "Jesus, what the hell is that?" somebody said. "Whoa" and "Look out" and V. M. paid them no attention at all except to dash and scoot around them, back and forth, like a football player running for a touchdown, laughing all the time. She felt exhilarated, pumped up, brilliant with excitement. When she burst onto a section of sidewalk that was empty of people she yelled at the top of her lungs: "GET OUTTA MY FUCKIN WAY!" She bolted around a corner, onto a side street that led away from the beach.

She ran as fast as she could all the way back to the fairgrounds. She had always been a very fast runner. There was nobody chasing her. The man in the souvenir shop was still standing there with his mouth hanging open, already framing the story he would tell for the next two or three weeks to anybody who would listen to him.

EMIL ACTED DIFFERENTLY TOWARD Lester Ray in ways that the boy could not quite figure out. He knew it had to do with Sheila, and Lester Ray had expected Emil to be angry, but he didn't seem angry, just distant, aloof, removed from any situation the two of them found themselves in. They were making preparations for the long trek down to Fort Myers where they would spend the winter. When Lester Ray had asked Emil if he'd have a job down there, Emil had looked at the sky and said, "Well, you never know." Which wasn't an answer at all. Lester Ray and Mrs. McCrory still had almost three thousand of the five they had started with, so it wasn't a question of money. It was a question of what Lester Ray would do with himself before the carnival started touring again in the spring, when he was taking for granted he would have his old job again. But he couldn't be sure of that either. Sheila told him that she and the girls would be working a club out at Fort Myers beach. The winter was the big season in south Florida, so they would do all right.

The carnival caravan would head south down the Dixie Highway, U.S. 1, running along the eastern edge of Florida, along the Atlantic, all the way to West Palm Beach, where they'd turn west and cross to Fort Myers on Alligator Alley, a highway that ran through the Everglades below Lake Okeechobee. Emil had told Lester Ray that some of the rides would join an amusement park in West Palm Beach for the winter season; others, along with the freak show, would attach to a park on Cape Coral near Fort Myers. Emil, himself, had a small house in Fort Myers where he would spend the winter months.

"I thought you told me your home was your trailer," Lester Ray said to him.

"It is, my man," Emil said dismissively. "Most of the time."

"That doesn't sound like what I've learned about Gypsies," Lester Ray said.

"The old ways are dying out, Lester Ray. Not many people live them anymore. I live in my house down there three months, so the rest of the year, three-quarters of it, I'm on the road, which is just about how much Gypsy I am, three-quarters."

"I thought you were always on the road, that your trailer was your home," Lester Ray said, "that you always have to be moving on."

"It doesn't matter what you thought," Emil said. "But now that I think about it I have to admit you're right, because three months is just about as long as I can stand to stay in one place."

"You get itchy feet," Lester Ray said. It was more a question than a statement.

Emil looked steadily at him. He didn't reply for a long time. Then, he said, "Yeah, it's the Gypsy blood in me. That's what you need to know, isn't it? That's what you want to hear." Lester Ray was just a boy, with his pale innocent eyes and his eager stance, no matter that according to Sheila he was a stud in bed. She needed to think of him as a man, to justify herself, to rationalize her lust, but he was a child, really, still attached to his mother, however thin the cord has been pulled, still fastened tightly. And what can I tell him? That his mother was a whore who would have left him even if she hadn't been a Gypsy, which she wasn't really, anyway, not in any real sense.

There was no question in Emil's mind that the woman in the photograph was Anna Maria Spiroski, and if, as Lester Ray believed, had been told, she was his mother, that didn't mean anything, really, because Minnie, as she called herself sometimes back then, was probably a world away by now, still determinedly moving, escaping whatever demons pursued her, staying one step ahead of them. So she did not die that day in those Mississippi woods, she did not bleed to death; he was not surprised. She was too tough. She was beautiful and he had thought at first he could love her but he could not get inside that iron protective shell, the barricade of fear that surrounded her, that sometimes made her shrink from his touch, as if she didn't trust him, couldn't trust him. All that was a long time ago. Lester Ray had told Emil that his father was a drunk and the Anna Maria Emil had known would not have been able to abide such weakness in a man. The boy was a good kid, but he was headed toward certain disappointment and heartbreak, with his mother—if Anna Maria was his mother and she was still alive and anywhere to be found—and with Sheila, too. Two whores. Two bitches. All women were whores and bitches. What the hell did it matter who your mother was? Maybe it was best just not to ever know.

"How is Sheila?" Emil asked.

"Whattaya mean, 'how is Sheila?'" Lester Ray replied.

"Just what I said. You seem to see a lot of her."

"You got a problem with that?" Lester Ray's fists were clenched. His eyes were narrowed.

"No," Emil said, "I got no problem with that. Settle down, why don't you."

230 of the Gypsies

"Sheila's fine," Lester Ray said. "If you need to know."

"All right. Good to hear it." Emil smiled, but Lester Ray didn't smile back. "What's eatin you, Lester Ray?" The boy just gazed at him, as if from a great distance. He wouldn't answer that, Emil knew. "Or maybe I ought to say 'what are you eatin?'"

"You son-of-a-bitch," Lester Ray said.

"Oh, come on, boy. I'm just teasing you. Why don't you relax?"

"I don't want to relax," he said. He sat stiffly in the folding aluminum chair. They were sitting outside the top, in the mid-morning cool. Lester Ray could smell the changing season in the air. The scent of autumn. Just this little bit further north and they had a much more defined autumn.

"Suit yourself," Emil said. He rose and went inside the top without another word. It was an act that Lester Ray knew was designed to get under his skin. To just walk off like that. Emil was so jealous of him and Sheila he could hardly stand it. A man pushing fifty, and he was jealous of Lester Ray, and that made Lester Ray feel kind of good. He sat there, absorbing the sun, thinking of Sheila.

"I like the way you talk," she had said to him. They were drinking beers—longneck bottles of Jax—out of a metal cooler she kept in her dressing room.

"How do you mean?" he said. "How do I talk?"

"You know. Tough." She looked away and then back at him. "Like Alan Ladd or something."

"Who the hell is Alan Ladd?" he asked.

"You never heard of Alan Ladd?" she asked incredulously. "You know, the movie star."

"I never went to many movies," he said. "There was no picture show in Piper."

"You're kiddin. You never saw *Shane?*"

"Oh, yeah, I saw that one," he said. "I hitched up to De Quincy Springs and saw that one. Was that Alan Ladd?"

"Oh, come on. You're shittin me. You know that was Alan Ladd."

"No."

"Well, it was. It was Alan Ladd."

"I don't talk like that guy," he snapped.

"Okay, okay. I didn't mean it as an insult, for God's sakes!"

He took a long drink of the icy beer. He sat there looking at her, admiring her. There was no imperfection at all that he could see. Her eyes were like windows to another world, one that was freely erotic, inflaming. She sat on the stool in front of her makeup dresser, facing him, leaning back against the dresser. She wore the overlarge man's work shirt and white panties, her long legs bare. He could see the narrow strip of white covering her crotch. She ran the tip of her index finger around and around the lip of the bottle, watching the progress of her finger. She looked pensive, sad.

"What's the matter?" he asked.

"Nothing," she said, "nothing's the matter." She sighed.

"Okay," he said, after a minute of silence.

"Bad things have happened to me, Lester Ray," she said. "And I have this . . . this depression, which is like having the blues but about ten times worse, and it just comes over me when I don't even expect it, when there's no reason for it, and it weighs me down like something physical, like I'm really sick or something. You know?"

"Don't think about the bad things," he said.

"God, Lester Ray, I don't have to think about em, I don't even have to remember em, but they're there all the same, inside me, like they're eatin me up from inside." He didn't know about that kind of thing, she thought. He couldn't know, because he was too young, he hadn't lived enough. "My family was rich," she heard herself say. "I come from a rich family. I always had everything I wanted. I was happy. I know what happiness is. I married a boy from another rich family, a boy that I met at the country club, you know? I had this huge wedding, with all these bridesmaids, fourteen of em, I'm not kiddin you, and flowers, you wouldn't believe the flowers, white orchids everywhere, and I wore my grandmother's wedding dress, studded with pearls, with this humongously long train. My husband was so handsome, and we were happy." She kept running her finger around and around the rim of the bottle.

"What happened?" he asked.

"Whattaya mean, what happened?"

"You're not married to him now, are you?"

"What? Oh, no, of course not," she said.

"Well, what happened, then?"

"You ask too many questions, Lester Ray," she said. "It's none of your business what happened."

"Then why're you tellin me all this, then?" he said.

"I don't know. I don't know why I'm tellin you. All I know is that Emil came along one day, and it was like he took me out of a raging, icy cold sea and laid me in warm, heated blankets."

"Emil?!" he exclaimed. Something began to dry up inside his chest. He felt disconcerted, confused. What was she saying? Why was she bringing him into this? "What are you talkin about?" he asked.

"I had been in Europe. Touring. They don't treat dancers in Europe the way they do here, Lester Ray. In Paris people look up to you, they think of you as an artist. I used to drink a lot, wine, people over there drink wine all the time, with every meal, even with breakfast, for God's sakes. 'Give me two croissants and a carafe of red wine.' So I drank a lot, and a lot of whiskey, too. And gin! When I played London—I danced before royalty, Lester Ray, and it was so exciting—I could have floated all the way back over here just on the gin I drank. It's not as strong as the gin over here. You have to drink more of it."

"Are you tellin me you were a drunk? Because I know all about that kind of thing."

"No. No, I'm not sayin that at all. I was never a lush, Lester Ray. I mean, I always knew when to quit. The life of a dancer in Europe is exciting, that's all I'm saying."

"Why'd you come back over here then?" he asked. "To this?" He gestured around at the dressing room, the tent.

"I told you. Emil," she said.

"You fell in love with him," he said.

"No, not that. I never said anything about 'love.'"

He looked long at her, his eyes slits. Furrows of concentration across his brow. "I don't know what in the hell you're talkin about," he said, "do you?"

She stood up. "You don't have to understand, Lester Ray. Get out, now. I need to get ready."

He sat there in the sunshine after Emil had abruptly left. Thinking of Sheila. There weren't many minutes of the day that he didn't think of her. He didn't know if he believed her about dancing in Europe. What did he know about the world? She was certainly beautiful enough to have danced before the royalty of Europe. The only other people he knew who had been to Europe were some old guys who hung out at Saddler's, drinking beer, who had been over there during the war, so he didn't know much about it. Did she mean that Emil had come over there and gotten her and brought her back? She didn't want to tell him all that part. Warm heated blankets my ass, he thought.

Sheila knocked heavily on the door to Emil's trailer. It was after midnight and the rides and shows had finally shut down and everything was quiet. The popcorn smells, the greasy food odors, still lingered. Emil opened the door and pale yellow light spilled out, illuminating her clearly. Emil saw at once that she was drunk. She held a jelly glass half full of whisky. She mounted the first step, a little stoop, and he stood in the doorway, blocking the way.

"Where're you goin?" he asked.

"I'm comin in," she said.

"I hope you're not mixin pills with that stuff again," he said.

"Get outta the way, let me in," she said. Her tongue was thick. Her makeup was blurred and smeared. Black tear tracks were visible on her cheeks.

He stepped back, gave her room to come in. She staggered slightly as she came through the door. She was wearing a silk robe, green with a yellow flowered pattern, tied in the front. He sat back down, where he had been reading the Savannah newspaper when she knocked. The air in his trailer smelled of garlic and parsley. She had not even known parsley had a smell until she started hanging around with Gypsies. There were icons—saints, the Virgin, Jesus—painted on slabs of wood and mounted on the walls. The first time she'd seen the inside of his trailer she'd asked sarcastically, "Where do you think this is, Heaven?"

"No," he'd replied.

"Don't it give you the heebie-jeebies to have all these pictures of dead people around you?"

"Not at all," he'd said. "They're a comfort."

Now she looked around at all the icons. She could smell coffee, too, and she could almost taste the coffee he made: rich and thick, strong, with chicory, very sweet. He leaned back in his easy chair, one socked foot over the other. His boots stood by the chair. He clasped his hands behind his head, elbows out. He was wearing button-front, flared jeans, a T-shirt. His belly was flat and hard. "Well?" he said. When she didn't answer him, he said, "What's on your mind, Sheila?"

"Nothing," she said, "I just wanted to see you."

"A social call?"

"I thought I might sing for you," she said.

"Sing for me? Since when?" He'd never heard her sing. In the years he'd known her he'd never even known she sang. "So what are you gonna sing? It's not my birthday, so don't sing that. It's ain't Christmas, so don't sing 'Jingle Bells.'"

"You're an asshole, Emil, you know that?"

"Yeah, so they tell me," he said. "What's this singing shit? Somethin new in your act?"

She took a drink from the glass. It looked like undiluted whiskey. She was already pretty drunk. "No, I was gonna sing just for you, but now I wouldn't piss on you if your pants were on fire."

"Good. I can do without the pissing and the singing." He could tell from the pattern on her cheeks that she'd been crying. "What you been cryin about?" he asked. "Your little stud-boy get mean on you?"

"He's not my little stud-boy. He's a nice boy. A good boy."

"I agree," he said. "So, what's wrong then?"

"I don't know," she said, "I don't know what's wrong."

"You're feelin all guilty and shit, I guess," he said. "I told you to leave him alone, I told him to stay away from you."

"I don't feel guilty, for Christ's sakes!" she said. "It just happened."

"Bull-shit. Something like that doesn't 'just happen,' and you know it."

"It's somethin special," she said.

He sighed. "Look, Sheila," he said, "I don't care how or where you get your kicks, and I know it is 'special' for him. I mean, how many fourteen-year-olds get to fuck somethin that looks like you? You still got your looks, even if you are an old drunk." He paused for a few seconds. "But I don't want anything happenin that interferes with the smooth runnin of this outfit. I've got to be accountable to old man Freeman, and if you get busted for foolin around with a minor, giving him booze and reefer and everything else, then it's not only gonna be your ass but mine, too! Everything'll all of a sudden open up, the stag reels and everything, and we all might be facin some serious jail time. You better give all that some careful thought."

"How'd you know about the reefer? Did he tell you that?"

"I didn't know. I was just guessin. But I know now, don't I?"

"He didn't even know what it was," she said. "He didn't even know who Alan Ladd is."

"Alan Ladd? Why should he know who Alan Ladd is?"

"Everybody know who he is, right?"

"I don't give a shit about Alan Ladd," he said, "and I guess Lester Ray doesn't either."

"But . . . well, never mind." She took another long drink from the glass. She didn't even frown. She might as well have been drinking Kool-Aid, for all it burned her. She was numb to it. Deadened to it from all the years of it.

"You know, Sheila, a lot sooner than you want it to, that booze is gonna start tellin on you. And when you start losin your looks, what are you gonna do then?"

She straightened herself up to her full height. She tried to look him in the eye but her own eyes were vague and unfocused. "I'll be beautiful until the day I die," she said.

"Maybe," he said, "but not stripper-beautiful. Lose your body and you're finished."

"You would take care of me, wouldn't you Emil?" she said in a little girl's voice. Her eye makeup had made large black circles around her eyes, making her pleading comical, like a cartoon raccoon's.

"Sure, baby. I'll take care of you," he said.

"I need somebody to want me," she said.

"Lester Ray wants you, doesn't he?"

"I need everybody to want me."

She loosed the ties in front and let her robe fall open. She was naked. She posed, almost losing her balance. "I still got it, sweet sugar daddy," she said.

"Yeah," he said, "you still do."

"I bet sweet sugar daddy wants a round-the-world, doesn't he? Huh?"

"That would be real nice," he said, unbuckling his belt, unbuttoning his jeans.

MRS. MCCRORY WAS ANGUISHED. She was losing the colors and contours of the physical world. As though everything, including her, was melting into a puddle, a liquid that could take no shape of its own. Sometimes she could see the things around her with great clarity, but most of the time it was as though she were looking through smoke or fog. Something was terribly amiss: she never saw or heard any birds anymore and she worried that they were gone. (Because she was asleep, she was unaware of the flocks of sparrows and pigeons and crows that descended on the grounds at night. They pecked among the trampled sawdust for dropped peanuts and kernels of popcorn, spilled Cracker Jacks and tossed away butt-ends of hot dogs, hardening and stale.) There was something in her mind she couldn't quite grasp that made it logical that there were no birds, something she should have known and could probably recall if she concentrated on it long enough, but before she ever got there her thinking would charge off in another direction, jerking back and forth and changing course randomly and haphazardly like a runaway wagon on a steep, rocky and uneven hillside. She would get agitated. Her hands would shake and she would cry. For long periods she would just lie around and cry, with no clear idea at all of what, specifically, she was sad about.

"I want you to smoke this," Lester Ray had said to her. He had propped her up on the edge of the bed, sitting up, with his arm around her shoulders.

"Lester Ray, you know I don't smoke cigarettes," she'd said.

"This is a different kind," he'd said, "it'll calm you down, mellow you out."

So he'd taught her how to draw on the wrinkled, fat hand-rolled cigarette, not anything that ever came out of any cigarette machine, she knew that. He instructed her how to draw the smoke in deep and then hold it for as long as she could. It burned her throat. It smelled like oregano and rosemary and old incense, a scent that she realized she'd forgotten, that had lain buried with everything else, her entire life that she'd lost any memory of. Sometimes it seemed as though she had just been born, created out of thin air just in the last minute, and before she realized it she'd already forgotten that minute, too. Her life had slipped away, evaporated. It might as well have never existed. The most frightening thing of all was that she was not sure that it had. She had no way of knowing.

As she let the harsh, sweet-smelling smoke fill her up she began to feel relaxed, soothed, and suddenly her thinking was remarkably lucid. She did not know when exactly her mind had snapped open, only that it had, and she was on a bed in a house trailer and the young man standing there in front of her was not just this vague, strange form that she knew only as Lester Ray, a combination of words that meant nothing to her and mystified her anew every time she remembered them, each time she associated them with the creature who would from time to time precipitately materialize before her. She knew him. She had a shared history with him. His name was Lester Ray Holsomback. And she was Imagene McCrory.

"Lester Ray," she said.

"Yes, ma'am?"

"Lester Ray."

"Yes, ma'am?" he repeated, puzzled.

He was smoking on the cigarette, too. He handed it to her and she sucked on it, trying not to appear greedy. She held it in her lungs like she was underwater. She was drifting. She wondered if she'd been drinking whiskey and didn't know it. She floated.

"Where are we?" she asked.

"We're in Savannah, Georgia," he said.

"Savannah, Georgia? What are we doing here?"

"Well . . ." She was different all of a sudden. It was as though the old Mrs. Mack, the one he had known ever since he was a child, had suddenly and without warning reappeared. He wasn't sure what to say, what to tell her. "We ran away," he said.

"Ran away?" she exclaimed. "Ran away?" She laughed merrily. "Lord help us!" She couldn't stop laughing. "We ran away from Piper. We ran away from that son-of-a-bitch Orville, and I ought not to say that cause I'm callin myself a bitch, ain't I?" She cackled.

"Yes, ma'am," he said, "we fixed up that old car and hightailed it out of there."

"Lord help us," she said again. They were both laughing now and couldn't seem to stop. After a while she got herself under control. His laughter trailed off, too.

"What is this place?" she asked.

"A carnival," he said.

"A carnival?!" she blurted, and that started them to laughing again.

"Yes, ma'am, we joined the carnival!"

"We joined the carnival!" she echoed. She looked around. "Where is that unfortunate-lookin little girl?"

"She's around. She's got her a boyfriend. Another midget."

"Well, good for her."

"Yes, ma'am," he said.

She seemed to be lost in thought for a few moments. Then she asked,

"Where's Orville?"

"Well, probably lookin for us," he said. "Don't you remember? He wanted to put you in an old folks' home and you didn't want to go, so you and me ran away."

"Yes, yes that's right," she said. "Did we bring Mrs. Wrinstine's cat with us?"

"No, ma'am."

"Well, and not her cow either, I hope," she said. She seemed to be slipping away again. "That little ugly girl turned into a boy, didn't she?"

"No, ma'am. She just got her some boy clothes."

He gave her the reefer cigarette again. She remembered how to do it.

When the smoke exploded from her mouth, she looked around again. "What is this place?" she asked again.

"Oh, you mean . . . We bought us a house trailer. We're travelin with the carnival."

"And we're in . . . where?"

"Savannah, Georgia."

"My, my," she said. She lay back on the bed then, her head on the pillow. She smiled at him. "You're a good boy, Lester Ray," she said.

"I try to be," Lester Ray said.

He sat on the edge of the bed and watched her drift off back to sleep. Just as he was about to quietly slip off the bed and away she opened her eyes. "Lester Ray?" she said.

"Yes, ma'am."

"I want to be awake when the fire comes again," she said.

"Ma'am? What fire?"

"You know," she said. "The fire of the Holy Spirit. God's love."

"Yes, ma'am," he said.

"You know about God's love, don't you, Lester Ray? Comin in fire?"

Lester Ray had never known that Mrs. McCrory was religious at all. He had never seen a Bible in her house and she had never talked about it before with him, in all those years. And Lester Ray had never been to church and Sunday school, except one time when he was in about the fourth grade, when he'd gone to a Church of God Sunday school with this boy he knew at school, Bobby Bobo, who had a fierce red and purple birthmark that covered almost the whole right side of his face. The preacher at Bobby Bobo's church promised a quarter to anybody who brought somebody new to Sunday school, so Lester Ray had gone with him and they'd bought a pack of Lucky Strikes with the quarter and split it, ten cigarettes apiece.

"Yes, ma'am," he said, "I reckon I've heard about it."

"Good," she said, "good," looking hard at him with her eyelids drooping. He watched her close her eyes again

LESTER RAY WAS SIPPING whiskey from a pint bottle, just outside the canvas flap that draped the doorway to THE STREETS OF PARIS top, when he heard the "Hey, Rube!" cry. It was late, the last show of the night, and he knew there were not very many men in there. He heard the "Hey, Rube!" again as he rushed inside. He saw the man who had a grip on Sheila, one hand rubbing one of her naked breasts, and he didn't hesitate. He ran over and grabbed the man's shoulder and yanked him back. The man spun around to face him. He was big, with a round, flat face, a day's whiskers on his cheeks and chin. A big belly. Stringy, dirty hair that sprang away from his head in looping, oily curls. "What the fuck?" he said angrily, and Lester Ray could smell the whiskey on his breath. He started toward Lester Ray. Lester Ray acted without thinking. He kicked the big man square in the balls. The man's mouth fell open with surprise and pain, revealing stained teeth, a tongue like a slab of liver, and he grunted and leaned forward, both hands going to his groin, and Lester Ray hit him with his fists, one, two, three, four times, alternating right and left, the man's head snapping back and forth, blood spurting from his nose and lower lip. The man slumped toward the ground, his eyes rolling back inside his head, and Lester Ray kept punching him, rapid rabbit punches as he fell. Lester Ray could hear the girls screaming, hear Sheila's voice, and he could think of nothing but the man's dirty hand on her breast and he was no longer reacting from instinct but from a violent and terrible fury that overtook him and inflamed him, scorched him. He began to kick the man, in the stomach, the ribs, then three times right in his bloody face. He felt huge hands on his shoulders, was pulled away, back.

"Lester Ray, stop it now," he heard the giant say. Bellarmine was holding him tight with one arm around his heaving chest. His breath was coming in gasps, each sharp intake of air like a sob. He was shaking all over. The man lay on the matted, trampled grass, still, not moving, his face a mass of blood, his torn, faded shirt stained with it. Lester Ray struggled against the giant's arm, trying to get back at the man on the ground. "Jesus, boy," Bellarmine said, "take it easy. You want to kill the guy?"

"Hell yes," Lester Ray grunted, panted, squeezing the words out, "I want to kill the son-of-a-bitch!"

"Hold him," Emil said next to them. "You all right?" he asked the girls.

"Yeah, okay," they chorused, shrinking back on the stage.

There were no customers; they had fled as soon as the fighting started. Emil knelt down next to the man on the ground. He shook him. "The bastard's not breathin," he said. He rolled the man onto his back. His arms flopped of their own dead weight. "Goddamit, Lester Ray," he said. He ripped his shirt open and put his ear against the man's bare chest. His skin was pasty pale, bloodless. "Goddamit, you've killed this motherfucker!"

"He was grabbin Sheila," Lester Ray said, "he was after her. He had no business . . ."

"But you didn't have to kill him, for Christ's sakes!" Emil said.

"He's pond scum," Lester Ray said.

"Jesus fuckin Christ!" Emil said.

"Are you sure he's dead?" Sheila said from the stage.

"You want to come down here and see for yourself?!" Emil growled. He looked around at all of them. Bellarmine had released Lester Ray. Malik had come in from outside. They all stood looking at the lifeless body on the ground.

Bellarmine said, "He was kicking him in the face. He probably drove the poor bastard's nose bone back into his brain."

Nobody said anything. After a few moments, Emil said, "Malik, tell everybody to shut everything down. Get all the marks off the grounds and out of here. Let's just hope this bastard doesn't have a family out there lookin for him."

"What are you gonna do?" Sheila asked.

"What do you think? Get rid of him." He stood there glaring at Lester Ray. "I ought to call the fuckin cops and give you up to em," he said.

"Well, why don't you, then?" Lester Ray said irately.

Emil gave a bitter laugh. "Because we're Gypsies, man. You think they'd stop at you? They'd be after us all, including your precious Sheila."

"Stop it, Emil!" Sheila said. She and the other girls had put on silky robes that shimmered in the bright spot lights which were still on.

Malik came back in. "Get some of the boys," Emil said. "Wrap this asshole in canvas and haul him out to some secluded spot on the beach and bury him in the sand. Deep. By the time anybody finds him we'll be long gone. And get somebody to put enough water on this blood to soak it into the ground." He looked at Lester Ray. "Ordinarily that'd be

Lester Ray's job, I know, but I got other plans for him."

"What plans?" Lester Ray asked.

"It ain't too complicated, boy," Emil said. "Tonight, right now, get hitched up and head out south. There's a state park, Frank Butler State Park, I think, or something like that, just south of St. Augustine, right off U.S. 1, pull off there and wait for us. We'll be along in a day or two. You got it?"

Lester Ray looked up at Sheila, where she stood on the stage. She nodded to him. "Go on," she said, "I'll see you then."

EVERYTHING HAD HAPPENED SO quickly—in such a furious, maddened rush—that he was almost to Brunswick—Mrs. McCrory asleep in the back seat—when it began to really dawn on him what he had done. He had killed a man, with his own bare hands. Taken a life. Something that was irrevocable, final, so that there was no going back, no second chance, no way to change it ever again. He couldn't even tell himself that it was self-defense, because he knew the man couldn't have really hurt him, he was older and out of shape. He wondered if the man had a family, a wife and children. He was a total stranger, his and Lester Ray's lives having touched, crossed, in a fraction of an instant, only a tiny moment, a mere tick on the clock of both their allotted times. And yet Lester Ray had held the man's life in his hands; it was like the man's grasp on Sheila was on Lester Ray's neck, squeezing the breath and the blood out of him, and he had to act to save himself, to save Sheila. A second was all it took. But it all already seemed vague and ephemeral, and faded, like an old dream that had unexpectedly reemerged.

He was remembering another recent time when he'd lost his temper and he knew he could have done damage that time, too, and that would have been against Emil. They were talking about Lester Ray's searching for his mother, whether or not he would ever find her. Lester Ray was tense, stressed. He had been crying some at night, something that he didn't want anyone else to know. Emil had seemed to guess it. At first he'd seemed calm, even compassionate.

"Lots of Gypsies winter in south Florida," he'd said. "Maybe she'll be there."

"I hope so," Lester Ray had replied. He had already thought of that.

Then Emil seemed to swell up, his mouth twisted, his eyes darting around the room and then back to Lester Ray. "Shit, boy," he said, "maybe Sheila's your mother, you ever think of that? Maybe you're fuckin your own . . ."

And Lester Ray had seen only white, had forgotten even who or where he was, and he had swung his fist, clipping Emil a glancing blow on the chin.

"Whoa, shit, boy," Emil had said, springing back and away from him. "I was only kiddin, man!" He rubbed his chin. He glared at Lester Ray. "You want some of me, boy, you just say so."

"Don't kid about that," Lester Ray had said, "or I'll kill you."

"Fuck," Emil had said, still rubbing his chin. "You would, too, wouldn't you?"

The old car's engine hummed. The mechanics at the carnival had practically rebuilt it and kept it in good shape. The car had been painted again, this time a bright yellow. It had reflecting mud flaps and a large chrome owl as a hood ornament, and two beaded pillows against the back window, except that now Mrs. McCrory was sleeping on one, her head gently swaying with the movement of the car. There'd been a thunderstorm earlier and mist hovered over the highway, the headlights like two tunnels into it, pulling them onward, away from the dead man whose bloody, battered visage Lester Ray did not want to recall. All he wanted to think about was Sheila. And his mother. But not both at the same time. He blinked back tears. He imagined that the fog was a curtain that would open and his mother and Sheila would both be there welcoming him.

ON THE MORNING AFTER Lester Ray left with Mrs. McCrory, there came a knock on Emil's door. When he opened it, he saw a tall, slight man smoking a cigarette. When she said, "Are you Emil Kirova?" he knew then it was a woman. Her hair was much shorter than his and she was dressed as a man, a white shirt and striped blue tie, dark blue gabardine pants, shiny shoes. She smoked ostentatiously like a man, as if she had practiced before a mirror like a teenager trying to be more grown up.

"Who wants to know?" he asked.

"I've been told that you're the big boss of this outfit, and I need to talk with you a moment."

"What about?" Emil asked. "And who the hell are you?"

She stuck out her hand. "My name is Millicent D. Roget, and I'm an insurance investigator for Boston Mutual Life. I'm looking for someone you may know, or might have known in the past."

"Who?" Emil asked.

"May I come in?" Miss Roget inquired.

"Sure," Emil said, stepping back. He motioned her inside. She was struck by the dimness of the interior, by the heavy, spicy odors in the air. It took her eyes a moment to adjust. Then she took in the icons on the walls. This man was a religious nut or a collector of old world art, one of the two, she thought. Or maybe both. She sniffed. She detected cooking spices, ginger and garlic, and the lingering scent of marijuana and stale tobacco. The inside of the little trailer was tight, crowded with just a couple of pieces of furniture. He motioned her toward a chair, the only one. He sat on the edge of the bed. There were no lamps on, the interior lit only by the muted sunlight that filtered through the small windows. Or portholes, she thought. The trailer was like a small, compact submarine. "How can I help you?" he asked when they were seated.

"I'll get right to the point," she said.

"Please do."

Sheriff Prudomme had called to tell her that the boy's father had finally come home. He had expressed no real surprise that his son was gone. He had told the sheriff that he guessed Lester Ray had gone looking for his mother, who had deserted them both when the boy was a baby. She was a Gypsy. The father said he told the boy she had gone off with a bunch of Gypsies. "I'm looking for an elderly lady named Imogene McCrory. I have it on good authority that she has been traveling with a tribe of Gypsies in the company of a young man."

"Familia," he said. "That means extended family. We don't run in tribes. You're thinking of Indians." He grinned.

"Family, then," she said, not smiling back.

He ignored her mispronunciation. "Why're you lookin for her?" he asked.

"The young man, allegedly searching for his mother, stole Mrs. Mc-Crory's car and kidnapped her, along with a fourteen-year-old girl. The police in De Quincy County, Florida, as well as the highway patrol in five states, are looking for them. At any rate, it seems the mother was a Gypsy, ran off when the boy was small, and now he wants to find her. I have to tell you, Mr. Kirova, I have it on good authority that a woman and boy matching their description have been traveling with your circus."

"It's not a circus, it's a carnival."

"Whatever," Millicent D. Roget said. There was very little air circulation in the trailer and she waved her smoke from in front of her face. "I want to find them before the authorities do. My company has an interest in proving that Mrs. McCrory is still alive, you see. They can put the boy underneath the jail as far as I'm concerned. But I don't want the old lady being subjected to the trauma of seeing the boy arrested. I understand they've been close in the past."

"How do you know he took her against her will?"

"She is not of sound mind, Mr. Kirova," she said.

"Well," he said, settling back on the bed, "there's nobody around here like that."

When she had smoked the cigarette down to a tiny butt, she looked around. He handed her an ash tray. She ground the cigarette out and immediately took out another. "I notice you are closing up here," she said, indicating outside with a wave of her hand.

"Yeah, it's the end of our season." Some of the trucks with the dismantled rides had already left. The tops for the oddities and the girly show, the stages and the bannerline, were broken down and folded on trucks.

"Where do you people go when you're not running around with a carnival?" she asked.

"If you mean us Gypsies, we go everywhere, all over the country. Hell, all over the world. No tellin where all. We put the show together again in March and start all over again."

"And where is this equipment stored until then?" She took out a chrome-plated Zippo and lit the cigarette.

"Various places," he said. "Look, Miss . . ."

"Roget."

"Miss Roget, I can't help you. You've got the wrong traveling show. Somebody told you wrong. You need to check out the others. Now," he stood up, "I'm kinda busy, so . . ."

"Of course." She stood, too. "You wouldn't object if I asked around among some of your people, would you?"

"No," he said, "help yourself." He knew none of them would tell her anything. Nothing would zip a carnival worker's mouth faster than some official-looking person coming around asking questions. Especially those who were Gypsies.

"I would have talked to them, anyway, you know." She paused in the doorway. "Mr. Kirova, I'm going to find her, sooner or later. And if I do, the police will find the young man. Lester Ray Holsomback. Doesn't ring a bell, huh?"

"No."

"He's going to be in a world of trouble when we catch him."

"Well, I wish you luck."

As she stepped down outside she said, "You wouldn't mind telling me where you're headed after this, would you? Where you're going?"

"Yes, ma'am, I would mind," Emil said.

"Why are you so secretive, if I may ask?"

"I ain't secretive," he said, "it just ain't any of your business, is all. I reckon that's the Gypsy way."

She smiled. "Well, bon voyage, Mr. Kirova," she said. He watched her walk off, stiffly and erect. She had missed them by less than twelve hours. If she was that close, the police probably were as well. She could follow him, but he knew that there were other carnivals in the area closing up for the season and she would probably check them out first, buying Lester Ray some time before she discovered—as she would—that most of them were going to the same place: winter quarters in West Palm Beach and Fort Myers, Florida.

15

PIPER, FLORIDA

JANUARY 1950

Mae Clair Belvedere Bean wrote on the pad and handed it to Minnie, "You're gonna need somebody to take care of you."

"Hah," said Minnie. They were sitting on the front porch of the PIPER TOURIST HOME, drinking coffee in the chill of the morning. Minnie's belly rested on her lap. She was still working at Saddler's, over the objections of Pearly, Gerald Saddler's wife.

"It ain't decent," Pearly'd said. "A woman don't show herself like that in public."

"Long as she can do the job," Gerald Saddler had replied.

Mae Bean rocked in her chair. She took the pad back. "I'm serious as a heart attack, Minnie Mouse," she wrote. She had taken to calling Minnie "Minnie Mouse." "That ere mouse is the only other person I ever knew name of Minnie," she'd written earlier.

Minnie read it and handed it back. "I can take care of myself," Minnie said. She sipped the hot coffee. Mae Bean made strong coffee, the way Minnie liked it.

Mae wrote again. "Yeah, but you gonna have a little crumb snatcher, too, right soon. What you gonna do then?"

"I'll worry about that when it gets here," Minnie said.

"What you need is a man," Mae wrote.

"You ain't got a man," Minnie said.

"I ain't got no rug rat, neither," Mae wrote.

"In my experience," Minnie said, "a man don't do anything but get in the way."

Mae laughed. "Hah!" she said. "That's the God's truth." She didn't bother to write that last. Minnie laughed, too. Mae wrote: "But you ain't got that way without a man, that's for sure."

That is certainly for sure, Minnie thought. Emil. It had to be Emil, it couldn't be anyone else. But he had no real connection to what she was carrying in her belly. He was not the father. Pure biology didn't make him the father. He was a stranger. And in those woods that day, when he had gone off and left her there, he had relinquished any claim on either her or her child, not that he would want one. Quite the opposite, she was sure. He would keep moving forever, and she would too, and it was a certainty that sooner or later they would encounter each other again and it was just as much a certainty that they would never see each other again. As far as she was concerned, it did not matter. She had forgotten even what he looked like. She would not even recognize him if she met him on the street. He was no longer real to her. She might as well have dreamed him.

All those things were true, and yet he had given her this living being growing inside her, this human who was already closer to her than any other person had ever been. Finally, she had encountered someone she could not run from, at least not in his or her present state. His present state. She knew it was a boy. Mae Bean had offered to get her cousin to drive Minnie over to De Quincy Springs to see a doctor, but she refused. (The only doctor in Piper was an old man, Dr. Taylor, who was semi-retired, who drank a lot of whiskey but still looked at sore throats and gave shots and wrote prescriptions.) She felt no need for a doctor. It was all very natural for her: she felt complete, one with the world. She and her baby were a unit, whole and perfect, complete and full. As though she were a new, fresh sculpture she was creating from the inside out, formed from artless stone from deep inside the earth. She felt that she was God, that this was what God was: simple, a love internal that needed nothing, no one, else. She didn't want anyone like a doctor touching her, violating her, diminishing what she thought she had finally grown to be, a person total unto herself.

Mae Bean wrote on the pad and handed it to Minnie. "Did you love him?"

"No," Minnie said.

Did I love him? Had she ever loved anybody? Did she even know what love was? She didn't think it was anything necessary to life. I've gotten along well without it so far, she might have said to Mae Bean. But she didn't. She sat looking out across the sandy street, thinly paved with light gray asphalt, potholes full of murky water. The street the house was on ran perpendicular to the highway. The house sat a block away from the cars speeding by—silently, to Minnie—on their way to the Gulf. There was no way anyone could see Mae Bean's sign, PIPER TOURIST HOME, unless they were standing in the narrow, weedy front yard, or maybe if they took a wrong turn and stopped to ask directions, or if they were having car trouble and looking for a mechanic. It was a two-story house, and Mae had her "studio," as she called it, on the second floor in the back, looking out over a grove of pine trees, where she wrote her poetry.

Mae Bean took out a Pall Mall cigarette and tapped it on her long thumbnail, which was painted the exact dark red of the cigarette package. (The shade of her fingernails clashed with the pink of her hair, making her hair look as though it might have once been red but had faded over time into its pastel hue.) She offered Minnie one and she took it, and the two women sat smoking in silence, rocking gently in the oversized wooden rockers that Mae furnished her porch with—a row of them, which seemed to be the only visible acknowledgment that the house was, indeed, intended to be a vacation house for tourists—sipping their coffee in the fresh, cool breezes that came off the Gulf sixty miles to the south.

Did I love him? Minnie sat pondering her relationship with Emil, the brief time they had lived together, traveled together. She had been fond of him; she had enjoyed being with him. The sex was good. Maybe that was enough to total up to a kind of love, she didn't know. Other people didn't seem to have a problem with knowing what love was. They just seemed to fall into it and out of it with ease without even thinking about it. "Did you love your husband?" Minnie asked. Mae was a widow.

"No," Mae wrote on the pad, "I didn't." She took a long drag off the Pall Mall, leaving dark crimson lipstick ringing the end, and blew the smoke softly toward the street, where the breeze picked it up and swirled it away. Mae didn't seem inclined to say anything else, to comment further. The women rocked, the chairs making faint squeaking noises on the boards of the porch floor. Minnie had no problem with the abrupt, short answer. She considered the "No" a quite sufficient response. She relaxed into the soundlessness that surrounded her, that had become a natural part of her world. Had she been suddenly able to hear the squeaking of the rockers she would have been startled by the intensity of the sound: it would have sounded to her like the feral cries of an angry, wounded animal.

MINNIE TOOK HER NOONDAY and evening meals at Saddler's Lounge. The cook was a porcine man named Alex Hardy, who was so fat that his eyes were only narrow slits in his bulging, balloon-like face. He was a huge man, and quiet. Like Gerald Saddler, he wore a white apron, but his was smeared not only with grease but with blood from the hamburger meat he was constantly forming into patties and flopping on the hot grill back in the kitchen, where they immediately began to sizzle. Alex Hardy never said anything, his hulking presence simply hovering about the place, peering out at the world through the squinted eyes. At any given time, it was difficult to tell what he was looking at. "He ain't right in the head," Gerald Saddler told Minnie, "he can talk but he just don't."

The close air in the bar smelled of bacon until just before noon every day, when it began to smell of seared red meat and onions, burnt grease, and stale beer that had been splashed on the floor and only cursorily mopped up by Alex, who was also the janitor. He swept and mopped during the hours close to midnight when the crowd would thin, leaving only the hardcore drinkers who were not distracted by the cleaning going on around them.

There was only one other employee of Saddler's Lounge besides Gerald, Pearly, Alex, and Minnie and that was a man named Earl Holsomback, who was the clerk in the package store and filling station that adjoined the lounge, that actually occupied one end of the long, concrete block building. Earl Holsomback was a slim man of medium height in his early forties. He wore his thinning, dark hair long, brushing his shoulders. He sat behind the counter listening to a country music station out of De Quincy Springs, sipping on a Schlitz that he kept hidden behind a cardboard display of spark plugs next to the cash register. He sold the six packs and snacks and pumped the gas for the beach-bound folks, kidding around with them, telling the boys and girls that they better watch out because the water was full of jellyfish and stingrays. And he would relate fictitious, sinister stories of the latest shark attacks. He even kept a shark's tooth that he showed people, urging them to rub their thumbs on the edge to test the sharpness. "Like a razor," he would say, "it'll rip flesh like a meat cleaver!"

"You like Hank Williams?" he asked Minnie one day.

"She can't hear you," Gerald said, "she's deaf as a post."

"Oh, yeah, that's right," Earl said. He motioned for her pad. "Do you like Hank Williams?" he wrote.

"Yeah," she said. "Back when I could hear him I did."

"Oh, sorry. I forget." He wrote "Sorry" on the pad.

"That's all right," she said.

Gerald handed Earl another cold Schlitz. Earl was not supposed to pull beers from the cooler in the store but get them at the bar so Gerald could keep up with how many he drank. Earl got every other beer from the bar. He thought Gerald didn't know he was doing that, but Gerald did; he had allowed for that in the salary he initially offered Earl when he took the job. "How come she talks like that?" he asked Gerald.

"She can't hear herself. Don't know how she sounds."

"You noticed how her eyes are funny?" Earl asked.

"Yeah. Can't miss that, Earl." Gerald laughed. He slung the damp towel he'd been using to wipe the bar over his shoulder.

"She's a good-lookin woman, too, ain't she?" Earl said.

"You might say that," Gerald said, "but don't let Pearly know I said so, now."

"Pearly don't give a shit," Earl said.

Gerald just laughed. It was late afternoon. Cigarette smoke hung in the air as though it were draped from the ceiling.

"Stung by a trouser worm, huh?" Earl observed, watching Minnie carry two beers to a back table. Her apron bulged in front over her expanding belly.

"You might say," Gerald said.

"Reckon her baby's gonna have eyes like that?"

"I don't know, Earl," Saddler said.

"I wouldn't mind gittin me some of that," Earl said.

"She's learnin to read lips some, Earl," Gerald said, "so I'd watch what I's sayin if I was you."

"No shit?" Earl said. "All right, then." He watched her come back and pass them. She sat on an empty stool and sighed. She swiped a few stray hairs back from her face. There were tiny drops of perspiration on her forehead. "Name's Minnie, huh?" Earl asked Gerald.

"Yeah," Gerald said. He moved down to get fresh beers for two men at the end of the bar.

Earl cut his eyes at Minnie. He held out his hand and wiggled his fingers. "Gimme that little note book," he said. She slid the pad down the bar to him. "My name is Earl," he wrote on the pad and slid it back to her. She read it. He could see no reaction at all in her face. She just looked tired. Then she looked up at him and smiled. "Hey, there, Earl," she said.

He nodded and smiled back. He saw through the front plate glass window that a car had pulled up out front at the pumps. He stood up, holding his Schlitz. "Scuse me please," he said, "duty calls."

She watched him go out through the package store. He had a stiff-legged, straight-backed gait, as though he wanted to appear taller. He was bald on top. He wore the rest of his hair long so that it hung down to his narrow shoulders like the fringe on a tablecloth. The sunlight outside was clear and radiant, even though the day was chilly. The lounge was overheated and her ankles were swollen. She had recalculated: maybe she was seven months. She had no idea what she would do when her baby came, she would figure that out when it happened. She saw no reason to consider changing the way she lived her life, day to day, place to place, the way she had always existed. She couldn't imagine any other way.

"I'm not running from anything," she had told Emil one day, "I'm chasin something."

"What?" he'd asked.

"I don't think I need to know that," she'd replied. "I'll know it when I find it."

"You're full of shit, Anna Maria, you know that?" he'd said.

"Fuck you."

It had occurred to her that maybe she'd found it, whatever it had turned out to be, inside her womb at that very minute, soon to be a breathing, thinking person, the first thing she would have ever produced, would have ever wanted or needed to produce for the indifferent and unloving world she traveled through, trying to keep from being touched and wounded by it. And it was not fair to the child, she knew. It was not possible to be fair to any other human being, no matter the circumstances. No matter how hard you tried. If she hadn't learned anything else in her life, she'd learned that.

Earl filled the car with regular Esso. It was a gray and white Pontiac with a snazzy sun visor over the windshield and fins on the back end. "Nice car," Earl said to the driver, a man traveling alone.

"Thanks," he said. "You got a men's room in there?"

"Round back," Earl said. There was a men's room in the lounge, too, but just for the hell of it Earl usually sent them around back to the grimy and odious one with the tilting toilet and the broken urinal covered with black, tarred canvas, a hand-lettered sign on it saying Do Not Use. Earl washed the windshield and then popped the hood, raised it, checked the oil. "Quart low," he said to the man when he came back to his car.

"I didn't ask you to check that oil, now did I?" the man snapped. He had on a tie, the knot pulled down and hanging in the middle of his chest.

"No, sir," Earl said, "we just give full service." He slammed the hood down as hard as he could. The man looked at the hood, then at Earl. "How much do I owe you, smart guy?"

"Three sixty," Earl said.

The man handed him four dollar bills. "Keep the change," he said and climbed back in behind the wheel. "Use it to pay somebody to clean up that filthy fuckin rest room."

"Why, thank you, good buddy," Earl said. The man scratched off so fast the car fish-tailed when it hit the highway and Earl could see the man wrestling with it, getting it back right, and Earl laughed out loud. "Fuck you, too, buddy," he said, "and thanks for the beer!"

Earl Holsomback had been born right there in Piper and had lived there, off and on, all his life. His parents had been old when he was born and had both died when he was a teenager. He had dropped out of school and taken a job in an ice house over in De Quincy Springs, running the big saw that cut the huge block of ice into small, icebox-size chunks. He had continued to work jobs like that—racking balls and sweeping out a poolroom; busing tables and washing dishes at a greasy spoon; working as a mechanics' helper; cutting right-of-way for the power company; running a country store (he'd been fired from that one for stealing from the till); being a driver's assistant on a beer truck, where he loaded and unloaded cases of beer. He and the driver enjoyed a free cool one that was often offered wherever they made a delivery, so by the time he went home he already had a good start on that evening's buzz. He lived in an unpainted frame house down near the river, close to the city dump, for which he paid rent of $10 a month.

Earl had never been married but he had had many girlfriends, mostly women he'd picked up in various beer joints around Piper and De Quincy Springs. Sometimes they would live with him for extended periods, a few weeks or months. He was a contented man, as long as he got a paycheck every Friday to buy beer and the next week's supply of canned sardines, Vienna sausages, potted meat, peanut butter, baloney, a loaf of white bread and a carton of Camel cigarettes. If he wanted something hot he would get him a catfish sandwich at a colored cafe a block from his house. He often wondered what more a man could want. He mostly wore cast-off clothes that he found in the city dump. Most of the furniture in his house came from the dump, too: an old iron bed and a mattress, found at different times, a perfectly good settee with just one small hole in the upholstery, a sofa missing two of its legs that sat on bricks, a metal kitchen table with the Formica surface worn down to nothing. He had found an ice-box—not a thing wrong with it—that some rich folks had probably thrown away just to get them a new one. He sometimes rode a bicycle around town; he had also, at different times, driven an old pickup truck, a motorcycle that made so much noise Deputy Al Lister had threatened to fine him if he didn't get it fixed or get rid of it. Even, on occasion, he'd ridden a mule that he borrowed from an old boy named Baby John who lived down the street from him. Currently, he was driving around in a decrepit old hearse that he'd paid a man fifty dollars for. He used it to haul old worn-out tires and batteries that Gerald Saddler paid him a little bit to haul off. He then sold them to Old Man Sims at his junk yard out on the edge of town.

Earl was intrigued by the pregnant waitress, especially her different-colored eyes. He'd never seen that before. He went out of his way every day to pass close to her in the lounge, to savor her face. He thought she was, even pregnant, one of the best-looking women he'd ever seen. Ordinarily he would have admitted she was way out of his league, but he had asked around and knew she was not married or at least didn't have a husband on the scene. She lived by herself over there in Mae Bean's rooming house.

And her being deaf fascinated him.

"She come in here one day right out of nowhere, askin me for a job in that squeaky voice of hers," Gerald Saddler had told him. "Where she comes from I don't know and probably won't never know, cause I just about wore out my fingers writin down shit for her in the first few days, and I don't do that no more unless I absolutely have to. You'll have to ask her all that yourself."

It didn't matter that much to Earl where she came from. He was just curious. He thought she had the skin tone of a foreigner. (Maybe she even had some colored blood in her somewhere, which made her even more appealing to Earl.) He wondered who'd knocked her up, how all that had happened, but he didn't have to know. He could just see that she was worn out and alone and lonely. And so pretty.

"A woman ought not to be by herself when she's got a baby comin," Earl said one day.

"Well," Saddler said, "it don't seem to bother her."

"It bothers me," Earl said.

"Well, ho, ho, ho, what the hell business is it of yours?"

"I make things like that my business," Earl said.

Saddler gazed at him, frowning. He swiped at the counter. Earl took a sip of his freshly opened Schlitz. After a minute Saddler said, "You better watch out, Earl, and that's all I've got to say."

Minnie was conscious of two sets of eyes watching her all the time when she was in the lounge, not counting the men who came in to drink beer and their women. Earl Holsomback, who was obviously not the brightest man in the world, contemplated her with such open longing that it was almost innocent. The other was Alex Hardy. Minnie only gradually became aware of his little beads of eyes behind the swollen, fleshy lids constantly fastened on her, when he was sweeping, or bringing cases of beer out from the back, even when he was in the little kitchen, which was separated from the bar area by a half wall. He watched her every move. She had the feeling that he was waiting for some sort of opening, that he would make some move on her, and she was preparing to refuse him gently, rebuke him, hopefully without hurting his feelings. Gerald had told her he was like a child. She had spoken to him but he just gazed back at her, his eyes, as much of them as she could see—which was a constricted little strip across the middle of his dark brown pupils— empty and expressionless.

He sometimes helped her bus tables and occasionally their hands would touch or he would accidentally brush up against her. Once he had paused and reached out his beefy hand and laid it flat on her stomach for a few seconds. She didn't mind it. She thought he was just curious about her pregnancy. Then he slid his hand up and touched the tip of her breast with his forefinger. It still seemed like a harmless, childish gesture. There was nothing sexual or menacing about it. She stepped away from him and shook her head. "No, Alex," she said, and she smiled because it was the way you would speak to a small child or a little dog.

He continued to touch her from time to time, and after too much of it she began to grow uneasy about it. She had not been afraid of a man since old Alexander Mossback Frill all those years ago, when she had learned that she could take care of herself. In the past, if some man made unwelcome touches, she would have kicked him in the balls or even punched him with her fist, moving quickly and dancing just out of his reach, or she would have thrown hot coffee in his face or hit him across the head with a beer bottle or a pool cue. But she couldn't dance and skip around now. She had a baby in her, grown almost into a person. She was awkward and slow. And she was protecting not just herself but that baby, too, and she carried it out in front of her, assailable and exposed, defenseless from the world. She would never before have cared too much if someone had gotten a gut punch on her, but now she knew she had no defense to that, no counter-strike because it would be too late. It was an opening up of herself that demanded even more trust than the opening of her legs to a man. She didn't completely trust anyone—especially a man.

These days, now weeks, that she'd been in Piper, it seemed to her that something threatening was always hovering just outside her peripheral vision. She couldn't identify it, but she knew it was there. It caused her relentless anxiety, interfered with her sleep so that she was constantly tired. Her legs hurt her all the time. Gerald Saddler allowed her to sit down as much as she could. "Maybe you ought to take some time off," he wrote on her pad one day. "I can't afford it," she said. She had started to worry about things like feeding the baby, buying it clothes, even getting it toys to play with. She knew nothing about taking care of babies and she worried about that. She felt nakedly vulnerable for the first time in her life.

"Have you figured out what you're gonna do?" Mae Bean wrote on her pad.

"No."

"Well, listen, I hate to have to say this, but I can't have any cryin baby livin in this place. I've got to worry about my other renters, my permanent ones," she said. Minnie had looked closely at her lips, trying to read them. She was getting better at it. But she still couldn't understand it entirely. Mae Bean wrote: "No baby living here."

"Oh," Minnie said. She had gotten the essence of it. She had never worried about places to stay in the past. She would just as soon crawl into a clump of roadside bushes to sleep. But she was being forced to change. And she was growing to resent it. She hadn't asked for this. All of a sudden her life was on course and she was no longer free. She fantasized about finding Emil, tracking him down, and flinging the baby in Emil's face. Flinging him. She was certain the baby was a boy. Maybe it's my ancient Gypsy fortune-telling gift coming out, she thought wryly, as if she could have ever escaped her Gypsy blood, her Gypsy soul.

One day she was bending awkwardly forward wiping off a table when she felt hands on her buttocks. She knew without turning around that it was Alex Hardy. She did nothing for a moment, hoping he would stop, but he didn't. His hands were large, and he cupped each cheek, hefting them, massaging them. "Alex," she said, "what the hell are you doing?"

She turned around. She was not alone with him, so she wasn't immediately alarmed. There were several men at the bar watching curiously and Gerald Saddler had turned at the sound of her voice to see what was going on. Alex's face was excessively broad, his cheeks round and pudgy. His lips were pursed, as if he were about to kiss her. Instead, he said (she was sure he said this as she read his lips), "Give me one of your eyes."

"Which one do you want," Minnie said, "the blue one or the green one?" She laughed.

He reached out then and grabbed her tightly by the shoulders and jerked her forward toward him. His fingers bit into her skin, hurting her. She was shocked more than frightened, because he had always seemed so gentle. "Stop it, Alex!" she said.

"Alex!" Gerald yelled from behind the bar. "Turn her loose!"

The big man pulled her to him, close, gripping her so firmly she couldn't move. His big soft belly was pressing against her harder one. It felt to her as if he were pushing her baby back inside her. Now she was scared, because the man's strength seemed inhuman. She saw his lips part, his heavy pink tongue protrude. He licked her across the nose. His tongue was warm, wet and slick, and his breath smelled like rancid bacon. She couldn't breathe. It felt as if he would crush her chest, squeeze whatever air she had left completely out of her lungs. His face was so close she could see the pores, the droplets of sweat, the dust of his new-growth beard, a tiny shaving cut with a smear of dried blood on it.

"That baby's mine," he whispered, "and I want that baby." She read his lips.

"Let me go!" she breathed.

"Alex! Listen to me, Alex," Gerald Saddler said. He pulled at the man's shoulders, but Alex held her tight.

"That goddam barrel of lard," Earl Holsomback said as he bounded into the room from the package store. He picked up an empty beer bottle from the bar and smashed it over Alex's head. The big man staggered, but he still held on to her. Earl grabbed another bottle and brought it down hard on the back of Alex's head. This one didn't break so he hit him again and then again. Alex's arms dropped to his sides and Minnie fell back and away from him, and Gerald caught her before she fell into the table. The big pale man just stood there. "You want me to hit you again, fat-ass?" Earl asked him.

"No," Alex said.

"What'd you think you were doin, Alex?" Gerald Saddler said, helping Minnie onto a chair.

"That fucker's crazy," Minnie said.

"He's got a fuckin hard-ass head, too," Earl Holsomback said.

Alex turned and walked calmly back into the kitchen. Gerald sat down at the table with Minnie. The other men in the lounge had turned back to their beers and conversations. "You okay?" he wrote on her pad.

"No," she said, "I'm not okay."

"He didn't mean no harm," he wrote.

"Shit, he said he wanted my baby. What the hell does he mean?"

"Nothing," he wrote.

"Shit," she said. She was just now getting her breath back. Her shoulders hurt where he had grabbed her, her chest where he had squeezed her. "Suppose he hurt my baby?" she said. "And what's the crazy fucker gonna do next?"

"He's alright," Gerald wrote.

"Hell, Gerald, if it was just me I'd kick his ass. But it ain't just me right now."

"Yes," Gerald wrote.

"'Yes'? What the fuck you mean by 'yes'? What I'm sayin is, you got to get rid of him. Fire his ass."

"I can't," he wrote.

"Why can't you? Listen, buddy, it's him or me, okay?"

"He is my wife's cousin," he wrote.

She knew, then, with a sinking finality. Either she was going to continue here with Alex watching her all the time, waiting, not knowing what he might do, keeping her in constant stress, or she was going to quit. But she had no place to go, and if she quit she would have no money to rent a place. Which eight months ago would not have mattered to her in the least. But now it did matter, and she hated Emil Kirova, hated him with a passion that surprised her with its depth.

"Then I quit," she said. She stood up and pulled her apron off and threw it at Saddler.

"Sit down. Just settle down a minute," he said.

She sat back down in the chair. Feeling lonely was unfamiliar to her. She did not need people. She owed them nothing and they owed her nothing. But now she felt the warm alien presence of her baby. She felt as helpless as the baby. Sometimes it was hard for her to believe that it was actually happening to her. She would wake up in the night and have to put her hands on her swollen belly to reassure herself that she hadn't simply dreamed it all. That's when she felt most alone, in those dark early morning hours of wakefulness, when she knew she'd never go back to sleep and would be tired all the next day, wearing her legs away for her meager salary and the ten-cent tips, sometimes just a nickel, that came her way.

"Here," Gerald Saddler said, setting a cup of coffee before her.

She looked at it, at the heavy white cup, the thick saucer, cafe-designed to withstand rough treatment. A thin wisp of steam curled up over the surface of the deep blackness—almost the exact shade of Emil's eyes— and then disappeared. She didn't want coffee. She didn't know what she wanted. She wanted to be away, on the road, headed to the horizon and whatever lay on the other side of it and she didn't care what that was or even if there was anything there at all. It was just away, removed from where she was at the moment. It was change, a longed-for transfiguration that she believed would give her her life back. Not knowing what lay on the other side of the permutation was what gave her energy, fired her existence, returned her to her comfortable role as misfit. Yes, misfit. She was not a mother. Being a mother was beyond her comprehension.

"That guy is an asshole," Earl Holsomback wrote on her pad and shoved it over in front of her. He sat down at the table with her. He was thin shouldered, hardly any chest at all. Today he wore a pair of faded overalls over a T-shirt that was grayed and thinned from too many washings. He took a package of Camels from a pocket on the front of his overalls and offered her one. She shook her head "no" so he took one out, stuck it between his lips and lit it from a book of paper matches. He leaned back and blew the smoke toward the ceiling.

"Thanks for lettin him have it with the beer bottle," she said. She concentrated on the movement of his lips when he answered.

"No problem atall," he said, "I been wantin to do that to the dumb motherfucker for awhile now." He grinned at her. He was missing one tooth in front, in the middle on the top, and his others were tobacco-stained. "Listen here," he said, "you can move in with me if you want to. I mean if you ain't workin and got that chap there on the way." He pointed to her stomach. She was getting much better at reading lips and she was sure she understood what he was saying, not missing more than a word or two.

But she hadn't expected him to say that. "No," she said, "I don't think so."

"Hey, I don't mean . . . like live with me," he said. "Not like a man and a wife, nor nothin. I just got this house I'm rentin, see, and it's got plenty of room, and I can get another bed for you and all, a whole different room. You can stay there till you get the baby and all."

"I don't think that's a very good idea, Earl," she said, "but I thank you."

"I mean, how you gonna pay rent at Mae Bean's place?"

"I'll figure somethin out," she said.

"I bet Gerald'd let you stay on here if you told him you changed your mind about quittin," he said.

"No," she said, "not long as Frankenstein back there is around. Once I say I quit, I quit." She sipped a little of the coffee. "Anyhow, Mae Bean has already kicked me out. She can't have no little baby cryin all night, she says."

"Well, all the more," he said. "If the baby's cryin gets to buggin me, I'll just go out for a few more beers."

"That's good of you, Earl. But I don't know."

"Okay," he said. "If you change your mind, just holler."

So she moved into Earl Holsomback's little house near the dump. Earl produced another bed from somewhere for her. She suspected he found it in the dump. It was wooden, old and peeling, the mattress sagging, but she didn't care. He established her in the living room of the little unpainted house, which from the outside looked abandoned, forsaken. She sometimes was nauseated because of the burning in the dump that produced a sickening, dead smell if the wind was right. Thank goodness it usually blew in the other direction, out over the river, away from the distant Gulf.

They sat at the dingy old Formica table in the kitchen with its three mismatched chairs. ("See here," he'd said, "one already for the baby!") He opened them both a cold beer and they lit cigarettes, two of his Camels. "It ain't much," he wrote on her pad. He waved his hand around to take in the whole house.

"No, it's fine," she said. "And go ahead and talk. If I can't understand, I'll tell you to write it down, okay?" It was chilly inside; she could see lines of bright winter sunshine through cracks in the rough boards of the walls. The house was like an old barn, but she had seen far worse in her life. She slumped in the chair: she couldn't sit completely up-right because of her belly. The baby surely was coming soon. That was a part of her that she would willingly relinquish, let go. She tried to feel those things that a mother was supposed to feel, those emotions that she knew instinctively she should feel, but they wouldn't come. It seemed to her that she was suspended in some sort of not-world, in a kind of not-time, away and separate from the normal progression of her life, which was a race to get nowhere and this was a time-out along the way.

"So when's at baby comin?" Earl asked. She was not looking at him, lost in her own thoughts, so he reached out and touched her hand and repeated it.

"So when's at baby comin?" He was jaunty. He seemed almost proud. It was as though the two of them—and the baby—were some kind of bloodless, negative reflection of a family, a twisted abstraction of one, all the elements there but not fitted together except in the most distorted and perverted way.

"Why?" she asked. "You gonna go out and buy a box of cigars?"

"I might just do that," he said. He grinned his gat-toothed grin.

"You're not the father, Earl," she said. She still did not know him well enough to know how to take him.

"Oh, hell, I know that. I'm just woofin," he said. "Listen, I been wonderin. You reckon that baby's gonna have eyes like yourn? Maybe one black and one brown this time?"

"I don't know." She took a long sip of her Falstaff. "It's called heterochromia."

"What?"

"This condition," she said, pointing to her eyes. "Heterochromia."

"That right? I didn't know that."

"My parents thought it was the curse of the devil," she said.

He cocked his head and peered at her. "You believe in the devil?" he asked.

"No," she said.

"I don't neither," he said. "I don't believe in much of nothin."

She planned to have the baby right there, on that old bed with its stained mattress and worn sheets. Earl didn't have a telephone, but he had promised he would go and get old Dr. Taylor for her if she needed him to. She hoped she wouldn't need him. She knew enough about the process of birth. She'd heard women talk, and one of the women in the Gypsy camp when she was with Emil had had a baby and the other women had tended to her, had done everything, and Minnie had watched the entire time. It seemed pretty simple, though she knew it was painful and could be dangerous both for her and the baby, and Earl's house was far from sterile, but if Jesus had been born around donkey shit and dirty hay and did all right she supposed her child—her boy—could, too. She would just get it over with and see what happened, what came about, and whatever it was she would accept it and go on about her business. She wasn't frightened. She was not afraid to die, she knew that. Death was natural, just another way station, but an important one—maybe the most important one—because death finally set you completely free. With death you no longer had anything left to lose.

Earl drank a lot of beer and ate almost exclusively out of cans. Minnie grew to like sardines on soda crackers, one of Earl's favorites, and he liked to fry Spam on a hotplate that someone had given him. "Some woman from the Baptist Church," he said. "Bitch. Like I'd want anything she could give me."

"You took it, didn't you?" Minnie asked.

"Hell yeah, I took it. But she was still a bitch."

Minnie suspected that he stole half the provisions they ate, maybe all of them, some of them surely from Gerald Saddler's little store and filling station. She didn't care, as long as they didn't get caught. She'd grown accustomed to living on stolen goods when she was traveling with Emil's familia, had become very adept at distracting a roadside store owner while some of the others helped themselves to the soft drink cooler and potato chips and candy. Every early morning on the day they were breaking camp the men would go out before daylight and come back with chickens, turkeys, sometimes a pig, ears of corn and buckets of peas and collards, peaches and pears, a watermelon or two. They would be long gone before anybody even missed anything.

ONE DAY, WHEN MINNIE was sitting on the little stoop that served for a front porch, taking the afternoon sun, a man came along the sandy road on a mule. He stopped the mule in front of the house and just sat there looking at her. She shaded her eyes from the sun so she could see him. He was more a boy than a man, but he was big, a soft heaviness that reminded her of Alex Hardy and she thought oh, no, not again. He wore overalls without a shirt, even though the day was cool, and sat astride the mule using a wrinkled croker sack for a saddle. He said, "I'm gonna sang in church." He lifted his index finger in the air and waved it around. She could not read his lips and had no idea what he'd said. She just nodded. He said again, "I'm gonna sang in church."

"Okay," she said.

He flicked the cotton rope bridle and the mule resumed its plodding walk on down the road. When Earl got home she told him about it.

"Oh, that's just Baby John," he said. "He ain't real bright."

"Who is he?" she asked.

"Lives with his parents down the road. Rides that mule up and down all day cept on Sundays and Wednesday nights when he goes out to one of these little country churches around here that's havin a dinner on the ground or some kind of refreshments. They tell me he'll get up in church and sing. Right in the middle of somethin else, the preacher's sermon even. He'll just stand up and go to singin and can't nobody understand what he's singin, but they just let him sing till he quits and sits back down. Everybody knows him. I reckon he figures he's earnin his dinner or his cookies or whichever."

She had been watching his lips attentively. She said, "I think I got all of that. Sounds crazy as hell."

"It is. He is. He's harmless, though. He ain't like that fuckin Alex if that's what you're thinkin," he said.

"It crossed my mind."

"Well, don't worry about him. He'll stop and speak to you, tell you he's gonna sing in church. He always says that."

"Yeah. I couldn't tell what he was saying."

SHE LOOKED IN THE front like a watermelon that was about to split open. Earl tried to do for her, but she didn't want him doing much. She let him fix her meals. Every now and then he'd bring her a hot sandwich from Saddler's or the colored cafe. But she didn't seem to want for much. He sensed that she wasn't about to become beholden to him any more than she could help. She was the first woman who'd stayed with him for more than a week who didn't nag him about how much beer he drank, even though all of them drank just as much or more. She was the only really beautiful woman who had ever given him the time of day and he figured she'd probably be the last. She didn't complain about the cold shower, didn't tell him he ought to fix up the place. She didn't care about the things most women in his experience cared about. She wore the same old stretched-out-of-shape T-shirt every day, just the shirt that hung low like a short dress because she couldn't get any of her shorts to button up around her. Her underpants wouldn't stretch enough either, so every now and then he caught a glimpse of her dark snatch, which just about drove him crazy. The two white dresses she'd worn to waitress in—swapping them out one each day while she washed and dried the other—wouldn't fit her anymore either.

She had a rich, fecund musk about her, like an overripe pomegranate.

Her skin had taken on a radiance, a buttery sheen, her breasts heavy with sustenance. Her face had filled out more, her features softer, not as sharp, though her eyes were still as alert and piercing as ever. The baby kicked and moved within her, and she called him and let him put his hand on her stomach and feel it. He couldn't believe you could actually feel the baby moving around in there.

THEN ONE DAY SHE said it felt like the baby clenched every now and then, like especially strong kicks.

"It's starting. I know it," she said.

"I can drive you to the hospital in De Quincy Springs in the hearse," Earl wrote on the pad and held it before her eyes. She was lying back on the bed, propped on pillows, staring up through the rafters.

"I won't go to a hospital," she said.

He made her move her face toward him so she could see his lips.

"You can lay down in the back," he said.

"No."

"I don't know what to do," he said.

She smiled. "You don't have to, Earl. I do."

"Shit," he said. He had bought a pint of Cabin Still blended whiskey. He poured a little into his beer and poured her a straight shot in a jelly glass. She downed it. "You want some more, just holler," he said.

She had started to sweat, beads of it popping up on her face like large summer raindrops. She moaned and then jerked and cried out. He poured her some more whiskey. "I can go get Dr. Taylor now," he said.

"No, not yet. I'm gonna be okay." She cried out again. He could see the power of the pain registering in her eyes. She was gritting her teeth, her hands grasping and bunching the sheets like claws.

"Shit," he said, "I'm gone."

IT TOOK THE OLD doctor a long time to get to the door. Earl pounded on it with the side of his fist until the door was yanked open. The old doctor stood there. He had on wrinkled, stained khaki pants and a white shirt, striped suspenders loosed and hanging down. Gray whiskers nearly an inch long protruded from his chin. His pale gray eyes seemed to be floating in yellowed water.

"You got to come quick," Earl said to the old man.

"Come quick where?" the doctor asked. "Don't be comin here . . ."

Earl interrupted him. "My . . . my wife is havin a baby. We need you." Earl didn't know if the heavy whiskey smell was coming from the old man or from inside his own nostrils.

"Since when have you had a wife, Earl Holsomback? You ain't stopped drinkin long enough to take on a wife," the doctor said.

"Never mind about that," Earl said, "come on!"

The old man stepped back and started to push the door to. "I don't deliver babies any more," he said.

"You got to," Earl said.

"I don't 'got to' do anything, young man," he said.

"But I'm scared," Earl said.

"You're also drunk," Dr. Taylor said.

"Not any drunker'n you are," Earl said.

"You got a point," the doctor said. He laughed merrily, as if Earl had told a joke that struck him as unexpectedly funny. "Wait a minute. I'll get my bag."

When the two men pushed through the door of the ramshackle house they pulled up short at what they saw. In the bed, the sheets below her waist bloody and rumpled, Minnie was propped upright on three pillows holding a red, shriveled baby to her breast. The baby was still covered with blood and mucus. She was smiling broadly. The baby mewed like a kitten, then let out a shrill, high-pitched cry.

"Well, hell, Earl," Dr. Taylor said, "if I'd known the baby was already here I wouldn't have hurried so."

16

Fort Myers, Florida

Winter 1964

They were sitting in Emil's trailer in the large winter camp outside Fort Myers. There were carnival people there from all over the country, many of them Gypsies. Lester Ray was certain that he would finally find his mother, or at least find someone who knew her, someone who would tell him something about her.

"You need to get rid of that car," Emil said to Lester Ray. "It's the only physical thing that really ties you to whatever you're runnin from back there. Or at least I think it is. I don't know shit about you, Lester Ray, and I don't want to know, okay."

"All right," Lester Ray said.

"And that old woman. You can't get rid of her, so I don't know what you'll do about her. And that dwarf seems to be Yak's problem now. If they catch up to you all Mrs. McCrory'll have to do is go home . . ."

" . . . to an old folks home," Lester Ray interrupted.

"Well, she's 'old folks,' ain't she?" Emil asked. "Listen, you know old Diego? He knows a place over in LaBelle, buys old cars for junk. They take em and crush em flat and stack em up. Thousands of old stacked up flattened out cars out there, seems like acres and acres of em, far as you can see. It'd take a man a hundred years to find a car out there. They sell em off for scrap. Get Diego to take care of it for you, okay?"

"All right," Lester Ray said.

"And listen, I've been meanin to ask you this. Do you have a birth certificate?"

"I don't know," he said. Sometimes he thought he hadn't been born anyway, that he had just appeared, out of the air, not born of a woman at all, and all the foggy, shadowy memories he had of his mother were not really memories at all, just nebulous projections of his own longing. "My daddy always told me my birthday was February 20."

"Because if you don't have a birth certificate, maybe you ain't even legally a person. I know a lot of Gypsies like that. There's never been any record of them anywhere."

"So?" Lester Ray asked.

"So why don't you change your name, just become someone else? Easy enough."

"Can you do that?"

"Yeah, sure. If you ain't really got a legal name, then you don't have to go all legal to change it. Just call yourself somethin else. Bingo, that's it." Emil was staring at him. "Then the guy the cops are lookin for just disappears."

"The cops?" Lester Ray exclaimed. "You mean for that guy in Georgia?"

"No, no. They won't find that fucker for a long time. Nobody'll connect him with us. The cops are lookin for you for stealin that car and kidnappin that dwarf and old lady. And there's some insurance investigators on your trail, too. Lookin for the old lady."

"Shit," Lester Ray said. He had been tormented by his memory of the man he'd beaten to death ever since they'd left Georgia. He remembered the stranger's strength, then suddenly his stillness as his vigor left his body. He'd never even imagined actually killing a man, and now he'd done it. "Maybe that man had a wife and children," he said to Emil. "Shit," he said again. He dreamed about the incident all the time, his sudden explosion, the power in his arms that surprised even him. He could hardly even allow himself to know, to realize, that the man had had his own life, a life that Lester Ray had destroyed in a moment of purblind rage. He shuddered when he thought of it, tried to push it from his mind.

"You just have to live with it," Emil said. "You were protecting Sheila. You did what was right. I know you didn't mean to kill him, but those things happen, Lester Ray." He looked at the boy, at his tilted head. The boy looked as if he were searching the floor for some sort of answer. "We all do things we're not proud of, Lester Ray," he said. That cool morning: driving away and leaving Anna Maria in that clearing, battered and bleeding. Running away from a bunch of bigots, scared of them, telling himself he was protecting his people, all the old people in the kumpaniyi, knowing at the same time that he was a coward. That morning, he was a coward, pure and simple. "We never forget things like that, son. We just have to learn to live with them." He sighed. "So you get rid of the car. Change your name. Don't claim to have a damn thing to do with those other two."

"Mrs. McCrory? I couldn't do that. I've got to take care of her."

"Well, she might have to be given up to those insurance folks, not much to be done about that. Nobody can do anything to her but put her in that old folks home. Hell, she won't know the difference, not as far as I can see."

"No, I ain't doin that," Lester Ray said.

"Suit yourself." Emil lit a cigarette. He sat for a moment inspecting the glowing end. "So," he said, "what do you want your new name to be?"

"You're full of shit," Lester Ray said. He laughed. Sometimes it was hard to tell if Emil was serious or joking. But he started thinking about names. He'd never particularly liked or disliked "Lester Ray." It had never really mattered to him what his name was, because he hadn't given it much thought. He'd always assumed his mother had given him that name and let it go at that. His mother!

"How'll my mother find me if I've got a different name?" he asked.

"Find you?! You think she's lookin for you? Shit, Lester Ray, she ran away from you, she doesn't want to find you!" Every now and then, when Lester Ray said something like that, Emil was reminded that the boy was only fourteen years old. Almost fifteen.

"How do you know? Maybe she's changed her mind."

"Don't be a fool, boy. I'm talkin about right here, right now! I'm talkin about fuckin cops!"

"All right! I hear you. Never mind," Lester Ray said. "I reckon there are school records," he said, after a minute. "I used to go to school."

"School records for Lester Ray Holsomback," Emil said. "Not for

... well, whoever. And you don't have a drivers' license."

"I don't know about this," Lester Ray said.

"We'll all swear you've been with this kumpaniyi since you were a baby. You can take a Gypsy name."

"Like what?"

"Well, like anything. Any name you've ever really wanted?"

"Maybe Billy."

"Billy?" Emil exclaimed. "That ain't really Gypsy. But you can take a Gypsy last name. You can take Kirova if you want. Let Billy be your American name."

"Your name?"

"Yeah. You can always be my cousin, or somethin. There's always a lot of Gypsies in the same kumpaniyi with the same name. It's vitsa. Extended family. All Gypsies are kin to each other."

"Billy Kirova, huh?" Lester Ray said. He liked the sound of it. He didn't really know why he'd said "Billy." It had just popped out. Billy the Kid. Billybob. Why not? He wasn't at all sure about the "Kirova," though. For the first time in a long time he thought of his father. The old man had probably not even missed him, had been drunk ever since he'd left. But he had his father's name: Holsomback.

THE ENORMOUS CAMP, EAST of Fort Myers just off Florida Highway 884, was a virtual city. Hundreds of house trailers, with many tents erected for housing. Some were set up as cafes, grocery stores, and produce stands, with vendors selling prepared food: hamburgers and hot dogs, souvlaki, huge iron pots of gulyás. The aromas of cooking wafted over the whole camp all day, and people sold clothing: the mufti of the Gypsies, cowboy boots, hats, scarves. Dancing went on day and night. The music was highly improvised: maybe two or three old men with fiddles, playing at breakneck speed, or individuals and groups singing a cappella. There were guitars, and many of the dancers, both men and women, used hand percussion. Most of the dancers were men, but the women and girls were the most showy and bright, with multi-hued skirts and petticoats whirling in a shimmering mix of color.

Many of the freaks from the oddities shows mingled with everyone else: midgets and giants; two girls (Cissy and Marie) who were joined together at the hips, facing in opposite directions, who moved about with a jerky, crablike motion (they were cheerful and friendly and sometimes joined in the singing); a woman named Myrtle who had four legs, two normal ones and two smaller, shorter, childlike ones growing out from between her legs; numerous people cursed or blessed with odd skin resembling an elephant's or an alligator's. There were ape-like geeks as well, several from different shows who all claimed the title "The Missing Link" or "The Wild Man (or Woman) From Borneo," who were all friends, glad to see each other again after a long season on the road, and who seemed, in the winter camp, easy with everyone and as sociable as everybody else. There were people whose bodies were covered in tattoos or excessive growths of hair. Nobody paid them any especial mind.

And the countless Gypsies were from all over the country. Lester Ray went around with the photograph of his mother, showing it to people, asking them if they knew her. Occasionally someone would ponder for a while, even admit to a shadowy, misty remembrance of someone who looked like that, who had eyes of two different colors, blue and green, but none could recall when or where they had known her or whatever had happened to her. Several of the older people said that yes, they remembered her, but they had never really known her.

Finally, one old woman sitting on the running board of a pickup truck, stirring a pot of gulyás, said, "That looks like Anna Maria."

"You know her?" Lester Ray said, a sudden, expectant heat seizing him, arresting his breathing.

"I knew her one time, yes," the old woman said. She was as lean and bony as a pile of twigs, her thin gray hair pulled severely to the back of her head and tied with a black ribbon. Her skin was as rough and brown as boot leather.

"You knew her? I mean, is she dead, or what?" The old woman raised her eyes to his. Her eyes were as gray as the smoke that escaped the fire beneath her pot. Lester Ray steeled himself for the answer.

"I don't know," she said, "it was a long time ago."

"It wasn't that long ago," Lester Ray exclaimed, "she's my mother and I'm just fourteen, so she was alive fourteen years ago, I know that."

"Don't raise your voice to me, little boy," the old woman said.

Lester Ray wanted to tell her harshly he wasn't any "little boy," but she was a link. He didn't want to sever contact with her. "I'm sorry," he said. "I didn't mean to raise my voice."

"You need to learn respect for the old people," she said.

"Yes, ma'am," he said.

She continued to stir the stew using a large metal spoon with a worn, wooden handle. The warm, spicy smell of the gulyás tickled Lester Ray's nose. He was hungry. He realized he'd forgotten to eat, but he didn't want to eat. He didn't want to ever eat again until he found his mother. He knew in his gut that the answer was here, in this odd, singular place that passed for a permanent town in the Gypsy world, and he only needed to keep going until he found it. Whatever it was. If she was dead, she was dead, and there was nothing he could do about that. But he would know. The dizzying drifting inside his chest could settle and be still. The elusive, lost cornerstone could finally be placed, to make him whole.

"What's your name, boy?" the old woman said, without looking at him now, her eyes focused on the stew. The pot sat on three bricks and the fire beneath it was all but gone, only slightly glowing bits among the ashes.

"Billy Kirova," he said, without thinking about it at all.

"Well, you come back to see me, Billy Kirova," she said. "I'll see if I can find out anything for you."

"All right," Billy said. "Tell me your name."

"Olevia Kaslov," she said. "I'll be right here. I ain't goin nowhere."

ONE NIGHT THEY THREW a fifteenth birthday party for Lester Ray. ("Or maybe it's the first birthday for Billy Kirova," Emil joked.) Mrs. McCrory, who was in a particularly lucid period along about then, made a cake. The giant Bellarmine was there, along with Joe-Josephine and Margie, the world's fattest woman, with her servant Careem, who pushed her around on her cart. Old Saartji came, and Yak with V. M. on his arm, both of them dressed up in the formal clothes they danced in. Other Gypsies: Malik and Diego and Artago, who brought girlfriends. Several people from other shows encamped nearby showed up: Chang Woo Gow, the dog-faced boy, whose face was completely covered with hair; a woman named Yo-Yo Mama, who had been born without arms but who could keep two yo-yos going for hours with just her stumps; an old Gypsy man named Shakadorius who played a little accordion and had a tiny monkey on a leash, who danced and held out its hand for coins. And Sheila was there, along with Angie and Judy. There was plenty of wine and beer and everybody got pretty drunk.

Sheila gave Lester Ray a big smack on the cheek and he grabbed her and turned his face and kissed her deeply and long on the lips, to the hoots and laughter of the other partygoers. Everybody laughed but Emil, who watched silently and moodily from the edge of the crowd. It seemed incredible to him that Lester Ray's mother likely was Anna Maria Spiro-sko. He hadn't allowed himself to give it much attention while they were on the road, but now he couldn't get it out of his mind. He had started to look for her himself, asking around among people he knew. One old man said he vaguely remembered seeing her years ago: "Pretty girl," he said, "different-colored eyes. She was sick, as I recall."

"Sick how?" Emil asked. "What was wrong with her?"

"I don't know that," the old man said, "and I might not even be right about her bein sick. It just kinda sticks in my mind."

"What happened to her?"

"I don't know that, either," the old man said.

And Emil, of course, could count. Lester Ray must have been born some time shortly after the last time he saw Anna Maria, so there was a possibility—a thin possibility—that he could be Lester Ray's father. That Lester Ray might be his son seemed even more improbable and unbelievable than Anna Maria's being the boy's mother. He and Anna Maria had been together only a matter of six months or less. He had always used a rubber. He was certain she had not been pregnant when he had left her that day. But how could he be certain? That day! Seeing Lester Ray and thinking of what he did to Anna Maria that day froze his heart and caused his brain to turn to slush. He couldn't believe his life which had been so patterned and evenhanded had taken this totally shocking, completely unexpected turn. It was as if that cowardly thing he'd done fifteen years ago was now taking its revenge.

But of course all this was not true. It was too inconceivable. He was letting his guilt over what he'd done power his imagination. It was easy enough to deny when he was busy, when he was traveling, running the carnival. He was just letting this remote contingency slip up on him during this lull, take him by surprise when his defenses were down. He was hoping that Lester Ray would find her so she could clear all this up and ease Emil's mind and conscience. But she might not even admit to Lester Ray that she was his mother, much less anything else. But what if she told Lester Ray what Emil had done to her, abandoning her in the woods like that? The shame would be too much to bear.

He watched the boy with Sheila. Lester Ray was only her boy-toy. Lester Ray didn't know that and he was headed for a crash. Emil could tell from observing him, talking to him, that he was in love with her, her almost twice his age, and she hadn't had the decency to discourage him. He remembered vividly when he, himself, was fifteen years old: he could go at it five, six times in a row. Hard for Sheila to give up. It was even rumored around that she was sharing him with the other girls, but Emil knew Sheila well enough to know that was untrue. Not a chance. All three of the girls were hustling at the strip club on the beach—Manny Lou's, it was called—they were hooking, and Lester Ray—he needed to start thinking of him as Billy—was bound to find out about it. Surely, some-where inside his mind, even at fourteen (now fifteen), Lester Ray sensed the truth about Sheila. He knew that Emil had been with her, because Emil'd told him. He knew that Sheila wasn't any virgin, that was for sure. But maybe he hadn't realized she was a hooker, that he was sharing her with every john with twenty bucks who came along. And had been, ever since he'd known her. Well, we all have to grow up sometime.

"Hey, I like the name 'Billy,'" Sheila said. She had worn a plain black dress to the party, tight, showing her figure. She looked good. She took a drink of wine. "I used to be married to a guy named Billy."

"You were married?" Lester Ray exclaimed.

"Hell yes," she said, "hasn't everybody been married?" She was drunk.

"Well, not me," he said. He was drunk, too, but not nearly as drunk as Sheila.

He had begun to notice that Sheila drank all the time, more and more since they'd landed here in south Florida. Sometimes when he came into her trailer in the late mornings she would be sitting forlornly, staring into space, her makeup from last night smeared, her mascara bleeding down her cheeks like sooty tears. "Make sugar a little drink, will you, hon?" she would say, pointing to the bottle of vodka sitting on her dresser. He would pour a couple of inches of vodka into a glass smudged with fingerprints, with lipstick on the rim, and hand it to her, watching her hand shake as she raised it to her lips and drank it down in one gulp. Sometimes her hand was shaking so bad she had to use the other hand to steady it, bringing the glass to her mouth like a little child with a cup of milk.

It was familiar to him, of course. He had done the same thing for his father, rarely hard liquor but beer and sometimes wine. If you wanted to be a serious drinker it was something you had to do. My morning medicine, his father had called it. Lester Ray had grown up with it.

One morning he realized how weary he was of that whole scene. "You look like shit," he said to Sheila.

"Honey," she said, "I just woke up. I'm a workin girl."

"But you're so beautiful. Why do you want to do this to yourself?"

"Do what to myself? I just didn't bother to take off my makeup before I went to sleep. Is that a crime?" She pouted at him and held out the glass for more. He sloshed another shot into it and handed it back to her.

"No," he said, "it's not a crime." He found another glass and poured himself an inch of the clear liquid. He sniffed it; it smelled like kerosene. "What the hell is this?" he asked.

"Vodka," she said.

"No, it's not," he argued. "It's white lightning. Moonshine." He sipped some of it. "Shit," he said, "this stuff must be a hundred and fifty proof!"

"It's the good stuff, baby," she said. She relaxed back onto the bed. She had on a light blue nightgown, so thin he could see her nipples and the dark shadow of her pubic hair. The room smelled of musty bed linens still reeking of sleep, the aseptic scent of the raw whiskey, the pink, cloying sweetness of her makeup table.

"Where'd you get it?" he asked.

"Some fellow," she said.

"What fellow?"

"Goddammit, Lester Ray, drop it, okay?! I've got a fuckin headache. What the hell difference does it make where I got this shit?"

"Okay," he said, "I was just curious, I guess."

"Well, don't be. It ain't healthy."

"Yeah," he said, "I remember about the cat."

"What fuckin cat?"

"You know, the one that curiosity killed?"

"Ha, ha," she said. "Very funny." She lay back on the bed and massaged her forehead with her free hand. Her eyes were closed. He sat gazing at her, taking all of her in. He was convinced that a more perfect body did not exist in this world. He had an erection just looking at her.

Sheila was drinking a lot of wine at the birthday party. She and Angie were flirting with Bellarmine Fagafoot. "Come on," Sheila said, "take it out and let us see it? Okay? Please?"

"I promise I won't touch it, Mr. Fagafoot," Angie said. She was plumper than Sheila or Judy, shorter, her hair dyed a copper red, her pubic hair dyed to match it. (Sheila had told Lester Ray about the dye.) For the party Angie had put on a white blouse and a red and gold Gypsy skirt.

"Go look at Yak's, if you really want to see something," Bellarmine said.

"Oh, hell, we've seen Yak's. Everybody's seen Yak's, in those movies."

"I've never watched those movies and don't intend to," Bellarmine said. "Excuse me, if you will." He held up his empty cup to indicate that he was going for more wine. He moved away with his long, loping strides, like the tallest of trees moving through a forest of bushes.

There were two old, dark Gypsy men with long, gray handlebar moustaches, one who played a violin and another a guitar. A lean but hefty man with large, dark eyes and his hair cropped close, sitting astride what looked like a wooden box, empty and hollow, which he played like a drum with his fingers and palms. An old woman in a long orange dress with a purple artificial flower in her hair sat on a stool between them; she sang and chanted to the music in some old lost language while the dancer moved in a blur of red. They had laid down planks on the sand to make a sort of dance floor, or stage. The dancer was a young woman, long black hair tied in a ponytail, intense black eyes. She wore all red: a tight silk skirt that flared just above her knees into pleats and lace; a formfitting bodice, red lace lined with the same silk of the skirt. She wore high, lace-up black boots with nails driven into the soles to make taps, so that the stomping of her feet made what sounded like small explosions. She wore castanets on her fingers, clicking them together over her head in time with the movements of her feet. She whirled, twirling her skirt, moving faster and faster as the music grew more frantic. The old woman grew more shrill. Many of the people watching made squeals of approval that sounded almost like catcalls. She danced several times, and when she was finished, to enthusiastic applause, Yak and V. M. did what Yak claimed was a traditional Gypsy dance from the Rodolphe Mountains of Bulgaria, called "The Bear Dance." He had taught it to V. M. They jumped around grunting and then dropped to all fours and crawled before they hopped back up, repeating these movements over and over until the song was over. The older Gypsies present said they had never heard of such a dance and had certainly never seen it before. Some of them were offended and those who were drunk got angry about it.

The party went on late into the night. Along about 3 A.M. Emil made a toast, with all the drunk partygoers shouting "Hear, hear," or "Chin, chin," or anything that came into their minds. Emil's toast was: "Here's to Billy Kirova, who was born on this night, this very night, and forevermore will be known to the world by that name! May he be blessed and protected from tsinifari, the evil spirits of the world, and forever remain pure and unashamed!" Drunken cheers and applause—heard over most of the camp—erupted then, disturbing the sleep of people and prompting several cries of "SHUT THE FUCK UP" to come bursting forth from the otherwise silent, sleeping darkness around them.

"ORVILLE," MRS. MCCRORY SAID, addressing Billy, "your grandfather is dying, and we have to go to him." She was trembling, trying to stand.

"I'm not Orville, Mrs. Mack," Billy said. The old woman's eyes seemed focused inward; they appeared to Billy to be empty of anything but pain. He knew her father could not still be alive. She had never spoken of him before. "Just take it easy, okay? I'll take care of it." He put his arm around her shoulders and pulled her against him. Her shoulder was only fragile bones covered by a thin layer of skin. He could feel the heat of her though his shirt.

She could see Orville sitting right there beside her. Or maybe it was that boy. She didn't know where she was, only that she was a long way from home, a long way from her father, and she could see him in her mind's eye, lying there in that big old four-poster bed just crying like a baby, with soft little sobs and tears running down his old rough cheeks. He knew he was dying and she wanted to tell him she loved him. She had lived eighty-three years on this earth and she had never known there were people who were born without arms. That ugly little boy turned out to be a little midget girl, and will wonders never cease? They had changed Orville's name to Billy, but that didn't make him not still Orville. Her sister would eat all her pudding real fast and then want half of hers. She liked to eat slow and savor the sweetness on her tongue. But she would lose half of what she had left, and that wasn't fair, so she would go and tell her father, except he had gotten old and feeble and was in the bed, dying. She saw her sister, sitting there smirking at her, holding two empty bowls. "I'm going to tell," she said. Her sister said, "Go on and tell. That old man's already in hell!" It made her cry. "You go to hell!" she said to her sister.

"What's that you say, Mrs. Mack?" Orville asked her. Where did he come from? I wasn't talking to him. He hasn't even been born yet. There was a rose bush in the corner of the yard, and Uncle Paul would tie his horse there and the horse would stick his head over the fence and eat some of the roses. She and her sister thought that was funny. This boy, Billy, I don't know him. What's he doing? "Get away from me," she said, slapping at him.

"Hey, wait a minute, Mrs. Mack," the boy said, "this is me."

"Me who? I don't know you!" She kept pushing him away. Then she forgot about him. I will go into my kitchen and polish my silver. Mr. McCrory, Winston, will be home from his office soon and I want things to look nice. Would you look at that? That damn jay is still after Mrs. Wrinstine's old cat, and I hope he kills it. That cat is useless and sorry.

Like her milk cow. She can't keep that cow fenced up and the old cow gets out and eats bitterweeds and ruins her milk, makes it not fit to drink, and Mrs. Wrinstine tells me she can't figure out how that cow keeps getting out and I tell her it flies over the fence and she says she ain't in any mood for joking. I'm living in a house trailer now. I never thought in all the world I would live in a house trailer. It might be parked in the middle of New York City, for all I know. This boy takes care of me. He's over there right now heating up some soup for me. Why, knock me over, that's Lester Ray Holsomback! What's he doing here?

"What are you doin here, Lester Ray?" she asked, and he turned around and smiled at her.

"Well, I'm glad you're back," he said. "I thought your mind had left you."

"It did. I'm stupid," she said.

"You're not stupid, Mrs. Mack, don't say that."

"I can't remember anything from one minute to the next," she said. Boys in school who couldn't remember anything were stupid. They got whopped on the head with a ruler and had to sit in the corner. They never got to be the ones to beat the chalk dust out of the erasers after school. One time Louis Hornberger begged and begged to do it, so finally Miss Fannie let him, and he went all around the outside of the school leaving white eraser prints on the brick walls. Mr. Hitchcock took his belt to him. Then all of a sudden Mrs. McCrory's mind went blank. It was like she was drifting inside a giant bubble, and there was no sound. She looked around her. She had no idea who this boy was. She couldn't think of what the thing he had in his hand was called. She had a faint notion that whatever was inside it was "food," but she was not sure what the word meant.

"I want to sleep now," she said, and she was not at all certain who had said it or what the meaning of it was either.

MILLICENT D. ROGET AND Cassandra Birmingham were sitting in a roadside restaurant called Peter Piha's Seafood Cafe in Crystal River, Florida. They had taken U.S. 19 out of Tallahassee on their way to south Florida, following the curve of the Gulf Coast.

"All indicators point to Fort Myers," Miss Roget was saying, slicing her broiled scallop. "Here is the scenario as I see it. The boy didn't really steal the car. The old woman gave it to him. And she's running away to avoid the nursing home, which her asshole of a son wants to put her in, that is if he is so unlucky as to discover that she, his own mother, is still living, which I would lay odds is true. Hate to disappoint the shithead. All we've got to do is find her alive. And the boy's mother was a Gypsy, and he's lookin for her. We have discovered that the biggest concentration of Gypsies in North America is now down near Fort Myers. So there you have it."

Cassandra Birmingham swallowed a mouthful of fried shrimp. "Yeah," she said.

"I really think they'd been with that carnival we inspected outside Savannah. I found a midget girl who fit the description of the one the boy took from Piper, ugly as a dead thorn bush. She denied it all of course and told me her name was Salome Diderot. It's hard to tell how old those people are. They all look like bizarre little children, don't they? She may have been fourteen, but she had mighty big tits. Who knows? Anyway, I'm not concerned with her."

The two women ate in silence for a minute or two, and then Cassandra Birmingham said, "Well, you know what I always say."

"What's that, sweetheart?"

"To find a Gypsy, go where the Gypsies are!"

BILLY WENT SEARCHING AGAIN for the old woman Olevia Kaslov. He found her sitting in the same place, on the running board of the pickup, stirring something in the pot over the open fire. Billy thought that must be what she did all day every day.

"Hello, boy," she said.

He watched her put the spoon down on a piece of newspaper and begin to strip meat from the bones of a boiled chicken, dropping it into the gulyás. "This one's got fish in it, too," she said, "lots a peppers. You hungry?"

"Yes, ma'am," he said.

"Got corn in it, too. You like corn?"

"Yes, ma'am." He sat down cross-legged on the sparse grass. She stirred the gulyás, peering intently into the iron pot. The fire was so hot Billy had to scoot back. He watched her as she stirred, being careful and precise as if she were performing some delicate surgery. She had two gold teeth in the front of her mouth and her cheeks were caved in. Her pointed chin curved upwards, making Billy think of a witch preparing some kind of magic potion. He could see her brown scalp through the spare gray threads of her hair, pulled back tightly to the ribbon at the back of her neck. Her worn green and gold skirt was stained with grease spots and flecked with ash from the fire. She wore an old blue sweater in spite of the warm weather. It was unraveling at the cuffs and the neck. She continued to stir, as if she had forgotten he was even there.

"Ma'am?" he said.

"What's that?" she asked, concentrating on the contents of the pot.

"You said you were gonna see if you could find out anything about where my mother might be, remember?"

"Course I remember. I ain't dumb."

"Well?"

"You just a child," she said. She looked at him, her eyes the color of rain clouds. "Where's your daddy?" she asked.

"I ain't got one," Billy said.

"Everybody's got a daddy, child," she said.

"I mean, I don't live with him anymore. I'm not a child. I'm out on my own." He wanted her to quit calling him a child. He was getting impatient. "Do you know where she is, or what?" he asked.

"There you go, gettin huffy again."

"I just want to know," he said.

"Yes," she said, "I know where she's at. I can send you right to her. Better yet, I can take you right to her."

"When?" he said. "Where?"

"Hold your horses," she said.

"Just tell me . . ." He stopped. He could tell by the look on her face that she was not going to tell him any more and that she would take him, if she were going to, in her own good time. He was trembling inside. He could not quite grasp that he'd finally found his mother. If the old woman was telling the truth. If she wasn't just crazy. He couldn't believe anything until his mother was right there in front of him and he could reach out and touch her and know she was real. But he was close. He could feel it in the quivering of his blood.

"When?" he asked again.

"In the morning," she said, "ten o'clock, be right here."

17

FLORIDA

SPRING 1950

Minnie had no idea what to do with a baby. She had thought maternal instincts would tell her how to go about it, but she was wrong. She didn't have enough milk. ("Maybe it's your diet," old Dr. Taylor had written on her pad, "beyond that, I don't know.") They had to put the baby on warmed cows' milk almost from the start. It was a little boy, and that seemed to make it even worse for her. Every time she looked at that tiny penis she felt alienated from the child. She knew it was not that she didn't love the little boy, because she did, as much as she'd ever loved anyone or any thing. What she felt was, she told herself, not good enough for a mother. She wanted to love her child. She tried to remember her own mother, her own love for her family, but she couldn't. She was unable to experience it again, even in recollection. It seemed a foreign concept, an intrusion.

Earl Holsomback pretended to be the father of the child, though anyone who was even a quasi-regular at Saddler's Lounge knew otherwise. Not one time in his hardscrabble life had he ever even dreamed he would one day have a wife as beautiful as Minnie and a child to show the world what they had produced together. But she would not marry him. She would not even listen to his pleading, his reasoning.

"A boy needs a father," he said. He had become accustomed to turning his face directly to her and speaking as plainly as he could so she could read his lips

"He has a father!" she snapped. "How the hell else do you think I got knocked up, huh? Unless I'm the Blessed Virgin, and I sure as hell

ain't that! So shut up about a father." She could see the hurt in his face.
She softened toward him. She said. "You already are his father, Earl, in
a lot of ways."

"But it ain't permanent," he said.

"Nothing's permanent, Earl," she said, "trust me on that."

So he had to be content just living with her, even though they were not
really living together, at least not in the way he intimated to his buddies at
Saddler's or to anyone else who would listen to him. He would even tell
perfect strangers at the gas pump about his beautiful wife and his baby.
But she continued to sleep on her own bed in the living room and she
made it clear that it would stay that way, despite his constant pleading,
his clumsy endeavors to seduce her, his sulky, besotted depressions, even,
on one occasion, a drunken attempt to rape her which she successfully
fought off because he was so drunk.

"What do you want to name him?" Earl asked one day a couple of
months after the baby was born. Up to then they had just referred to
him as "it" or "the baby."

"Why don't you name him?" she replied.

"I can't rightly claim no kin to him," Earl said.

"You're his father, Earl, come on. You can name him if you want
to."

Earl thought about it. He decided to name the boy for his grandfather
and his father.

"Lester Ray," he told her. "That's his name, Lester Ray Holsomback."

"Fine with me," she said.

The house was drafty and dusty. It stank of dirty diapers and rancid
food. The closets had a dry-furry mice smell. The house cried out for a
good cleaning, but it wasn't something she'd ever done and wasn't anything she'd ever be willing to do. The longest she'd lived in one place,
other than her time with the Frosts and at the Cedar Key Hotel, had
been the months with Emil in his trailer, and the old women in the
familia cooked for them, washed their clothes, even cleaned the trailer.
Now and again Earl made a feeble gesture toward cleaning the house:
washing up dishes, sweeping out with a ratty old broom that left bristles

all over the floor. (Once, when they had let dirty dishes accumulate into a huge pile in the sink, Earl carried the whole mess down the road and threw them into the dump.) He was good to wash the baby's diapers in an old galvanized tin washtub on the narrow back porch, which had to be done frequently. He used the same tub to wash their few clothes. He hung everything out to dry on an old wire back fence, overgrown with honeysuckle. It was Earl who got up in the night to heat the bottle and feed the baby. Minnie couldn't hear the baby's crying. Earl didn't want to wake her up. He hummed a tuneless chant to the baby as he rocked him in a rickety rocker he'd retrieved from the dump. From the same source he'd gotten an old iron baby bed with one side that went up and down, and they made a mattress from pillows.

"That dump's my Sears and Roebuck," Earl said. "Folks throw away good shit."

Minnie grew restless just hanging around the house looking after the baby. As spring came on, the house became hot and airless, and it seemed even more so in the thick silence she lived in. Sometimes, the soundlessness seemed to swell like a hollow bubble in her ear.

"I want to go back to work at the lounge, Earl," she said one day.

"Hell, no wife of mine is gonna work," Earl said. "Your place is here with the child."

"Hah!" she said. "In the first place, I'm not your wife, and in the second place, you don't tell me what my place is. Clear?"

"This is my house," he said, "you supposed to do like I tell you to."

"Earl, are you a complete and total damn fool?" she asked, laughing.

"You ever hear of common-law marriage?" he asked smugly.

"Now I know you ain't got good sense," she said.

She felt the old familiar feeling of tendrils coming out of the floor and wrapping around her ankles, trying to hold her there, wherever she was, wherever she had to get away from. It was the sure sign that she needed to move on. And she knew she would. And probably soon. She would sit for long hours holding the baby, looking at it. The little boy looked nothing at all like Emil Kirova, and sometimes she wondered if she hadn't gotten mixed up, confused one place with another, one man with another, jumbled time all around. Looking back, her life seemed to her one long string of people, their faces all blended together, melting into one another. She realized that she had no solid reference points for so much of her life, because places seemed, in her memory, too often no different from each other. She had the sensation of mostly passing by, without slowing, without stopping. Of not absorbing anything. Of not allowing anything to invade her and capture her.

Now she felt trapped, interrupted. Blocked. The days hung on her like wet clothing. The child was a mystery to her, a conundrum she could not grasp, could not even reach. She held its warmth to her breast but she was not connected to it. As the days passed, the child seemed to grow further and further away from her.

"We can take it to work with us," she said to Earl, "you can keep it in the package store."

"How you know Gerald'll take you back?" Earl said, pouting.

"He will," she said.

"Why don't you get Mae Bean to keep it?"

"Hah!" she said.

So they took the baby to work with them and kept it in a peach basket behind the counter in the package store, where Earl could watch it as he sipped his beer. Gerald quickly rehired Minnie because he didn't have a waitress for the late shift, which his wife Pearl had been working. Pearl made over the baby, cooing and baby talking to it. Earl brought him out from time to time and set the peach basket on the bar so the customers could look at it. Earl told Alex Hardy, when he came near it, "You touch that baby I'll cut your fat guts out!" So Alex kept his distance. He stayed mostly in the kitchen, anyway, since Minnie had returned. Gerald had told him that one more incident like what had happened with Minnie would get him fired in a minute, cousin or no cousin.

Sometimes Minnie's eyes would grow so accustomed to the dim lounge that when she went out into the sunshine she would be blinded for sometimes as long as five minutes. That had never happened to her before Lester Ray was born. It was as though her entire physical makeup—not just the droop to her boobs and the stretch marks she tried not to notice—had been severely altered. She would have to sit on a bench outside the door for a while, both deaf and blind, helpless, until her eyes adjusted to the light. She felt terrified until her sight returned. Every time it happened she thought that would be the occasion when her sight refused to come back. All this contributed to a nagging sadness, an uneasy despondency that wouldn't go away.

After one of those episodes, when her eyes had slowly adjusted themselves to the high, bright sunlight, several of the regulars came out, laughing and joking and poking one another on the arm. With them was Pearl Saddler, who had just gotten a Kodak box camera and several rolls of film for her birthday. Three of the boys posed for her, making faces, holding up their beer cans. One of them, a man named Harold Tucker, said suddenly,

"Hey, take Minnie!"

The boys and Pearl came boiling toward her, all chattering at once. Minnie, who had not heard or seen them had no idea what they were doing.

"Yeah, take a picture of us and Minnie," one of the others said.

"Hell, you could sell one of her to a magazine!"

She picked up enough to catch on. "Oh, no, you don't want to do that," she said.

"Come on, Minnie," Pearl said. "Pose. Come on."

"No."

"Come on. Please!"

"Well, okay," she said and stood up. She had a feeling of giving up something substantial, of acquiescing to something far more important than a simple photograph. She didn't want to do it. She was willfully forcing herself.

"Take your apron off," one of the men said.

"Take it all off," Harold Tucker said, and everybody laughed.

Minnie removed her apron. She held her hands out to the side. "Okay," she said, "here you go." She felt exposed, unprotected. Almost as if the camera were a loaded pistol.

"No, wait a minute, I want you to pose!" Pearl said. "Hey, Harold, where's your car?" Harold drove a dark gray Chevrolet.

"Parked around there in the shade," he said, "why?"

"Go get it. We'll make a picture of Minnie sitting on your car." They all thought that was a great idea, so Harold went around the side of the building and drove his car out to the front. Minnie was wearing a pale, yellow dress. They helped her mount the bumper and sit on the front fender. She crossed her legs. Pearl had her lean forward, her elbow on her knee, her chin propped in her hand. She was limply passive, allowing them to arrange her as though she were no more than a mannikin. "Smile at the birdie," Pearl said, and the camera clicked.

Minnie couldn't remember ever having had her picture made before. It was disconcerting. She didn't understand why it disturbed her so. The idea of briefly stopping the progress of time, capturing that split second of eternity that would exist as long as the picture did, made her uncomfortable. There was something unnatural about it, as though it somehow was not meant to be, as though that fraction of time was now gone, was now history, and was meant to stay history. She had heard or read of primitive people who were frightened of cameras, fearing that photographs stole something of their essences and captured parts of their souls. She felt some of that. She knew the camera had taken her image, her visage—that she looked at in the mirror every day. A developer would transfer it to slick paper and make it into a picture, so that it was no longer merely a reflection of her but something that was her but that existed separately from her. It was almost like someone stealing her shadow.

"Why don't you take a picture of the baby," she said to shift the focus. She rarely called Lester Ray anything other than "the baby."

So THE WEEKS, EVEN months, went by with a stultifying sameness and a deadening routine. The little boy grew alert and heavier, active, with surprising strength in his small hands. Earl liked to get down on the floor and wrestle with him. Especially when he was drunk. Minnie worked as many hours at the lounge as she could, mainly to stay away from the depressing house and to put off as long as possible Earl's persistent campaign to get her into his bed.

Eventually, a whole year had passed, and she still scarcely ever called her child anything other than "the baby."

Evo ASIMOVA DROVE A black 1941 Cadillac, a long and sleek car with

mud flaps and a squirrel tail waving from the radio antenna. On the dash
were two little iconic statues, carved from bone and delicately painted:
the Virgin Mary and St. Christopher. They had been brought to America
by Evo, a young man of twenty, and his family, Bulgarian Gypsies from
the mountainous country around the little town of Gotse Delchev, a
hundred and eighty kilometers southeast of Sofia. The three of them
had managed to escape, in 1941, just before the Nazi occupation. His
parents had spoken only Bulgarski and Roma, no English. After the
death of his parents, both in 1945, Evo had continued to travel with
their familia of migrant farm workers, from Florida to North Carolina
and back, following essentially the same circuit as Minnie's family had
all those years ago. He learned to speak English and became an expert
mechanic, specializing in tractors, caterpillars, combines, any large farm
equipment. Evo had taken it especially hard when his familia, which in
the last years had been made up of mostly elderly Gypsies, had broken
up, many of the elderly going to live in the cities where the children had
taken work. He was proud of the Gypsy culture and history, proud of
himself for being a Gypsy. It saddened him greatly to see the old ways
of the Romani people fading into little more than memory. Evo was on
his way to the large winter camp of his people in south Florida, hoping
to get on with a familia traveling with a carnival, which was becoming
more and more the norm. Though all the vitsas there would welcome
him, he knew his expertise with large engines would allow him to choose
the familia he most wanted to be a part of.

Evo had been working his way gradually south doing jackleg mechanic's work as he went. He worked on sawmills, at cotton gins, even a
short stint at TCI in Birmingham until he ran into union problems. He
worked at several car repair places, then spent three months at a chop-
shop in Valdosta, Georgia, where stolen cars from all over the Southeast
were brought to be dismantled into parts that were then resold. Luckily,
he left there two days before a raid by the police. Perhaps it was a coinci-
dence, he thought, but he believed it was really divine intervention. When
he was a boy he had served as an acolyte for four years at an Orthodox
church in Gotse Delchev, and he still considered himself devout, though
Orthodox churches were hard to find in America outside the big cities.

He attended Roman churches when he could but of course he could not take the Eucharist, which did not bother him too much because he was an outsider anyway. He was a Gypsy.

Evo Asimova was short and lean, though he was thick through the chest and shoulders, with very little neck so that his head appeared to sit flat on his shoulders. His complexion was dark, his beard heavy, his midnight black hair thick and curly. He wore a gold earring in his left ear, a gold chain as a necklace and a brown leather wristband. On the day he pulled off the highway into the gravel parking lot of Saddler's Lounge, he was wearing a red, western-style shirt with pearl buttons, flared blue jeans and sharp-toed, spit-shined brown cowboy boots. Sunglasses. When he stepped out of the Cadillac, which was spotless and gleaming, he ground the butt of a Chesterfield into the gravel with the heel of his boot.

Inside, he removed his sunglasses and sat down at a table. There were several men hunched over beers at the bar. The air was cool but filled with smoke. The jukebox, turned down so low he could barely hear it, was playing Kitty Wells's "Honky Tonk Angel." He realized, as he listened, that it was not a jukebox, but a radio playing in an adjacent room. He watched the waitress approach him. Talk about an angel! She was the most striking woman he'd ever seen and he knew from her olive skin and coal black hair—and her bearing—that she was a Gypsy. When she leaned down and said, "What can I get you?" in this funny, squeaky voice, he looked at her eyes to see how deep brown or black they would be. He was startled to see that they were two different colors, neither one of them brown or black but one blue and one green. She stared at his mouth.

"Falstaff," he said, "and a cheeseburger, no tomato."

"Comin right up," she said. Her voice was high, slurred, the words run together but plainly understandable. He watched her write the order down as she walked back to the bar then pass it through to the cook, a large, fat albino. She wore a tight, light blue dress that hugged her figure, a nice one—curvy and voluptuous. All woman. He knew her body would be soft, not muscular. Her face, the regal cheekbones framing her eyes, was remarkable. And her eyes: He knew, once he had caught even that brief glimpse of them at the table, that they could never have been any other way. Had they had been uniform, had both been one color or the other, it would have been a violent disruption of God's order of things.

When she brought his beer, in a can with a frosted glass, he said, "Can you sit down with me for a minute?"

"Sure," she said. She sat across from him.

He stuck out his hand. "Evo Asimova."

She took it and they shook. "Minnie," she said.

"That's not your real name," he said, "because you're a Gypsy."

"It's the name I go by," she said. Her voice was not a lisp, more the speech of a child just learning to talk.

"What are you doing," and he indicated with a quick sideways jerk of his head, "here?"

"I work here."

"I mean . . . well . . ."

"I know what you mean," she said, "excuse me." She went to wait on another table. He watched the way she carried herself. She was luminous. In the dim lounge, she seemed to have her own spotlight to follow her around. His spirit felt fully enmeshed with hers. Maybe it was that they were the only Gypsies in this room full of gaje. Had he known her before, in some other time, some other place? He didn't remember ever seeing eyes like that and he doubted he would have forgotten if he had. She went back to the bar and sat on a stool. She gave no indication that she was coming back to his table, at least until his cheeseburger came. Then very subtly she cut her eyes toward him, a quick glance, but it was enough.

After a few minutes she set his cheeseburger before him. It was on a platter with French fries and a dollop of cole slaw. "Need another beer?" she asked.

"Yes," he said.

She stood looking down at him with her solitary eyes. "What makes you think I'm a Gypsy?" she asked.

"Because you are," he said. She smiled. Her teeth were even and white. She moved away and left him to eat his sandwich. That's when it dawned on him, hit him: the reason she focused so intently on his lips was that she was deaf! She was lip-reading. That's why her speech was so peculiar. It was quirky, it was strange and unusual because she couldn't hear herself. Like her speech, her eyes were bizarre, beautifully freakish. All of these things together signaled a deep and profound mystery, something singular and extraordinary. He was intrigued. He knew he had to know more.

When she brought him his second beer he nodded toward the chair she'd sat in before. "Sit down, why don't you?" he asked.

"I've got customers," she said.

"I think I know you," he said.

She frowned. Then she just gazed at him for a long moment. Finally she said,

"No, you don't." She turned and went back to the bar. She did not look back. He realized he'd made a mistake. He didn't know what he was trying to do. Was he drawn to her sexually? Was he trying to pick this woman up? No, he didn't think so. If so, sex was only part of the attraction, maybe a very minor part. He just wanted to talk to her. Maybe get to know her a little bit. He was fascinated by her. What was she doing in this sandy, sun-bleached, nowhere town, a remarkably beautiful Gypsy woman like her? He felt as though he had to know.

He finished his lunch and his second Falstaff, picked up the check and walked over to the bar where she was. She was talking quietly to the bartender, a bullet-headed man who could have been a professional wrestler. "Minnie?" he said, sliding onto the stool next to her.

She didn't respond. Then he remembered and touched her on her shoulder. She turned her head quickly. "Yeah?" she asked. Her eyes were cold, unfriendly. Not at all they way they'd looked when she'd sat down with him.

"Could we talk a little?" he asked.

"About what?"

"I'm sorry. I didn't mean to offend you when I said I knew you."

"I wasn't offended," she said. "I was just nothing. Excuse me again," she said, and she went to take care of a table. When she came back she sat on the same stool, next to him.

"Another beer, bud?" the bartender said.

"Yeah, please," he said. "Falstaff." He looked at her profile. Her hair was long, parted in the middle and swept down shoulder length. She busied herself totaling up a check. She was using a stub of a yellow pencil. Her fingers were tapered, slender. She finished the adding and turned around, her eyes darting, checking on her customers. She sat leaning her back against the bar, her elbows propped on it behind. She spoke without looking at him.

"I just don't want another fuckin Gypsy in my life," she said.

Her bitterness surprised him. He put his finger on her chin and turned her to face him. "I'm not trying to intrude in your life," he said.

"Yes," she said, "you are. That's what you're doing."

"Well," he said, "I'm sorry, really I am. I'll just finish my beer and be gone."

"Fine," she said. Someone waved to her from one of her tables, and she was gone. Without another word. He left the bottle half full on the counter, along with his check and three wrinkled dollar bills.

Evo Asimova spent that night in a weather-beaten old hotel in the little village of Grayton Beach, on the Gulf. He lay on his bed, wide awake, the ceiling fan turning above him, the mosquitoes whining and bumping against the rusty screens of his second-floor room. He'd eaten his dinner in a ramshackle crab house on the beach, two dozen raw oysters on the half shell followed by a fried red snapper filet. Ordinarily he would have thought it was the food keeping him awake, especially the oysters, but he knew that was not it. He could not get the image of the girl—the woman—Minnie out of his mind. Her oddly matched eyes peered at him out of the darkness. There was some curious connection between him and Minnie, but he couldn't grasp what it was. He thought of the old Gypsy saying: We voyage to meet relatives as yet unknown. Could they be related in some way? No, that wasn't it. It was simply that they shared the same soul. The Gypsy soul. But he knew nothing about her. She was him, and he was her, and they were strangers at the same time.

He barely slept all night, and the next morning, after a breakfast of an omelet with fresh shrimp, he pondered returning to the little town where she lived. But then he reluctantly turned his Cadillac east on U.S. 98 toward Apalachicola.

One day Minnie awoke with a sharp pain in her lower abdomen, so severe it caused her to double over and grab her stomach. She told herself it was only gas pains. She got Earl to bring her some milk of magnesia, and that seemed to help some.

The next day the pains were worse. She went to see the old doctor. Dr. Taylor's office was two rooms walled off in the front corner of a general store on the main street of Piper, which was also the highway that ran through it. The front room was the waiting room containing a wilted, leaning wicker sofa and matching chair along with a desk in a corner for a nurse or receptionist. The second room was where Dr. Taylor saw his patients. It was all white: white walls, a padded enamel table covered with a white sheet, enclosed glass shelves of medical paraphernalia and rows of medicine bottles, all smelling heavily of rubbing alcohol. Minnie sat on the table. The old doctor listened to her heart and lungs and looked in her throat. He pressed on her abdomen. She flinched with the pain.

"You had your appendix out?" he asked.

"No," she said. "I've never been sick. I've never had any kind of operation."

"Well, you've probably got appendicitis," he said. "You ought to have it taken out. I can arrange the surgery in Panama City."

"I can't have any surgery," she blurted. She was leaving, going back on the road, she had already made up her mind.

"Well, you need to. This infection might pass, but it'll come back."

"How am I gonna pay for it?"

"I don't know that," he said, "I'm just tellin you."

"Could it be somethin else?" she asked.

"Could be, I guess, but I don't think so. I'm gonna give you this penicillin shot and some antibiotic tablets. And I've got some morphine capsules here I'll give you for when the pain gets really bad. Enough to last you awhile, to get you to the doctor in Panama City. But don't wait too long. It might rupture, and then you'd be in trouble."

"Maybe it'll just go away," Minnie said.

"I doubt it," Dr. Taylor said. "The pain might, specially with this morphine, but once those things start to get infected, they don't quit."

MINNIE TRIED NOT TO let on around the lounge how much she was hurting. She didn't tell anybody. Earl knew it, of course. When she brought home the morphine he wanted some of it.

"Come on, Min, you got to share," he said.

"Fuck you, Earl," she said, "this ain't dope, it's medicine!"

"It's good stuff. I had some one time," he said.

"Earl," she said, "you're just about pond scum, you know it?" She kept the pills on her person all the time, even at night, and didn't let Earl near them. They gave her quite a bit of relief, so she rationed them. Usually the most intense pain came on in the middle of the afternoons, so she could get by on one dose a day. When she took the morphine she could more successfully deny that anything serious enough for an operation was wrong with her, that it was mostly an inconvenience because she was more than ready to move on. She had already made up her mind that she would leave Lester Ray with Earl temporarily. She couldn't take him on the road with her. Maybe she was going to have to give in and settle some place for a while, get another job, until the boy got older, but it wasn't going to be in Piper, Florida, and it wasn't going to be hustling drinks in Saddler's Lounge.

She didn't know where she was going, just that she was going, and that certainty made her feel better. The knowledge that she was leaving worked almost as well as the morphine. It made her feel like her old self again, before Piper, before the baby, before Emil. It put her back in control of her own life. She had just about convinced herself that the pain would go away if she just gave it enough time. And one day it did. It didn't return on the second day and she was overjoyed. She almost threw the rest of the pills away to finalize her recovery and keep them away from Earl. Then, on the third day, the pain came back.

THE DAY THE PAIN returned, Minnie was in the process of bringing two hamburgers to a young couple at a front table when she saw the man walk in the door. He was so familiar she knew she had seen him before, even recently, but she couldn't immediately think where. Then it hit her. It was the man who had been in a couple of weeks ago, who had tried to talk to her. She glanced at him and nodded a hello. He was good-looking. Maybe that was why she remembered him. He sat down at the only vacant table. She went back to the bar to get beers to go with the sandwiches she'd just delivered. Then she went over to his table. She swiped the top of it with a damp towel she kept tucked in the sash of her apron. "What can I get you?" she asked. She looked him directly in the eyes. They were black and deep, like tiny pools with no bottoms. They were very sad eyes, the most melancholic she'd ever seen. She watched his lips for his reply. They were full, reddish, almost like a woman's.

"Do you remember me?" he asked.

"Do I know you?" she asked back.

"I was in here before. We talked. You're Minnie."

"Yep," she said, "that's what they tell me." She smiled. His black hair was thick and tightly curled. It was only late afternoon and he already needed another shave. She could smell his cologne, an earth scent, like ginseng roots just pulled from wet ground. She flashed back to the old ladies in Emil's familia, in the camp, gathering "sang" as they called it, boiling it over the fires. They mixed it with their spittle and put it on the shoulders of the girl having the baby, to ease the birth pangs. And to ward off evil spirits. Maybe that's what I need, she thought.

"I am Evo Asimova," he said. He spoke with a stiff, formal accent that she recognized as eastern European. It was the accent of the old people in the camps.

"And you're a Gypsy," she said.

"That's right," he said, "you remembered."

She took him all in with a glance: the earring, the tight leather band on his wrist, his boots. She turned and pointed her short yellow pencil at a chalkboard behind the bar. "That's it," she said, "and beer, of course. Or Coca-Cola. But I remember you drinking beer before, don't I? Falstaff?"

"Yes, good memory," he said. "A cheeseburger and a Falstaff."

He watched her walk back to the bar to get his beer and put in his order. She was as stunning as he recalled, even more so. Even in his imagination she had not been more desirous. After he got his food he kept watching her, his eyes following her wherever she went, from table to table, back to the bar. When he was finished with his sandwich he asked for another beer. He sipped it. She wore a worn cotton dress that had once been bright yellow but had faded to a soft gold, the color of sunlight. She wore a white apron over her dress, with a pocket where she kept her order pad and her pencil. Her long hair, parted in the middle, was pulled back and tied with a blue ribbon at the back of her head. The hairstyle accented her high, sharp cheekbones. Evo sat sipping his beer for a long time, then had another. He sat there until the supper crowd had thinned out, until it was pitch dark outside, leaving the serious beer drinkers, most of them sitting at the bar.

She stopped at his table. "You don't seem to be in any hurry to get somewhere," she said. She sat down across from him. When he looked at her face he was inclined to recoil, just as if someone had shined a bright flashlight in his face. Her eyes were tired, though, and for the first time he could see the sagging skin around her mouth. And she was pale, paler than he remembered. He was relieved that she was not perfect. Still, he could have sat there and looked at her forever.

"I'm not," he said. "What time do you get off?"

"Hah," she laughed, "Mr. Originality you are, buddy."

"No. I'm not trying to make a date or pick you up. I want to take you away from this place."

"And that's not a pickup?" she asked. Her eyes were laughing, but it was a weary amusement.

"No. I mean away. Far away. For good."

The smile faded from her face. She tilted her face to the side questioningly. She stared at him with her awesome eyes, the query there, too, buried in those two astounding colors. "You're serious, aren't you?" she asked then, barely above a whisper.

"As serious as I've ever been in my life," he said. "You're not . . . well, married or anything are you?"

"Would it matter?" she asked. She had not changed her posture. She continued to gaze at him.

He was lost. Pulled into her visage and vanquished. There was no recovery for him even if she rejected him. He had relinquished what he was, everything he had been up to this moment, to her. He had given her his soul. She could accept it or stomp on it, whichever she wished, and he could do nothing about it. "No," he said, "it wouldn't matter."

MINNIE LEANED BACK AGAINST the leather seat in the Cadillac. It was late, close to midnight, when they drove away from Piper, heading south toward the Gulf. Minnie did not look back. All she had was the faded yellow dress she wore. She had not wanted to go to the house, to confront Earl. She wanted to just be away. The image of her little boy raising his stubby arms to her, the way he would do when he wanted to be picked up, burned in her mind and she swallowed hard. She took a long drink from the Jack Daniels bottle that Evo had handed her.

"I'll buy you anything you need," Evo had said. She didn't need much, she had thought, but she had said nothing to him beyond, all right, let's go, when he'd made the proposition. Now, thinking of Lester Ray, tears rose up, stinging her, blurring the passing scenery, the dark bungalows sitting back in sandy yards dotted with patches of tangled liveoaks, the closed fruit stands, the occasional bursting bright lights of an all-night filling station as they passed it. She could hardly lie to herself that she was leaving the boy in better hands, leaving him to a better life, but she wanted desperately to believe that. Earl wasn't a bad person. He was a drunk, but he stayed home with the boy and kept him while Minnie was at work during the six months or so he had been out of work. (Gerald had finally fired him because of the steady stream of beers he helped himself to.) He would watch over the child, surely he would. He loved the boy. He thought of him as his own son. He played with him, tickled him until his giggles filled the house. She couldn't have carried the child with her, and she had to go. It was way past time.

She felt the whiskey warming her, relaxing her. The whiskey helped to ease the pain in her belly, which was now a dull presence that had persisted for most of the day. She looked at the two icons on the dash. They reminded her—against her will—of Emil. She took another drink from the bottle, feeling the liquor burning pleasantly down her throat. "You religious?" she asked. It was dark in the car and she couldn't see his lips, so she didn't hear his answer. Or even if he answered. It made no difference, one way or the other. Two strings of beads, green and gold, hung from the rearview mirror. The immaculate interior of the car smelled like cedar trees.

Just as the sky was lightening in the east, he pulled off at a motel.

The sign said: MINT SUNRISE MOTEL, VACANCY. He stopped before the office and opened the door, and when he did the dome light came on. "Where are we?" she asked. She realized she'd been sleeping. Her eyes were dry and scratchy.

"Perry," he said. "Nowhere. Just a place to sleep."

"I've been asleep," she said.

"But I haven't. I need a bed." He got out.

She felt around and found the whiskey bottle. It was still half full. She took a long swig. Then she swished some around in her mouth like mouthwash and spit it out the window.

When they were in the room she said, "Listen, I've got this terrific stomach ache."

"I know," he said. "You were mumbling about it in your sleep. It's all right. We'll just sleep, okay?"

"Okay," she said. She sat on the edge of the bed. She was exhausted. She was still holding the bottle which she set on the bedside table. The room had green, painted concrete block walls, the bed a pink chenille spread. There was a picture of some palm trees on a beach over the bed. An old Philco radio sat on a table across the room. She went into the bathroom and relieved her bladder. She was wearing a slip, so she pulled her dress over her head, then lowered the slip enough to get her brassiere off before pulling it back up as a nightgown. When she reentered the room Evo Asimova had pulled the spread down and covered himself with the sheet. He appeared to be fast asleep, facing the wall. It was not, of course, the first time she'd been in a hotel room with a man she knew nothing about. She sighed. She crawled onto the bed, beneath the sheet, her head of its own accord dropping to the thin, flat pillow smelling faintly of dust, her arms and legs aching with fatigue. She sank into a deep and dreamless sleep.

They had breakfast in a diner next to the motel. She'd had diarrhea earlier in the morning and her stomach still felt queasy, so she ordered poached eggs on toast. Evo had a huge breakfast: a short stack of pancakes, three fried eggs, bacon and biscuits. He watched her poke at her eggs. She was ashen, her face drained of most of its color. When they got out of bed he had noticed that she was thinner than he'd first thought. Her shoulder blades stuck out, her collar bone was prominent at the base of her neck. Across her back, beneath the slip straps, were scars that looked like whip scars, still a vague pink, not yet fully bleached out white by time. He was curious but he didn't mention it.

"In answer to your question," he said, chewing, "yes, I'm religious."

"Oh," she said. She'd forgotten asking him about it. "I'm sorry. It's none of my business."

"You spend the night with a man in a motel room, you're entitled to a few questions," he said. He laughed. "You saw the icons."

"Yes."

"The Virgin Mary, of course, and St. Christopher, the patron saint of travelers, but being a Gypsy you already know that."

"No, I didn't know that," she said.

"Oh, come on, 'Minnie,'" he said. "You're a Gypsy, so you knew that." He took a bite of his pancakes and chewed. When he swallowed, he said, "Tell me your Gypsy name."

She just stared at her plate, the poached eggs like colorless blind eyes looking back.

"You can run, Minnie, but you can never get away from what you are," he said.

"Anna Maria Spirosko," she said.

"Good. I'm gonna call you Anna Maria then."

"All right."

He ate in silence for awhile. Then he said, "We're headed for Fort Myers in south Florida. It's where the carnivals have their winter quarters. They're mostly Gypsies, and I want to get on with one of the carnivals. Travel with them."

"Always traveling," she said. She sounded very tired.

"Yes. Jesus said, 'Foxes have holes, and birds of the air have nests; but the son of man has nowhere to lay his head.' That's in the Gospel of Luke. He was talking about Gypsies, Anna Maria. We have no home. We are the lost tribe of Israel."

"You tellin me you're Jewish?"

"Jews are the found tribe of Israel, we are the lost."

"I'm not a Jew," she said. "I'm not anything."

"You're a Gypsy," he said. He crumpled his napkin and dropped it on top of his dirty plate. He pulled out his cigarettes, offered her one. When she shook her head he lit his own. "So let's hit the road," he said, smiling.

HE BEGAN TO REALLY worry about her when they were south of Sarasota, in mid-afternoon. She was pressed back against the seat, her eyes squinted shut. She moaned with pain. She had been drinking Jack Daniels from the bottle since before noon. When they stopped at a little roadside drive-in, she'd wanted nothing to eat. He had felt her forehead. She was hot with fever.

"You need to see a doctor," he said. "We'll find one in this town, okay?"

"No," she said. "I've seen a doctor. I'll be all right. It just comes and goes."

"You sure?"

"Yeah. The pain'll be gone in a few minutes." She took a capsule and drank some water. He ate his hotdog, watching over her, relieved when he saw her body relax, her closed eyelids cease fluttering.

Fragmented dreams bristled in her mind, darting shafts of light from Lester Ray's face, Earl standing naked with a monstrously gigantic erect dick, pointing to it and grinning, great masses of labyrinthine live oaks and dense sawgrass. She was asleep and not asleep. All she had to do to be awake was open her eyes. She was only distantly aware of the car's swaying as Evo guided it back onto the highway. The rush of wind was a soothing balm. As long as she was mobile she was all right. Her head on the back of the seat rocked with the movements of the car. She was leaving everything painful behind her. Again.

They arrived at the huge Gypsy camp at first dark. Anna Maria was asleep, had been for a couple of hours. Evo began asking about for Olevia Kaslov, a woman who had been a friend of his parents, who had known Evo since he'd first come to America. Several people pointed the way, and he guided the big Cadillac down the narrow passages between the tents and house trailers and trucks. He squeezed by cars, most of them old and worn and dusty, but decorated with reflecting mud flaps and squirrels' tails like his own. He stopped in front of a battered pickup truck. It had a small living area with a curved roof built onto the bed. It was made to look like the old horse-drawn wagons their people traveled in for generations. Evo knew exactly what it would look like inside: the walls draped with colorful scarves and strings of beads, a box containing cooking utensils and food against the back of the cab, a small bunk bed against one side, a chair. Between the scarves would be icons—depictions of the saints, the Sacred Heart, the Blessed Virgin—hand-painted on pieces of wood, many of them tiny, some of them brought from the old country. Those were coveted, and they were priceless.

He leaned over and shook Anna Maria's shoulder. She did not respond. He had been anxious and frightened for some time now. She had been sleeping all afternoon, sometimes mumbling, sometimes crying out in pain. He had not known what to do. He'd kept telling himself that everything would be all right when they got to the camp. Olevia would know what to do. She would have some old folk methods and medicine that would cure Anna Maria overnight. He got out and went up to the narrow back door and knocked. Olevia Kaslov, looking older than he remembered (of course she did; he was sure he looked older as well) opened the door. She recognized him immediately.

"Evo Asimova!" she exclaimed. She stepped down and took him in her arms and hugged him, her bony arms strong. "Evo Asimova," she repeated, "you make these old eyes happy!"

"It is so wonderful to see you, Olevia," Evo said.

"Please come inside. I will make tea."

"You must come and look at Anna Maria. She's sick."

"Anna Maria? Oh, you dog, you have a yourself a little baro muy," she said and laughed.

"This is no joke. She's very sick, Olevia. I'm afraid she might be dying!"

"Dying?" She hurried out behind him to the car.

Anna Maria's head was reared back on the seat, her eyes closed. The old woman shook her, but she did not respond. She was limp. Her face was sallow, bloodless. Olevia felt her forehead. "She is burning up with the fever, Evo," she said, "how long has she been like this?"

"Ever since we left north Florida. Night before last. Or was it yesterday? I don't know."

"You have to get her to a hospital," Olevia said. "There are no doctors out here. None would come. The gaje despise us."

"I have no money," Evo said.

"That is no problem. Wait." Olevia went back to her truck. In a moment she was back, holding a thick roll of bills. She thrust them toward Evo. "They know at the hospital that we always pay cash."

"But . . ."

"Take it, Evo! It is not mine. It is ours. Have you forgotten the Gypsy way?"

A NURSE AND TWO orderlies lifted Anna Maria out of the car and put her on a gurney. Before Evo could park the car and get out they were gone with her into the emergency room of the small hospital. At the desk he gave the nurse her name. "How much?" he asked, pulling the money from his pocket.

"Oh, yes, you people always pay cash, don't you?" she said, and behind her smile he caught the condescension and distaste of the "you people." "Take a seat," she said. "They are with your wife now."

He didn't bother to correct her. He sat down and clasped his hands in front of him. His mind surged: anger, frustration, fear, regret. Regret that he had not forced her to stop and see a doctor. Guilt: he was in charge; he should have done something. Anna Marie was very sick, he could tell that from looking at her. When they'd put her on the gurney she'd looked like a corpse. He looked around. There was only one other person in the waiting room, an old man slumped in his chair, asleep. He closed his own eyes. I will never sleep again, he thought. He waited a long time, how long he had no idea, but he must have dozed off because he was jerked awake by a doctor's hand on his shoulder. The doctor, a young man with reddish hair and a reddish mustache, sat down next to him.

"Mr. Spirosko," he said. His words seemed to come echoing from deep within a concrete tunnel. "I'm Dr. Vance." Evo said nothing. The doctor went on. "Your wife has a ruptured appendix. She must have emergency surgery."

"Surgery?" Evo asked, still deep in the fog of sleep.

"Yes. We've already sent her up to surgery. How long has she been in pain?"

"I don't know. Since yesterday, I think."

Dr. Vance looked quizzically at him. "You don't know how long your wife has had these symptoms?"

"She is not my wife," Evo said.

"Oh," the doctor said. He frowned. "But you are the responsible party?"

"Yes. I . . ." Evo paused, thinking. "I am her brother," he said. "I am her only living relative."

"Then you have to sign all the papers. Go to the hospital office down that hall right there."

"Is she . . . will she . . . ?"

"She'll be fine," Dr. Vance said, "we just need to get the poisons out of her as quickly as we can."

EVO SIGNED PAPERS GIVING them permission to do the surgery and guaranteeing payment. He knew that Olevia would see to it that the money was paid. He was told that the operation would take an hour and she would be in recovery for at least another hour afterwards. Then she would be moved up to room 310. He found the cafeteria and got a cup of coffee. How had he so quickly gotten himself into all this? When he thought of Anna Maria under the knife he flinched as though the scalpel was touching his own skin. Was it possible that he really, truly loved her? He had thought so when he'd gone back to see her. Gone back to get her and take her away with him. He felt as though he had known her and loved her for years, not just days. What if she should die on the operating table and he would never look into those mysteriously mismatched eyes again? He could not bear to even think it. His hand shook as he raised the heavy, clunky white cup to his lips. The coffee was scalding hot. It seared his mouth and was bitter, as though it had been brewed hours ago and had been sitting in the pot all that time absorbing it own acidity.

Evo, after all, knew very little about Anna Maria, who she was, where she came from. It had not mattered to him when he had returned to Piper for her and it did not matter now. He was so captivated by her that none of those things even crossed his mind. He could see only her beauty. He loved her: why else would he have gone back?

There were plenty of desirable women. He had never been for very long without one. But Anna Maria, from the first moment he saw her, had lodged herself in his heart, in his mind, so that when he closed his eyes he saw only her. They had not made love; they had never even kissed. Yet he was certain he loved her and always would. He sat staring at the wall of the cafeteria for so long his coffee got cold and he couldn't drink it.

He looked at his watch. It would be awhile before she was in her room, but he went up to the third floor anyway. The hall smelled of rubbing alcohol, and faintly of feces. A nurse directed him to the waiting room on that floor. It was empty of people, orange plastic chairs against the walls, a table of worn and wrinkled magazines, a cheap Bible on an end table. He was tired. Exhausted. He stretched out across several of the chairs, his boots in one chair, his head on a pile of the magazines in another. The next thing he knew someone was shaking his shoulder. He opened his eyes to the glare of overhead flourescent lights. He had no idea where he was. He sat quickly up. It was the nurse who had sent him here.

"Your sister is in her room now," she said. "Dr. Vance is with her. He'd like to speak with you."

Evo stopped by the men's room and splashed his face with cold water and dried it with a paper towel. He went into room 310. It was a double room, a white plastic curtain dividing it down the middle. Anna Maria was in the first bed. There was a tube in her nose. An IV drip was attached to her arm. Hanging just beneath the sheet at the side of the bed was a plastic bag that he assumed was attached to a catheter. Her face was a pale, spectral white, her hair matted and tangled, greasy and dirty. She was asleep. Or still unconscious from the anesthetic. Dr. Vance was standing at the foot of her bed writing on her chart. He looked up when Evo came in. He smiled, a forced grin that Evo knew was meant to be reassuring but was stiff and slick, like a poor actor on a stage.

"She did very well," he said, nodding his head with a jerk, as though Anna Maria had taken some kind of test and passed. Evo didn't reply. He just looked at Anna Maria on the bed, the unwrinkled sheet tucked neatly around her at shoulder level, as if she had not moved for a long time. "Just as we thought, the appendix was ruptured. Had been ruptured, probably, for several days. When a person has appendicitis there is intense pain, and when the infected appendix finally bursts, the pain goes away, like lancing a boil. But the pain comes back because, unlike with a boil, there is no place for the pus to go except into the body. She was lucky. A membranous sac formed around the toxins that prevented their release, and we got to it just in time, just before it, too, ruptured. Otherwise, she would have developed peritonitis and it could have been fatal."

"But she's all right?"

"Well, in a case like this, the incision is especially large, since we took so much out. It's pretty open. We stitched her up, of course, but the way that works is this: when we close a patient up we stitch the first layer of skin down inside, then the next, on up to the surface." He illustrated this with his hands, flattened one on top of the other. "So her outer layer of skin, her epidermis, is still pretty open. She'll have an open wound for a while that'll have to be dressed twice a day, bathed with an astringent, the bandages changed. We'll do that here in the hospital, of course, but she'll be dismissed long before the incision is healed, and someone will have to do it at home. Possibly for three weeks, maybe more. Is there someone who can help you?"

"I can do it myself," Evo said.

"Complete bed rest for at least six weeks. And then she should be good as new. I'll stop by on my rounds in the morning. Any questions?" He was already moving toward the door.

"No," Evo said, "no more questions," but by then the doctor was gone, the door swishing to behind him.

There was an elderly lady in the other bed who'd suffered a heart attack, so Evo couldn't stay in Anna Maria's room with her.

"Go home, get some rest," the nurse told him. "We'll take care of her."

"I don't want to leave her," Evo said.

"Then you'll have to go back to the waiting room," she said.

So Evo spent that night, as well as the next three, stretched out on the plastic chairs, sleeping fitfully. Anna Maria was awake the next morning, though still in pain. "What happened?" she asked him. She looked beautiful even in the stained white cotton hospital gown. Some color had returned to her cheeks and her hair was brushed. He told her all the details, all he knew. Olevia Kaslov came to visit her that day, bearing a bouquet of roses (the perfume of them took Evo back to the Bulgaria of his youth) and with more money for their expenses. She wore a blue scarf on her head, heavy gold hoop earrings, dark red lipstick thickly applied. The skirt of her yellow dress touched the floor.

"Evo, you need a shave," she said. "I will come back tomorrow with a razor for you, and a change of clothes."

"How can we ever repay you?" Anna Maria asked her.

The old woman seemed momentarily shaken by the shrill timbre of her voice. "You have already repaid us," she said, "by being alive."

So Evo CARED FOR her in the weeks after she left the hospital. They lived in a borrowed trailer down the road from Olevia. When Evo changed her bandage, which often was stained through with light colored blood, he could see where her pubic hair had been shaved, where it was growing back in little black specks. It was still lush and thick further down. Anna Maria noticed him observing her. She could not raise up very far on the bed or bend at the waist, so she couldn't see herself. "Am I ugly down there?" she asked.

"No, of course not," he said seriously. "You could never be ugly, because you're beautiful."

"A raw, open bloody wound, and being shaved on top of that, is beautiful?"

"Yes," he said. He looked up at her face. His eyes lingered on her for a long time. Big eyes, round and deep. A fawn's eyes. Large black pearls.

"Evo," she said gently, "you have very sad eyes."

"I have eyes," he replied, "that are full of love."

18

FORT MYERS, FLORIDA

WINTER 1964

Just at ten o'clock, on a morning that was clear and cool, Billy knocked on the door of the old woman's trailer. The sun's rays, aimed like a spotlight, warmed Billy in the gentle chill, heated the air toward the comfort of noon. Billy smelled bacon and strong coffee mixed with the scents of incense and perfume that seemed to always hang over camp. The old mobile home was rusty at the seams and there were patches made with flat squares of tin screwed to the sides, the once-silver color faded to a papery, spotty white. The metal door rattled when Billy knocked on it. He had not slept much. His anticipation had battled all night with his nagging doubts. The biggest part of him knew the old lady was probably wrong, maybe even intentionally misleading him for her own eccentric reasons, or she could be as removed from reality as Mrs. Mack, who was drifting further and further into some remote world known only to herself. At any rate, it seemed to him highly unlikely, after all, that he had found his mother so quickly. He had daydreamed so many scenarios of himself, middle-aged and graying, finally encountering her, an old lady like Mrs. Mack or this Olevia Kaslov, after half a lifetime of searching, which he was fully prepared to do. That he had found her so soon, if indeed he had, was almost a disappointment. Not that he wasn't excited. He just knew to hold it in check.

He had no idea how he would feel when he saw her. Would he love her, a stranger, simply because she was his mother? And how would she feel? Anger? That he had caught her, found her out, exposed her as a woman who had deserted her baby? He didn't know what to expect. Would she look the same as she did in the picture—which could have been made just a little over fifteen years ago, or might have been made long before that time—or would she have changed, become a different person altogether?

The door creaked open and there stood Olevia Kaslov. She had on a long orange skirt and white shirt tied at the waist. Her weathered brown face looked like boot leather. She wore a purple scarf tied around her head and gold hoop earrings. She had put on a dark red lipstick. The effect, to Billy, was startling, even grotesque. As much as he had been around women in his young life, they were still a great enigma to him.

"What do you want?" she asked. He was still standing on the ground, and she looked down at him with watery, melted-chocolate eyes.

"You said you would take me to my mother," Billy said. He added: "If I was here at ten o'clock."

"It's noon time," she said.

"No, ma'am, it's ten o'clock. Right on the dot."

"It is?" she asked.

"Yes, ma'am."

She grinned, her two gold teeth glinting. She had been teasing him, but he didn't especially appreciate it. He was too nervous for joking around.

Olevia Kaslov's pickup truck was as old and worn-out as her trailer. The floorboard was so thin with rust that Billy's foot went right through it when he mounted into the passenger seat.

"Sorry," he said.

"Don't worry about it," she said, cranking the pickup, which rattled mightily with the turning of the engine. The truck had a floor stick shift, on the knob a picture of a naked woman. Billy figured it was probably left over from a previous owner. There were strands of different-colored beads of varying lengths hanging from the rearview mirror. The upholstery was fake leopard fur. Olevia ground the gears and the old truck leapt forward when she released the clutch, throwing Billy's head back. She guided the truck down the narrow lane. She was hunched over, peering through the steering wheel with narrowed eyes, driving with both hands. She could barely see over the dashboard. When they reached the highway she turned toward Fort Myers.

AT THE PUBLIC BEACH in Fort Myers, there was a long concrete abutment that served both as a type of boardwalk and as a seawall against the hurricane storm surges that came hurtling out of the Gulf of Mexico. There were benches, observation spots with coin-operated spyglasses, as well as hot dog stands, small souvenir shops, cold drink places, sno-cone stands, beach equipment rental places. There was one small shop, its front open to the passers-by, that sold Gypsy crafts: handmade jewelry, beads, hand-painted icons, carefully arranged bouquets of artificial flowers. Sitting behind the counter of displayed wares was Evo Asamova. And Anna Maria Spirosko.

Anna Maria had one streak of white in her dark, still luminous hair. She was dressed in typical Gypsy garb: a white sleeveless blouse, a knitted off-white vest that tied in front, a long red and black patterned skirt. She wore gold earrings and a gold chain around her neck. She was thin, almost skinny, as thin as she'd ever been in her life. Evo's hair was cropped short. He wore a navy blue western-style long-sleeved shirt, jeans, and boots.

The two of them had been together for fourteen years. They had sold their crafts in the little booth for the past six years. Before that Anna Maria had worked for a while as a waitress at a restaurant on the beach. Evo had hired on with various construction companies building beach houses and had worked as a freelance maintenance man, repairing roofs and porches, doing small remodeling jobs.

It had taken Anna Maria a long time to recover from the trauma of her surgery. Her incision had become seriously infected and she'd had to go back into the hospital. The doctors had discovered that she was severely anemic and also borderline diabetic. Both her eardrums had been punctured by that shotgun blast and she had gone so long without treatment that she would be deaf for the rest of her days. Before her hospital stays, Anna Maria's only visits to a doctor were when she'd been examined regularly for venereal diseases at Miss Ida Hooten's place in Cedar Key, her visit to the doctor in Mississippi to treat her lash wounds, and the one visit to the old doctor in Piper. She had never before had a thorough physical examination, not even when she was pregnant or afterwards.

During all her physical trials, Evo was at her side. He never seemed to tire of his caretaking. He was devoted to her. When she would awaken from her fevered dreams the first thing she'd see was his worried face, his melancholy eyes. She would think: What does he want? He didn't want anything. He was giving: he was the first person she'd known in her life who seemed to want only to do for her. At first she was wary, suspicious. But she had no choice but to be dependent on him. She had never before totally relied on someone else. By the time she was stronger, when she could get up and walk around without pain, when she no longer needed him to dress her incision and take her temperature and bring pans of warm water for old Olevia Koslov to bathe her with, she realized she had a choice. She knew that she was free again. She could leave anytime she wanted to.

And yet she didn't.

They couldn't stay permanently in the borrowed trailer, so Evo found a small furnished bungalow near the downtown area of Fort Myers, where he would be more likely to find work. The cramped space stank of mildew and mold. They opened all the doors and windows to let in the salty air from the gulf. While Evo was out, Anna Maria mopped and scrubbed, another new experience for her. There was just one bed, a double one, so they began sleeping together, and as soon as Anna Maria was recovered enough, they began making love. It was as easy and natural as moving into the house. She would study Evo, watching him for long periods of time. He had an ease of movement, a grace that was rare in men. He was gentle. But his gentleness was not soft, or weak; it was a form of kindness.

He was the one who brought up the nature of their relationship. "I'm not asking you to make any promises," he said. "I'm content, hour by hour. One day, one week at a time. I love you, but if you ask me to go tomorrow, I'll go." Unlike other Gypsy men she had known he didn't seem to feel the need to prove anything. He was confident as a man. He was like her, in that he didn't care what anybody else thought about him. "I don't care about marriage," he said, "I'll be happy as long as I can have you."

They walked on the beach a lot at sunset, and she began to collect colored pieces of sea glass that would wash ashore along with broken sea shells and clumps of seaweed. "I wonder what this came from?" she would ask him, holding a piece of teal or pale-red tinted glass. He offered guesses from time to time ("an old medicine bottle; a broken set of glassware from an ancient shipwreck; a mirror"), but she wasn't looking at him and didn't hear him, scrutinizing the glass as though it held some secret message for her. Soon she had quite a collection, and Olevia Kaslov taught her how to make jewelry out of it, how to mount it for necklaces and bracelets, studs and dangling earrings. When she quit her waitressing job she opened the little shop on the beach. Evo had always painted and he took it up in earnest again. Soon they had a supply of crude and primitive—but colorful and pleasing—oil paintings on wood, some religious icons, some beach scenes, and some portrayals of activities in the Gypsy camp. The shop became very popular with the winter vacationers and the Northerners who lived in the area for the season.

The day was warming. The beach was swelling with its usual crowd of sunbathers and swimmers: young people with coolers of beer, families with packed picnic lunches. They paraded up and down the beach in shorts and sunglasses, up and down the concrete boardwalk, many stopping to look at Anna Maria's and Evo's wares. Women, especially, would exclaim with delight, even awe, at the charm of the jewelry and the craftsmanship with which it was made. They had some old icons mixed in with Evo's—they had collected genuine articles brought from the old countries in the Gypsy camp—and the little paintings, as well as the larger scenes, proved to be popular, especially Evo's representations of the Virgin of Guadalupe, with her golden halo and her head tilted reverently to the side. Often they were sold out of a day's stock by midafternoon and they could go home before the late, declining sun became unbearable in their eyes.

OLEVIA PARKED THE RATTLY old truck in the crowded parking lot of the public beach. She got out and beckoned to Billy to follow her. He climbed carefully down, avoiding the rusty floorboard. The two of them mounted the steps at the end of a long, concrete abutment. She pointed down the row of shops facing the beach. Billy felt a nervous trembling inside, like someone shaking a marimba in his chest. The old woman was pointing down the row of shops. Billy shaded his eyes with his hand. The blinding sun was like brass horns blowing in his ears.

"There," she said, "down there."

"Where?" he asked. "What?"

"A shop. Jewelry. Gypsy stuff," she said, "for the gaje."

His legs refused to walk.

"Go," she said. "I wait for you here."

What will I say? he thought. He was hot and uncomfortable in his jeans. His T-shirt was already damp with sweat. His hair had gotten longer and shaggy. The T-shirt was tight across his chest and around his upper arms. He swallowed, already thirsty in the heat. "All right," he said. But still he didn't move. Olevia looked kindly at him, smiling, her gold teeth glistening in the bright sunshine.

"Go," she said, "go!"

He was walking then, his legs stiff at the knees. He passed a row of shops, nothing like Olevia had described. And then he saw it, up ahead. A temporary shop, canvas overhead, the kind you would see in a carnival. A woman in khaki Bermuda shorts and a light blue cotton blouse stood in front of the counter with her little girl, who wore a green and yellow, polka-dot bathing suit. They both wore white sandals. They were looking at a piece of jewelry, the mother holding it, showing it to the little girl. The woman's toenails were painted a bright pink.

Billy raised his eyes from the woman's feet to the two people sitting behind the counter. He recognized the man immediately: he was the man who had sat astraddle the box, playing it like a drum during the dance at his birthday celebration. He focused on the woman. She was thin, her skin creamy, tan, not as dark as the man's, but darker than Billy's. Her thick black hair had a gray streak at the top. He stared at her face, transfixed. She looked like the woman in the photograph. She was beautiful, as beautiful as Sheila. More so. Her cheekbones, her nose and chin, were delicate, fine, as in a pen-and-ink drawing. Her eyes: one blue, one green. Her eyes hit him with the force of a sucker punch to the back of his head. He had not expected them, had forgotten about them. His breath caught; he could have counted to thirty before he finally released the air from his lungs. She looked up then. Their eyes met across the few feet of steamy concrete. There was communication of some kind, not recognition, nothing he interpreted as anything more than mild curiosity, yet his body wrenched tensely against itself, his scrotum tightened and his testicles sucked up inside his belly. Then the shopping woman with the little girl moved over between them, shutting them off from each other.

SHE KNEW WHO HE was immediately. She did not "recognize" him, as she had no idea how he must look now, but she felt something move in her breast, a flutter or a stab. Maybe it was the expression on his face: open, expectant, strong and defiant yet vulnerable. He did not look like her but his face mirrored something of herself that she had never before seen in anyone else. She could not have articulated what it was. But it was there. She was sure it was him, and she was not even surprised, as if every day for the past fifteen years she had expected it, had always known that in the next second she could look up and there he would be and she would instinctively know him beyond any doubt. She supposed she had known that if any son of hers came looking for her he would not stop until he found her. She would have done the same thing. No, she thought, that was not right. She didn't do that. She had done just the opposite. She had said, all right, I will find my own way, make my own life, all alone, because if you don't need me I don't need you.

The customer moved over between them. The woman wore glasses with white plastic frames. The little girl couldn't decide if she wanted a necklace or a bracelet. Her indecision annoyed Anna Maria. Anna Maria's mouth felt sticky, coppery. She was aware of the sentient smell of her own warm body, fecund and plenteous, the vessel that had given existence to that spectral boy who stood there staring at her. He had lived inside her for the first nine months of his life, the closest that two human beings could possibly be. He had been a stranger to her after that, tied to her only by distance. The woman took from her straw purse a billfold.

"She'll take them both," the woman said. Anna Maria was only dimly aware of the woman's lips moving.

"What?" Anna Maria looked up at the woman's mouth, at her eyes behind the glasses. They glowered at her impatiently.

"I said, 'she'll take them both,'" the woman said.

"Oh, yes, certainly," Anna Maria said. She took the woman's bills and put both the bracelet and the necklace in a paper sack and handed it to the little girl. Without a word they moved away. Anna Maria's glance darted back to the boy. He was not there. Only an empty space. He had vanished. She had the unsettling thought that she had imagined him. But she knew better. The throbbing inside her womb was too real. He had found her now, and she was certain he would be back. He would greet her, or confront her. Punish her. Whatever he might do would be in his own time. She would wait on him. She sat there enshrouded in her own profound silence.

"You see her?" Olevia said when Billy walked back down the concrete steps into the parking lot.

"Yeah," he said.

"What she say?"

"Nothin," he said.

"Nothin? What is this 'nothin?'"

"I didn't say anything to her. I chickened out. But it was her. I know it was."

"Well," she said, "go back and talk to her."

"No," he said. "She'll be there again. She probably comes there every day."

"She does. She and Evo. But you're here now. Go and talk to her." Billy did not respond. "Did she see you?"

"She saw me, yeah," he said. "But she didn't know who I was." He climbed up into the truck. "I'll come back. Now that I know it's her, I'll come back. I . . . I just wasn't prepared."

The old woman labored up behind the wheel. She sat there for a minute looking at him, not saying anything. Finally, she said, "She knew who you were."

"No way," he said. "Unless . . . hey, you didn't tell her, did you?" He glared at her.

"No," she said, "I did not tell her." She cranked the truck. It sat there idling. "But if she saw you, she knew who you were. Nobody would have to tell her," she said, and then she released the clutch and backed out.

BILLY COULD NOT GET the image of her out of his mind, as if the photograph had finally fleshed itself out and taken human form and lodged itself so solidly before his eyes that he could not even turn them away or close them, because if he did it made no difference at all: she—her face—was still there before him. He felt misty, floating, as though he were half drunk or just finished with a joint, yet he had had nothing. At the same time he felt an increased pull of gravity, his legs heavy. Everything had an unreal quality: their trailer, Mrs. Mack, his own hand if he held it up and looked at it. It was as if the earth had shifted slightly, had paused imperceptibly and then started turning again on a slightly askew axis, faster or slower, so that time—minutes, hours, fifteen years—became irrelevant. He had closed his eyes as a baby and opened them here, now, and the intervening years had dried up like a rain puddle in the sun, disappeared, vanished, evaporated back into the dim reaches of forgotten memories. He had not existed before now. He had sprung full grown from that one glimpse of her face.

He made dinner for himself and Mrs. Mack. Macaroni and cheese. Tomorrow. Tomorrow he would go back out to the beach and he would walk right up and look at her, look her in those arresting, riveting eyes, those spellbinding hypnotic eyes, and he would say, hello, I'm your son Lester Ray Holsomback, except I'm not Lester Ray Holsomback anymore, I'm Billy Kirova, and I've been searching for you all my life and now that I've found you I have no words, no tears, nothing but me. So here I am. He was consciously delaying any real emotions he might eventually feel, because they would be so unfamiliar he would not know how to deal with them. He would just have to intuit his way through that passage like a blind man on a strange street.

After Mrs. Mack finished with her dinner and he removed the dish towel she used as a bib, she sat at the table staring at the wall. What was she thinking? What was she seeing? It was a game he played with himself, trying to imagine it with her. She was thinking of her son Orville. She obviously still loved the guy, for whatever reason Billy did not know. What she was seeing was this: the sunset at the beach, from a bench right where his mother's shop was. (His mother. Different now, like words from another language.) Through the little window in their trailer Billy could see only the glowing golden tops of clouds, but in her emancipated mind Mrs. Mack could see vast streaks of amber and orange against the giant thunderclouds that were forming out in the Gulf, purple and heavy near their flat bases, moving inland. The sun was just a bright red sliver on the horizon, between cloud banks, and the water had turned from blue-green to waxen and pallid, had lost its color as if it had been sucked up by the low clouds. The waves picked up, spraying whitecaps further and further out from the beach. The colors in the sky were like immense brush strokes. The gold of the dying sun formed a sparkling path to where she sat. It beckoned to her. She sat completely motionless, her eyes unfocused, as though she were looking at something far beyond the painted edge of the sea.

♣